THE TASKMASTER

The Plot Bandits

Book 1: *The Disposable*
Book 2: *The Merry Band*
Book 3: *The Narrative*
Book 4: *The Taskmaster*

THE TASKMASTER
Copyright © 2023 by Katherine Vick.
Cover design by Nada Orlic.

Thinklings Books
1400 Lloyd Rd. #552
Wickliffe, OH 44092
thinklingsbooks.com

For my readers,
Thanks ever so for joining the Quest.
I hope you enjoyed it!

And for my publishers,
For giving me a chance to fulfil a dream
and share the Quest with everyone.

The Plot Bandits, Book 4

THE TASKMASTER

by

Katherine Vick

Thinklings

Thinklings Books, LLC
Wickliffe, OH

Meanwhile, the princess refuses to be left behind and, with Zahora's help, disguises herself as a man and rides into battle. The High Lord of Sleiss is Craxis's general and he ruthlessly kills the King of Nyolesse—furious, Islaine rides forwards and defeats him in combat, saving the pathetic and floundering Tretaptus in the process. But, greatly outnumbered, all seems lost for the five kingdoms until Halheid makes a suicidal final charge and Islaine rallies the dispirited troops and drives them forwards.

"Dullard!"

The world seemed to freeze. Prone on the floor, for a moment Princess Pleasance could only stare at the empty doorway through which her—*whatever* he was, that was a matter for another time—Prince Dullard had just been hurled by the spitting, furious form of his cousin, Count Bold. It had started out so well, rallying the servants of the Imposing Castle to confront the complacent, self-centred family of Royals and Nobles they were obliged by the social structure of the Realm to work for. That they were *her* family, a family that up until very recently she would have felt obligated to stand with, was a matter she was still struggling with, but following an attack by her own sister and now Bold's charge, it seemed her side had very much been chosen.

She needed to move, to find Dullard and step up before things got too out of hand. Scrambling desperately, Pleasance tried to leap to her feet but the silk underskirts of her dress caught solidly around her ankles and sent her tumbling with a smack back against the bearskin rug. Even as she stared, shocked, into the muzzle of beautifully crafted teeth, she heard Valiant's scream of "Get them! Get the traitors!", saw Valour and his nameless cohort of disposable minor Noblemen leap into action, heard Dauntless's cry for calm and Stalwart's roar of war, heard the clatter of the Servants' footsteps as they too leapt into the fray, some vanishing down the stairwell after Dullard and Bold, others shaking the floorboards as they rushed bravely forwards to meet the Nobles' charge.

They have ladles and broom handles! She could not escape the treacherous thought. *My family have swords and rapiers and Quests' worth of training! We'll be picking up pieces of Servant for days and even if they heal, will that Duty Pixie even be allowed to fix the loose pieces back on?*

What have we got these poor people into?

She tried to rise again, but the sweep of Valour's sword missed her head by inches and drove her for the third time into the bearskin's embrace. As she scrambled on her hands and knees out of the line of fire, heart pounding in her ears like thunder, a hefty metal shape crashed against the blade—Sour's cleaver, which slapped the blow away. Even as Valour staggered in shock, his eyes widening at the impudence of a Servant daring to challenge his attack, Jolly's ladle descended with a hearty crunch and sent him reeling backwards.

"Stop this!" Dauntless's voice cut through the noisy chaos of unexpected battle with determined grit. Pleasance caught a glimpse of him standing tall and strong, his arms outstretched in a placatory manner, his shape silhouetted against the narrow stone window. "Stop this at once! What good will it do? We are only going to—"

"Silence, you traitorous dog! You side with them, you suffer with them!"

Like a carrot-topped projectile, Baron Stalwart slammed into his relative, thrusting him backwards in the kind of dramatic, limb-flailing arc that any Narrative would have been proud to lovingly describe. Pleasance caught one brief, eternal glimpse of his face, frozen in a mask of shock and horror before he crashed through the lattice of heavy glass and delicate metalwork and—with a scrape that must have left a good amount of his cloth and skin on the stonework—he tumbled backwards through the window and vanished out of sight.

I have to help! Pleasance gritted her teeth as she dragged herself away from the rug at last and battled with her skirts to find her feet. *This is my fault...Uncle Dauntless! And Dullard, I have to... A weapon! I need a...*

This time, she made it three quarters of the way upright before the liveried back of Scrape came hurtling through the air and slammed her with a crunch against the elegantly painted wall plaster. On instinct, she grabbed his shoulders, flinging them both to the floor as Valiant's sword slashed round in a vindictive swipe that tore a violent chunk out of the décor. Her cousin's husband towered over them, dark hair dishevelled, teeth gritted and eyes intent as he did as he did best—did battle. Dragging his sword free of the wall, he prepared for a more decisive strike. Scrape's face was inches from hers, his eyes rich with ripe terror, his cheeks puffed by hyperventilating breaths, his knuckles white as they grasped the shattered broom handle that Pleasance could only assume had taken Valiant's first blow…

Broom handle. *Broom handle!*

Valiant's sword whipped back behind his head, gathering the momentum for a double-torso-splitting blow. There was no time for pleasant by-your-leaves. With all her strength, Pleasance ripped the broken wood out of Scrape's unresisting hands and thrust mightily upwards.

Valiant's face turned purple, then mauve, before slowly draining out to white, his sword teetering above his head in suddenly stilled fingers. His eyes drifted down his own body to where Pleasance's blow had done its utmost to dam any future ebb from him into the Royal gene pool. Slowly, with his eyes crossed and his legs clamped together, he swayed, staggered backwards, and teetered sideways through the open door.

"I'll get him! I'll get him!" Suddenly emboldened, Scrape took on an expression of almost beatific glee—grabbing back his makeshift weapon, he scrambled to his feet and hurled himself through the door in pursuit.

And suddenly the room was still.

With bemused shock, Pleasance stared around the suddenly quieted solar, heard the wind whistling through the shattered glass of the window, saw the gentle rock of a tumbled chair, a fallen silver candlestick, the bearskin rug turned over, a tapestry ripped and torn, bits of broken broom and glass—though luckily not of Servant—scattering the wooden floor. Sweetness was a motionless heap of velvet and blonde hair nearby. In the distance, through the open door, she could hear yells and crashing and the clash of steel as the battle moved out into the remainder of the castle, leaving behind the carnage of the solar and Pleasance herself in its wake…

"Ma'am!" Pleasance jumped violently as Menial, her coif dislodged and crooked allowing her mousey hair to spill over her face, thrust into her line of sight with outstretched hands. "Are you all right, ma'am?"

Pleasance took several deep breaths. "I thought we established," she declared more crossly than she felt, "that you were going to call me Pleasance."

Menial was breathing fairly hard herself. "Sorry, ma...Pleasance. Force of habit, Pleasance."

With a grateful nod, Pleasance accepted her former Maid's offer of a hand up, untangling herself from the damned awkward skirts of Sweetness's troublemaking dress as she finally found her feet again. More from habit than need, she brushed at the plaster-dust scattered over the silk and quite successfully spread a long white smear down her bodice front. She felt a shiver of horror from her internal Islaine, but since it wasn't her dress anyway, Pleasance found that personally she didn't care.

"Have you seen Prince Dullard?" she asked, surprising herself with how calmly the question emerged.

Menial nodded, her lip caught in her teeth. "Last time I saw him, he was fighting Count Bold, Pleasance."

Pleasance fought down a shiver of concern. Impressive as Dullard's swordsmanship could be, he hadn't a ruthless bone in his body, whereas Bold, whilst probably less skilled, could and would do things to a hapless sparring partner that simply weren't pretty. She had to find him...find them before Dullard's niceness got him skewered.

"Come on," she said, pausing briefly for a last scan of the solar in case any handy weapons had been left behind. "We'd better..."

Her voice tailed away. She froze. She stared.

"Father," she said.

King Paragon hadn't moved. There he was, seated on his low stool near the fireplace, his bearded face blank and his eyes full of a strange, bewildered sorrow. His dogs had disappeared—presumably, they at least had had the common sense to vanish up the narrow spiral stairwell to the sleeping chambers when the trouble had started, but Pleasance couldn't help but wonder, from her father's empty demeanour, whether he had noticed any of what had happened at all.

"Father," Pleasance repeated softly, turning away from the door as she took one, two, three steps back into the room towards Paragon's unmoving form. "Father, are you...?"

"Bitch!"

Clawing fingernails dug into her scalp, her hair, yanking and tearing and grabbing. Pleasance screeched and lashed out, flailing desperately over her shoulders as she caught a glimpse of Sweetness's face, her teeth viciously clenched and eyes full of fury flashing in a blood-stained face as she latched on to her sister with unexpected strength. Knees dug into Pleasance's back as Sweetness flung her whole weight down on top of her, nearly driving her to the floor. Fervent, frantic hands scratched at her throat, her face, her eyes, clawing like a feral animal as she shrieked with rage and kicked at her stomach. Bruising blows echoed against Pleasance's ribs, her scalp burned as though on fire as her sister's vicious hands roamed everywhere, tearing stinging strips of flesh from her neck, her arms, her cheeks, catching in her nostrils and digging ruthlessly inside, snatching at her eyes, and she could only struggle and shriek and stagger as she battled to throw her sibling harpy off.

"Let go of her! Let go!"

This time it was Sweetness's turn to shriek with pain. The spitting weight of her sister vanished as suddenly as it had appeared—spinning sharply on her heel, Pleasance was just in time to see Menial crash back against the floor with sizable chunks of her sister's enviably shiny hair clamped between her fingers. Sweetness herself was sprawled on top of the Maid and she struggled madly, pushing herself free of Menial with a stinging slap as she reeled and staggered to her feet. Her breath came in short, violent gasps as her hands stretched out like claws before her.

"How could you?" she rasped out acidly. "How could you *do* this to us—your own kin, your own flesh and blood? How could you betray us, make a mockery of us, leave us to suffer vile indignities at the hands of lackeys and pot-scrubbers? And for whom? For what? For that ridiculous buffoon Dullard?" She paused a moment, dragging the trickle of blood from her damaged forehead away from her lips with a sweep of her fingers and an unladylike spit. "Why do you tolerate him,

Pleasance? You've always thought him a pointless idiot, like we do! What has he done to you to so corrupt you, to turn you against everything in your life that is good and worth holding dear?"

Pleasance's skin was awash with pain—she could feel warm blood against her own skin and her hair felt matted and mangled and tender, but she had no time now to assess the damage that Sweetness had done.

"He woke me up!" she declared in retort. "He made me see sense, made me see things the way they really were! I was trying to do the same for you, Sweetness! I was trying to help you!"

"Help?" Sweetness flung out the word like an accusation. "We didn't need your help! Everything was fine until you and that absurd fool of a Rejected Suitor came and ruined our world! He hasn't helped you see sense, Pleasance! He's brainwashed you! He's broken your mind!"

"No!"

"Yes! I don't know how he's done it, how he's got under your skin—"

"You have no idea what you're talking about—"

"How he's managed to mangle your poor brain—"

"You can't understand!"

"How he has corrupted you!"

"You'll never understand!"

"You should despise that man for what he's done!"

"He keeps me myself!"

Silence. Even the distant roar and crash of the fight suddenly seemed an infinite eternity away.

Sweetness was staring at her sister in genuine, dumbfounded shock. Pleasance was staring back with almost the same emotion. She hadn't meant to say it, she'd never meant to say it, but it had been there, it was waiting, and it had just spilled out.

"Keeps you *yourself?*" A hint of disdain crept in Sweetness's shocked tone. "What's that supposed to mean?"

Pleasance took a deep breath. After their earlier discussions, there was no way in the world that Sweetness was going to understand what she was about to say, but the residual part of her that looked back on their shared childhood felt she owed it to her to try. "When I first stepped into The Narrative," she said softly, "Princess Islaine was there waiting for me, planted in my head; and at first, I welcomed her. But the more I saw of Islaine, the more I realised that Islaine *wasn't me*. I didn't want her to be me, but I could tell that the longer I spent with her, the more I would be Islaine. Not only in The Narrative. Forever."

Her sister's voice, when it came, was only a breath away from silence itself. "You cannot be serious."

Pleasance steadied herself carefully, reflexively brushing the front of her dress. She saw her sister's eyes dart down to the white stain, her fingers clenching, but the apparent shock of the revelation appeared to have stayed her murderous sartorial impulses for the time being. She wanted to tremble and it took all her strength of will to keep her body still. "Well, it would seem that I am."

Sweetness stared at her, baffled. "But that's what *happens*, Pleasance," she said incredulously. "You go into The Narrative and it makes you a better person. That's the way it works. That's the way it's supposed to work. It makes you into the person you're supposed to be."

You should listen to her. You know it's true.

The soft, inviting voice—*her* voice—rose from within and curled around her psyche. Pleasance pushed her away but the sense of her hovered alarmingly.

Think of Dullard. Think of that smile he gave you...

Think of how ridiculous it made him look. You can do so much better than that.

NO.

No.

No?

"I don't think Islaine *is* a better person." The tremble was there now; there was no expelling it. "I like who I am without her, and being around Dullard keeps her out of my mind."

But you'd be stronger with her, braver, more resolute. You wouldn't need to cling to the memory of some lanky under-bred fool with a nose with more kinks than a cornucopia to feel powerful...

"All the more reason to *get away* from him," Sweetness exclaimed with sudden passion. "Pleasance...*dear* sister...perhaps you haven't spent enough time In Narrative to understand, but life here and now, in the grey and dull without its light—it is *nothing* to life within. You say what happens outside of Narrative is what matters, but, Pleasance, that simply isn't true. Until you feel the warm embrace of your Narrative self surround you, until you feel the intensity of emotion, of joy, of despair, and of pure true love that it can spark within your heart, you have never *lived.*" She shook her head slowly. "The common breed, the Ordinary—they can never understand that because they have never earned the right to that moment of magnificence. Don't throw away your chance at such a wonderful gift over the words of an unworthy man that, I assure you, once you've shared the gaze of your *true* Narrative love, you will understand was nothing more than foolish fancy."

I know you're afraid. But you should embrace it. You know you'll feel it and you'll not regret it once it is done. Forget this nonsense. Be who you were born to be.

Be me.

Pleasance could feel her body shaking from head to toe, the pain in her skin and her scalp suddenly very far away as her mind whirled in frightened fog. It would be so easy, so simple, and everything would be right again...

And then Sweetness smiled, soft, sweet, sisterly, as she gently extended her hands. "Come to me," she said soothingly. "Come with me. I will take you to your rightful place, to your Narrative honour, and this will be forgotten. I promise you, Pleasance. Everything will be perfect again."

Her hands were rising, slowly, shakily, and she could feel her legs itching to take the two steps, just two steps, all she needed to take back all she'd ever wanted...

"Pleasance, no! Don't do it, Pleasance! Think of Dullard! Think of Dullard, Pleasance! You watched him in the corridor, you watched him, you watched him, *think about when you watched him!*"

The lone voice, so familiar but meek no longer, cut through the fog of Pleasance's mind like a lighthouse through a storm. The memory crashed like waves upon a stormy shore, from just before they'd burst in to the solar, watching him stood at the end of that corridor, leaning against the stone, askew but occupied, one leg always twitching and slightly bent, his upper arms pressed awkwardly against his sides in stark contrast to the constant motion of his lower arms, the clasping of his hands, the gesturing of his fingers. His face had been so intent, his lank hair brushing at his ample nose, his eyes serious as he talked, his jaw in relentless motion. His features would flash from one emotion to the next in rapid succession, nervous, serious, thoughtful, embarrassed, awkward, apologetic, enthusiastic, encouraging, coaxing, caring, kind. His voice had rippled to her ears, soft and precise, the crisp, clean edges of his words tempered by his gentle tone. And he'd smiled warmly.

Dullard.

Inside her mind, a voice was screaming at her. But it sounded suddenly very far away.

As she shook herself, staggering backwards and snatching her hands away, she heard her sister shriek, saw her lash out viciously and send poor Menial flying back over the fallen chair with an almighty crash. She crumpled in a heap and lay still.

"No! Menial! Leave her alone!" Pleasance started forwards but suddenly strong heavy arms had clamped around her body, lifting her helplessly off her feet as she struggled and fought. Her father's face, sorrowful and weary, pressed over her shoulder.

"Pleasance, she's right," he said, and even as she fought his grasp, she could hear regret in his tone at what he was doing to his younger daughter. "I'm sorry but she's right. This is for your own good."

"What are you doing?" Pleasance shrieked, tearing desperately at his skin, his doublet, anything she could reach; but her father's arms, strong from the legacy of his heroic past, held her firmly.

Sweetness's face filled her vision, the trickle of blood from her wound cutting a scarlet swath across her pale, perfect skin. Her eyes were intent. In one hand, she held the silver candlestick.

"The right thing," she breathed fervently. "We're going to *save* you."

And the candlestick descended with a violent crunch and everything went dark.

* * *

It was, it was fair to say, not exactly an even fight.

On the one hand, herself. Flirt took a moment to assess herself, her mail as ever chafing in uncomfortable places, her dark, curly hair tucked safely beneath her helmet as she fingered the elegant hilt of her beloved sword for reassurance that she was doing the right thing. Her head ached from Poniard's blows the night before but, luckily, he had only half-caught her and knocked her out briefly and the damage was already healing nicely.

What a night. She had to confess she was still struggling slightly to process the events of the evening before with Preen's approval of Poniard's vicious attack on their little band of rebels, intended to leave them as close to genuinely dead as was possible in a Realm where death was generally regarded as a minor blip in one's day. The fact that they had somehow managed to fight off their world's most vindictive killing machine, who had then proceeded to set himself accidentally on fire in a gruesome echo of their intended fate, was strangely unreal—indeed, if it were not for the slight scent of singe still lingering in the air, a part of her might have wondered if the whole thing had been some insane nightmare.

And it had not been her nightmare alone. Ranged behind her were her newfound companions-in-arms, the stalwarts of the Rural Guard: Donk, enormous and towering, an army in himself but with a heart too gentle to be so; Tumble, with his knobbly face and strangely thoughtful outlook; Dunny, a scruffy, food-stained bundle of bad habits; Thump, a meaty bulk of dim-wittedness and lecherous humour clinging to a cudgel named Ronald, who she had never expected to find made up for in conviction what he lacked in wit; and Clunny, who fired out waves of antagonism and sardonic retorts almost as strongly as his ever-present odour of beans. And, of course, there was Shoulders, his loose head balanced awkwardly beneath its supporting helmet as he stared out at the horror ranged before them with barely concealed dismay.

But he had surprised her. When Clunny had rained down a bucketful of protests on hearing her plan, it had been Shoulders who had stepped up, had told his fellow Disposable to suggest a better plan for him to back, and when he had failed, had strongly suggested he therefore shut the bloody heck up and live with this one. It was strangely as though, with Clunny to make protest for him, Shoulders felt more comfortable standing up for the rebellion he had until now struggled to tolerate. It was not the wholehearted and fervent defence of their position she might have liked. But the world had not shuddered and come to a stop yet, so that was a while away. And there was no denying that it was progress.

And so here they were, abandoning their hijacked pavilion to stand together in a loose line before the scrappy canvas tents and smouldering fire pit that a mere day before had been a place of repose, staring out at the entire force of the Realm's Disposables ranged out before them.

To her right, the City Watchmen, as was traditional, were a ragtag band in rusty, mismatched armour, although they did look in a tiny bit more careful nick than usual after prepping for the Final Battle to come. Beside them, the Buccaneers, friends of her uncle Reel, with their plaits and flowing moustaches, looked uncomfortable dressed in armour and short swords, their traditional flowing shirts and curvy cutlasses left behind. The smaller band that Flirt assumed was the Garrison of the Grim Fortress had banded together with Disposables from the Plains and her occasional customers, the Bandits of Bandit Pass, to form a mass of disgruntled-looking manpower in the centre. And as morning had come, even the Garrison from the Imposing Castle had appeared, looking somewhat bewildered at this turn of events but backing up the line all the same. To their left, the Palace Guard, their armour shining brightly, set their companions in contrast with their neat two lines of men. And finally, ranged around to complete the ring behind them were those sent to Bulk Up—Trappers and Ordinary folks in search of a change, unhappy elves in heavy hoods, and Desert Tribesmen and Exotic Islanders with their natural ethnicity concealed ahead of the potential Final Battle, looking, it was fair to say, not precisely themselves.

It was...*imposing* wasn't the word exactly, although there was an air of that in Sentinel's gleaming Palace Guard. *Intimidating* could have perhaps been applied had she not already spotted three different guardsmen picking their respective noses (and one inspecting the contents), another four scratching their backsides with a certain involved satisfaction, and one using the point of his halberd to pick between his sandaled toes. *Bone-shatteringly terrifying* could hardly be applied to a horde staring with such a strange mix of boredom, irritation, and weary despair at the blond-headed figure in striped hose, a rainbow-slashed doublet, and a feather-bristling cap who stood poised before them with one hand raised delicately to the sky as he extolled tales of heroic virtue upon the world's most unreceptive audience.

But that was Preen's idea of inspiring his troops, wasn't it? Tales of heroes they would never be and never cared for told by Bard, whom they had to fight the urge not to duff up whenever he crossed their path. He didn't understand his men. He never had and he never would because he didn't care to try. And deep inside, they knew that.

Which was why she knew she had to test their loyalty, had to test their fealty to their so-called leader against a fundamental of their lives. If she played this right, she wouldn't need to break Preen's tenuous hold over them. Preen would do that for her.

And that would be her chance.

But for now, she had to concentrate. Squick had taken her message nearly ten minutes ago. Surely, it couldn't be long before…

And then, with a reluctant ripple, the horde parted and Preen strutted into view.

His hair was slicked back. His hands were clasped together. Gracing his face was perhaps the most self-satisfied smirk that Flirt had ever seen. His eyes were glowing with triumph.

He thinks we're going to surrender.

That had, of course, been part of the idea. When she had sent a subdued message via Squick requesting negotiation on the matter of surrender, she had always intended to make Preen feel the upper hand was slipping back towards him, especially following Poniard's spectacular failure the night before. If Shoulders's testimony was anything to go by, it would make him more off-balance.

She took one last look at the nervous faces of her Disposable companions, at their weary workmates gathered in a loose ring around them, and at the gloating face of the Officious Courtier they were instructed to obey, and steeled her shoulders. This was her moment, her time to prove to herself that she had it in herself to be who she wanted. She wasn't going to mess it up, was she?

"Well, well, well." Preen's voice slithered across the intervening air as he sauntered to a halt a prudent few yards out of their weapons range. "Isn't this interesting?"

His tone was the verbal equivalent of his smirk. Flirt allowed herself a brief moment of fantasy about walloping it off his face using a giant haddock—but, alas, the dream would die unfulfilled, for such action would hardly be prudent, especially since Preen wasn't alone. A little way back, Squick was hovering uncomfortably as he stared down at them with something close to pity. Summoned from his companions by a casual curl of Preen's long finger, Sentinel marched swiftly and neatly over to the Courtier's side, although his expression was sternly disapproving. And over his shoulder, unremarkable as ever but for the ridiculous sight of a field captain's insignia on his shoulder, Midlin was watching them with an expression fervently bland. Thrash, it seemed, had paid for his insolence by demotion.

"Interesting how?" Flirt offered casually.

Preen's brow creased slightly at the ease of her tone, but it was not enough to kill the smirk. "That here we are, after your strutting and posturing and insolence, with you calling me here to beg for a lenient surrender," he drawled. "How the self-proclaimed mighty are fallen!"

Flirt struggled to hide her smile. "If you say so. How lenient a surrender are we talking about?"

Preen gave a dark chuckle. "Oh, not very, I assure you. After all, this is hardly the best position from which to negotiate."

Finally, Flirt allowed herself to smile. "Oh, I agree completely. But don't worry, we'll go easy on you, won't we?"

The words skimmed straight over the deafened heights of Preen's ego, but the wide eyes and dawning realisation of the faces beyond him told Flirt that her target audience had heard her loud and clear. Preen, however, was ploughing on. "In truth, there is scant room for negotiation!" he exclaimed victoriously. "Incarceration is an inevitability!"

"If you insist. Though I can't say where we'll put you all."

"A suitable punishment for defiance of the worst kind must be publicly seen to be done!"

"I suppose we could deny your men their ale rations for a week or so, couldn't we? Though I'm not sure what we'll do to you..."

"There will be horse-whipping! Parading through the streets stripped naked! Peltings with rotten fruit at every stocks in the land!"

No open mention of trying to burn them now, though. And Poniard's mission had apparently been secret. Interesting... "Well, if that's the kind of thing you're into..."

"They will talk for Quest upon Quest about the fate of those who dared to stand against that which was right and good! And they will remember it was brought about by *me!*"

"I'm sure they will." Flirt tapped her sword hilt easily with her fingertips. "So, do you have any more requests? Or shall we just accept your surrender like that?"

Preen's fervent, misty-eyed reverie came to a crashing halt. He blinked hard. *"What* did you say?"

"Your surrender?" It was hard, so hard to keep a straight face. "Do you want us to take it on condition that the men lose their ale and get locked up and you get horse-whipped and paraded naked while being pelted by rotten fruit? Or are there any more conditions you'd like to add?" Flirt beamed beatifically. "We'd hate to deny your wishes, wouldn't we?"

Preen's mouth gaped open like a bewildered guppy as a gratifying titter of laughter rippled through the ranks of the men. *"My* surrender?" he managed, his voice laced with incredulous shock. "I have come here to negotiate *your* surrender!"

Flirt let out a carefully crafted chuckle. "Oh, I don't think so. We're hardly going to give up when we're in such a strong position, are we?"

"Strong position?" Preen's teeth came together with a grinding crash as his jaw snapped shut. "You are horrendously outnumbered!"

From Flirt's right, bang on cue, Tumble gave an enormous smile. "We know."

"Right slap bang in our favour, it is," Dunny added cheerfully. His bandaged arm had already begun to heal. "It's almost embarrassing."

Preen stared from one grinning Disposable to another. His face creased like a screwed-up parchment. "You are utterly mad!"

"Nah. It's the First Rule, mate." Thump was looking at Preen with something not far off pity. "You can't deny the First Rule."

A ripple of nods followed hurriedly in the wake of the murmur of agreement that was trickling through the horde of Disposables around them. Although the more Ordinary recruits looked bewildered, every fighting man, scruffy City Watchman to shining Palace Guard, uncomfortable Buccaneer to seasoned Garrison man, had understanding in their eyes. Oh, not all of them liked it—Midlin's face was screwed up with discomfort, Sentinel's with resignation, and there were others mirroring their mood amongst the crowd. But all of them understood.

And Preen clearly did not.

"First Rule!" he spat. "Not that ridiculous nonsense again!"

Under different circumstances, Flirt might have punched the air. That was why she had insisted that when the conversation spilled around to their precious Rule, the lads should take the lead. She had gathered the concept, vaguely, by now, but the Rural Guard believed it, lived it and breathed it in a way she could not, and that was something they and the rest of the Disposables had in common. It was not something that those who did not should discuss.

A point highlighted by the fact that the vast majority of the troops Preen called his own were now staring at him as though he had kneecapped their sainted mother.

"Please do not dismiss the First Rule." Sentinel's voice was strained. "As Thrash and I informed you—"

"Shut up!" Preen's voice cracked like a whip. "I told you already that I don't want to hear another word about that absurd notion! I am here to negotiate their surrender and that is all!"

Tumble was shaking his head. "You shouldn't knock the First Rule, mate. It's the *First Rule.*"

There was a rumble of approval from the ranks. Preen ignored it.

"Enough!" he screeched, spittle spraying with little dignity from his lips. "I will hear no more of this ridiculous… You will surrender! I am the one in authority here, you sad, pathetic, witless ingrates, and you are going to surrender to me! Immediately!"

There was a long, slow, epically drawn-out silence. And then, his head lolling loosely within its nest of bindings, Shoulders took one soft step forwards.

"Will we bollocks," he replied.

It was crude but the sentiment was pure as the ring of a freshly cast bell. Preen visibly winced, his eyes skirting along the line of the Rural Guard, skipping past Tumble and Dunny who had already defied him as he sought desperately for a weak link. His gaze fell onto Thump.

"You will surrender!" he ordered rampantly. "Now!"

Thump looked worryingly uncomfortable for a moment to be so singled out, fingering his cudgel nervously, but his face settled into a determined rut and his jaw hardened stubbornly.

"No, thanks," he replied, his defiance slightly forced but sincere in spirit. "I don't want to."

"You don't *want* to?" Preen chewed over the words incredulously. "I don't care what you want! Just do as I say! *Surrender!*"

But Thump made no move towards him, his grip on Ronald tightening as he shook his head with more conviction. "No," he repeated. "Not going to do it, mate."

Preen's intently burning gaze dismissed him instantly, flicking on to find first Donk's torso and, after a small height adjustment, his face. Flirt could see the strange pity on the gentle giant's face as he stared at the Courtier's sudden desperation.

"Then you do it!" Preen's words were shrill and cold. "You tell them to surrender! Tell them what fools they are and make them obey me!"

But Donk was shaking his head, slow, enormous, its movement seeming to send shocked vibrations through the air.

"I'm sorry," he said with sincerity. "But you've proved why I shouldn't."

Preen gasped. Presumably he had assumed that Donk, ever the peacemaker of the group, calmer of sarcasm and quiet tower of strength, would put an end to this. And when he hadn't…

His gaze tripped along one final time. It visibly wilted when it found Clunny but, desperately, he pressed on.

"You!" he barked out and his voice was trembling in his rage and his disbelief. "You will surrender to me right now!"

The Disposable snorted. "If they won't do it, what makes you think that I will?"

Preen gaped, apparently appalled at the man's failure to grasp the basic facts at hand. "Because I gave you an *order!*"

He laughed. Clunny gave a casual chuckle and Flirt could actually see the way the sound of it scraped at the very core of Preen's soul. "So?"

So.

So.

Such a simple word. So small, so lightly spoken, barely more than a dash of breath to make it come to be. But that one *so* seemed to slip down beneath Preen's skin and set fire to every droplet of his blood.

"I ordered you!" The words erupted from the Courtier's lips, slashing at the air. "I ordered you and you *will* obey me, you will obey me, you will *obey!* I am your leader, your guardian, the master of your instructions, interpreter of the words of our very Taskmaster! You *must* do as I say! You must, you must, you *must...*" He took a violent gasp of breath. "I am the holder of your book!" he hissed. "I hold the words of the one who rules this world, the instructions that must be followed! And while I hold those words, I deserve obedience, I deserve respect! As long as that book is under my command..."

"What?" Shoulders was apparently taking an inordinate amount of pleasure from the simple act of drawing a brown leather rectangle from the pouch at his waist. "You mean *this* book?"

If it had been possible to puncture a man with a needle and watch him deflate, Flirt suspected that Preen's expression would have been a remarkable likeness. The pomposity and screeching air of authority whistled away into nothing as his eyes fell upon the source of his power resting casually in Shoulders's dirty fingers. It was apparent that the reason for the standoff had momentarily escaped him.

And his voice, when it came once more, was suddenly subdued. "Why are you doing this?" The words were shrill and fearful and painfully small. "What do you want?"

Flirt took a deep breath. If she was honest, this strangely defeated-looking Preen had not been part of her plans—she had expected screeching and spittle and a rain of insults. He looked so lost without his precious book.

I must be going soft, mustn't I? But can even Preen be reasoned with? Can he understand?

"We want what's fair," she said softly. "That's all. We want a fair chance to be more than bit parts. We want the chance to show what we can do, for Heroes to be chosen by merit, not by birth. We want the bad jobs and the good jobs to be shared around more evenly, for talent to be used, not wasted. We want a say in things. And we want some respect."

"Respect?" The word was close to a whisper. "You want respect?"

There was something in his eyes, a kind of frustration, a kind of hunger that Flirt didn't understand. But she nodded anyway. "That's about the size of it, isn't it?"

"But you don't care what happens to anyone else in the process, do you?" Preen's voice hardened. "You don't care what happens to *me!*"

Flirt opened her mouth to phrase a reply but, alarmingly, the smirking Clunny got in before her. "Not really, mate," he retorted easily. "It's not like you care what happens to us. And after last night…"

"Clunny," Donk reproached him gently. "This is hardly the time."

"Why not?" Clunny gave a shrug as he roughly folded his arms. "He's up against the wall now. And we know that's about the only way the bugger will ever listen to us."

"He's right, Donk." Thump stepped forward a pace, his chin stubbornly firmed as he stared at the Courtier intently. "He needs to know he can't keep treating us like this."

Preen blinked, as his trepidation gave way to visible bemusement. "Treating you like what?" he asked with confusion writ large upon his face.

The three Disposables exchanged looks that were sincerely incredulous. Shoulders very pointedly rolled his eyes. And beyond them, Flirt could feel the burn of intense gazes around them. The Disposable horde was taking a great interest in this turn of the conversation.

"You've been yelling at us," Tumble offered.

Preen stared at him in astonishment. "Of course I do. You need firm guidance. You need to be told."

"You insult us," Clunny added more coldly.

Preen shook his head slowly. "You need to know your place. The chain of command is essential. Besides, you generally deserve it."

"We deserve to get yelled at and insulted and pushed around?" Donk interjected, his voice a soft rumble.

The expression on Preen's face suggested he couldn't quite believe that they didn't comprehend. He also appeared completely deaf to the wave of muttering that was rising up behind him. "Of course you do," he replied incredulously. "It's the only thing you'll understand."

"And you didn't think that maybe we might understand you treating us with respect and thanking us every once in a while for the work we put in?" Donk spoke again, his tone oddly sad.

Preen noticeably bridled. "No one treats *me* with respect or thanks *me* for the far more important work I do," he snapped in return. "Why should *you* deserve it if I don't?"

And I was almost feeling sorry for him...

But the conversation could go either way—both Plans A and B were still on the cards and perhaps B was worth one final shot. It was time for Flirt to intervene. "Do you ever bother to earn it?" she inserted firmly. "Because that's how you get respect—you earn it. These lads, now, they've earned some, haven't they? They've done all you've ever asked of them and more. But what did you ever do to earn theirs?"

The rumble was growing. Midlin was looking worried. Sentinel was looking cross. Preen, however, looked irritated and his irritation sparked a sudden burst of bravery. "You want respect without earning it!" he retorted harshly. "You just told me!"

The Barmaid gave a cold grin. "We are earning it, the hard way, aren't we? By showing what we can do to those that don't want to see. And it sounds to me as though you could use a bit of that yourself, couldn't you?"

Preen blinked. "I beg your pardon?"

"You say you want thanks and respect." She had to be careful now—if she played what she was about to try badly, she might wind up alienating the very men she was seeking to convince. "Maybe you should go and get it for yourself rather than waiting for it to come to you."

Instant suspicion creased Preen's face, although there was a certain spark of interest within his eyes. "What do you mean?"

"I mean, maybe you should think about helping us." The Barmaid pulled a face. It was like pulling teeth to try this, especially knowing he had approved their murder the night before to save his own hide, but there was no denying he would be useful. And he was the only one who could open the damned book that was her last hope of tracking down the fate of Fodder and the others. "It pains me to say it, Preen, because frankly, you get on my nerves, don't you? But I think we have more in common than either of us think."

Preen's expression flared indignantly. "I can earn my own respect! You think I need your help for that? When I destroy you and bring this rebellion to an end..."

Destroy... *Nice choice of words there; what happened to 'capture'?*

Shoulders snorted loudly. "Yeah, because that's going to happen. I don't imagine your Assassin friend's in much of a state to help you right now. How much respect and thanks do you think they'll be heaping on you when they see you've lost your oh-so-important instructions to a pack of rebels and then botched taking them out?"

Preen winced noticeably but his features remained dark. "You actually want me to help you?" he snapped coldly. "And how do you suppose I can do that?"

"For starters"—Shoulders hefted Preen's precious book with a casualness that made the Courtier shudder—"you can show us how to unlock this little blighter."

It was his face. It was the look on his face, the sudden light in his eyes, the brief, intense smile—Flirt could smell the sudden surge of glee that rolled from Preen as he felt the pendulum of power swing back in his direction. Coldness swirled around her insides like a snake.

Oh no, oh, Shoulders, you shouldn't have said that...

"You can't open my book." It was a statement of fact that Flirt could not deny. "Of course you can't. Once it's locked, only my touch can be the key." The Courtier's smile spread, cold and predatory, as he saw the looks of discomfort that crossed their faces. "You don't want my help. You *need* it." He released a wild giggle at their expressions.

"You can't threaten me and you can't force me to do it. And without me, that book is nothing."

"The book doesn't matter now." Flirt stepped in, eager to neutralise Preen's sudden grab for power, but the look on his face told her she wasn't fooling anyone. "What matters is what this could mean for you. There's more that you could do, more that would get you noticed, get you respected..."

She wanted his hunger, and he felt the pang. "Such as?"

"Speak to the other Courtiers." This was it. Would he turn or would he flare? Either way, the name she was about to say would turn this whole business one way or the other. "Speak to Strut. Everyone knows he's the one who *really* runs things, and he could..."

"Strut?" She had said the magic word. Preen ignited. "Strut, Strut, Strut! I'm sick of the sound of his name! I'm sick of his stupid work and his ridiculous voice! I'm sick of the way everyone bows and scrapes and panders to him as though he's the most important person in the world!" Flirt stepped back as the Courtier gesticulated wildly, venting his spleen over his hated cousin. "He doesn't deserve it! I deserve it! *Me! It should be me!"* Abruptly, furiously, he wheeled on Flirt, one bony finger thrusting sharply in her direction. "You want my help?" he screeched. "Well, you can have it, on one condition. *I get Strut's job."*

There was a moment of shocked silence. Preen glared at them in return, breathing hard, his eyes glowing with a heady cocktail of fury, pent-up frustration, and just a glimmer of desperate craving. And he meant it. There was no denying the yearning on his face, writ bold and bright for all to see. Preen's true face was showing.

And around him, the men he had been badgering and haranguing and insulting to insure they obeyed their instructions and the chain of command without question or hesitation were staring at him.

Midlin seemed hardly able to believe he'd spoken the words. Sentinel's expression was disgusted. Squick's was nearly pitying.

Flirt kept her expression serious. But inside, she was crowing. *See that, lads? See how much he respects his so-called betters?*

"That's not how it's going to work," she said softly, cautiously, keeping her voice as neutral as she could. She couldn't believe she'd considered trying to recruit Preen when he clearly didn't really understand. "We aren't in this to put ourselves on top and tear others down—"

"That's exactly what you're in it for!" Preen retorted fiercely before she could finish her words. "You can couch it in whatever words you choose, but I see your meaning! You want to live in the Palace, swigging wine and playing Heroes and Heroines whilst you take your revenge and set those who once stood above you grubbing in the mud! Don't deny it! And I agree with it!" He ploughed on, cutting over the Barmaid's attempt to refute it. "We should make them pay for what they've done to us! Everyone who has ever looked down on us, not respected us, sneered at us! Every snobbish Noble that considered me beneath them should be made to clean every garderobe, every cesspit and rubbish bin! Hauteur, that smug bastard—he should be made to run naked through the streets of the Magnificent City—let's see how dignified he is then! Quibble, bloody Quibble, my own brother, thinking he's above me—he can play Disposable and get chopped up in a ditch. And as for bloody, bloody, bloody Strut... Let him come down here, to my level, and see how he likes it! Let him be the one to herd these...these witless cattle to the slaughter!" Preen swept an arm around to encompass the dangerously rumbling mass of his men. "Let him listen to their pathetic gripes, to their pointless ramblings, to their absurd notions! The *First Rule!*" He sneered openly. "Running in fear when you outnumber your enemy! Ridiculous! Let him face off their idiotic cowardice whilst I move in the circles of the elite, the talented, the heroic! Let him live my life and me live his! Give me that, give it to me and I'll give you whatever help you need!" He stared at Flirt, his eyes gleaming madly, his fingers curled from outstretched arms. "What do you say?"

Flirt stared at the wild, breathless figure before her, stared at the almost obscene craving on his face and felt a little sick. This was the bad side of Fodder's dream, the selfish side, like Poniard, who took their ideas and twisted them vilely to please himself. It was not a pleasant sight and she suspected that even if they succeeded, it wouldn't be the last time she saw it.

And there could only be one reply.

"No," she said. "Like I said, didn't I? That's not why we're doing this."

Preen's face froze. His fingers curled slowly and dangerously into fists.

"Then you will pay!" he shrieked insanely. "You will pay for your insolence! Guard!" One hand whipped out, grasping Sentinel by the arm. "Fetch your men! Fetch them now and attack!"

* * *

Erik had always been a clean boy, happy to scrub behind his ears at the insistence of his uncle and to take lazy dips in the pond behind his since-ruined childhood home. He had always admired the shining ripples of bouncing streams and the mirror reflections of a still lake surface. But right in that moment, he was quite happy to admit that he'd just as soon never see any kind of water again.

It had been so close. Had it not been for Elder's frankly heroic spell-casting that had held the ragged remains of the rapidly disintegrating ferry boat together long enough to fling them to the shore, Sir Roderick and Zahora at the very least would have been in a great deal of trouble, and the man of Sleiss's vindictive scheme to trick them onto a sinking vessel and abandon them to the unkind mercies of the river would have proved an unqualified success. But fortune had smiled— although they had suffered a cold and unpleasant dunking, none had been the worse for it as they had gathered on the bank in a damp huddle, shivering and emptying copious amounts of river weed from their clothing, armour, and other, less comfortable places.

After retrieving the disgruntled horses from the shallows, they had set about drying themselves, stripping off their wet tunics as Elder sparked a roaring fire to life to bring warmth and chase away the moisture. Even Zahora, in an uncharacteristically immodest display, had stripped down to her lower garments in an effort to dry herself properly; and although Erik had, with the best of intentions, fought to keep his gaze averted, he found himself unable to help but track her honed, curved figure out of the corner of his eye. A glance told him that Roderick and Slynder were similarly, if discreetly, transfixed; and to Erik's surprise, only Svenheid of all of them proved able to remain a true gentleman as he kept his gaze firmly pointed in the direction of where Erik, along with the knight and the thief, had settled together after hanging their stripped-off tunics by the fire.

"Whither hence do we ride?" Sir Roderick asked at length as, with the worst of the water dried from them, the companions set about pulling on their unpleasantly clammy clothing and distinctly rusted armour once more. "We have been travelling with scant aim for near a day now."

Elder was shaking his head as he emptied out the last dregs of water from his long boots. "We must learn what Craxis plans. His forces may already be massing." He glanced up the low, sloping, wooded rise that hemmed in the river valley. "Beyond that horizon lie the Paltas Flats, open scrub and grassland that stretch for many miles from the Swamp of Craxis to the Plains of Nyolesse. It would make an easy passage for an invading force to reach the lands of those he would destroy. With the Ring so close, I cannot imagine Craxis will wait in his stronghold much longer. We must make haste to find his men and carry warning, if needs be, to our allies in the south."

Erik felt a well of cold within his breast. "What of the princess? Have we abandoned her?"

Elder stared at his young charge with genuine sorrow. "Her trail is lost," he conceded with apparent pain. "There is nothing we can do there but hope. And with the strange nature of this man of Sleiss, this Fodhelion as he would call himself, you have even lost your sense of the Ring. We can but fight the enemy we can see."

Battling a surge of hopeless, painful rage, Erik pulled himself into his saddle. He felt the gauntleted hand of Sir Roderick land gently against his shoulder, saw his sad eyes at the abandonment of his mistress, but the knight said nothing. Erik was grateful for that. He had no wish for further words.

And so it was in silence that Erik and his companions made their way up the lightly wooded hillside, the afternoon sun a gleam against gathering clouds that mustered like a wall of troops across the surrounding sky. As the ground began to level, the trees thinned out and before them stretched the expanse of the Paltas Flats, a sheer horizon filled from end to end with remorselessly smooth, unbroken plains of grass that arched away until swallowed by the blue touch of the far sky. It seemed to Erik that if one were to cross that great, level, featureless expanse, one would find a domed wall of azure and fluffy white that burrowed into the earth and brushed against the out-stretched fingers of he who dared approach it.

"The Paltas Flats," Elder said softly. "There is no hiding here. We will see the troops of Craxis or any other enemy long before they come."

Erik smiled in satisfaction as he reined in his horse by the edge of the trees. Not a hummock, not a sapling, not a bramble or bush could be seen beyond that point. The man of Sleiss would not sneak up on them so easily out...

"All right there?"

Erik gasped; Zahora reined in her horse so sharply that it reared and bucked violently. Slynder swore, Svenheid growled, and Sir Roder-ick's sword was already near out of its sheath as Elder's fingers glowed. But the man of Sleiss, who was leaning casually up against the last scrubby patch of trees before the spread of flat grass, merely cocked a half-smile and shrugged at the sight of their efforts.

"Are you going to bother, though, really?" he said easily. With a glint of red, he twiddled the Ring of Anthiphion with shocking disre-spect between his fingers. "Because, you know what'll happen, so why waste your effort?"

"Impudent wretch!" Roderick's sword was quivering in his grasp. "What foul plan do you seek to inflict upon us now?"

"Inflict?" The man of Sleiss pulled out a distinctly insincere expression of affront. "That's hardly polite, is it? Besides, mate, don't you think if I was going to rain down some terrible fate upon you, I'd have done it before I let you see me?"

There was a thoughtful pause as this point sunk in. But Elder was glaring at their nemesis, lightning arcing between his fingers like a terri-ble maelstrom locked in his palm.

"Then what do you want?" he barked angrily.

The smile was back, soft, easy, infuriating. "I want to do you a favour."

"Really?" Slynder exclaimed cynically as he shifted his bad leg in the saddle.

"Yep." The man of Sleiss pushed himself upright, gesturing with a flourish like a street magician's sleight of hand to the tree against which he had just rested. "I wanted to suggest you make use of this tree. While you have the chance, I mean."

Erik blinked, and he wasn't alone.

"Make use of it?" Svenheid rumbled. "What nonsense do you talk now?"

"No nonsense." The man of Sleiss was couched in a mask of sincere concern. "It's a nice tree and the last place of discretion you're going to come across for a while." He gestured out across the flat, open expanse before them. "So I thought you lads might want to stop and take a piss."

The silence that followed was as vast as the plains stretched out before them. It whistled like a scud of wind through unimaginable distance and unspoken-of places. And only at great length, and somewhat cautiously, was it broken eventually by Slynder.

"Pardon?" he managed.

"I thought you lads might want to piss behind the tree." The man of Sleiss repeated the words with abominable casualness. He was still smiling that awful half-smile. "And for the lady, there is this charming selection of wind-dappled foliage." He swept his hand in a cheery arc. "I mean, seriously, do you want to leave it until you get out there into the unbroken nothingness without so much as a tuft to crouch behind? Imagine the draft..." He shook his head with mocking concern. "And no privacy, of course, and no way of getting any—you do a piss out there and everyone's going to see you. You could circle the horses for a bit of discretion but that seems a bit daft when you've a perfectly good tree back here. So why not make use of it while you can, hmm?"

Elder's face had gone slightly purple. His voice, when it rippled from the depths of his beard, was distinctly dangerous. "What, in the name of all that is holy, makes you think we have the slightest need for...that?"

The man of Sleiss cocked his head. "Well, you did take on a lot of water recently," he offered innocently.

Elder's eyebrows knitted into one giant, angry caterpillar of white. "And why do you assume we have not already...taken care of such matters?"

The man of Sleiss shrugged. "Well, because you didn't, did you? I was watching from up here—you pulled yourselves out, lit a fire and dried yourselves off, goggled at harridan when you thought she wasn't looking, then mounted up and rode up the hill. No pissing about there." He pulled a thoughtful face as Erik shifted in the saddle, trying to ignore the strange discomfort that was welling at the foot of his belly. "In fact, as far as I've noticed, there's been no pissing about anywhere. You've got a big hairy barbarian over there who drinks gallons of ale every chance he gets, but where does he put it away because it never comes out again." He shook his head. "I've seen a lot of quests," he remarked inexplicably. "And I know there's not much let-up for you merry people, not much time out of the glare of the good old light to take care of such things. But you know what? It needs to be taken care of, you know. You can't ignore it, but yet it doesn't happen. I don't ever remember seeing the big, brave hero nipping behind a bush for a quick moment of relief. I don't recall catching a princess having a discreet squat in a hollow. And the amount of ale that gets put away in every inn, but does anyone ever nip out to use the privy? No!" He tutted grimly. "And the thing is, that liquid has to go somewhere, doesn't it? Sweat doesn't cover it and if no one ever goes, well... Where is it? Sitting there maybe? Waiting?" He gave a sigh as his gaze shifted from face to face, rich with an odd kind of pity. "I hate to bring this up, I really do, but it's for your own good. I mean, think about it, seriously. When's the last time any of you people went to the toilet?"

Erik was speechless. Partly it was the crude impudence of the question but partly it was also because of the sudden, disconcerting appeal of the tree. He wriggled in his saddle, trying to shift the weight that had settled over his bladder like a boulder of pure granite. It was to no avail.

And the man of Sleiss was still smiling. "So, like I said," he remarked, patting one hand against the bark. "I thought I'd offer up this tree. While the chance is there. In case you need to go."

Elder drew himself up. "We have no need of your ridiculous offer! We have no need to go!"

"Ummm…" The heat of Elder's eyes could have ignited the grasslands into a raging inferno as they swung to find Slynder hunched over in his saddle, hand half-raised and with a painful expression on his face. "Actually, I wouldn't mind a minute…"

His voice trailed off under Elder's thunderous glare. The sorcerer's voice was as stormy as his face. "You do not need to go," he declared, his tone rich with menace.

Slynder's expression was pure pain and his voice a strained squeak. "Fair enough! I can probably…hold it…"

He doubled over in the saddle as Elder's eyes swung dangerously across the others. For the first time, through the haze of his own discomfort, Erik noticed the way Sir Roderick's lips were clamped together as sweat dripped down his face, that Zahora was switching her gaze between the empty expanse and the cosy foliage with an expression close to yearning, and that Svenheid's eyes had slowly but distinctly begun to cross. Erik winced. How had the man of Sleiss managed this? What was the absurd lunatic doing to them?

"Everyone all right?" The man of Sleiss was raking his eyes over their suddenly crippled company with insincere concern. "Look, there's no shame in it. It's a natural bodily function! When you've got to go, you've got to go!"

Elder turned fully purple. "No one needs to go!"

"Now, I don't know about that." The man of Sleiss hooked his hands casually behind his back. His gaze switched to Roderick. "You're looking a bit uncomfortable there, Sir Knight. Feeling the call of nature, are we?"

Sir Roderick's expression was a mixture of strain and steel. "I will not fall prey to your blandishments, fiend!"

"Your bladder will probably burst then," the man of Sleiss noted clinically. "Look, I'm not doing anything here. There's no spell, no magic. You've just realised that in however many weeks you've been riding out on this quest, none of you have ever relieved yourselves." He shrugged. "That kind of thing…well, it's going to build up, isn't it? And after being dumped in that water, all that sloshing, splashing water going tinkle, tinkle, tinkle when it gushed out of your clothes…"

"Oh, bugger this!" Even as Erik grimaced in pain, Slynder had already cracked—the little thief flung himself out of the saddle, landing heavily on his injured leg as he dropped to the ground with a cry. But he was not to be thwarted—scrambling on his hands and knees on the dusty track, he crawled into the bushes. A moment later, a huge sigh of relief drifted from behind the tree along with the sound of…

"Gods have mercy!" Roderick was next, vaulting from his war horse as he bolted for cover, his hands already yanking back the relevant gaps in his armour. An instant later, with a pained gasp, Zahora dived into the greenery.

Elder was incandescent with fury. "Don't even…" he started to scream in Svenheid's direction, but the barbarian had already toppled sideways out of the saddle, landing with a crash on the road. After a moment's scrambling, he too found a tree and…

No, no, he couldn't, he couldn't hold on anymore, he was going to have to…

"Erik!" Elder's roar could have felled an army. "Don't you dare!"

The pain was excruciating, the need immense, and only the sheer, terrifying weight of Elder's will kept Erik in the saddle. He was going to burst, explode in a hideous, messy heap as he battled to contain more liquid than any human being could reasonably survive…

And then the man of Sleiss, with slow, deliberate care, drew a bottle of water from his belt and shook it gently. It sloshed.

"Want some?" he asked sweetly.

It was more than a scream. It was a primal, echoing, desperate cry of one past the edge of despair. Erik could stand no more.

He heard Elder's voice screeching at him, but he didn't care. He heard a chuckle too and felt in that instant an urge to turn, to fight, to smite the hated enemy who had inflicted such horrors upon him. But his need was too urgent, too pressing, and revenge would be too late; for even as he hurled himself from the saddle and darted into the last of the trees for desperate, sweet relief, he saw the flash of red that meant the man of Sleiss was...

Gone...

* * *

It was a sad and tragic fact of his family, Dullard had to concede. So many—too many—members of the Royal and Noble families who had spawned him were so lost in their stereotypes that they'd completely forgotten how to be people.

However, there were probably better times to mull that fact over than when one was tumbling head-over-bruising-heel down a wooden staircase tangled with the spitting, snarling shape of one's homicidal distant cousin. Dullard filed the thought away and turned himself back to the business at hand.

With a jarring thud, Dullard slammed down against the small wooden landing. He could feel his fingers still digging tightly into the hilt of his sword as he scrambled desperately, shoving himself aside moments before the weight of Bold slapped, sword blade first, down beside him. He heard his cousin's winded *oof* as he curled up in a shocked ball at the feel of an actual impact—clearly he was more accustomed to engaging in dramatic combat In Narrative, where the magic light would wipe away any pain from such a minor thing as tumbling the length of a flight of stairs. Far more at home in prosaic reality, Dullard limped and groaned his way to his feet, grabbing the banister as he staggered towards the final few steps into the open expanse of the Great Hall. Open ground, room to defend himself—that was what he was going to need if Bold was determined to press this ridiculous urge for violence and...

Fingers snatched around his ankle, dragging him off-balance. Dullard kicked out instinctively at Bold's screech of triumph but it was already too late—reeling like a drunkard, he flew forwards, slapping face first into the wooden floor of the Hall as his body walloped the length of the remaining steps with painful clarity. Certain that lines of precisely spaced bruising lay in his not-too-distant future, Dullard nonetheless managed to snatch his ankle free of his cousin's grasping fingers, slithering forward as hurriedly as he dared until the momentum of his feet overtook him and sent him somersaulting heels-over-backside into a heap on the floor.

He could taste blood against his tongue and feel its warm slither down his face. His entire body was a blossom of potential purple waiting to erupt into bruises.

This was not going at all how he'd hoped.

Heavy footsteps on wood. Bold was on his feet.

Oh dear.

The swing of the sword missed his nose by less than an inch and sent splinters hurtling from the wooden floor with the power of the impact. Dullard rolled reflexively, stumbling to his feet, his hand fortuitously still grasping his sword as he blocked the second blow Bold had just aimed for his neck. His cousin was glaring at him like a man possessed, teeth gritted within the cradle of his blond goatee, eyes wild—with a warlike shriek that echoed through the Great Hall's rafters, he dragged his sword away and swung yet again with demonic fervour. Dullard managed to deflect the blow once more as he danced backwards, but he could already see the next strike lining up, a mighty double-hander aimed right at his torso; and he knew, heavy in his heart, that he would not be able to bring his sword around in time to stop it.

So he did the only thing he could think of. He leapt.

And in a motion that Dullard was quite certain he could never have pulled off had he been consciously trying, he landed two-footed and with perfect balance on the end of the mighty banqueting table.

There was a brief, shocked pause from both combatants. Neither of them had expected *that*.

Bold stared at him, inhaling sharp, rasping breaths as his eyes filled with indignation.

"How dare you?" he hissed. "That's *my* move!"

Well. It seemed that Sweetness wasn't the only one in that marriage with a possessive nature. "Sorry," Dullard offered diffidently, not particularly wanting to antagonise the already seething ex-Hero any further. "It was an accident."

That, however, proved the wrong thing to say. "Accident?" Bold's voice topped the next octave. "Accident? I spent a month, a solid month, perfecting that trick and even then, The Narrative had to help me! But now you have the blazing gall to stand there and tell me you did it by *accident?*" His jaw hardened viciously. "Well, maybe I should show you what else I've perfected!"

Other feet had appeared down the stairs now, Sir Valour and a couple of his lower-ranked cohorts locked in a bizarre battle of kitchen-implement-versus-swordplay with Jolly, Sour, and several others from the Servants. But heedless of these newcomers, Bold dashed backwards, shoving aside a hapless Servant with one hand and an unfortunate Knight with the other as he gained the height of the dais. His lips were twisted into a manic smile as his eyes fixed on a point just above Dullard's head.

On the *iron chandelier.*

Oh goodness. This probably wasn't going to end well.

Dullard prudently backed his way down the vast table. Bold, apparently believing he'd scented fear, let out a whooping holler and hurled himself forwards.

In all fairness to him, it wasn't a bad effort. The power of adrenaline had given him a launching strength that Dullard hadn't quite expected and by some miracle, he did indeed, with a handy boost from the end of the table, manage to get his hands around the candle-lined ring of iron and start to swing forwards. In Narrative, Dullard was certain it would have been a thing of beauty, a magical arc that would have ended with his own body being catapulted backwards by a pair of well-cobbled boots and landed on with a fairly decisive crunch.

In reality, however, the impact dislodged several candles, splattering Bold's hands, arms, and face with hot wax. Even as he gave a bellow of shock, the tumble of a flaming wick slapped against his fingers and his legs flailed haplessly in mid-air—hollering an unmanly screech, the ex-Hero lost his grip and landed with a crunching thud on the tabletop.

Giving a wonderfully musical quiver, his sword point dug into the wood around an inch to the left of his ear.

There was a brief cessation of violence. Even the red-faced Stalwart, who'd appeared at the top of the stairs, couldn't help but take a moment to drink in the sight of Bold lying on his back on the banqueting table, whimpering and clutching his fingers like a wounded toddler.

Politely, Dullard waited for his cousin to get his breath back, pausing a moment to wipe the blood from his face with his handkerchief in order to distract himself from a powerful and unworthy desire to burst out laughing. He diligently tidied his aching nose and restrained his twitching lips as Bold lurched onto his elbows and then his knees, winded and gasping. Around them, the fight resumed in pockets of random violence—Sir Valour was fending off Jolly's dangerous ladle with a bewildered expression as Bow and Sour rounded on the once-more-rampaging Stalwart and pursued him onto the dais. The prince even saw Duke Valiant stagger through the solar door, clutching himself in a somewhat inappropriate place as he lurched his way down the stairs. A moment later, a wild-eyed Scrape appeared in hot pursuit, brandishing a broken broom handle with a distinct air of intent.

The feel of eyes burning against his skin turned him back to the matter in hand. Bold was resting on his knees, one hand wrapped around the hilt of his imbedded sword as he glared at Dullard with furious humiliation rampant in his eyes.

Carefully, Dullard tucked his scarlet-stained handkerchief away in his doublet, taking a firmer grip on his sword once more.

"Are you all right?" he asked cautiously.

Bold's expression flared. "Don't patronise me, you cretinous little worm," he snapped in retort. "You knew that was going to happen, didn't you?"

Dullard shrugged awkwardly, fighting down the inappropriate flood of satisfaction that was running circuits in the back of his mind. It was unbecoming to be so unkind, even if the man *was* an obnoxious tit. "I had a feeling. That kind of move works beautifully with The Narrative to back it up, but in real life, it's highly improbable. Sorry."

"Sorry?" The acid behind that word could have dissolved metal. "You *will* be sorry, you bottom-feeding ne'er-do-well, you filthy maggot, you pompous, self-righteous, turncoat scum!" He lurched to his feet, sword gripped ruthlessly in his hand as he straightened himself, shoulders flung back, chest thrust forwards, legs locked in their

best heroic pose as he flicked his hair back from his face in one dashing sweep. "You should have run me through when you had the
chance! You will never have the chance again! I will rend your limbs
from your body and decorate the walls with them! I will strip the skin
from your traitorous bones! I will make bellows of your lungs and feast
upon your liver! I will have your bones for my dogs and make a trophy
of your heart! I will eviscerate you, make a rope of your guts, and hang
you with them as you gasp your last! I will spread your quivering flesh
across every inch of this hall! I will destroy you so utterly they will
struggle to find as much as a fingernail to bury! I will make you sorry
you ever dared to breathe a word beyond your place! I will make you
pay!" With a gorgeously twisting flourish, he thrust his sword point
towards Dullard, dropping into a crouch as he poised himself for
battle. "Have at you, cur!"

With a precise twist of his wrist, Dullard lashed out, catching the
hilt of Bold's sword and snatching it from his grasp. It landed with a
clatter against the tapestry-lined wall.

Bold stared blankly for a moment at the hand that had seconds
before held his weapon. He blinked.

Dullard gave another shrug. "You were holding it wrong," he
offered politely. "That stance looks lovely In Narrative, but again, this
is real life now, and, well..." He flashed a brief, apologetic smile. "You
did rather leave yourself open." Bold's blank stare was rising to his face
now, features fixed and eyes stunned as Dullard ploughed on. Perhaps
this was an opportunity, common ground, a chance to build a bridge
with his distant relative. "I'd be glad to show you how if you wanted—
I've made an extensive study of swordplay over the last few Quests,
especially Narrative techniques as opposed to what works without it.
Or if you'd like to start the fight over when we're both a bit more
ready, I'm perfectly happy to wait here for a minute while you go and
get your sword..."

Bold was still staring at him. A hint of horror was tinting the edges
of his eyes.

"Not that I want to keep fighting, of course," Dullard conceded.
Maybe something could be salvaged from this; perhaps in shock, there
could be logic. "As I said, we didn't come here to fight, which is why I

made no effort to incapacitate you while you were down. All I want to do is talk." He risked a smile but Bold's oddly haunted expression offered nothing in return. "I'm sure between us, you and I could bring an end to this madness. All we have to do is calm everyone down and be reasonable." Lowering his sword, he widened the gentle smile as he offered his free hand to his cousin. "What do you say?"

Bold was staring at him. The hint of horror in his eyes had become a flooding confirmation.

"The Narrative!" he screeched wildly at the top of his voice. "We need The Narrative! Help!"

Before Dullard could catch hold of him, Bold had turned on his heels and fled, flinging himself off the table with a stumbling leap. He slammed into the wall, scooped up his fallen sword, and lurched with an ungainly barge through the Great Hall's exterior doors. Cries of alarm sounded from the courtyard beyond.

Dullard sighed. Oh, good grief...

The gates and secret passage were well guarded, he knew. But Bold was teetering on the edge of crazy and there was no guarantee that Strut would permit any limb- or indeed head-removing damage he did to Chopper, Cleave, or the Artisans guarding the gates to be fixed. Healing bashes and scrapes was one thing, but even out of Narrative, hacked-off limbs needed a pixie. No, he had to stop him and he had to do it quickly...

He leapt from the table, managed two steps forward, and was flung to the ground as a heavily built lesser Noble who Dullard believed was called Stance barrelled into him, staggering, bewildered, with his doublet ripped. An Artisan and a dishevelled serving Maid tackled him to the ground as one and started relentlessly beating his head against the wooden floor.

"Gently!" Dullard would have stayed to ensure his words were heard—judging by the grim determination with which the Maid was yanking on Stance's hair, the prince suspected she either hadn't heard or was working out some previously unheralded grudge—but Bold had already disappeared and right now, he had to be the priority. Hurrying back onto his painfully achy feet, Dullard started forwards once more.

"No more, please! No more! I *surrender!*"

Hands grasped the sleeves of his doublet, desperate fingers pulling at the fabric. Dullard staggered and wheeled to find himself staring at the pale and terrified face of a young Knight called Sir Venture.

"I never wanted to be a Knight!" he sobbed, his hands clinging relentlessly to Dullard as the prince fought, as politely and sympathetically as he could, to extricate himself from his grip. "I hate fighting! All that running around makes me feel awful! I suffer from horse sickness! I want to do something quiet and peaceful like gardening or tapestry weaving or flower arranging! Please can I do that, *please* don't make me fight any more! Have mercy on—"

"Look out!"

Dullard didn't even think about what he was doing. He heard Jolly's scream, saw the furious crimson face topped by manic red hair that belonged to the charging Baron Stalwart, and simply used the first weapon that came to hand.

It was unfortunate that weapon was Sir Venture.

Hurling the young Knight round in a mace-like arc, Dullard flung his poor young supplicant into the rampaging Baron's face. The young man's metal cuirass slammed into Stalwart's ruddy features and hurled him backwards to the ground with a crashing thud. There was a painful-sounding tear of thread and suddenly Bland and Nameless hurtled into view, dragging the tapestry they had just liberated from the wall and flinging it over his struggling body. For a moment their efforts seemed doomed to fail as they fought to contain the fervent flailing and muffled roars from beneath the fabric; but with an almost stately determination, Jolly the Plump Cook waddled over and, after delivering two firm raps with her ladle, settled her substantial backside quite firmly on his head. The struggling ceased abruptly.

Grasping a shocked-looking Venture by the elbows, Dullard hauled him over to where Bland and Nameless were rolling their suddenly subdued captive up a little more securely. From her new seat, Jolly glanced up warily.

"Jolly, this is Venture and he's surrendered." With far less care than he would like to have taken, Dullard thrust the bewildered young man into the arms of the cook. "I have to go, but can you please look after him—gently?" he added, seeing the alarming gleam in his old friend's eyes. "He's no danger."

Jolly nodded. "Course I will, love."

"Thank you!" Turning rapidly away, Dullard hurried once more to the door that Bold had fled through a short but alarming while ago. Surely nothing else could possibly...

"Scrape, move!"

Bow's bellow echoed from the rafters even as a bizarre, three-headed creature lurched and limped into Dullard's path. In spite of his apparent earlier incapacity, Duke Valiant had recovered enough to put up a...well, *valiant* battle, his broadsword swinging wildly as Bow and Scrape clung to his body. Scrape was wrapped around his knees with his eyes tightly shut and Bow latched like a limpet to his shoulders as he wrestled with him for control of the sword. And the reason for Bow's cry became immediately apparent as Dullard saw Valiant wrench his hilt free of the serving man's grasp and swing his sword in a dangerous downward arc towards...

Dullard stared. No, surely, he couldn't be that...

Scrape too had heard the call. And as he saw the blade descend, he yelped and hurled himself flat to the ground.

Valiant's knees, it was safe to say, were unable to follow suit.

For, with a beautiful forehand sweep, Valiant sliced straight through his own legs.

There was a brief moment of shocked pause for all concerned. And then slowly, inevitably with the weight of Bow on his back, Duke Valiant teetered and slid forwards like a felled tree. Like the stump of a mighty oak marking its passing, his shins and booted feet remained defiantly upright.

Certain that Bow and Scrape would easily have the legless Valiant in hand, Dullard vaulted over the Duke's supine form and finally reached the door that Bold had bolted through. Bubbling with frustration and fear at the delays he had suffered, he yanked it open and stared.

The gates were still locked, thank goodness, manned by determined-looking Artisans grasping the hammers and saws of their trade, although several of the lesser Nobles were making a spirited attempt to breach them. At the forefront of the defenders stood Cleave, laying about him with a length of wood that was driving his wary attackers back with bold vigour.

They were doing well enough. But where was…

Bold.

There. Dullard could see him now, at the far end of the stretch of battlements that started from this very stone stair, above the giant wooden shape of…

Oh dear, no. A trebuchet.

Dullard hadn't realised that any of the siege engines had been completed by the Artisans. He supposed they hadn't thought it mattered enough to mention. But there it was, a fully completed and—oh no—armed trebuchet, waiting to be wheeled out into battle or, alternatively, fired directly at the gates at which it was coincidentally aimed, shattering them and any who stood before them into tiny pieces and opening the way for Bold to…

No one from below seemed to have seen the danger. Bold had only to descend one flight of stairs and he would…

"Hold, foul fiend! Now, I have you!"

An armoured figure jumped into Dullard's path, tall, broad, perfectly formed, chin cleft and hair blond, eyes flashing with heroic rage as he jabbed his sword against Dullard's chest. Sir Valour grinned fiercely.

"Now you will pay for your misdeeds, traitor!"

But over his shiny, muscular shoulder, Dullard could see Bold starting towards the steps, his eyes locked on the catapult with fervent intent…

Dullard's eyes flicked to Valour, this strutting, this ridiculous, this…*Pleasance-courting* fool in his way, and something inside of him snapped.

"I don't have *time* for this!" he cried out, and suddenly his hand was lashing forwards, catching Valour's badly held blade, and slapping it back into his unnaturally handsome face. Even as Valour reeled in shock, Dullard drove his shoulder into his body, charging him backwards, *backwards* and back against the battlements, *through* the battlements as his prince-pushed momentum and the weight of his armour drove the apprentice Knight, with a high-pitched screech, over the wall and out of sight.

Ah. Oops.

As Dullard staggered away, half-turning back towards his destination, the adrenaline that had driven him forwards moments before vanished like an unplugged dam. In its place came the default state of guilt.

What *had* he done? There was a gorge out there! Valour was a nuisance and an irritant but he hadn't deserved that! He couldn't just leave without...

Biting his lip, Dullard scampered rapidly back to the part of the wall from which the apprentice Knight had been hurled. Grabbing the stonework, he cupped a hand to his mouth and leaned out.

"Sorry!" he called down anxiously.

There was no response. He hadn't expected one. But he felt a bit better for having apologised.

Duty done, Dullard turned and hurtled after Bold once more. But to his surprise, he found his cousin not on the stairs down, but poised on the battlements. And he wasn't alone.

He was standing, no, he was struggling with someone, locked in a desperate fight with a hangdog figure brandishing a dangerous-looking cleaver.

Sour!

But he was no match for Bold! He had to help him!

Cursing himself for hesitating, Dullard rushed forwards once more. Even as he ran, he could see Sour was now pressed against the battlements as Bold grabbed the cleaver-grasping hand and slammed it against the stone, once, twice, three times...

The cleaver tumbled. And Bold was lifting Sour, pushing him, shoving him through the gap as Dullard himself had accidentally done to Valour moments earlier; and the drop below, though nothing to a gorge, was hard cobblestones and a skull-dashing fall to the stable yard and days of painful recovery...

He had to stop him before it was...

Too late.

Limbs flailing, Sour plunged head first from the wall. He slammed into the roof of the stables, smashing the rough thatch aside as he vanished in a hail of straw. He did not emerge.

"Sour!" At Dullard's wild cry, Bold's head snapped up. He gasped and grasped his sword as he backed down the battlement.

"Get away from me!" Bold's sword flapped and slashed madly in his direction. "Leave me alone, you freak!"

"Freak?" Dullard could feel his hands trembling as he advanced down the stone walkway towards his cousin, his voice low and dangerous, too worked-up to stay polite. "From you, Bold, I'll take that as a compliment! Because I'd rather be a freak than an obnoxious, selfish, self-deluded, vain, conceited, strutting, pompous, arrogant, bullying bastard like *you!*"

The look on Bold's face at his insult was almost worth the lifetime of taunting and victimisation that had provoked it. His bearded jaw dropped and flapped like a limp goldfish.

"You can't speak to me like that!" he exclaimed indignantly.

Dullard, who had surprised even himself, shocked himself further with an incredulous laugh. "Actually, it's remarkably easy," he retorted cheerfully. "I just opened my mouth and out came the words!"

Bold clenched his teeth. "I will not be humiliated by you!"

Dullard raised an eyebrow. "I don't think there's much need. You seem to be doing a remarkably good job by yourself."

"Oh yeah?" With one admittedly impressive dashing leap, Bold landed on the edge of the wall, balancing carefully as he thrust his sword point towards Dullard's nose. "Well, we'll see who's laughing when I fire that trebuchet and level the walls and those gates to rubble!"

Dullard had had quite enough. "And how do you plan to get down there?" He gestured to the stairs behind where Cleave, who had finally subdued his attackers, was advancing rapidly up the stone steps with a stern-looking Lathe as a furious Bow approached from the hall. "I think you'll find you're trapped, Bold. Step down and surrender and no one else needs to get hurt—"

"Never! I will never surrender to the forces of infamy!" Dullard stepped back as spittle was flung in a wide arc from Bold's maddened lips. "See!" He gestured frantically downwards, towards the broken roof of the stables—Dullard could see poor Sour's battered form being carried clear by Jolly and Bland as the Nobles' horses milled around, looking confused. "My noble steed will catch me! He will carry me to safety!"

His noble steed…

Oh no. Surely he wasn't going to…

"Bold!" Dullard darted forwards desperately. "Bold, don't…"

He jumped.

And, insanely, he was grinning. Legs apart, sword aloft, his expression smug and beatific as he waited in expectation for the unnaturally gentle impact and impressive ride to safety he was anticipating. Indeed, he continued to grin right up into the moment when he bounced off the tall stallion's backside, did a full somersault, and landed face first on the hard floor.

The horse trod on his head.

And he'd still continued to grin as Cleave and Bow had bound up his badly bent body and dragged him like a sack of potatoes to join the heap of groaning, damaged Nobles that was amassing in the centre of the courtyard. Dullard had a nasty suspicion that he might be a bit broken in more than his body.

He sighed, stretching his bruised and aching form as he stared over the battered mass of his distant family—Stalwart's red hair sticking up out of the green tapestry in which he had been rolled like an inverted carrot, Lord Stance hunched in a heap with a large dent in his skull, Duke Valiant looking lost as he stared at his legs propped up beside him. Dullard had already suggested to a couple of Artisans that they could go out to collect the undoubtedly battered form of Valour and had been shocked to learn from Scrape that they'd need to pick up poor, brave Dauntless as well. They'd made a few conversions— Venture was sat with one of the Maids, wearing a beatific smile as he wove daisies into her hair; and Duchess Vanity's rejected ex-Hero, Defiant, had sidled up to Dullard and asked if they were planning on doing the same thing at the Palace where said Vanity was, and if so, could he help? Given the presence of her apparently uninformed husband, Dullard had diplomatically opted not to make a fellow rejected suitor's day by revealing her recent dragon-pancaked state but instead focused on several other minor Nobles who had also expressed an interest in a change of status quo. And, apart from Sour and one unlucky Artisan who was sat having his guts sewn back into his belly by a Maid with a resigned expression, no one from the Servants had been badly hurt.

They had done it. They had taken the castle.

But it wasn't how Dullard had wanted to take the castle. He hadn't wanted a fight. He'd wanted people to understand.

Well, maybe now the situation was clarified, now that they could see that these Servants were as courageous as the Nobles' Narrative roles, there would be more understanding, there would be a change of heart. Now they could see this was real, that the Servants weren't going to be pushed around anymore...

They could try to talk to them again and this time, the Servants themselves would do the talking, although obviously he and Pleasance would help out wherever...

Pleasance.

Where was Pleasance?

He glanced around once more. But no blonde, curly head appeared, no purple-clad figure marshalling their troops or berating her foolish family. The fight was over. Why was she not here?

And... He felt a cold, terrified snatch against his heart. Where was Sweetness? And where, oh where, was King Paragon?

He caught Bow by the arm. "Have you been back up to the solar?"

Bow frowned at him—perhaps Dullard's expression was betraying the sudden fear that had grasped his insides. "Not yet. Do you need us to?"

Dullard's grip tightened. He was overreacting. He had to be. Pleasance and, yes, Menial too, for she was also absent; they were probably sitting with the captured Sweetness and Paragon, waiting for someone to come. "Yes, very much. Because Countess Sweetness and King Paragon are unaccounted for."

Bow's eyes widened. "I'll get the lads. We'll..."

"Prince Dullard! *Prince Dullard!*"

Menial. He saw the Maid stumble through the door from the Great Hall, her head bleeding and her eyes full of fear, and he knew. He knew as his heart plunged and his ears roared, he knew as he rushed forward unbidden and caught her stumbling form as she reached the bottom of the steps, knew as she grabbed his arms and stared him in the face with a horror-filled gaze.

"Oh, sir!" she exclaimed.

"Where is she?" Dullard couldn't quite believe himself how calmly the question came out. He could barely hear his own words over the tumult of his own heartbeat. "Where is Princess Pleasance?"

Menial's face was pale and bloody. "They took her, sir!" she gasped out. "Her father and sister, they took her away! They knocked her out and dragged her off, sir!" She took a deep, rasping breath as she stared into his eyes, seeing the question he asked silently whilst already knowing the answer. "Oh, sir! They're taking her back to The Narrative!"

* * *

"No."

Sentinel's single word was softly spoken, but it rang across the Camp like a struck bell. His face was a mask of cold disdain.

"What?" Dishevelled and wild-eyed, Preen's features contorted as he stared up at the stony face of the captain of the Palace Guard. "I gave you an order!"

"And I choose not to obey it." Sentinel's expression could have been carved in granite. "My orders come from the instructions. You no longer have the instructions." His eyes performed a languorous dart in the direction of Shoulders and the brown book clasped in his hands. "And based on the disgrace I have witnessed, I do not consider you a worthy person to interpret our commands. My men and I will take no further part until there is someone here who is."

Preen gaped. "But...but I'm your Courtier!" he almost shrieked. "You can't speak to me like that!"

"I think you'll find I can." With a sharp, precise yank, Sentinel snapped his arm clear of Preen's grasping hand. The tiniest hint of a curl appeared in one corner of his lips. "Indeed, I believe I just did."

And with a sweeping turn of his heel, Sentinel marched away from the open-mouthed Courtier and back to the shiny ranks of his men. A moment later, to the jingle of kit and the uniform stamp of boots, the ranks of the Palace Guard turned and marched back into their camp.

For a moment, Preen seemed only able to stare at the sudden gaping hole in the flank of his perimeter. Flirt didn't blame him. She'd always doubted that Sentinel was likely to be swayed to disobedience, but she'd never expected that he and his men would actually abandon the siege.

Well. That makes things easier, doesn't it?

Her gaze quickly raked the ranks of the men left behind. Most looked nervous. Some looked angry. Many looked shocked. But none looked particularly inclined to be the first to step up and lead the charge in Sentinel's place. Flirt fought not to punch the air. It was working! Facing a choice between their orders and the fundamental rules of their life—they were hesitating. They were thinking! And once the thinking had started…

"You!" Preen's harsh exclamation cut into her thoughts—she glanced up to find that he had wheeled dramatically on Midlin, marching up to his bland-faced new field captain with fire in his eyes. "You do it then! Get some men and attack them!"

But Midlin was staring at him. Midlin the obedient, Midlin the unimaginative, Midlin who lived and breathed orders from a higher power, was making no move to obey. His chin was trembling slightly.

"Is it in the instructions?" he said desperately.

Preen blinked. "What?"

Midlin's hands were starting to shake as well. "The instructions…" he managed, his monotone voice suddenly wavering. "The instructions must be obeyed."

Preen manically rolled his eyes. "I'm giving you instructions, you ridiculous man! Get some men and attack them!"

"But…" Midlin's face contorted painfully. "But you don't have the book. Instructions come from the book. And if you don't have the book…" His lips quivered. "How do you know what the instructions would say?"

Preen exploded. "I *just do!*"

"But…but the First Rule!" Midlin's words stammered out of blood-drained features. Sweat pooled on his brow. "The instructions always follow the First Rule and…*ack!*"

Preen lunged like a cobra. Long fingers clamped around the front of Midlin's mail shirt and, fuelled by the strength of frustrated rage, he hauled the Disposable up onto tiptoes and shook him like a ragdoll.

"Will! You! Just! Do! As! I! Say!!!" he roared into Midlin's bland face, punctuating each word with a violent shake. Even as the Disposable stared at him in bewildered horror, Preen flexed his wrists and hurled his victim down into a heap on the grass, stalking forward with fists clenched as he towered like a beanpole over the hunched, shadowed figure before him.

"*Enough* of this first rule!" he screeched. "*Enough* questions! *Enough* disobedience!" One hand lashed out, grasping the now terrified-looking Midlin and dragging him onto his knees. "You will *get* to your feet!" With another yank, Midlin was forced to stagger upright. "You will *fetch* some men!" Hauling the Disposable by the armpit, Preen strode across the grass with Midlin stumbling in his wake. Ahead, the massed ranks of the Disposables rippled backwards like a breath of wind in an effort to subtly retreat from his path, but Preen was clearly in no mood to be merciful—he tore into the front rank, snatching and shoving as one after another, bemused armoured figures were thrust tumbling forwards. "And *now!*" Preen's voice slashed through the air like a saw-edged blade. "You will damned well *attack* them or you will share their damnable fate!" His manic eyes swung from one startled face to the next, his jaw clenched and his face twisted as his voice rocketed up several octaves. "*Now!*"

The small, befuddled clutch of a dozen or so men exchanged wary looks with each other. Flirt could see them rolling the choices over in their minds—did they attack a band that they outnumbered, though not by much, and risk the wrath of the First Rule? Or did they disobey the incandescently furious form of Preen, who looked about ready to rip them into tiny pieces with his fingernails?

Tough choice, lads...

And it was time to make it tougher. "Stay back, boys," Flirt called to her Disposable companions, drawing her beautiful and significantly heroic-looking sword from its sheath. "If they come, I'll take them *alone.*"

Ouch. The stricken looks on those poor lads' faces were actually painful to behold. But Donk was right. One man—or woman—holding a lone defence with a very shiny sword meant *nobody* wanted to go first.

But behind them, there was Preen, panting like a rabid dog and looking fully prepared to rip out their livers and eat them. Slowly, and with undisguised reluctance, Midlin and his unfortunate troop began to edge their way forwards.

Flirt didn't edge. Flirt strutted. Flirt sauntered. Flirt worked her wrist so that her sword arched in casual circles in front of her as she closed towards them, playing every inch the Narrative threat.

Fight or flight, boys, fight or flight...

She knew she should want them to flee. Running would mean a snap of Preen's control, a break from his ever-tenuous command and her chance to step in. But at the same time...she hadn't had a decent scrap in a little while, and with her shocking lapse and head wound from last night, she wanted to be sure she was back up to speed.

But which way would they jump? Which way would it...

"Will you *get on with it?*"

And as though the screech of Preen's voice had galvanised his very blood, one of the reluctant Disposables hefted his short sword above his head and, with a desperate, high-pitched, almost plaintive screech, he charged.

With a simple flourish, Flirt deflected his down-swinging blade, ducking aside as she pushed the blow aside. She caught a glimpse of his pale, wretched face, sweat-stained and miserable as he brought his sword back up for a fresh assault, but Flirt had already anticipated the move, slashing the blade away as her foot rose with a well-aimed, upwards knee strike. As her opponent whimpered, she shoved him into a heap on the ground and turned.

And her next attacker was there. Spurred on by the brave stupidity of his comrade, the bulky figure of a Garrison soldier had lowered his halberd and stormed at her like a charging bull. Flirt sidestepped the move, knocking the blade down as she extended her foot and sent the soldier tumbling head over heels. Ignoring the jarring pain in her knee that resulted, she brought up her sword quickly to catch the descending axe of a tatty City Watchman, a sweaty, unshaven figure who pressed down hard as he fought to use his strength to buckle her. A frantic, half-toothed, halitosis-riddled grin flashed across his face.

"You know!" he gasped out loudly. "I like a girl with—"

Flirt's teeth gritted. "You even think about saying *spirit*, arse-wipe, and I'll rip off your ears and make you *swallow them!*"

She thrust upwards, slamming both axe and sword blade into the Watchman's chin. He staggered, reeling backwards, and slumped to the ground. Several more of his teeth lay scattered in the grass beside him.

Sword clenched in her fist and trying to ignore the painful throb of her healing head, Flirt turned as a mail-clad Buccaneer stumbled forwards uncomfortably, his moustached face riddled with disconcertion as he struggled to work with a sword so unlike his familiar cutlass. He started to charge and...

"Wait, wait! Stop! Stop it!"

The Buccaneer staggered to a halt. And Flirt stared.

What the...?

For Preen it was who had shouted—Preen, who had harangued and bullied them into making this attack, who had suddenly screamed it to a halt. He was staring at the cluster of eight or nine remaining Disposables with an incredulous look on his face.

"What are you doing?" he exclaimed, his voice rich in disbelief.

Midlin and his remaining men exchanged a series of uncertain glances.

"Ummm..." one of the remaining Garrison soldiers ventured. "Attacking her? Like you told us to?"

"Yes, yes, yes!" Preen waved away this statement of the obvious with one dismissive hand. "But I meant you should rush her together and butcher her as one! Why, *why*, for pity's sake, do you insist on running in to get slaughtered *one at a time?*"

"Well." The Garrison man glanced around at his companions for support but all of them, including Midlin, had suddenly discovered an intense fascination with their shoes. "Because of the Second Rule?"

Preen's expression, such as it was possible to interpret the range of twisting emotions that arched across his features, could best be described as dangerous.

"*Second* Rule?" he drawled darkly.

"Yeah." The unfortunate Garrison man swallowed hard at the black menace in the Courtier's eyes. "You know? When a superior force attacks a lesser band, they..." His voice faltered under the onslaught of Preen's glare but bravely, or perhaps foolishly, he ploughed on through his sentence. "They...they must...always attack...one...one at...one at a time?"

Preen stared at him. His eyes flicked around the range of nodding heads and thoughtful expressions and slowly, but very noticeably, they bulged in their sockets.

"What..." he said, his voice a very distinct and very desperate whisper, "...is the *matter* with you people?" He wheeled in a circle now, eyes wide and oddly dangerous as he wrung his hands together. "You can see what they are!" he snapped frantically. "Rebels, abominations, set to destroy us all! You saw what they did to the poor, innocent soul I sent last night to engage in *peaceful* negotiation with—"

"Peaceful negotiation?" Shoulders's indignant voice cut harshly into the Courtier's attempt to rouse his troops. "You sent Poniard the bloody Assassin to chop us up and burn us! How is *that* peaceful bloody negotiation?"

Mutters rose from the ranks, encouraging mutters, as nervous looks were exchanged at this revelation. Flirt dived quickly upon the opening. "Yeah, Preen, most people send a diplomat by daylight for peaceful negotiation, don't they? They don't send a well-armed and psychopathic trained killer in the middle of the night!"

Preen's tone was creeping back towards hysteria again. "Nevertheless, you treated him with violent and uncalled-for brutality! You set the poor man on fire..."

"No, we didn't!" Thump's yell was indignant. "Stupid bugger set *himself* on fire trying to set fire to us! Only time we touched him was to stop him trying to *mince* us!"

"Yeah, he stabbed me!" Dunny gestured fervently to his bandaged arm. "And he stabbed Donk too and kicked Shoulders and smacked Flirt round the head! All out of Narrative too! He was nuts!"

"But that was the plan, wasn't it?" Now was the time, Flirt knew, time to let these men know how far Preen would go against their fellow Disposables. "Have Poniard incapacitate us and then set us on fire?

And leave us like that? Forever?"

Gasps of horror rose from the massed ranks as Flirt ploughed on.

"And you didn't ask Strut, did you? You just went ahead and approved it without his say-so because you were too scared to get in trouble yourself! And you didn't care, did you, if anyone innocent got caught up in it! Because what do a few Disposables matter, what do even the Merry Band matter, as long as *you're* okay?"

"You, you…" Preen's voice flipped up an impossible couple of octaves, his hands balled in fists and shaking, his eyes filling his whole face with manic wildness. "You abominable…you dreadful…*you*…"

And slowly but surely, his face turned purest purple.

His eyes were bulging as they scanned in circles, until they fixed upon a City Watchman who was staring at him from behind his halberd with a nervous expression on his face. Laughter began spilling from Preen's lips, first a few giggle explosions followed by a frantic whirl of sound.

"Ah ha!" Laughter dissolving into maddened cackling, Preen lunged forwards towards the alarmed Watchman, snatching his halberd from his grip and swinging it wildly round in a manner that sent the men around him scattering out of his way.

"I'll do it myself!" he screeched. "No Assassins, no witless cattle! You'll be sorry you ever messed with me!"

Grasping the halberd in his scrawny arms, teeth gritted fiercely and spittle flying in lumps, Preen the Officious Courtier lowered his weapon and charged.

And indeed, he made it an impressive three whole steps before the weight of the weapon overwhelmed his less-than-muscular physique, plunging the base of the halberd into the soft earth and tangling it around his soft-shoed feet. Preen managed a childish squeal, limbs flailing as he tumbled, before the heavy weapon slammed into his forehead and sent him, dazed and reeling, to the ground. The halberd spun delicately for a moment longer before descending to whack across the stunned Courtier's head a second time, knocking him unconscious completely.

And there he stayed, his eyes staring skywards but seeing nothing. Tentatively, the Garrison soldier edged forwards and nudged his shoulder with his foot. Preen rocked slightly but made no reaction. His tongue lolled unpleasantly over his lips.

"Blimey," Flirt heard Tumble mutter. "I think we broke him."

Well, that's one way to create a power vacuum, isn't it?

And this was the moment. Flirt could see it, feel it, sense it in her bones—this was what all she had striven for in the last few days had been about, what she had been waiting for, what she needed: to stand up, call out, and sweep away the doubts of these men, to find her friends and lead her new recruits onward to drag down the Quest and finally earn the rights and respect she had always known that she and they deserved. A sea of bemused faces ringed her, lost and confused, and she would give them direction, give them purpose, give them life. This was what she was here for.

It was time. Time to step up. Time to be heard.

"Preen asks a good question!" Her words rang out across the Camp, carried to every corner of the tents by the shocked silence that had followed Preen's dramatic downing. "What *is* the matter with you people?"

Eyes. Eyes everywhere, darting towards her, curious and confused, worried and hostile but all looking now, all listening, and this was her chance. An upturned crate was lying nearby—ignoring the disconcerting creak it gave as she placed her foot upon it, Flirt sprang up onto the makeshift platform and stared out at the mass of troops.

"Preen thought there was something, didn't he?" Her voice rippled in the air as she stretched her hands, one still grasping her ornate sword, out before her. "Cowards, he called you. Idiots, imbeciles, witless cattle not worthy of his time or respect! Well, I say *no.*" She hurled the word towards them, feeling the passion of her belief flow through her as she fought to craft it into words. "I say *no* to instructions that favour the few and grind down the many! I say *no* to the shackles of oppression they clamp on us every time they call us Ordinary! I say *no* to a society that denies talent by labelling who we are and what we will be before we are even born! Now is our time! Now is our moment! Now is the day, now is the hour that we stand up to be counted, that we prove we have a voice that deserves to be heard! Now is the day we throw off the shackles of our forebears, we rip up our labels, and we show the world who we are! I say we show all of those who think we are nothing but Ordinary that there's nothing ordinary about us!" With a glorious flourish, she thrust her sword blade high into the air. *"Who's with me?"*

Silence.

Absolute silence.

Somewhere in the nearby grass, a cricket started chirping.

She had expected excitement, exultation, a tumult of fervent cheering and caps thrown in the air. A round of applause would have been nice. Hell, she would have settled for heckling.

But this?

Blank stares assailed her from every direction. Many pairs of eyes blinked.

Her sword arm started to tremble from the effort of holding it aloft. The wood beneath her feet gave an alarming lurch. With an echoing crack, her foot went through the crate.

"OW! Bloody..." Thrown off-balance by her thrust sword, Flirt scrambled for several undignified moments to extract herself from the broken pieces of wood. Ignoring the throb of her ankle and calf, she staggered back to a semblance of upright, straightening her mail shirt as she scrabbled to cling on to the tattered shreds of her dignity.

And then, she saw the hand.

It was tentative, to say the least, barely half-raised as it hovered around the height of its owner's head. It was attached to a spindly arm which curled up to meet a pair of bony Watchman's shoulders under a worried-looking, scruffy face that was watching her with a brow so furrowed it could have housed a wheat crop.

Flirt stared at him. "Yes?" she managed breathlessly.

The Watchman crinkled his nose as he let his hand slip back down. "So..." he said, his voice a welter of hesitant confusion. "These shackles, right?"

Flirt nodded slowly. "Yes..."

"Why're they putting them on *bears?*"

Flirt blinked, hard. "Sorry?"

"Well, you said it, din't you?" The man made a strange gesture with his hands. "That we had to throw off the shackles on the four bears?"

The last, lingering shred of hope that Flirt had been clinging to made a hurried break for the exit. "That wasn't what I meant, was it? I..."

"But you said it." The little Watchman had an alarmingly persistent look about him. "And you din't answer my question. Why shackle up bears, hmm?"

"There's a dancing bear down in Salty Port that they shackle." This random injection was provided by a bearded Buccaneer a few yards down the line. "But that's only for Narrative scenes. The rest of the time he hangs about, harmless as anything, practising his juggling. Plus, I'm told he plays a mean hand of blackjack."

"Seems mean to shackle them up," one Garrison man offered thoughtfully. "I mean, poor wild animals. What have they ever done to us?"

"They could use ropes instead. Less chafing."

"Maybe some kind of rudimentary cage?"

"Seems mean to me."

"And why do it, hmmm? 'Cos she still din't answer my question!"

Flirt could actually feel her brain trying to curl up and die. "Can we just forget about the bears? I..."

"Forget about them? After they've been shackled and roped up and made to play blackjack? That's a mighty cavalier attitude you've got there, missie!"

"Maybe we should look after them instead. We've got a decent yard up at the castle."

"Yeah, but is there enough room for four of them?"

She wished there was a wall. A nice, sturdy, solid wall of brick or stone—she wasn't fussy—so long as it would make a satisfying thump when she started to beat her head against it. For a brief, disconcerting instant, she could actually sympathise with Preen.

"Please!" The pitch and volume she thrust into this one word brought the rambling exchange to a glorious halt. "Please," she repeated more softly. "Apart from the bears, did any of you actually take *anything* from what I just said?"

There was a pause. A young, stringy-looking lad in chain mail, his

Adam's apple bobbing wildly, was the first to venture into it. "Well..." he offered cautiously. "It seemed a bit...negative to me. All that saying no?"

"Lots of throwing stuff around too," injected a Garrison soldier. "And ripping stuff up. Sounds a bit messy."

"Would we have to stand up for long?" a Watchman said suddenly. "To be counted? Only I have trouble with my bunions, see, and it'd take bleeding ages to get through everyone."

"They gonna count us then?" a dark-browed guard from the Grim Fortress queried curiously.

"That's what she said."

"They counting everyone?"

"Dunno. Maybe."

"Is that how come they knew there were four bears?"

"Enough bears!" Flirt's eruption, alas, was only enough to briefly distract their attention.

"How would you get bears to stand up and be counted anyway?"

"I dunno. Prod them with something?"

"Would they need to stand up? I mean, if there's only four of them..."

"But if you know there's only four, why bother to count them in the first place?"

If she hadn't considered it would be a betrayal to her principles and a decidedly W-word-like thing to do, Flirt would have undoubtedly gone off to find a quiet corner to cry in. But she couldn't give up. Not quite yet.

"Please, please!" she intervened again, and other than a few random bear-related murmurings, the conversation calmed down once more. "Look, I was trying to explain something, wasn't I? But you haven't heard what I was saying! You've taken it wrong!"

"In that case." The casual voice that drifted over belonged to the Grim Fortress ruffian whom Shoulders had identified as Thrash. "You can't have explained it very well, can you?"

And he was right. He was absolutely right.

It was as though she had been smacked between the eyes by a thunderbolt. The briefly dimmed bear discussion erupted back into life once more but Flirt no longer cared, lost in the realisation that had swamped her.

She'd been such a fool.

She'd listened to Preen harangue them and Bard try to inspire them and she'd learned nothing. She'd assumed all along that it was what they were saying that had alienated them, and to a degree, it was. But it was also the way that they said it.

It was about the way that people thought.

Those who lived The Narrative the most followed grand designs, epics of thought and deed, the actions of Heroes. Shoulders had unwittingly pointed it out, in the sarcastic way he'd annotated Bard's distant speech in Preen's tent, stupid and pointless words that meant nothing to those of a practical bent. Because Ordinary folk didn't think like that. They didn't live like that. They didn't waste words on flowery nonsense. They said what they meant. They followed the routines and rules they knew, the habits of a lifetime ingrained within them, and got on with it. But she'd got so caught up in the need to show what she could do, in the thirst for the kind of heroic deeds she'd always been denied, that she'd done exactly what a Hero would have done. She'd tried to inspire her troops with rhetoric.

And in The Narrative, driven by its syrupy encouragement, it would have undoubtedly been a triumph. But in the real world?

The Disposables obeyed Preen because he gave them their instructions. They didn't need to be inspired into it. They knew what they were doing already. It was their job.

They weren't ready for it to be anything else.

More words from Shoulders's scribbled transcript swam before her eyes, spoken, he'd said, by Thrash, the very man who had a moment before brought her crashing back to earth.

We're Disposables! We just want a nice quick fight, our entrails sewn back in, and a big, frothy tankard of ale when we're done! And we don't want to be bloody patronised!

Shoulders had underlined that final word. Three times.

She'd known that too. She'd always known it. How had she come so far from what she'd been?

She'd wanted to prove she could be more than a Barmaid and

she'd certainly done that. But as she'd said herself to Preen—she couldn't order people to respect her or do as she desired. They didn't want to listen to a troublemaking rebel preach sedition. They didn't want fancy words that they wouldn't be bothered to understand. Thrash had been right in the words he'd flung at Preen, transcribed by Shoulders for her to read. Unlike Fodder, most Disposables didn't want to be Heroes. They just wanted a quick fight, a big tankard of ale, and not to be patronised.

She'd tried to be their leader. But once upon a time she'd been their friend. And they'd listened to her.

And then she realised. She'd been so caught up in trying to prove what parts of being a Barmaid she wasn't that she'd forgotten the part of it she *was*.

And that was when she knew what she had to do.

A part of her was screaming at herself, that she couldn't go back, that she'd come so far, that all she had achieved would be wasted. But she knew also that that wasn't true. She knew who she was now. She knew what she could do. She knew what parts of herself she liked and what she didn't. There was nothing wrong with her aspirations for greater things as long as she didn't forget what she'd had in the first place.

Slowly, deliberately, she walked back to where Shoulders and his fellow Rural Guards were clustered in a bewildered huddle. Shoulders gave her a highly cynical look.

"That went well," he drawled sardonically.

Flirt ignored him. "Donk, Tumble, Thump," she said quickly. "While they're distracted, I need you to slip out and get down to the supply tent. Bring back as many barrels of ale as you can, understand?"

Thump's eyes lit up. "Will do!"

As the three of them made a hasty exit, Flirt turned on their companion. "Dunny, I want you to keep an eye on Preen."

The mucky Disposable pulled a face. "Must I?"

"Yes." Flirt clamped down firmly. "I don't want him coming to his senses and getting in the way, do I?"

Clunny was staring at her with narrowed eyes. "What are you up to?" he asked suspiciously.

Flirt sighed. "I'm going to start talking your language, aren't I? Shoulders, do you know where my pack is?"

Shoulders looked notably alarmed. "In the pavilion. Why?"

It stung, it did sting, but she knew that it was necessary and she knew that it would work. It had to.

"Because," she said wearily, "I think I'm going to need my apron."

* * *

The sky was boiling. Lightning skittered through the clouds in frantic flashes, darting, spinning, jabbing at the deep-purple clusters of cloud as though to puncture them and drain them dry. Thunder rolled in sonorous waves from above, striking the skin with almost tangible force as it set their eardrums vibrating. In the vast emptiness, the scrubby grass rippled like ocean waves against the harsh surge of the wind, spinning up spirals of dust that scuttled past with a scatter of soil and breeze. The air smelt of impending rain.

Hunched down in his saddle, Erik stared wearily ahead to the cluster of unfamiliar tents, decorative cones lined with beads and tassels that danced and tossed in the blustering weather. And before them stood the threatening knot of horses, their occupants shaven-headed, leather-clad, sabre-wielding men who bore their tattoos like a shield, unflinching before the weather. Elder was less stony-faced, wincing when his long beard whipped in the rising storm as he spoke with fluent eloquence to convince this fierce horse tribe of the plains to allow them passage through their territory. The wind carried only brief snatches of his words, but from his tone, it sounded as though he was making progress.

Erik hoped so. The wind was burning at his skin and his scalp was prickling uncomfortably. He longed to move on to a place where electricity did not spark the air, where his skull was not the highest point for miles around at which the storm could aim its golden forks of death. To his side, encased in his heavy steel, Sir Roderick's face betrayed even greater trepidation at the prospect of an attack against which he could not defend.

"How much longer will this take?" Canted uncomfortably in the saddle, Slynder dug his fingers deeply against the bandages that wrapped his healing leg. Itching had of late become an issue. "I want to be well away from this place before that storm decides to shed its load. I've seen hailstones the size of mace-heads on these plains before now."

"It will take as long as it takes, so hold your tongue and have some bloody patience!" Svenheid's voice was a bad-tempered growl—his temperament of late had been greatly uncertain, varying between foul moodiness and disconcerted uncertainty. It seemed at times to Erik as though he was fighting some strange inner battle that no other, perhaps not even he, could understand. The man of Sleiss and his odd ways had had strange effects upon them all.

"Don't bicker." Zahora cut in harshly before Slynder could deliver the retort half-hanging on his lips. "You're like children! It's pathetic."

"Pathetic?" This time Slynder's retort was not to be restrained as another bright, vaguely reddish flash lit up the sky behind the gathering of tents. "So, concern for our safety is pathetic? How dare—"

"Desist!" This time it was Roderick who intervened. "I have more reason than any of you to fear, but do I moan and argue? I do not!"

Zahora's expression was harsh. "Of course you do not! To fear would take a brain…"

Roderick's eyes bulged in their sockets. "Why, you…"

"Enough!" At last, silence fell. In the force of the argument, Elder's return to their group had been overlooked. He stared from face to face, his eyes fierce—he had not entirely forgiven any of them for the incident at the edge of the wood, although Erik had observed that after he had done scolding them all, he had taken an unusually long time behind the tree that had started it all, where he claimed to be regaining his composure.

Elder cleared his throat pointedly. "If you are quite finished," he said with a voice that dripped with ice, "Eoin-Har is the son of the local tribal chief, patrolling their borders against invaders. He has offered us shelter from the storm in his patrol's tents before we continue our journey west. He also reports he and his men have lost young horses and indeed young children to flying beasts that have been strafing these Flats. Craxis, I fear, is not far away."

"This storm may even be his doing," Roderick suggested. "I have heard it said that he has such power, even without the Ring."

"It is possible," Elder conceded. He gestured to the tents. "So, we would do well to take shelter now, while we have the—"

"Shelter? Are you having me on?"

The weight of oppression in the air was as nothing to the weight that pressed on Erik's soul at the grating sound of that casual voice that had haunted their last few days. Even as his companions jerked, their faces rich with the same cocktail of fury, alarm, and resignation, the man of Sleiss sauntered casually out from behind the nearest tent, his fingers picking at the beaded fabric with an expression of mild disdain.

"I mean, you've been brewing up the storm of the century here, right?" The man gestured towards the lightning-strafed sky. "Howling winds, hailstones like mace-heads, thunder and lightning and everything you'd expect from a real monster of a weather system. But you seriously think you can take shelter from that in a tent?"

Elder's expression was one of raw rage as he flung one arm towards the bewildered-looking huddle of horsemen. "The men of this tribe have used these very tents to survive the storms of these Flats for generations past! They are strong, durable, well-planted…"

The man of Sleiss's lips twisted. "No, they haven't," he interrupted with a snort. "They all live up in smoky hall, on the border with the mountains, carousing and enjoying the shelter! They only come out onto this miserable expanse when they have to and for as little time as they can get away with; isn't that right, sabre, old mate?"

This strange address was directed at Eoin-Har, the chieftain's son, who was regarding the man of Sleiss with a mixture of surprise and trepidation. He raised his hands in a pacifying manner.

"Please leave me out of this, yeah?" he said pleadingly. "I don't want any trouble."

The man of Sleiss looked oddly sympathetic, but it did not stay his tongue. "But it is trouble, isn't it?" he said, rather more softly. "When we had that ale together after the last battle, you were telling me about saddle sores, what a pain in the arse shaving your head is, what so much riding does to your spine, the sweat of horseback, the smell of you afterwards..."

"That was different!" There was a shrill note to Eoin-Har's voice now, the stony composure of moments before wiped away in an instant. "That was just moaning! Everyone moans! And you weren't the enemy!"

There was an almost sad tinge to the man of Sleiss's face. "I'm not the enemy now," he said quietly. "You know me, you know that. You think I'd be doing this if I didn't have a bloody good reason?"

"You know him?" The harsh exclamation, a vocalisation of the dawning truth of the exchange, came from Zahora. Her curved sword was already in her palm. "You are his friend, you treacherous—"

"No!" Eoin-Har's face was frantic as he waved his hands madly in the air. "No, I don't know him! Well, I do know him, but not in this quest and...oh bloody hell!"

He yanked sharply on his reins, wheeling his horse around madly. "Sod this!" With a whip of leather, his horse burst into a gallop—a moment later, his bewildered-but-loyal men also turned their horses and launched after him. The dust of their departure streamed away in the swirling wind.

The man of Sleiss arched an eyebrow, his expression, strangely, looking slightly guilty for a moment before he firmed his jaw and turned back to Erik, that awful mocking half-smile slipping once more onto his features.

"Oh well," he said with faux cheer. "At least they left you the nice storm-proof tents, didn't they?"

Was it the smile? Was it the tone? Erik wasn't sure and probably never would be what it was about the man of Sleiss that turned his soul to lead. He could feel the rage at his intrusion building in his chest like a kindled fire.

"Why do you do these things?" He had not realised he meant to speak until he had. "Why do you torment us like this?"

The man of Sleiss shrugged, and that casual gesture sent another splinter of anger to fuel the fire building inside Erik. "Because I can. Because somebody has to."

"Speak straight!" It was Slynder who snapped out. The man of Sleiss regarded him slowly.

"I do," he said calmly. "You're the ones who twist everything up. You and your instructions. I'm playing by ear and seeing what happens."

"Did you play by ear when you stole the poor princess?" The rage glowing in his heart spilled into Erik's voice. "When you snatched her from those who cared for her, subjecting her to infamy and torture?"

He was smiling. How dare he smile in the face of such a question? "I wouldn't worry about the princess, mate," he replied with a grin. "Trust me, that girl can take care of herself."

The fire was burning through the dry tinder of Erik's fears with wildness. "Where is she? What have you done with her?"

He shrugged again, the hated, hated shrug. "Dunno, mate, sorry. I haven't seen her since you chased us off that bloody mountain. But don't worry..." There was something so mocking in his smile. "She'll be with the prince. And they've been getting on famously."

Erik's skin would catch fire, he was sure of it, for he could not contain the inferno rising within at the thought, the implication of what the man of Sleiss had said, of his Islaine alone with that reprehensible, that amoral, that foul prince who might...who would...who could...

"I tell you what." And then, the voice of the man of Sleiss slipped like a dose of lantern oil over Erik's flames. "This storm looks like it won't be much fun. But hey-ho, you've got your lovely tents right here..."

And in that moment, flames roared like a volcano through his skull as something inside of Erik snapped.

"Storm? I ask of my love and you talk of the storm?" It was his voice, it must be, for it was passing through his lips; but Erik was barely aware he was speaking, let alone in such a harsh, infuriated tone. The air around him, so heavy with the latent power of nature, suddenly seemed to flow into his skin, to fill him, engulf him, to link itself to that strange, secret part of himself that did things that he could barely understand. He felt the storm, shared the storm, was the storm, the thunder rippling in his voice, the lightning flashing in his eyes, the weight and force of wind and scudding cloud wrapping into his flesh as all became a part of him, a part he could touch, use, control. And there was only one use to which he cared to put it.

"I will show you the storm!" The wind howled around the thunder of his voice, eviscerating the plains as it passed—vaguely, he saw his companions clinging to their saddles, but his eyes fell only on the man of Sleiss, staggering back under the force of nature's blow. "I will show you its heart and soul and rip it through you! I will make you wish you had never dared to cross my path and take from me my love! I will make you pay for what you've done! Now!"

It was as though the very sky had ripped apart. Hailstones, bigger even than the mace-heads Slynder had suggested, thundered earthwards in a tight, white column from the sky, trained on the man of Sleiss like an arrow from an archer's bow. Even as the man flung himself down amidst their ground-churning impacts, Erik felt himself call lightning that arced from above, scorching the earth as it blasted craters from the grasslands where his hated nemesis huddled. Black, menacing, rippling with terrible power, one after another they came spiralling down from the sky, dark twisters that set the very air screaming as they touched the ground in a circle around the cowering figure and began to dance in a deadly spiral that closed upon his form. The remains of the now-battered horse tribe tents ripped, dragged, and were sucked but for a few scraps up into the nearest howling vortex.

His friends had retreated past the wreckage of the shredded tents, wrapped in the glow of Elder's magical protection. Erik cared not, other than it was for the best. Lost in the eye of the storm, he had no need to flee, trusting his horse to trust him as he raised his hands to the sky, absorbing the lightning that arced into his fingers, feeling the deadly winds that curled destructively just beyond his safe lull as he moulded the twisters' dancing, closing, closing the circle, ready to rip the now-invisible form of his hated enemy into atoms of the very wind. The power consumed him as he exulted as at last the tables turned; at last the man of Sleiss was tamed; at last the evil, mocking fiend who had stolen away his Islaine would...

Red light exploded.

It was a vicious slap across every inch of Erik's skin—he lurched in the saddle, winded and shocked as the overwhelming power of the raging storm tore like the ruined tents. As the glare across his eyes faded, Erik gaped and stared upon an unbelievable sight.

There was a hole in the storm.

There was no other way to describe it. It was a shaft, a sunbeam-washed lull, and though the hailstones battered, the lightning smacked, and the circling tornadoes surged, no hint of even a breeze could touch the shining shaft of light that tumbled from the pinprick hole in the vast thunderhead above.

And standing in the centre of it all, washed in scarlet, the Ring of Anthiphion thrust towards the sky like a talisman, stood the man of Sleiss.

And then, he began to laugh.

It was slow at first, a hiccupping giggle that slipped into a chuckle, then a chortle, and then suddenly there was full-blown laughter, rolling, rippling, disbelieving laughter that tumbled louder even than the thunder as it echoed across the Paltas Flats from end to end. His eyes were fixed upon the sky as he laughed and laughed and laughed and laughed, apparently unable to stop as the seizures washed through his body again and again. His fist, ever grasping the Ring, tightened as he thrust it with renewed vigour towards the heavens above.

"Come on!" he screamed wildly. "Is that all you've got?"

Power surged once more through Erik's body. Gritting his teeth, he hurled out his storm once more, but although the twisters darkened and roared more deeply, although the hailstones ripped great clods from the earth and lightning tripped alight the dry grass into a wind-whipped tornado of fire, nothing could touch that peaceful sunbeam. The man of Sleiss's hair was not so much as ruffled by the breeze.

And he was still laughing.

"That's it, isn't it?" he roared, not at the bewildered form of Erik but at the scudding sky. "That is all you've got! You're throwing it all at me, magic, heaven and earth, and you know what? I can hold you! Ha!" He punched the calm air of his haven with one fist. "You tried fighting me with men and with magic! You've tried using stupid dragons and playing cruel tricks! You've even used the bloody weather! And you can't stop me! Me, the little man, the nothing! Seven words! Adequate! Hy-bloody-gienic! I'm the rusty link in your precious chain and look how it's breaking down! Have you noticed me now?" His face was as wild as his voice, his features creased with passion, his eyes burning madly. "Well, I'm coming for you!" he screamed out. "I'm coming! And maybe I won't just ask nicely for a fair deal! Maybe I don't have to beg and plead and kick up a bit of a stink! Why should I? I can do anything you can do! So why not be you as well?"

It was as though the very air dissolved. In an instant, the storm was gone, the fiery twisters evaporating in a puff of air, the thud of hailstones silenced, the lightning darkened, the wind slashed away into still nothingness. Erik lurched as the power that had filled his body to its core vanished in an instant—gasping in shock, he could do nothing as his horse reared wildly, hurling him with a breath-stealing smack onto his back in the dusty grass. Even as he lay, gasping and stunned, he saw the figure of the man of Sleiss, shrouded in red light, his face set with grim determination.

"You may have set the tasks." His voice was soft, but it echoed with the power of the silenced thunder. "But you're not the master anymore..."

With a flash of scarlet, as always, the man of Sleiss was gone.

Erik couldn't move. He could barely breathe, his body shaking as light danced before his eyes. The scudding clouds twisted as they sealed once more the tiny gap rent within them, spinning and swirling as the wind began to rise once more, whipping dust over Erik's eyes...

What was the man of Sleiss? How could he do the things he did? How could they hope to stop him? How could Erik ever dream of finding his precious Islaine?

Dust... Islaine... Dust... Islaine... Dust...

Islaine...

Suddenly, as his eyes carried him with shocking suddenness away from the horror of moments before and into a new vision, there she was.

Islaine.

Chains. Chains wrapped her beautiful body, trapping her with heartless cruelty against the dusty earth. A gag dug against her face and he could see across the porcelain perfection of her cheeks, the silvery tracks of tears. And there, lying over her as though to seep the very goodness from her soul, he saw a shadow that could only be foul Prince Tretaptus backing away, a key grasped in his silhouetted hand, a mad cackle of a voice crying out in lunatic torment that if she would not be his, she would not be any man's. And then, overhead, shadows, shadows formed of wings and claws began to circle hungrily...

"No!"

Erik was on his feet instantly. His brain was on fire and he knew, knew in his heart and soul that the abominable scene he had witnessed was true, was real, was happening now. He could not wait to find his retreated friends, he could not wait for anything—rushing forwards, he grabbed the reins of his contrite-looking horse and threw himself into the saddle. Power filled him, more potent than any storm—guided by the instinct that had carried the vision of his love to him, he wheeled his horse, digging his heels into his flanks as he spurred his mount ahead.

Islaine needed him and no power, no force on earth, no man, no monster was going to keep him from her side.

His true love was finally coming home.

* * *

It was entirely his fault.

Thud-thud, thud-thud, thud-thud, thud-thud...

The hooves of Dullard's borrowed horse pounded roughly against the earth, kicking up billowing clouds of dust that swirled in his wake like turbulent waves, the tempo of its passage vibrating through his sore-and-aching body like an echo of his galloping heartbeat. The wind slapped his face like nature's rebuke, the occasional unpleasant splatter the mark of an insect not rapid enough to escape from his path. He knew his velocity was reckless. He didn't care.

It was entirely his fault.

Thud-thud, thud-thud, thud-thud, thud-thud...

Focused as he was on maintaining a pace both rapid and horse-feasible, and upon keeping his gaze fixed upon the dark shape that was kicking up a cloud of dust on the horizon before him, that one thought was haunting Dullard's brain. He couldn't be free of it. He wasn't sure that he deserved to be.

Because he knew it to be true.

He should never have left her alone up there. What had he been thinking? He should have asked a Servant or two to stay with her at all times, should have avoided Bold's impetuous charge and stayed with her himself, should have taken better care of her...

Pleasance's pale, indignant face, crowned in a swirl of dishevelled curls, rose up before his mind's eye, her expression filled with scolding as she informed him with a wild flash of the eyes that she was perfectly capable of watching out for herself. And whilst circumstances had contradicted the insistence she would most certainly have made, he knew that, of course, she would never have accepted such molly-coddling, would never have permitted herself to be guarded and followed and protected. And any attempt by him to insist would certainly have ended badly.

So perhaps he was not to blame in that respect. But he certainly was in others.

Thud-thud, thud-thud, thud-thud, thud-thud...

Gentle swirls of dust, tumbling slowly to their rest after the turbulence of the prior passing, were whipped into the air once more by the tumult of his pursuit. He strained to see past their larger counterparts on the road beyond, to clear a sight to his target, to be sure that he was closing in...

Why had he not left a guard to watch over Quibble? And why, oh why, oh why had he not had the common sense to keep hold of Quibble's book?

He couldn't quite believe his own stupidity in leaving it right there on the kitchen table. He recalled a vague idea that it might get damaged if trouble arose, that if a Noble got their hands on it, they could use it to call for help, and so he'd deposited it on the table with barely a thought as they'd started upstairs. And there it must have still been after Sweetness and Paragon had battered down the locked door to their private chambers with a discarded mace, fled with Pleasance down the service corridor, and found themselves in the deserted kitchens where the muffled cries of Quibble, sealed up in the unlit oven, had come to their attention...

And now Quibble and his book had gone too. Certainly, he'd started scribbling a call for aid before they'd even left the kitchen. Dullard had no doubt that Strut and his Taskmaster knew full well that the princess had finally been retrieved, and plans would be thoroughly afoot for a rapid reintegration.

The Narrative would already be on its way.

Thud-thud, thud-thud, thud-thud, thud-thud...

His limbs were screaming at him with indignity, the promise of erupting bruises—his legacy from his fight with Bold—a blossoming reality. His nose throbbed and although the tide of blood that had trickled from within had ebbed, the potential for further leakage was undeniable. Dirt and wind and insect matter battered his beleaguered eyes and set him desperately blinking.

He was in no state for this greater fight that lay before him. But that was his own fault too.

For even with Pleasance captured, all might not have been lost. The castle had been supposedly locked down, after all. So why had he ever thought that only one guard would be sufficient to watch over the only secret passage out of the castle?

Poor Chopper. The dent in his head when they'd found him had been big enough to hold an apple. Leaving Jolly and Menial to patch the poor man up as best they could, Dullard had rushed to the walls. He had no clear idea of where this passage was likely to emerge—it varied as much as the design of the castle did—but from a quick assessment of the passage's direction, he surveyed the landscape for a likely exit point and found a stand of sturdy-looking rock sticking uncomfortably out of the plain about a mile to the west. And then, when he'd spotted the carriage hurtling in the same direction from the Manor House nearby, he had been certain.

The call for help had been made. The race was on.

Every Servant who could ride had been mounted on a steed and sent to intercept. Dullard himself, along with Cleave, had darted down the passageway, hoping to catch up with Pleasance and her captors before they could reach their escape route.

But he'd failed. He'd failed her. Again.

For as they'd stumbled out into the light, tripping over themselves in the haste of their rapid descent, the carriage was already dashing away.

His heart had plunged in that awful moment, forcing up depths of despair he had not even known he possessed. It was only the clattering arrival of the horses that had snapped him back to his senses.

And so, they had chased.

Thud-thud, thud-thud, thud-thud, thud-thud...

Although no horseman of particular renown, Dullard was easily the most experienced rider of the party and, having hurriedly mounted Valiant's famously swift black war stallion, he had quickly outstripped his companions. Under less urgent circumstances, he might have perhaps stayed his pace a little, held back and kept the group together, but this was no normal ride and his prudent brain—the part that might have prodded him and suggested it would be wiser to wait for backup rather than charging in alone—was no longer the part giving orders. He had to reach Pleasance before The Narrative did.

He had to. He had to. Because he couldn't bear to think what would happen if he...

The fear on her face whenever Islaine rears herself within her... Her horror and repulsion at the thought of marrying Bumpkin...

What if she loses herself? What if the Pleasance I know and...and care for becomes Islaine?

What if I lose her?

No, don't think about that. *Don't think it.*

She'd said she thought that she had her alter ego under control. She'd seemed as sure as he'd ever seen her. But for how long? How well could that resolution stand up against The Narrative? He knew she was strong but was she yet strong enough? Did she believe what she said?

Weak from injury, confused and angry and upset by her sister and father's betrayal—she would be vulnerable. He couldn't risk her exposure to The Narrative in such a state...

Thud-thud, thud-thud, thud-thud, thud-thud...

The horse was starting to pant beneath him—he suspected it

would be hard pressed to keep up this frantic pace for too much longer. But the glimpses he was catching through the veil of dust ahead were clearer, closer, a few hundred yards now, wild and helter-skelter but not so far away.

The carriage. He was gaining on them.

Frantically he spurred his horse on, wiping the sweat from his brow as he dug his knees in and tried to ignore the mad clamour of his heartbeat. How far away was The Narrative? Even aided by mysterious powers, could it really get down from wherever it had been lurking and reach Pleasance before he did?

And, of course, reaching her was one thing. Regaining her was another.

A glance over his shoulder told him his companions were almost out of sight behind him. He'd told the Servants to stay safely away and not to get involved if it came to a Narrative fight—he didn't want to risk what might become of them there, but that did mean that he would face any Narrative challenges alone. His bruised body gave a resentful, full-length throb as though to remind him of his diminished health. And the maelstrom of anxiety and guilt that tortured him was playing havoc with his frantic attempts to focus on the task in hand...

But it isn't a task. It's Pleasance.

Which is exactly why you have to concentrate.

Think. *Think.*

Thud-thud, thud-thud, thud-thud, thud-thud...

What is there that you can do? Where can you find an advantage?

The Vast River. He could see it now, a thick ribbon of blue in an undulation that tucked the flat landscape through which he had been riding into a brief and shallow dip. It was perhaps a half-mile ahead. And it was empty. There was no boat.

Of course! Punt's ferry post was always supposed to be the only crossing point in times of Quest—any other boats had been tucked away out of sight and wouldn't be readily accessible. There wasn't one ready and waiting. They wouldn't be able to cross the...

And then the world erupted with *green*.

The ground was shaking like a leaf in winter gales as a whirlpool of dirt and sparkling emerald lightning lanced up to fill the skyline. Dust and a mighty, crunching roar crackled and echoed through the air as Dullard's horse reared and pawed violently at the sky. Half in shock himself, Dullard scrambled, clinging to the reins as the eruption of particles and the horse's black mane obscured his vision, his knees digging desperately into the leather flanks of the saddle as he battled to keep his seat. For a few more terrifying seconds, his mount bucked, hooves slashing before it dropped, panting and sweating, to all fours once more, prancing nervously and spooked on the spot.

Dullard couldn't blame it. He felt much the same himself.

With a deep and powerful rumble, the shaking slowly subsided, the fog of earth gently settled, and the air began to clear. Waving one hand furiously in front of his face as he coughed, Dullard couldn't help but see the too-familiar sparkles of green that danced through the debris that had engulfed him.

Higgle. The Duty Pixie in charge of Landscape and Architecture had just made an alteration.

He couldn't have diverted the river. That was a long and arduous business that required much care and planning, for even when moved, rivers still had to go somewhere. Had he made a ford? He'd heard no splashing. The Vast River was too wide for a bridge to have been built. So, what on earth had he…

The last tumbles of dust cleared. And Dullard gaped.

In all his Quests as a Principal, in all his studies of landscape, he had never seen anything like *this*.

For where a moment before there had been river, there now lay solid land, dusty, bland, and dim like the Battle Ground beyond the far bank. The shallow dip of a valley through which the Vast River had flowed was gone.

But not completely. For the river remained, flowing serenely along the self-same course to the north and south, vanishing beneath a low arch into a tunnel that flowed heedlessly under the new piece of land-scape to emerge unscathed beyond. And from this new earth, low ridges rose on either edge, a gentle rise of hill that cut off sharply at its crest to drop sheer and unhindered to the water once out of sight.

They hid the river from view completely.

What The Narrative didn't see, The Narrative didn't know. As far as the Merry Band would be concerned, there would be no river at all.

Higgle had made a *land bridge*.

Genius. Utter genius.

But it also rather killed Dullard's plans for a waterside confrontation. But he couldn't give up. He'd never give up. Whatever happened, he had to press on, he had to do it, he had to do it for...

And then he saw her.

The carriage had stopped at the very centre of the bridge but was turning to leave as he stared. Two brightly clad figures—Paragon and Sweetness; it had to be—were settled inside with the battered Quibble, a couple of white-clad Priests, and—oh dear, he'd had no wish to get him in further trouble—the slender form of his Uncle Primp beside them. Crouched like crows over a banquet, the winged forms of his friends from the Assorted Freakish Creatures were lining the crests of the two ridges, shuffling their feet with a discomfort notable even from this distance. And there, alone, wriggling madly and trussed-up from head to foot in heavy chains, a purple-clad, blonde-haired figure lay staked out in the centre of the land bridge. Her bonds trapped her entirely.

Pleasance!

His uncle was running this scene. His friends the AFCs appeared to be the antagonists. If he barrelled in there and ruined it all, they were likely to suffer for it.

But it was *Pleasance*. Pleasance! He couldn't leave her!

He...

She...

Vivid light arced across the horizon from the north, glowing against the northern ridge of the land bridge. Fingers of brightness crept towards them.

The Narrative!

No!

He hesitated no more. Digging his heels into the flanks of his horse, he charged forwards.

Thud-thud, thud-thud, thud-thud, thud-thud...

They saw him coming, of course. He saw Sweetness's thunderous face as he hurtled past her carriage, saw King Paragon stare blankly as he galloped away. He saw Quibble dive for cover, saw Priests gesticulating wildly, saw poor Primp's expression of weary despair, saw the AFCs as they launched into the air and began to circle, their eyes fixed very conspicuously upon the approaching Narrative light as they gathered themselves with steady hesitancy to swoop.

And he saw Pleasance. Saw her confusion and her rage, saw her frustration and her fear, saw her hurt and saw her horror. And for an instant, as she saw him rush towards her, saw him rein in and leap from the saddle, saw him running towards her with every ounce of speed he could find, their eyes met.

He saw her yearning. He saw her desperation. He saw her terror at what she knew was to come.

But he saw her hope. And he saw in her eyes, oh, just for one moment he saw…

Light…

Islaine!

And there it was, laid out exactly as his vision had foretold, his beautiful princess gagged and chained ruthlessly to the dusty earth by her foul suitor, left as mere fodder for the brutes of the monster he now served! He could see them circling above, dark shapes of tooth and claw, their hungry eyes fixed upon their prize like ravenous hunting wolves. They would not wait for their feast much longer.

But the most extraordinary sight lay before him. Foul Tretaptus, the mad villain who had himself, Erik was sure, been the very man to chain the wan, terrified form of his princess to the earth, was scrambling to her side, hacking at her chains with his sword in desperate madness as though he himself did not hold their key. Had he discarded it in some fit of rage? And why free her when his vision had shown him so resolved to her death? Had he had a change of heart? Or could he, like the Lord of Sleiss, not bear to see something so divine destroyed so utterly?

But nonetheless, Erik could not stand by and allow her to fall into his clutches again. Tretaptus had to be stopped once and for all.

And this was no man of Sleiss, armed with power that challenged even Elder's gifts. And Erik was no longer a mere amateur with his magic.

He saw Tretaptus's hand reach out, saw it touch the delicate porcelain skin of Islaine's cheek, and his mind burst into flames.

How dare he touch her? How dare he lay one hand to her? He had no right!

Golden fire erupted from his fingers, screaming through the air as it slammed into Tretaptus and hurled him backwards, weaving around him in ripples of shimmering, half-invisible light as he was trapped in a heap upon the floor. As Erik threw himself from the saddle, a flick of his hand was enough to dissolve the chains that bound Islaine, sending them tumbling away in a cloud of dust, filling the air with silver sparkles as she staggered free, ripping away her gag and stumbling to her feet. She blinked with a strange, bewildered desperation.

She was a vision. All that he had ever wanted, all that he had ever dreamed, her golden hair, laced with fiery flashes of fire, glittering in the silver-strewn air. Her skin was pale and delicate like a drift of pure new-fallen snow and as for her eyes...

"Pleasance!" Tretaptus's inexplicable cry slashed through the air as he battled and struggled like a demon wrought from fire and blood against his bonds of light. "Don't look into his eyes! Don't meet his eyes, pleasance! Concentrate! Fight her! Fight her, pleasance, you have to..."

With a snap of Erik's fingers, golden light rose like a serpent, solidifying into a gag that smothered the prince's nonsense into silence as the silver in the air congealed into bands of chain once more, snaking from the earth to wrap around the traitor's wrists and ankles and binding him to the very rock. But Islaine, his Islaine was staring at Tretaptus like a woman lost in a world of dreams, one hand rising, slowly, shakily, stretching tremblingly towards her captor, her kidnapper, with a strange and twisted yearning.

"Dullard?" he heard her gasp. "Help me, dullard! I can't... Please! Please help me!"

She was staggering towards him. Each step was a strain, an effort, as though fighting against the essence of her very bones, the desires written on her soul, but she was moving, jerkily, like a tortured marionette, taking herself as though against her own will back to the man who had ruined her life for her.

Erik stared in horror. What had that brute done to this poor flower? What evil perversions had he wrought upon her mind to make her so compelled to return to him?

He had to help her, he had to save her, for he knew deep in the depths of his soul he was the only one who could.

He was meant for her. She was meant for him. And he had known it always.

And soon she would too.

He rushed forwards, anxious and desperate, and tenderly caught her by the wrists.

"Islaine!" he exclaimed, thrusting every inch of the love that welled up from his soul into that one lyrical name. "Islaine, all is well! I am here to save—"

"No!" The screech that ripped from her lungs burst into his eardrums like a savage beast intent on slaughter. Suddenly her hands were slapping at his face, her fingernails ripping and tearing at his grasp as his beautiful, delicate princess erupted into a banshee before his very eyes. Her feet stabbed at his shins and ankles as she wriggled to pull herself free from his hold, kicking and writhing like a woman possessed as she screamed and shrieked and scratched. Her fragile face was screwed into a despairing ball, her lips twisted and her features filled with horror. And her eyes, those wonderful eyes that Erik longed to sink himself within, were pressed shut so tightly that it seemed to Erik a wonder that her eyelids did not bleed into their sockets.

What was the matter with her? What had Tretaptus done?

"No!" she shrieked once more even as poor, bewildered Erik fought desperately to calm her, to still the torment in her heart and bring her at last to peace. "No, I won't! Get your hands off me, bumpkin! Get away from me, let me go! I won't do it! I won't be Islaine! I don't want to, you can't force me, get your hands off me!"

"Islaine, Islaine, please!" Despair clutched as his heart. "Islaine, please, I'm here to save you! I know you know me not, but please, please look at me! I'm here to help you, Islaine! I'm here to—"

"No, no, no!" With a terrible shriek, Islaine's foot lashed out once, driving into his knees and sending him stumbling backwards. Her hands whipped up, dragging her wrists from his tender grasp as she wheeled in a frantic circle, staggering once more bizarrely towards Tretaptus. And as Erik gasped and reeled, she reached the prince in a tumbling rush, dropping to her knees beside him as she clawed madly at his gag.

"Help me!" he heard her cry out again. "Please, dullard, please, I don't know if I can hold on! She wants me to look, dullard, she wants me to look!"

Tretaptus was straining desperately at his chains as the gag was dragged away.

"I know you can do it!" he gasped out. "I believe in you, pleasance!"

"I don't!" Islaine was sobbing. "I don't, I need you to hold on to, I need you because I—"

"Islaine!" Erik could take no more. Hurling himself forwards with all his strength, he grabbed his princess by the arm, dragging her to her feet and swinging her around as his hand clasped her chin and forced her face up to his.

Her horrified blue-violet eyes met his and held.

And the very world shifted.

Her mouth dropped open, her lips working in small, frantic gasps as her body trembled and shivered. As though locked in a fit, she shook from crown to sole. Her blue eyes were a maelstrom, a violent, tortured chaos as a war that even Erik could not fully understand was waged fiercely within their depths. Although her head did not, could not turn, her loose hand rose in a trembling arc, her fingers reaching, stretching almost desperately to where the dumbstruck Prince Tretaptus was watching her.

"Dullard..." she whispered mysteriously, her voice little more than a gasp of breath. "I'm...I'm sorry..."

"No!" Somewhere away in the distance, Erik heard Tretaptus's despairing cry. But it no longer mattered. Nothing mattered but Islaine.

It was as though he was watching her awaken from a nightmare. For the turbulence behind her eyes was melting away and beyond that terrible storm lay a beautiful, dawning sunrise. Islaine, his Islaine, was staring up at him with love; oh, for the sweet, forlorn love that he had borne alone for far too long was shared between them now, blossoming up from her soul to entwine it with his for eternity. Her tormented trembling of a moment before slipped suddenly into fervent shudders of relief, her gasps of horror blending into the gentle sighs of joy. Her hands, no longer reaching or fighting him away, rested tenderly against his chest as she gazed up rapturously into his face, a blissful smile lighting up her features like the very sun itself.

"You have saved me," she whispered breathily. "You have saved me from the cruel, binding enchantments his foul allies planted upon me, from their torture and their games." One delicate hand stretched up and stroked his cheek with tender passion. "You are my hero."

As he pulled the princess into a soft embrace, her golden curls caressing his cheek, Erik caught a glimpse of Prince Tretaptus, slumped in a heap in his chains, his face crumpled with wretched anguish. It was no more than he deserved.

All too soon, Erik was forced to end the glorious embrace. "My lady, we cannot stay here!" he exclaimed, gesturing to the sky, where thick clouds of monstrous creatures circled them overhead. "It is only fear of my magic that holds them back and it will not do so forever! Quickly, to my horse!"

"Pleasance!" Tretaptus's voice cut into their hurried motion. "Pleasance, please! I know you can hear me! You can still fight Islaine! You can..."

But Islaine had already turned, her perfect face awash with sudden, fierce fury. "You will not address me, foul traitor!" she declared imperiously. "You tried to steal what was rightfully mine! I condemn you! I condemn you to rot in the jealous trap you meant for me! Let the beasts you summoned to consume me make short work of your flesh instead! For your death means nothing to me! I hate you!"

For an instant the broken pain upon the wretched man's face was so absolute that Erik felt a strange glimmer of pity. But no, the villain had brought this madness upon himself. And though he would raise no hand to the man himself, he would not reverse the sentence of the princess either. She had suffered more than any at his hand and she deserved the right to choose his fate.

He caught her hand and she turned to him, suddenly shaking but her eyes resolute.

"Islaine, we must go," he said softly. She nodded.

The creatures were close now as they mounted his horse, Islaine cradled in Erik's arms as they turned and rode with frantic speed out of the confines of the little valley. The princess's face was pressed into Erik's shoulder, shrinking from the horror she had permitted in her rage as he glanced behind to see the monstrous beasts circling the chained prince like a vicious whirlwind. Even as he watched, a creature dove towards Tretaptus, claws outstretched in vile intent as it swooped upon its prey. The prince was swamped from view in a flurry of leathery wings. Erik heard scraping and a shriek of metal and, shockingly, Tretaptus ran free, his nose and face bloody, slashed from his bonds by an ill-timed strike. He raced and scrambled his way up the nearby slope, the creatures pursuing with casual, determined intent as they swooped and leapt from rock to rock behind him. They knew this meat would easily be theirs.

He'd reached the crest of the hill when they caught him.

Piling on top of one another in their anxiety to eat their fill, the creatures dove as one. There was a shriek as Tretaptus flung himself to the ground with claws tearing at the air around him and suddenly, in a flood of wings and teeth, they set upon him in a single, fervent leap. Even as Erik gasped and the princess winced, a bloody human hand clawed at the sky from beneath two flapping wings as a final, lingering scream rent the air. And then the mad prince, the foul traitor, the torturer of Islaine was…

Gone…

* * *

It was the strangest feeling.

Flirt stared down at herself, stared at the frills of her low-cut white blouse, at the ripple of her long red skirt, the dangle of her brown apron, touched one hand to the white mobcap balanced on her heap of dark curls. These were the clothes she had worn for a large chunk of her life, her everyday normality and a far cry from the jangle of her chain mail with its oppressive weight pressing on her shoulders and the reassuring bash of her sword against her legs. It was familiar, comfortable, like slipping back into wakefulness after a long and vivid dream.

A dream that had bloody chafed.

The chain mail had made her feel powerful. It had also made her feel sore.

Whereas this...

Wolf whistles, groping hands, pinching fingers, and unshaven lips drenched in ale, the coarse cries to summon the wen...

Flirt shivered. Familiar and comfortable it might be, harking back to a simpler time, an easier way—but most definitely not what she wanted to be. No, she wasn't going back, not to that life. She had never liked The Narrative's idea of a Barmaid as a cheap form of exercise for a randy companion, though she was fortunate in that she'd never been required to go further than the preliminaries. But away from The Narrative, it hadn't been so bad. The Humble Villagers had respected her, chatted to her, liked her, and she'd always enjoyed the chance for a laugh and a discussion on armed combat with Fodder and the lads. They were her friends. And caught up in the need to prove herself and the urge for adventure, she'd almost lost sight of that. She knew them. She could see the way their minds worked, and if there was one thing that Disposables understood, it was ale. And they always had time to listen to the person providing it.

All the same, to ensure there were no misunderstandings...

Reaching down, Flirt grabbed her sword belt from her pile of discarded armour and strapped it hurriedly into place. Immediately, she felt better.

With a deep breath, she braced her shoulders and strode out of the tent.

"But why would anyone need to count the bears when there's only four?"

Flirt grimaced. Yes, she knew Disposables. And she knew how very, very hard it was to get them to let go of an idea.

"But how would you know there's only four, hmmm? If you ain't counted them?"

"'Cos it's *four*, you daft beggar! You don't have to count four! You can *see* four!"

"Course you can see four! But you only know it's four if you count it!"

Ignoring the spiralling discussion to her left, Flirt looked right and found Donk rolling in the last of a pile of ale barrels. From some mysterious place on his person, Thump had managed to produce a tankard. He already had foam on his chin as he glanced up, spotted Flirt, and started to leer. One drum of her fingers against her sword hilt killed the expression stone dead.

Flirt grinned. Now that was fun.

And it was time. Again.

She pushed her mind back to those evenings with the lads at the Archetypal Inn, to their thoughts, their moans, their needs. Mostly that had involved thinking about ale, moaning there was not enough ale, and needing more ale; but beyond that, just sometimes...

Sticking her thumb and forefinger between her lips, Flirt belted out an almighty whistle. The bear conversation staggered to a halt.

"Hey, lads!" Flirt called out. "Who fancies an ale?"

For an instant, there was silence. Stillness. A pause to adjust.

And then, the earth beneath her feet lurched, trembled, and began to shake as footfall after footfall set the very ground aquiver. A stampede of faces stormed into her sight from all directions, every one wiped clean of the bewilderment, the confusion, and the anger that had characterised that day so far, to be replaced by a pack of bouncing, happy puppies. She could actually taste their relief on the air—here was no perplexing tangle of conflicting orders, of turning on one's fellows at the exhortation of a man they disliked, of disobeying basic facts of their existence. This was just ale. Simple, straightforward ale.

And they needed that.

It didn't take long to distribute her wares. Like Thump, no self-respecting Disposable would be caught without the means to drink ale somewhere about their person; and in no time at all, the grass was strewn with happy Disposables, sat on their backsides laughing and quaffing as they joked with their mates. The Buccaneers and Ordinary folk had joined in with enthusiasm, and even a couple of the elves had acquired drinking vessels and were venturing tentative sips of the brew. The Exotic Islanders, not great drinkers of mainland fare, were nonetheless not to be left out and had sent runners back to their own corner of the Camp to return with drums of their own special, fruity intoxicant. Only the Desert Nomads had resisted the urge to indulge but they had laid down their weapons, pulled off the uncomfortable chain mail, and joined the general lounging around with broad, relaxed-looking grins. Even Midlin, shaken and off-balance from Preen's behaviour, had accepted a reassuring cupful to calm his nerves.

How to break up a siege, Flirt thought to herself with a grin as she topped off the frothing tankard of Pounce the Bandit's and sent him off to join his brother Thump, who had already sailed past three sheets to the wind and was tearing into the rest of the laundry basket. *You don't need mangonels or trebuchets, do you? You don't need a mass of soldiers and some brave soul to lead the charge either. You need confused troops and a great big pile of* free booze.

Stage one had been successfully completed. Now it was time to move on to stage two.

Shoulders was standing nearby, watching the revelries with a painfully wistful expression on his face; joining in the chugging was not really an option for a man whose mouth was no longer properly attached to his throat—while nourishment and breath always continued to make mysterious passage between the two disconnected parts in such circumstances, there was a certain degree of leakage that generally proved unpleasant for all concerned. Flirt approached him hurriedly.

"I need the book," she said softly.

Shoulders pulled a face. "What for? Now Preen's imploded, we've no way to open it. It's nothing but a glorified paperweight."

"I know that, don't I?" Flirt grimaced. "But like it or not, to a lot of these lads, it's the be-all and end-all, and I want them to remember we've got it."

Shoulders gave a lopsided shrug that sent his head rocking back and forth in the confines of his helmet, but he handed over the brown book without further comment. With an awkward nod—she was still finding the resigned-but-compliant and ever-so-slightly brave Shoulders that had replaced the lord almighty of moaning a tad disconcerting—Flirt tucked the book into the pocket of her apron and returned to the upturned row of barrels. Scooting her sword to one side, she pulled herself up onto the nearest barrel, settling with her feet dangling down as she stared out over the lounging mass of men before her.

It's not a field full of soldiers, is it? It's a tableful of lads having a crafty pint at the inn between jobs. That's how you've got to think of it, haven't you? That's how you've got to talk to them...

She cleared her throat. "All right, lads?" she called out cheerily. "Everyone got what they need?"

A chorus of approving murmurs and cries of assertion rose from the grass around her. Flirt grinned. "Glad to hear it! I thought we could use a relaxing drink after that palaver, couldn't we?"

"You said it, Flirt!" Pounce piped up to a roar of general acclaim.

"I mean, that man! Blimey!" Flirt let out a whistle. "I always knew Preen was a bit of an arse but..." She let out a huff of breath. "I had no idea, did I? I mean, the way was talking to you lads." She shook her head. "Disrespectful. That's what it was. Who's he think he is?"

The rumble this time was more ambiguous. A definite ripple of approval formed a strong core, but a nervous air danced around the edges.

"Well..." One hesitant voice piped up from within a nearby knot of soldiers from the Castle Garrison. "He is our Courtier..."

"But it's not his job to judge you lads, is it?" Flirt leaned forwards knowingly. "I mean, if you weren't doing your jobs properly, fair enough. But he was the one not doing his! Officious Courtiers, they're supposed to pass on the instructions, aren't they? Get us lined up in the right place in the right kit for when The Narrative comes? But where in the instructions does it give him the right to yell and bully and call you lads every name under the sun?"

The rumble strengthened, the core of approval hardening, but it had not lost its uncertain undertones. Flirt picked out a few nearby voices.

"The lass has a point, you know…"

"…pain in the bloody arse, I've always said it…"

"…stuck-up oik, strutting around, yelling at us like we're nothing…"

"…bit of respect, is that too much to ask?"

"…but he does pass on the instructions…"

"…maybe he's an arse, but what would we do without him to tell us? How would we know what to be?"

"…we need his instructions. The instructions are the law…"

Midlin's voice. Flirt stepped in quickly.

"It's all very well, him calling himself the voice of your instructions," she said loudly, dimming the chatter to a dull mutter around her. "But the thing is—he hasn't had any instructions, has he? Because we've had his precious book right here!" She didn't bother to pull it out with any kind of flourish—she'd learned her lesson there. Instead, Flirt simply eased the dowdy book out of the pocket of her apron and balanced it casually on one palm. "So, this fuss, this siege, these insults, these orders, trying to kill us—that was Preen by himself, wasn't it? And worse than that—Sentinel, he wanted to get you instructions, didn't he? He wanted to send word to Strut and call in help from a higher authority, even from the Taskmaster! And what did that arse Preen do? He ignored him! He was too scared for his precious dignity, wasn't he? Too scared of what it would say about him!" She puffed out her cheeks. "And that rant about Strut, well…" She shook her head pensively. "You know what, lads? It seems to me that if anyone round here's been disobeying the instructions, it's Preen."

The rumble was losing its uncertainty. There was a definite hint of darkness to its tone now.

"…she's right. That bloody git had the nerve to shout at us when all along…"

"...selfish bastard! Just thinking about himself, he was..."

"...wouldn't trust him to watch grass grow! The weasel..."

"...always thought if his brains were paint, they wouldn't cover a flea's boudoir, but this..."

Ah, the Buccaneers, such a wonderful turn of phrase they had. Flirt bit back a grin as she ploughed on.

"I've always thought you lads never deserved to be saddled with him, did you?" she said thoughtfully, casually hefting the book in her hand. "Because he's never understood you, has he? You Disposables, you're a family, aren't you? All in it together? One for all and all for picking up each other's limbs afterwards? It's camaraderie, isn't it? It's being able to stand together, fight together, moan about it together over a pint in the pub afterwards whilst your limbs get sewn back on! You stand by each other because no one else will! *That's* the Disposable way!"

In spite of a creeping hint of rhetoric to her tone, this time the clamour of sound was definitely an assertion. Flirt took a quick, deep breath in order to haul herself back down to the mundane and then rushed on.

"And that's what I've always liked about you lads," she said with an approving nod. "You respect each other, don't you? You respect a job well done. Because you get so little credit from the high-uppities or from The Narrative for your hard work, you make sure to share it amongst yourselves. You're good lads who do a good job and don't get appreciated except by each other, do you?" The rumble died back to a pensive murmur as her words flowed out. "And you know, I've always thought..." She shook her head slightly. "I can't help it but I have. I've always thought you deserved better. Better than what you got from the likes of Strut and Preen. And better than the miserable lot you get in the instructions..."

"But the instructions *are the law!*"

Flirt started noticeably, thrown out of her casual, conversational air by the shocking sound of a voice familiar but yet so suddenly rocked with actual emotion that she could hardly believe it was Midlin's. The sentence he flung out was rife with desperation, with fervour, with conviction, and with anger, and it seemed almost to echo around the sudden silence that it had blasted in its wake. "They are *everything!* We don't...we can't...they *run the world!* What would the world be without them? What would *we* be? What would *anything* be?" Midlin's face was contorted now, tears streaming down it. "I've said it and said it and you *never listened!* I see what you're doing and I won't have it! We have no worth without the Taskmaster! We have no purpose without The Narrative! The Taskmaster *is this world.* The Narrative *is our life.* And you would declare war on them, attack them, chase them away, and put yourselves in their place? Without them, would we even have a world *at all?"*

Uh-oh. The rumble had changed tone abruptly, a strong, worried thread snaking through its heart at Midlin's violent exposure of the destination of her conversation. She'd been trying to be gentle, to ease them into the idea gradually so it could settle comfortably in their minds, but Midlin had barrelled in like a battering ram and smashed her carefully constructed pathway into rubble. Rapid running repairs were definitely in order.

She crinkled her nose. "Now, Midlin, did I say—"

"You were *going to!"* The Disposable clambered to his feet, waving an accusing finger in her direction. "I know you were! You said it before, I was there, I heard you! Your words, Flirt, you said them! *Why do we have to obey the Taskmaster at all?"*

A shocked gasp ran through the lounging horde around her. Several pints were actually lowered.

Bugger, not good...

Less running repairs and more fighting the tide. But Flirt could see a causeway.

"I said that; I admit it." Placing the book down beside her on the barrels, she raised her hands palms forward towards the alarmed and wary faces of the men. "It was impulsive. I know this is a world of instructions. I don't know what it would be without them but..." She took a deep breath as Poniard's frenzied face, the weird behaviour of the delusional Gods, and Preen's mad eyes flashed across her mind, and she knew in her heart that she truly meant what she was about to say. Perhaps she hadn't always seen it in that way, but the last few days had drastically shifted her perspective. "But I don't think we're ready to find out. I've learned my lesson since I said that, haven't I? We *do* need a Taskmaster and we *do* need instructions." She took a deep breath. "We just need those instructions to be fairer."

And it was true. Ever since Fodder's desperate exclamation on the Mountain of the Gods, the feeling had been growing, and the stockade Barbarians, Preen and Poniard, and the Disposables themselves had only confirmed to her what she was now sure of: life without the Taskmaster wasn't going to be practical. These were the people she knew the best and she knew that they were not ready to have the safety of all that they knew, that they'd always known, torn away from them. The world they'd lived in their whole life was too ingrained inside of them, and weaning them to thinking for themselves would take time and guidance that she knew no one down here would be able to provide.

It was the Taskmaster or carnage. They simply needed the Taskmaster to do better.

Silence, but for the occasional slurp of ale, had fallen.

And then, rising from the grass nearby, a hard-faced lifeline spoke out.

"Fairer how?" asked Thrash of the Grim Fortress.

With a push, Flirt dropped from her barrel perch and moved forwards, weaving her way between the patches of men watching her like one enormous, badly groomed hawk. She gave the almost plaintive-looking Pounce a gentle punch to the shoulder as she passed, smiled at Thump's unfocused expression and Tumble's worried smile, Clunny's sardonic stare, Donk's enormous bulk and Dunny's beer-stained jerkin—even at Midlin, sat once more, his previously blank face stained shockingly with tears. And she could pick out less-familiar faces now: Lurk and Twister, the Bandits of Bandit Pass and her occasional customers; Thrash the demoted field captain; the bear-obsessed Watchman and the Garrison man who protested bear rights; the Buccaneer with the sardonic turn of phrase; and the stringy-looking lad in chain mail who'd called her negative...

They were people within themselves, each with their own ways and their own character, and it was unfair of her to lump them together as *the troops* or *the lads*. Each one deserved his moment, if he wanted it, each one his chance to shine. And even if he didn't, even if all he wanted from his life was rescuing his entrails from a tree and having a pint afterwards, he deserved the right to decide for himself. That way was only fair.

"You get a choice," she said, her voice soft but carrying well. "That's what we want—a choice. The right to say yes or no. The chance to be Heroes if we want, or go home and live our old life if we don't. And for whatever we decide to do, to be respected for it. That sounds fair to me, doesn't it? Does it sound fair to you?"

Silence. More silence.

"Would that mean...?" The nervous voice broke off, but it was too late to hide. Flirt followed it and found a pale elf, his mass of perfect blond hair spilling messily from under a rusty helmet as he gripped his barely touched tankard of ale with shaking hands.

"Carry on," she encouraged gently.

The elf bit his lip. "Would that mean..." he ventured once more. "They might let me live...in a *house?* On the ground? In a city? No leaves, no wind, no bark burn?" His voice was filled with a desperate yearning. "No *badgers?*"

Flirt smiled softly. "If that's what you wanted."

"D'you think they'd let me be a merchant?" another voice piped up suddenly, the dark-browed Grim Fortress soldier earlier involved in the bear debate. "Just once, that's all. 'Cos merchants, they always get good hats." He grinned wistfully. "I love a good hat."

"I wanna be a sailor," a pale little Watchman injected suddenly. "I'd love to go out on the sea. Only ever been once, but it was so beautiful..."

"I want to get *off* the sea," a Buccaneer offered fervently. "Makes me sick to my stomach, that motion, but I can't do a thing until The Narrative's gone. Saves itself up, it does. I can be puking for hours..."

"I'll take *anything* else," exclaimed a Desert Nomad. "You know all we ever do? Cover our faces, surround the Merry Band, and shake our weapons. Most of the time we don't even speak!"

"At least you get seen!" injected an Exotic Islander. "Who comes to our islands these days? And no one much wants us over here except to hide at the back of the horde. How often does anyone in this Realm see a face like mine?"

"Hours, I'm telling you! It comes out like a river, you wouldn't think one body could hold..."

"So, you're saying..." Thrash injected, thankfully cutting off the Buccaneer, who was now involving gestures, "that if we wanted to step up and say, 'I fancy trying out to be a Principal'...we could?"

"What?"

An audible groan rippled across the grass, part of it belonging to Flirt herself. Somewhere along the line, presumably at either the prospective threat of violence or the uncouth distribution of ale, Bard the Minstrel had abandoned his attempts to inspire the troops and melted out of sight. But if his sudden shrill exclamation was anything to go by, he hadn't escaped out of earshot.

And then he appeared, bursting from a nearby tent in an eye-aching flurry of colours, his golden hair whipping in the breeze as he stormed his way to the edge of the lounging troops. Wrinkling his nose, he picked a rather daintier line between them, making sure to keep his arms pressed close to his body and his hands well away from any possible contact as he wound his path towards Flirt. His expression was one of indignant rage.

"Did I hear you correctly?" he projected vibrantly in his rich voice. "Did you actually propose the possibility of allowing men such as these the chance to offer themselves up as Principals?"

Flirt raised an eyebrow pointedly. "I did. Problem?"

"Problem? *Problem?"* Bard's voice spiralled beautifully upwards. "Why, of course there's a problem! You'll ruin me!"

Flirt blinked. Of all the objections she had expected to hear, that was a new one. "Ruin you how?" she asked curiously.

"Well...*look* at them!" Bard spluttered furiously, his rage seemingly sapping his desire for flowery prose. "You can't expect me to work with this kind of material!" With his fingers wrapped firmly in the dangling end of his sleeve, he batted the brown, mundane locks of Pounce's head. "There's nothing remarkable about them! Nothing lyrical, nothing fanciful, nothing I can wrap my words around and use to burst into flight! Where are the flowing locks, the flashing eyes, the hair like fire, the voice like thunder? Where are the bulging muscles, the perfect skin, the distinctive noses, and the melting stares? There's no colour, there's no beauty, there's normal, boring, scruffy, ugly! Even the forces of evil are ugly in a strangely attractive way but this...*this!*" He took a deep and wavering breath. "This is a travesty! You are so...so...*so Ordinary!* There's nothing appealing here, nothing pleasant, nothing attractive to the eye or likely to set the soul on fire! There's no great depths of character, no moral rage, no yearning tragedy, no soulful angst, no pure romance! I mean, look at yourselves!" He smacked his wrapped-up hand down on the head of the confused-looking Lurk. "Can you see this twisted, bizarre specimen of a man staring longingly into the eyes of a beautiful princess and her loving him in return? Can you? And him!" He turned a jabbing finger on the bewildered stringy youth. "No creature with an Adam's apple that protrudes so uncouthly could possibly wield a Sword of Destiny and decimate the forces of evil! And as for you!" The hand—at great peril, to judge by the expression it was received by—was thrust in the direction of Thrash. "What would you be? A noble Knight, perhaps, would be your dream, a great Hero on horseback retrieving damsels in distress? But yet you possess no flowing locks, no eyes that beg for justice, tormented yet wondrous, tough and yet caring! All you have is that nose, and no nose should be at that kind of angle! You're *just a man!* An unappealing, undistinctive, utterly unremarkable man! I ask you! I ask! How am I supposed to make beautiful, flowing heroic prose out of *people like you?*"

For a moment, there was nothing but silence. Bard stood, panting, arms outstretched in artful agony, his face tortured as he gazed in yearning appeal towards the sky.

Thrash stood up. It was a slow uncurling of his body as he pulled himself with deliberate care to his feet, his eyes fixed upon Bard with a cool, almost thoughtful detachment. Bard's reaching eyes swung down to more mundane reality as he realised the presence of the Fortress Guardsman towering before him.

They arrived in time to see the fist.

And to judge by the way in which Bard's eyes glazed over as he keeled backwards like a cut sapling, it would be the last thing he would see for quite some time.

The cheering lasted several minutes. The clapping, backslapping, and handshaking for Thrash after he'd folded his arms and settled back onto the grass with a half-smile on his face went on quite a bit longer. Tumble was amongst the more enthusiastic.

Flirt stared down at the thumped Minstrel and shook her head. Some people never learned.

Dunny had joined the cluster around Thrash now, wiping the smear of beer foam from his face with his grubby sleeve as he offered a hearty smack on the shoulder before meandering over to poke the motionless Minstrel with his foot. Flirt sighed. Squick had also disappeared—he had probably found a nook to rest his wings by now and watch events unfold from safe neutrality—and Flirt wondered if she should send someone to find him so he could look Bard over. Satisfying as it was to see a longtime dream fulfilled, it was hardly fair to leave the poor idiot lying there. Perhaps if she grabbed Dunny and...

Dunny. Dunny, whom she'd already given a job to. Dunny, whom she'd told to watch Preen...

"Dunny!" she exclaimed loudly. "I told you to watch Preen!"

The Disposable glanced up in surprise, his face confused. "Well, yeah, but...there was ale..."

Flirt needed to hear no more. Her eyes swung round, searching for the patch of grass where she had last seen the purple-clad, glazed form of the Officious Courtier. And he wasn't there.

And...

Oh no.

Her hand slapped down on her apron and found nothing more than cloth. She'd taken the book out. She'd taken it out and left it on the barrels and...

Her gaze swung frantically round to the barrels. She found the sight she dreaded.

No book. *No book.*

She barely realised she'd started running until she slammed into the barrels, feeling frantically around the edges, plunging to grope the grass on either side, but there was no book and no Preen and surely that had to mean...

"Looking for this?"

Flirt froze. Flirt turned her head. Flirt stared.

Shoulders grinned.

For in his hands, he was holding the book, its pages crinkling in the breeze...its pages—yes, the book was *open*. And beneath one foot, gagged and bound in a heap and glaring with a great deal more conscious awareness than he'd earlier displayed, was Preen.

Flirt darted to his side in an instant. "What happened?"

Shoulders gave an incredulous snort. "What do you think happened? You gave Dunny a job and then offered him ale. You can't expect miracles!" He pulled a distinctly smug face. "You're lucky I was here. Sober, responsible..."

"Leaky."

Shoulders chose to ignore that. "While you were chatting with the lads, I saw matey-boy here open his eyes, spot the book, and start crawling that way on his hands and knees, groping about to grab it. I was going to just sit on his head but I thought to myself—what if he's after some instructions?" He beamed at Preen's foul-tempered expression. "So, I followed him instead. Let him crawl all the way on his knees until he was behind the tents and, lo and behold, if he wasn't good enough to open the book for me. So, I went and bopped him on the head, tied him up, and took it off him. Ta-da!" He offered the book with a flourish. "Does this mean we can find Fodder and the others now? Only I really want to track them down so we can finally put this whole bloody mess to bed!"

"I hope so." Flirt quickly flipped the book the right way around, leafing hurriedly past page after page of regular writing, but she couldn't help but notice the amount of crossings-out, of insertions and alterations in the later pages; and though she had never seen instructions laid out like this before, the early pages were so regular that surely the mess could only be because of their rebellion. And she needed to find the latest instructions, she needed to know what was happening now and...

    ...with foul Tretaptus dead and Princess Islaine at
    last safely in the arms of her true love, Erik, the
    companions resolve once and for all to ride to the
    Swamp of Craxis and ambush and destroy the trouble-

some Man of Sleiss in order to retrieve the Ring of
Anthiphion from him...

Her heart froze. Her stomach plummeted.

"Shoulders…" she whispered.

He pushed Preen to the ground and was at her side at once. "What?" His eyes followed her gaze and widened, his loose head rolling in horror. "Oh…oh no…oh…oh, we're *doomed.*" His voice was filled with purest horror. "We're so doomed. We're beyond doomed, we're epically doomed, we're as doomed as it's possible to be without being impossibly doomed." He clenched his fists. "They've got the princess and seen off Dullard, and Fodder's going to be next! And then it's us! Disembodied forever! Doomed, doomed, *doomed!*"

And to think she'd almost been missing the moaning. "Stop getting hysterical!"

"Why should I? I *want* to be hysterical! I *like* being hysterical! I'm *good* at being hysterical!"

"Enough!" Flirt could only imagine the look on her own face but it must have reflected enough of her frustration, her fear, and her fierce anger to silence him. "We're not giving up!" She bit her lip, her eyes raking over the painful words once more. "It doesn't look like there's much we can do for Dullard or Pleasance," she admitted painfully. "But the swamp will be the Stinking Marsh and that isn't too far from here. We still have time to save Fodder."

"Save him?" Shoulders gasped incredulously. "How?"

Flirt jerked her head towards the cheery, laughing, half-pissed mass of troops behind them. "With their help."

Shoulders wobbled his loose head in his best approximation of a shake. "You've barely started talking to them! They're interested but hardly converted! You really think they'll be ready and willing to ride off and face the Merry Band?"

"Not all of them," Flirt was honest enough to admit. "I'm no Preen." She shot the bound-up Courtier a hard look that he was glad to return. "I'm not going to bully them into something they don't want to do. Those who want to come can come and the rest can stay. No pressure."

"They don't want to go against the instructions!" Shoulders pointed out fiercely. "It's too much!"

Flirt smiled sweetly. "But I have the instructions, Shoulders." She waved the book pointedly. "And nowhere in them does it say they have to stay here. They are supposed to prepare for the Final Battle and, unless I'm mistaken, isn't the Battle Ground just south of the Stinking Marsh?" She squared her shoulders. "Besides, one of their own is in trouble." She turned towards the happy Disposables, painfully aware she was probably about to ruin their mood. But it had to be done. For Fodder's sake and for the sake of them all. Before it was too late.

"Come on, Shoulders," she said firmly. "It's time to rally the troops."

* * *

This time, Elder was certain, everything would finally be put to rights.

Erik's abrupt disappearance the previous afternoon had been an unpleasant and concerning mystery. But for a sorcerer of his skill and power, it had not taken long to fold his vision through the layers of air, to reach out and to witness his young charge's dramatic rescue of the poor Princess Islaine. It was a great relief to realise the tormented lamb was safe at last in the arms of those who would protect her and that soon, very soon, she would at last be joining their party to stand against the evil of Craxis. And so, before entering and with a brief touch of his mind, Elder had sent guidance to call Erik and his damsel to meet them when morning came here.

Not that here was the most pleasant of spots. But it was necessary. Oh, so necessary.

His eyes raked over the bubbling pits that surrounded them, damp boggy earth and dead, bent rushes clinging to heaped tussocks as they ringed the thick greenish pools of liquid that barely warranted the title of water. Sluggish, circular ripples that spread with slow, laboured difficulty across the foul expanse of gloop to their right marked the expulsion of small jets of foul-smelling marsh gas that only added to the miasma of eye-watering odour that permeated the air in such poisonous volume that it gathered in clumps of ill-smelling, moistened mist that blocked the world about and the morning sun from view. Every so often, out in the misty, half-concealed stretch of swamp a bit further away, the brackish, heavy surface of the water appeared to undulate.

The Swamp of Craxis. The first line of defence of the forces of evil, the stinking gateway to the desolation of their refuge, the border between humanity and the jaws of hellishness. A place of secrets, of darkness, of abomination and somewhere that few if any would ever willingly go.

Until now.

Elder smiled. In spite of the stench, he couldn't help himself. It was amazing, really. Why had he never thought of this before?

He glanced at his companions. Slynder, his fingers still absent-mindedly tearing at the bandages encasing his wounded leg, had wrinkled his nose with such fervour that Elder was surprised that the whole contraption did not fold back into his face altogether. Zahora's expression, so often shaped as though a foul smell had drifted beneath her nose, was even further exaggerated. Svenheid was making every effort to breathe solely through his beard. Sir Roderick's expression was a mystery, given that he had, rather futilely, closed his visor the moment they had entered this reeking morass, but the tight set of his armoured body spoke volumes on his behalf.

"Why must we be here?" As on the last three occasions, it was Zahora's voice that broke out over the gentle glooping of the water and hiss of escaping gas. "Why wait in this abomination of a place? Why could we not stay out on the Flats where the wind was clean and the air was fresh and we could see any danger of ambush? Why this place?"

Elder stifled a sigh behind his beard. He cared for Zahora as a companion, of course, but there were moments of late when he had started to find her shrill protests somewhat tiresome.

"As I have already told you," he replied wearily. "We have a purpose here, a valuable purpose, but I cannot at present say more. I would appreciate it if you would simply give me your trust."

Zahora snorted. "Trust? What of your trust for us? Has what we have endured together not earned us the right to the truth?"

Elder gritted his teeth, silently wishing that he had had to endure a little less of Zahora. "Of course, it has. But as experience has shown us, it is hard to know who may be listening and I have no wish to expose my hand before the round is played."

"And so you keep us in the dark? Out of some petty fear of eavesdropping?" Zahora drew herself up angrily. "Who could you possibly believe would be lurking in this fetid pit?"

"Oh, for pity's sake, you half-wit. Can't you tell he's talking about me?"

It was a strange sensation. That voice that had come to characterise dread and wary fear, that unassuming face as it bobbed up from behind a particularly large clump of dead reeds nestled on a hummock this time brought Elder only a surge of satisfaction. He was here. He had come.

The game was afoot.

The man of Sleiss raised an eyebrow. "My, my," he drawled curiously. "Aren't we cocky all of a sudden?"

"Hark who's talking." Slynder's sardonic retort did not quite remain under his breath.

The eyes of the man of Sleiss darted in his direction but he chose not to respond. Instead, he folded his arms as he wandered to rest his foot against a tussock by the side of the shifting green waters, watching Elder with unusual seriousness. "You must have some serious faith in this mysterious plan of yours," he said dryly.

Elder smiled. "I consider it quite foolproof, yes."

The man of Sleiss cocked his head. "In spite of the fact even the weather failed to take me down? In spite of the fact you've thrown everything you've got at me and more and haven't even dented me? In spite of the fact that without bumpkin boy to offer the only hint of defence you have, I could take the lot of you out with a snap of my fingers if I wanted to?"

"Why do you not?" Sir Roderick's voice echoed tinnily from behind his visor. "Why do you not simply end this instead of prodding and poking and playing with us like insects in a jar?"

The man of Sleiss gave an easy shrug. "Because at the end of the day, you don't really matter. It isn't your attention I'm interested in.

Wiping you out would put a nice dampener on the plot, but what would it prove in the end? The game's almost through now—you could be wiped off as tragic sacrifices and it wouldn't be the end of the world. And the end of the world is what matters." He gave an offhand shrug. "It would be pointless. And anyway, I don't want to win by force anymore. I want an acknowledgement. I want a surrender."

"We will never surrender to you, fiend!" Roderick's metallic voice retorted. "Never if the sky should fall and the earth should burn! Never in a thousand years!"

The smile was slow, knowing, smugly irritating. "Did I say anything about wanting a surrender from you?"

Elder stiffened in his seat, his shoulders thrown back as swamp mist teased at his dampened beard. "Then whose surrender would you have? The Lords of the Six Kingdoms? Erik's? Perhaps Lord Craxis himself?"

The look that the man of Sleiss fixed upon him in return sent a shudder through the very core of the world. "You know who," he said.

Elder fought to conceal the shivers that ran the length of his skin and set his nerve ends tingling. "You are quite mad!" he whispered with fervour.

The man of Sleiss shrugged. "Maybe. Maybe not. We'll just have to wait and see, won't we?"

"You would destroy us all!" The words slipped from Elder's lips spawned by a corner of himself that he was barely aware of. "You would ruin everything!"

"Or make it better." The man of Sleiss's gaze was relentless. "But we aren't going to know until we try."

"You think we will permit you to fulfil this abomination?"

The impudent wretch had the gall to chuckle. "Seems to me you can't do much to stop it. You ride at the whim of one, and that one isn't running at full tilt, thanks to me." He gave the tussock against which he was leaning a gentle kick as he pushed himself upright, sending ripples across the greenish surface. Bubbles rose and burst in a spiral. "It's not like you folks can do anything but ride around in circles at the moment. I've got all the shiny, end-gaming cards in my pockets now.

You don't have the Ring and without that, you can't face off with Craxis. And you don't have the princess to lead your big, brave battle to the finish in the meanwhile. So, without the Ring and without the princess, what do you think you can possibly do about anything?"

"But you do not have the poor princess. I do."

Elder's heart leapt. For in that moment, the foul-smelling mist parted like a curtain and out of its concealment rode Erik, seeming at once a young boy no longer but a young man, his shoulders thrown back and his face firm and bold, one arm wrapped with tender, loving care around the purple-clad waist of the slender form of Princess Islaine. For a moment, her pale, beautiful face, ringed in red-gold curls, seemed lost, bewildered; but at the touch of Erik's hand to her chin, at the meeting of their eyes, her expression blossomed into a glorious smile of content-ment. She sighed deeply.

"As you can see," she breathed warmly, her eyes never wavering from the young man's face, "my love has rescued me. I no longer stand in the foul clutches of your fiendish ally, Prince Tretaptus." She spat out his name as though poisoned by its touch upon her tongue. "I am no longer your pawn."

For the first time, Elder saw genuine shock flood over the features of the man of Sleiss. His jaw dropped open with surprise and, to Elder's joy, consternation flowed over the overwhelming confidence that had until that moment filled his eyes.

"Pleasance?" he ventured inexplicably.

Where a moment before loving contentment had gleamed, sudden irritation surged in the eyes of the princess. Her head snapped round to face her former kidnapper.

"Why do you persist in using that strange designation?" she retorted with sudden fierceness. "He used it too." A flicker, brief and barely there, crossed her face for an instant but it was quickly swallowed by her rage. "It is not mine! It has nothing to do with me! I am Islaine, heiress to the lands and title of Nyolesse, princess of the blood, the most noble lady of the Six Kingdoms! It is not difficult to remember!"

The man of Sleiss closed his mouth with a snap, his jaw firming, but alarm still ran rampant across his features. "No, it's not," he said carefully. "But neither is pleasance. And unlike that dung you just spouted, that one is actually your name."

Islaine gave a disdainful huff and turned her face away. "Witless nonsense!"

But the man of Sleiss was staring at her unrelentingly. "Where's the prince, pleasance?" he said, his voice steady but strangely uncertain. "Where's dullard?"

"You refer to your master, the dullard, Prince Tretaptus?" She turned to him once more, her chin lifted, her face filled with an odd relish. "Gone. Dead. Torn to shreds before our eyes and those shreds now lie scattered to the very breeze or lost to the bellies of his destroyers. He will trouble me with his rancid attentions no longer."

It was as though the man of Sleiss had been struck. He took a step backwards, his eyes filled with horror as he shrank from the bragged-up self-confidence that had so recently filled his steps with swagger. "He died in front of you?" he gasped. "In the narrative?"

Ignoring this strange statement, Elder was surprised to see this apparently heartless man so affected by the death of his mad master. Had he held some kind of power over him or held him ready for some great plan that his death should wound him so visibly?

"Before my eyes." The princess glared haughtily down at the first of her tormentors. "And you will follow him."

And Elder struck.

The man of Sleiss, for once, had not been ready—shocked by the death of his ally, the attack caught him completely by surprise. But it was not a move of magic that Elder made, a blow of light or power, but a simple sack of powder hurled with great force. The yellowish dust exploded over their nemesis's face and chest as he yelled with surprise, staggering back as he clawed at the stinging effect on his nose and eyes. With a sweep of his arm, Elder called his companions back and quickly, they spurred their horses away over the boggy terrain, withdrawing hurriedly if carefully to a distance of perhaps forty yards and the upthrust of a lonely outcrop of rock. As they reined in on this small piece of solidity, the man of Sleiss had regained his composure, wiping yellow smears from his cheeks as he glared at their retreat through red-tinged eyes.

"That's the master plan, is it?" he called out, his voice thick with irritation as he coughed loudly to punctuate the sentence. "Death by bloody allergies?"

He didn't know. It was almost too good to be borne as a smile slipped unbidden onto Elder's cheeks. "Not at all," he said cheerfully. "But that powder in which you are coated is the ground remains of a flower called the Night's Blood Trefoil, also nicknamed the Tempter of Demons. Most sane and sensible people destroy it whenever they see it. I was lucky to acquire this much from a rogue patch of the flower on the Flats."

"So you got busy while matey-boy was hogging the attention. Clever." The man of Sleiss spat fervently into the bubbling green morass over his shoulder. "So come on then, because I know you're dying to. What's the ominous flower of doom going to do to me? Dissolve my flesh or boil my brain? Leach out my blood through my ears? Make my bones ignite in a big, messy explosion?"

"To you, it will do nothing." He caught the surprised expressions of his companions out of the corner of his eye—Svenheid in particular looked put out that it would cause no immediate gore. "It is, however, utterly irresistible to creatures of unnatural birth. The slightest scent of it will drive them to a frantic fervour until they have consumed it."

The man of Sleiss gave a rasping chuckle. "Freakish creature time, is it? That's nice, I could use a sing-song."

Elder ignored this strange statement as a matter of course, his eyes drifting to beyond where the man of Sleiss lurked, to the expanse of greenish murk behind him that was less bubbling and more boiling as explosions of gas rent the surface into chaos. "I was thinking more of the guardian beast placed here by Craxis to protect the gateway to his citadel. The one that, unless I am very much mistaken, has been sleeping beneath the surface behind you."

But the man of Sleiss had already turned, observing the wild sloshing and burping of the water with, insanely, a smile touching once more against his lips.

"That's it?" He gave a mighty snort. "That's your wonderful, oh-so-confident plan?" A peal of laughter broke madly above the ablutions of the swamp. "You're going to set the ravaging swamp monster on me? You couldn't stop me with mysterious powers, with tricks or with thunderstorms! What makes you think a monster's going to be any different?"

And there it was. The final piece of the puzzle.

Elder raised one hand and swept it in an elegant arc across the swamp. "A monster...in this place."

The puzzlement on the face of the man of Sleiss was gratifying. "In this place?" he repeated disdainfully. "What's this place got to do with it?"

Elder gave a beatific smile. "This place that, according to the ancient texts that I have recently consulted, contains as a result of the overspill of Craxis's foul experiments a natural immunity to all possible forms of magic." He met the man of Sleiss's distant eyes. "No spell or talisman of any kind will ever work here, upon any part of this place or upon the beast that lives here. Including the Ring of Anthiphion."

He saw the moment. He saw the dawning realisation in the eyes of the man of Sleiss, the appreciation of the trap he had so blithely swaggered into and now could not escape. He saw the horror cross his face as his fingers groped at the Ring he had used for so long to torment them, shaking it, jabbing at it, his face filled with increasing desperation.

But there was no glow of red in reply. The ancient texts had spoken. It was powerless here.

And so was he.

His head snapped down. And then the floating tussocks beneath his feet erupted.

The earth of the Swamp of Craxis was little more than a crust—Elder knew that, for it had prompted his retreat to sturdy ground. The man of Sleiss, it seemed, had not been aware.

Elder could see his expression almost in slow motion, his mouth agape with terror, his eyes wild as he reached out, his hands clawing the air in his desperation to escape. The silent Ring was still clamped on his finger, sharing his fate as he craned himself towards the last dregs of freedom.

But it was already too late.

An enormous maw—green, rounded, vast, and slimy—exploded from beneath his very feet, rancid lines of teeth slicing upwards towards closure as the gigantic gullet yearned to make this tasty, irresistibly scented morsel its own. The man of Sleiss did not even have time to scream before the arching tongue engulfed him and the terrible jaws clamped shut, dragging him down, swallowing him whole, for utterly, completely and irrevocably, before the watching eyes of Elder, the princess Islaine, and all of their companions, the man of Sleiss was finally...

Gone...

Meanwhile, Erik and his companions, having battled past the monster guarding the swamp, have reached Craxis's citadel, where Vagg has arrived with the Ring — they sneak inside with Slynder's skill but they are discovered. Slynder kills Vagg but not before the Ring is handed on to Craxis. Eldrigon gets between Erik and Craxis and tries to hold the evil one back, but is killed. Distraught, Erik lets rip with all the power he has, knocking down Craxis before he can use the Ring, and claiming it for himself. Their power now even, Craxis challenges the callow youth to a duel but with the power of right on his side, Erik succeeds in killing the inhuman monster in combat. When he dies, his minions, built from magic, crumble to dust and the kingdoms are saved.

"No!"

The voice flew out of nowhere. Even as the giant green bulk of the beast slammed its mighty jaws together, a lone figure burst out of the mist just beyond it, a figure so ridiculously ordinary for such a place that Elder could scarce believe she was not some wild figment of his overwrought imagination. For it was a woman, simply dressed, her hair a messy mass of dark curls beneath a lacy cap as she hurled herself across the boggy, undulating ground, her red skirt ripped up the side to facilitate her velocity, her chest heaving with breathlessness against the low-cut bodice of her blouse. The only thing about her that carried her a step beyond the mundane was the glittering, finely wrought sword that rattled at her strangely-belted waist and tangled at her legs as she ran, with startlingly stupid bravery, directly towards the monster.

"Oi!" she screamed out. "Yeah, I'm talking to you, aren't I, swampy-boy! Where do you think you're going? Why don't you stand and fight like the stinking green blob of teeth you are?"

And then Elder heard Zahora's gasp of shock. "It's her!" she hissed between her teeth. "That slattern in chain mail who struck me in the woods! The ally of the man of Sleiss!"

"It cannot be!" Svenheid snapped in response. "She fell to her

100

death! You are mistaken!"

"I would know her face from a million!" Zahora's voice was a snarl. "As should you! She made impression enough on you that day!"

"How should I know her? I was not there when she murdered my brother Torsheid!" Zahora flushed strangely at his pointed retort. "And even if I had been…" Svenheid's bearded face was for a moment a mystery. "They all look the same to me…"

"Should we stop her?" Slynder exclaimed, his hands gripping his dagger hilts.

"For what purpose?" Sir Roderick's armoured shoulders gave a rather unchivalrous shrug. "Let the foolish woman join her friend in the belly of the beast!"

For she had, there was no doubt, captured the creature's attention. The giant, slimy, amorphous bulk of the monster had hesitated, its two enormous, bulbous eyes blinking slowly. It stared at the strange figure screaming at it as she hurtled towards its mindless bulk, her sword whipping from its sheath.

"I'll teach you to swallow my friend!" she roared madly. The beast gave an ominous rumble, as a giant webbed foot splashed out of the water and clawed at the unstable moss. Its toothy maw parted dangerously.

"She is insane!" Sir Roderick exclaimed, actually pushing up his visor as he stared at the madwoman charging. "The beast will slaughter her in an instant!"

And astonishingly, the woman stopped, wheeled and, apparently oblivious to the rumbling green mass of menace mere yards in front of her, turned to glare at the cluster of companions who were watching her.

"What?" she bellowed across the intervening air. "You don't think I can take this thing?"

"Madness…" Slynder breathed. Zahora was less discreet.

"Of course you cannot!" she snapped out sharply. "It is an absurdity!"

"Why?"

Elder gaped at the woman's ignorance, unable to help but respond.

"Do you not realise what it is you face?" he burst out impatiently. "This is the guardian at Craxis's gate! The beast is ancient, hungry, implacable, with skin like steel and teeth like diamond! No blade can break its skin nor arrowhead pierce it! In this place without magic, it is impossible!"

The towering mass of creature was advancing now, awkward and slow as it hauled its bulk against the floating earth, tearing it aside, but the ridiculous woman did not move.

"Impossible, hmmm?" she bellowed back. "So, what? It would take an army?"

Elder shook his bearded head in quiet disbelief at her insanity. "More than an army! Most likely it would take every armed man under the sun!"

The mossy ground dissolved beneath the beast's advance, cracking open all the way towards the rock upon which they stood as the monster lumbered forwards, mouth agape, foul breath staining the air, frog-like eyes bulging as it scented fresh meat.

And still she stood there. Smiling.

"So there's absolutely no chance it could be taken out by forty-two common soldiers and a barmaid?" she said brightly.

Elder gaped. "Of course not!"

The smile blossomed, broadened until it was a beaming grin even beneath the shadow of the roaring bulk closing down on her.

"Thank you so much!" she exclaimed. "That's just what I wanted to hear!"

With her free hand, she reached out, grabbing a trailing silver tail and whipping it—Elder realised with sudden shock that what he had taken for a belt was in fact only the beginning of a long metal chain that dangled out behind her, vanishing into the murk from which she had emerged. Her sword-grasping hand thrust up into the air, arcing over her head.

"You heard him, lads!" she roared. "Hopeless, impossible, it would take an army! You can't lose, the narrative says so! Believe it! First rule!"

"She's right! She's bloody right!"

"Blimey! We can do this!"

"We have to do this!"

"For the first rule!"

"For the four bears!"

"For no more badgers!"

The shocking, sudden chorus of coarse male voices echoed out of the concealing mists with startling abruptness. Sudden shadows moved in the gloom behind.

But Elder could already see that they would be too late.

For in that moment, the beast struck again.

Rearing high, its mouth agape, it arced with terrifying weight, the vast chasm of its maw plunging downwards towards the now horizontal sword of the hapless barmaid, who, insanely, was staring up at its lunging mass without a trace of concern. Her lips parted for what Elder was certain would be a horrendous final scream.

But he was wrong. Instead, came four bellowed words:

"Shoulders! Don't let goooooooooo!"

And then, she vanished too. The chain at her waist, tangling in the teeth of the creature, snapped sharply taut.

"Come on, boys! Let's get it!"

And suddenly there were soldiers, a charging troop of men surging out of the mist, their swords waving, billhooks, spears, and halberds stabbing at the gloomy sky as they trampled along the rippling ground and surged towards the swallowing beast. One heavily helmeted soldier hurtled into view oddly involuntarily, his body jerking like a marionette as he clung to the end of the taut chain, dragged across the unstable ground as his grip failed, his fingers scrambled, the metal links treacherously pulling away as the shocked monster writhed...

"Help!" he screeched. "Help, I can't hold it! It's got me, it wants me to let go!"

"I've got it!" A blond, somewhat effeminate-faced archer with oddly shaped ears pounced upon the trailing chain, followed hurriedly by a meaty-looking soldier and his knobbly-browed companion. A moment later, two more had joined the cluster heaving to keep the dancing chain in hand.

"Come on, lads!" the knobbly soldier exclaimed. "She's right, the urge to obey ain't half what it was! We can do this!"

It was not easy. The beast was writhing strangely and Elder, shocked beyond measure at this sudden turn of events, suddenly realised why, as he glimpsed the golden hilt of the woman's sword jammed between its curving rows of teeth. Even as it wriggled and squirmed, the men had reached it and although, as warned, their blades bounced harmlessly against its tough hide, one after another they leapt, with an insane lack of fear, onto the slimy skin, clinging to the edges of the mouth as they yanked at it with their weapons.

"Get the mouth open!" bellowed one hard-faced soldier. "Quick, before it digests them!"

The creature roared and the very air screamed, vibrating against the skin of Elder's distant cheek with the sheer force of its fury. Its massive bulk was shaking madly from side to side, sending swamp water churning and roiling as it struggled to free itself from the clinging web of soldiers scratching at its hide. The stunted, webbed fingers lashed out as best they could, catching a soldier as he charged and tossing him away with a violent blow—he hurtled, with a gasp and a tremendous splash, into the boiling mass of swamp water, floundering helplessly as the weight of his chain mail dragged him down. A wild toss of the monster's head claimed a second victim, flung in a hail of shrieking and limbs in a wild arc that ended with a bruising thump against the moss. A heavy, lunging charge over the weakened ground sent three men plunging in a screeching huddle into the thick swamp water; another staggered back, one arm hanging limply as a swiping blow tore both his weapon and his shoulder joint away. But still they came, these ridiculous men, their faces set with an obscure confidence and foolhardy courage as they hurled themselves into the face of slimy death and, impossibly, held their own. And Elder and his companions could only stare.

"Shouldn't we do something?" Erik was champing in his seat, his grip around the princess tightening as she stared out over the carnage with shocked eyes. "Shouldn't we help?"

"Help who?" Slynder's bemused, sardonic voice cut straight to the heart of the matter. "Whose side are we on here?"

And Elder could only shake his head. "I don't know," he whispered. "I've no idea."

And ahead, the bizarre battle was intensifying. A vicious, metallic twanging rent the air as the chain, threaded painfully around the creature's rows of teeth, was slapping like a whip through the air as the beast writhed intensely, hurling back waves of soldiers in a rain of chain mail and curses. The cluster of half a dozen men trying to hold the chain's loose end were struggling now, staggering from side to side, stumbling almost off their feet as they fought to hold their increasingly painful grip against the overwhelming power of the creature. Elder could virtually feel their fingers straining against the malicious bite of metal, their footing scrabbling on the unstable moss as they gasped and lurched; but in the face of these agonising odds, they refused to let go.

And that would be a mistake, Elder was certain, for the beast was whipping up the chain now as though to swing a morning star, lifting them from their feet with the power of its jerks. Out of nowhere, the solid metal whirled, danced, leapt upwards, and snapped back tight towards them with the force of a warrior's blow. It was the heavy-helmeted soldier who was caught completely unawares—there was not even time for him to try and duck before the chain smacked into the side of his head like a ballistic weapon.

And sliced it clean away.

As though flung from a catapult, the neatly severed head hurtled into the foggy sky in a long, delicate arc. And from some strange corner of the battle, Elder heard a mysterious, keening cry fade with its departure.

"Bollllllloooo...!"

And then it vanished into the mist and was lost.

His companions gaped. But what could they do? For a moment longer, the headless body wheeled in circles, its hands groping helplessly at the empty air. But, yielding inevitably to the laws of nature, it stiffened and keeled over in a heap.

"Oh, great," Elder heard one of them sigh. "That's torn it! Flirt's going to kill us!"

"Keep going!" the hard-faced soldier bellowed out, dragging the briefly faltering attention of his companions back to the business in hand. "Don't stop now! Donk, help with the mouth!"

"Okay, thrash!" A lumbering giant of a soldier responded to the strange moniker and, backed up by a stringy-looking companion, he waded his way into the fray. Wielding his billhook over his head, the giant man swung it forwards, lodging it in the beast's teeth as he dragged at its mouth. His companions rushed to mimic him and suddenly, the struggling creature was set upon once more from all sides, thrashing in a bewildered manner as a horde of men ringed it, battling in clumps to prize its maw apart. Unable to bring its lethal jaws into play, the monster was struggling as its attackers, emboldened, dragged its mouth wider. Elder glimpsed again the sword blade, impossibly strong, jammed between the green-stained ivory; and yes, dear Gods, a hand clung to the hilt, the chain snaking around the wrist as straining fingers clung on for dear life. She was still there, the strange woman, hanging on for dear life; and the beast, impossible as it seemed, was weakening.

And suddenly, the hard-faced soldier rushed into the mix, grabbing one of the billhooks as, in an act of bizarre daring, he dragged himself up the side of the slimy hide and stared down directly into one of the blinking eyes of the beast they fought. And, insanely, in an almost friendly manner, he addressed it.

"Sorry, slurp," he said gruffly. "Nothing personal. But do us a favour, yeah? Spit them out and bugger off."

The creature gave an agonised howl, thrashing wildly in reply to this strange invitation. Elder shook his head in disbelief—surely the fool did not believe that he could talk the horrific and senseless guardian at Craxis's gate into...

The beast gave a terrible jerk, hurling back many of those who had clung to it like limpets so tenaciously. With a burst of sound strangely like a whimper, it shrank back and, mouth painfully agape, sank from view into the swamp.

The soldiers were caught by surprise. The hard-faced soldier who'd summoned this retreat launched himself off the plunging beast like a pouncing cat and reached landfall, rolling as he staggered upright. Many of his companions, however, were less lucky—the giant man and a few others successfully disengaged their weapons in time but a half-dozen others were too slow and, with a mixture of shrieks and flailing arms, they tumbled into the swamp.

But even as their fellows dived to rescue them, a cry rent the air.

"Pull! Bloody pull!" The knobbly-faced soldier and his companions on the chain ran backwards as the creature vanished, dragging on the tightened metal links with all their strength. With a jerk and the lever of the suddenly freed blade, it lashed free of the grip of the teeth: a golden sword thrust upwards out of the greenish murk as though offered by a siren's hand. Several soldiers, the hard-faced captain and his stringy-looking companion amongst them, rushed to her aid; and first an arm and then a sodden body followed as the woman was hauled, slimy and coughing, onto the moss. But her free hand trailed behind her as she was pulled free and her eyes, though slightly shocked, were intent.

"Help me!" she cried out frantically. "Help me pull him free! He weighs a bloody ton, doesn't he?"

Hands dived from all directions, lancing into the water, and suddenly another hand emerged, a hand wearing a glittering ruby ring that shone even in the green, murky light. The rest of the figure followed like a beaching whale, covered in unpleasant gunge, clad in chain mail, his face stunned as he was manhandled onto the moss and lay there, gasping like a fish and staring shocked and wild at nothing...

Elder heard Slynder's hiss between his teeth. "The man of Sleiss! He lives!"

A horrified gasp rent the air. Islaine, her eyes wide and one delicate hand poised against her lips, was staring at her kidnapper with terror-filled eyes. "No!" she cried out painfully. "No, he cannot! This cannot be! He should be ended! They all, they all must, all my tormentors, they must be destroyed! You must get them all away from me!" She swung around in the saddle, clamping her delicate fingers against Erik's chin as his eyes misted with love at the sight of her forlorn features. "I cannot bear it, dearest Erik! You must deliver me from their hold forever! You must kill them once and for all!" She tossed back her hair, her eyes sweeping over the company. "Noble warriors, I beseech you! Let not this evil any longer stalk our lands! Now is our chance! Now is our moment! We must finish this forever!"

Her words were like an injection of verve to the blood, a violent jolt that filled the very bones beneath his skin with fizzling energy. Elder felt sudden renewed purpose skid the length of his spine and surge within him and he knew that he was not alone; even as his own hands closed upon his staff, Slynder's knives darted from their sheaths as Zahora and Sir Roderick dragged free their swords. Erik's own short blade, too, was drawn and even delicate Islaine, her eyes rich with determination, had accepted Zahora's spare blade into her soft hands.

A moment before they had not known what to do or how to act. But now, he had nothing but ice-cold certainty. The man of Sleiss must die. It was time.

"Yeah? Try it!"

The woman was quite a sight. For a moment, she remained bent over the kneeling form of the man of Sleiss, one hand on his back as she whispered something with seeming concern to his haunted, unresponsive ghost of a face. But she rose, dripping green as though risen from the depths herself, her clothes a slimy ruin, her hair a sodden knot, but her face was as fierce as any warrior maid that Elder had ever seen. Her golden sword was gripped in one green-knuckled hand like a talisman as she strode out in front of the slime-soaked, heavily breathing clusters of soldiers behind her to glare at the seven armed figures clustered on their outcrop.

"You think you can take us, do you?" she shouted furiously. "Didn't you see what we did? Impossible odds, you said! It would take an army, you said! Well, it didn't take an army, did it? It took thrash and the lads to come good! It took shoulders to hold on and..."

Her voice trailed off as she glanced suddenly over her shoulder, her fierce expression faltering briefly into one of confusion. "Hang on. Clunny, where's shoulders?"

"Where do you think? There was a fight and it's shoulders." The stringy, weasel-faced soldier regarded her slowly as her face remained blank and then dryly shook his head. His expression sardonic, he pointed to the headless corpse slumped nearby.

The woman's shoulders dropped sharply. She sighed mordantly as a wave of resignation swamped her face. "Where's his head?" she asked with slow weariness, rubbing one slimy hand across her brow in the manner of one who knew she would not like the answer.

"That way somewhere." The stringy soldier gestured into the foggy mist that had earlier swallowed the flying head. "It flew for miles. Didn't see exactly where it landed, though."

"Great." The word was thrust out from between gritted teeth. "Well, he'll have to bloody wait, won't he?" She turned back to face Elder and his companions. "Because like I was saying—if you want our friend, you'll have to take the rest of us down first! No magic, remember, no mystical powers, your own rules, they said so! A straight fight, that's all! You really think you can take all of us?"

Islaine sat proud and strong in the saddle. "Right is on our side."

The woman stared at Islaine for a long moment, her expression filled with sudden pity. "You know that's not true," she said softly. "Better than the rest of us, don't you? What happened, pleasance? An accident, was it? Did you just slip up? Or was shoulders right all along? Were you playing us the whole time and waiting for your chance? Did poor dullard know what you'd done before you tossed him to the wolves? Did he see you trample on his good nature first?" The woman's stare was relentless. "I can see the look on his poor, trusting face now, can't I? How much it must have hurt him when you…"

"No!" Islaine's voice was a shocking, gasping scream. "No, never! I…" The princess was shaking wildly in her saddle now, her hands clamped against her face. "No!" she whispered again, painful and intense. "No…"

Erik's face faltered at her distress; reaching out with gentle fingers, he touched her cheek with loving tenderness. For a moment, it seemed to Elder that she would pull away from his caring ministrations, but then her eyes met his and she melted into his arms with a sob.

"Destroy them!" she cried out, her voice ripe with pain. "Please, please, we must destroy them! They must be torn to pieces just as cruel Tretaptus was! I cannot be at peace until they are no more! I cannot be free!"

The companions needed no further incentive. Their eyes met and they nodded to each other, drawing their steeds together as they prepared to advance.

"You know what?" The woman gave a hysterical laugh. "I've had enough of this posturing, haven't I? You want a fight, you can bloody well have one!" With a cry, she thrust her sword powerfully into the air. "Come on, boys!" she bellowed at the top of her lungs. "Let's get them!"

In a sweeping, beautiful arc, she flung her sword down as though to start a race but worse, to start a charge of men who would have certainly surged forwards like a fervent tide, ready to take on all that came in the fire that filled their blood from their conquering of the creature.

That was, if any of them had moved.

The woman's cry died away as realisation dawned across her face that there was no cheer of death or glory, no trampling of feet or waving of weapons as her forces surged at her back. Her expression darkened as she wheeled around on her heel, her gaze raking over the suddenly still and distinctly nervous-looking clusters of men gathered behind her.

"Well, come on!" she exclaimed. "What are you waiting for?"

It was the stringy soldier she had earlier addressed who proved brave enough to step forward in the face of her blatant ire; but his face, although wary, was also set with stubborn determination.

"Bollocks to that!" he said with feeling.

The woman's eyes widened. "What?" she exclaimed.

"We're not charging them down!" The stringy soldier reiterated his point with breathless urgency. "Are you crazy? We'll get our arses kicked all the way back to humble village!"

The woman gaped at him. "Clunny, we've defeated an undefeatable monster! You've dragged me and fodder from the very jaws of death while they watched helplessly! They can't use magic here, no tricky spells, no mystical powers, and you lads can take them on without that! You can do anything, can't you? Why would you be afraid of them now?"

"Why would we be afraid?" The soldier shook his head in wild-eyed disbelief. "Can't you bloody count? There's only seven of them!"

The woman's face was quite a sight. It was as though she had raced towards the light at the end of the tunnel only to discover it was a blazing fireball of death.

"Oh no..." she groaned. "Clunny..."

"We said we'd help get fodder back!" There was a shrill note to the soldier's voice now. "He's our mate and he was in trouble! But we told you, we aren't breaking the basic rules and this is as blatant as you get! They are seven and we are forty-three and a half! We outnumber them, flirt! We'll get slaughtered!"

There was a pleading note to the woman's voice. "But you've seen what you can do now!"

But the soldier did not budge. "And we know what we can't! First rule!"

A chorus of nods and assertions rose from the clusters of men. Once again, weary resignation rose to swamp the woman's fierce determination. Her eyes fluttered closed as she slapped one hand against her forehead.

"But if you believe in yourselves..." she started heavily.

"I believe in what I know!" The stringy soldier threw his hands in the air. "We outnumber them! We will lose! Simple as bloody that!"

"Hang on, though." The unexpected intervention came from another soldier, the meaty-looking man who had helped with the chain. "Maybe we can help."

His stringy companion looked cynical. "How?"

"Well..." The man's heavy brow creased with slow thought. "What if we attack flirt and fodder instead?"

The woman's head rocketed up. "What?" she hissed dangerously.

The meaty soldier gave a half-hearted smile of apology. "It'd shift the odds," he offered tentatively. "I mean, you'd be surrounded, wouldn't you? The first rule would...be...on...your...side?"

His voice tailed nervously away under the sheer, rock-melting force of the woman's glare.

Several of his companions were also staring at him with incredulity, though it seemed to Elder, not quite for the same reason. The knobbly-faced soldier was the first to voice it.

"Fight against flirt? I'd rather go for the seven!" he exclaimed with feeling. "Forty-two against flirt? She'd obliterate us quicker than they would!"

"Yeah!" another scruffy-looking soldier intervened. "I thought the plan this time was not to get killed?"

Elder could have sworn that for an instant a flash of satisfaction danced over the woman's face. But a moment later, her expression was deathly once more.

"I'm going to say this only once, aren't I, thump?" she said, her tone soft but ripe with menace. "Don't you bloody dare."

That apparently did the trick. With hasty apologies, the man backed away.

But now it was the stringy soldier's turn to look thoughtful, glancing between the seven armed figures waiting politely for the debate to end so they could take their righteous revenge and the angry form of the woman before him. And suddenly, he grinned.

"I've got a better idea," he said, beaming blithely. "What if we shift the odds another way? Lads, what do you reckon to us running away?"

Elder had not thought it was possible for the woman's expression to darken any further. He was wrong.

"What?" she said, with real threat lancing through her tone.

But this time the enthusiasm of the soldier was not to be subdued. "We run away!" he repeated brightly. "If we bugger off and leave you and fodder to face them alone, then suddenly it's two against seven, isn't it? The odds swing back to you and you'll be gloriously victorious! First rule!"

And suddenly, his companions-in-arms were nodding.

"He's got a point, you know!"

"Bloody hell, he's right!"

"How could we be so selfish?"

"We're holding them back!"

"No, no, no!" The woman was shaking her head, her face shifting from menace to alarm in a matter of seconds as the ragged edges of her troops began to back towards the misty edge once more. "No, you can't!"

But they could and they were. One by one, the soldiers were backing off, slowly at first but with increasing velocity as they began to dart, one after another, into the concealment of the murk. The hard-faced captain looked less enthused than his companions but, occupied with aiding his arm-wrenched fellow, he moved with the crowd. Most of the others were smiling, many more waving back at the woman with confident expressions and cries of encouragement.

"It'll be all right now!"

"You'll slaughter them! It's inevitable!"

"You go for it, girl!"

"No!" the woman cried again, staring after their happy, retreating forms with abject disbelief. "Fodder!" She wheeled upon the man of Sleiss in one swift motion. "Fodder, do something! Say something! You're a disposable, they'll listen to you! Fodder!"

But the man of Sleiss did not respond. He remained instead on his hands and knees, staring blankly at the mossy earth, his expression distant. He looked like a man who'd seen a ghost.

With a huff of frustration, the woman wheeled once more on the final cluster of men moving hurriedly towards the safety of the mist.

"Clunny!" she bellowed, desperation rife in her tone. "Tumble! Thump! Come back! Please! This is ridiculous, isn't it? Don't be so bloody stupid!"

The stringy soldier wheeled as, with happy grins and waves, the last of his companions vanished from view.

"It's not stupid!" he hollered merrily. "It's perfect! Trust us!" He thrust two thumbs gleefully up in the air. "We're doing you a favour!"

And the thumbs faded into the mist and were gone.

The woman stared open-mouthed for a moment at the empty murk into which they had vanished. But her gaze darted sideways to the headless corpse slumped on the moss and her eyes rolled.

"You could have at least taken shoulders with you!" she bellowed after them. Her shoulders slumped. "Oh, bloody hell," she swore quiet-ly. With one foot she nudged at the side of the motionless man of

Sleiss. "And despite the fact you got me into this..." she declared firmly at his motionless face. "You're not going to be any bloody help, are
you? And shoulders certainly isn't..." She cast a rueful glance at the
corpse. "So..." Slowly, wearily, her sword glittering in her fist, she
turned to face the seven companions who had watched the scene play
out before them with weapons drawn, waiting for their chance to strike.
She sighed.

"All right," she said with resignation. "Bring it on."

* * *

".........ooooccccckkkkks!"

The vivid light of The Narrative vanished in a hail of fog, but that
was all Shoulders managed to register in the whirling, sickening tumble
that currently passed for his life. His body was down—he'd felt it
submit to the weighty demand of The Narrative that headless bodies
not wander around independently, and he'd been able to do nothing to
prevent it. He'd tried, he really had, but the sky had been churning and
spinning as his catapulted head danced through the air and that wasn't
the kind of thing that helped one's concentration.

He was never going to do it, was he? Defy The Narrative... That's
what they said, that's what his friends did, but still his fingers slipped
when they were told to slip, his body collapsed as soon as his head was
removed, he *couldn't* do it...

But more immediate concerns swamped self-pity with dizzy
awareness. Through a hail of rushing wind, of spinning greys and
greens and browns, Shoulders caught a glimpse of the ground
approaching at speed. Oh bloody hell, this was going to hurt...

The first bounce buried moss in his nostrils to a depth of a good
inch. The second, skimming a pool, filled his mouth with brackish,
foul-tasting water. And the third bounce...

Stopped him dead.

There was a thunk as something solid injected itself into his path,
halting his bouncing progress and bringing him to a standstill. But he
didn't ricochet. He didn't spin away. The strange clamp that had
arrested his momentum pressed down with gentle force and held him

firm.

There was a pause. Slowly, through the dizzying tumble of disorientation that passed for his senses, Shoulders became aware of something soft and leathery clamped against his ear.

Hang on. Was that a foot?

Warm fingers reached down, carefully lifting him upwards and away as he battled desperately to clear his vision to get some glimpse of whose hands he was caught in now, at whose mercy he stood, friend or foe, friend or foe...

Of course it's foe! We haven't got any friends!

"Get off me!" he yelled wildly, struggling to twist his head, to bring anything soft and fleshy into biting distance, but the fingers held him firm. "Get off! Oi! Let me go!" But his shouting was ignored as a fuzzy face swam up out of the whirling gloom.

And then Shoulders's vision finally cleared. His mouth dropped open.

"Bloody hell," he said.

* * *

The woman was waiting. Her golden sword, as beautiful a piece of work as Elder had ever seen, was grasped in her hands as she dropped into a defensive crouch. She was waiting for them.

The man of Sleiss remained unmoving. The corpse was even more so.

But it was not right. Elder was a good man and in spite of everything, the situation nagged at his soul. They could not charge down a lone woman en masse like brigands, like cowards...

"We will give you one more chance," he called out boldly. "We have no taste to attack a woman standing alone. But you protect the man of Sleiss and we cannot allow him to live any further. So surrender to us now and pass us the Ring your companion wears upon his finger and we will allow you to go free."

The woman's eyebrow tilted sardonically. "Don't do me any favours," she drawled grimly. "And if you think I'm handing over that Ring or my friend, you've got another think coming, haven't you?"

Elder shook his head. "Look at yourself, woman! You are outnum-bered! Three amongst us stand as great fighters of renown within this land. Do you really believe you can defeat us?"

The smile that slipped across her face was manic, the laughter that burst from her lips hysterical. "Course I can!" she exclaimed. "First bloody rule!"

She was quite mad. Of that Elder was sure, and he pitied her for her affliction. But he could not let it damage his judgement. This had to be done.

"I give you one last chance," he called out compassionately. "Please, take it. Surrender."

But the woman was staring at him, her head tilted, her eyes narrowed, and suddenly a fresh burst of laughter slipped from her lips.

"You don't want to do it, do you?" she said, comprehension dawn-ing in her voice. "You don't want to attack me!" She shook her head slowly, a manic grin plastered on her face. "What is it? Bloody first rule got you worried too? Or..." Her eyes widened sharply. "Or is it the plot? I mean, you're the good guys, aren't you? Destroyers of vast hordes of evildoers, not sodden women dressed as barmaids standing up for their mates. What's the matter? Don't want my blood on your precious reputations?"

Elder's bearded lips stiffened. "We have no wish to take any life. But we will do what is necessary. If your life must be sacrificed to save us all, so be it."

"So that's how you're going to justify it, is it?" The woman shook her head. "Good for you, one death in the name of thousands. Well, you know what? It's bollocks, and you know it, don't you? You know exact-ly what this is." She straightened herself, head held high, chin braced firmly, sword hefted boldly. "It's murder. And maybe I am going down." She smiled coldly. "But at least I'll be taking your whiter-than-white reputations down with me."

Elder fought down the uncomfortable squirming in his stomach. Two violent forces fought a war within his head, one the overwhelming necessity to put an end to the madness that had beset them, but the other, the swing of his moral compass that demanded it not be brought about in such a way that it compromised his honour. It had to be done. But yet...

"We cannot." Sir Roderick's voice was a pained whisper. "In the name of the Gods, we must but we cannot!"

"We can." Zahora's eyes were already fixed upon the woman who had twice bested her and once escaped her, her sword blade carving ominous lines through the air. "Or I can. Let me ride against her alone, woman against woman, sword against sword. There is no dishonour in that. And she owes me a battle."

"Can you defeat her?" Elder asked softly.

Zahora shot him a furious look. "Of course I can! I am ready for her now. I will not be fooled again!"

Elder sighed. "If you are sure. Do not kill her if you do not have to."

Zahora's sharp features contorted. "Only if she bids me the same favour!"

The woman's face had taken on a sheen of irritation. "Fine, you've found your bloody loophole, haven't you? Now can we please get on with this?"

Elder dropped his voice to a whisper as Zahora pushed her horse forwards, turning to his left. "Stay here, Erik. Protect the princess."

"But..." Erik's face was a picture of youthful indignation, but one glance at the still-stricken face of his Islaine persuaded him to obey. Elder turned to face the others.

"Stand ready to help Zahora and once they are engaged, ride with all haste to catch the man of Sleiss while he lies stricken. We must have that Ring."

Sir Roderick nodded as he dropped his visor with palpable menace. Slynder had already loosened his knives. Svenheid's beard was bristling as he clamped his hands around his axe.

Elder took a sharp breath. Physical combat was not his forte but he held enough talent, he was sure, to conquer such odds if needs be. And for now...

"Zahora," he said softly. "Go."

The warrior woman's eyes darkened. Sword grasped tightly, she whipped her horse into flight.

The mossy film of false ground rippled under the weight of her charging horse's hooves, but it did not give way as Zahora thundered forwards, bright sword swinging and eyes intent upon her target. The woman stood her ground with surprising courage, dripping green slime as she braced her feet against the unsteady earth and readied herself for the impact that...

And then Zahora screeched, lurched in her saddle, and went flying.

Where had it come from? Elder did not know. But through the air, whistling and turning out of the murk, the strange object had hurtled into the side of the warrior woman's helmet, bouncing off and flinging her with an undignified flailing of limbs into a boggy pool of green. She screeched again, shrieking and spluttering as she grabbed hold of the mossy edges and stared with shocked indignation at the object, clattering to a halt beside her, that had laid her so dramatically low.

Slynder's voice cut through the shock of the moment. "Is that a ladle?" he said.

"Attack!"

Elder did not even have time to turn. For from behind his horse, a mossy lump that he could have sworn had not been there earlier erupted into life as a banshee figure dressed, insanely, in a serving man's livery, hurled himself onto his horse. Fingers grabbed at his staff, his robes, his beard, extracting chunks with painful enthusiasm as the sorcerer struggled with his sudden attacker, with the hail of hands that pulled at him from all directions. Through the haze of battle, he glimpsed Svenheid, pitched out of his saddle and to the ground beneath the muscular bulk of a man dressed like a woodcutter—the barbarian did not seem to be putting up as much of a fight as he should. Erik, the screaming princess wrapped in his arms, had spurred his horse frantically in the opposite direction. Another serving man, his face anxious, was pawing at Slynder's knife hilts as another man, dressed as a simple craftsman, wrestled him in the saddle and clamped his arms in place. Even Roderick was struggling with an angry-looking serving maid, bolstered by a sallow youth in cooking clothes who leapt behind him on his horse and yanked his helmet back to front.

Elder could only gape at the chaos. What in the name of anything was happening now?

He heard Zahora's voice shrieking out, splashing helplessly as she struggled in her armour to climb out of the clinging swamp.

"They're getting away! Help me, you fools, they're escaping!"

As Elder batted bravely at his attacker, his vision briefly cleared. He saw the woman, her eyes wide and mouth gaping as she stared at a slender figure, a laden canvas bag dangling at his side, half-concealed as he hauled upon the headless corpse and heaved it painfully onto his back. But a shout from the stranger, unheard but sharp, burst her into motion—grabbing the shoulders of the man of Sleiss, she manhandled him to his feet and rushed after her rescuer.

"Stop them!" Zahora's cries were nearly drowned out by her frantic struggles in the water. "Do something!"

But Elder could not. Svenheid was still pinned to the ground, Slynder still clamped, Roderick still flailing blind, Erik still fleeing. And he could not get free of the constant grasp of the determined man in livery's hands…

"Go!" he cried out from just behind Elder's ears, near-deafening him. "Run for it! We'll hold them as long as we can!"

"Thank you!" The cry drifted out of the distance. Elder caught one final glimpse on the edge of the mist of the stranger hauling the corpse over his shoulders, of the woman, her eyes disbelieving but joyous, and of the blank face of the man of Sleiss. But the murk closed around their bodies and the shapes of those they had so nearly finally bested were…

Gone…

Flirt gasped as the clinging feel of The Narrative was snatched away by the sudden embrace of the concealing fog. For a moment, she could only stumble onwards across the unsteady ground, her hands planted firmly on the unresisting shoulders of the unresponsive Fodder, the events of the last thirty seconds tumbling incomprehensibly in her head. But a muffled voice cut into her daze and dragged her to her senses.

"Let me out! Let me out! Quick!"

Hauling Fodder's stumbling body to a ragged halt, Flirt wheeled in time to see Shoulders's headless body, dumped seconds before upon the mossy earth, staggering drunkenly upright with arms outstretched. His fingers groped at the air only for an instant before his head, dragged from a canvas bag, was held out to him. He snatched his own head out of the waiting hands and pressed it to his chest.

"Bloody hell!" he swore loudly. "I hate being in two bits!"

But in that instant, Flirt wasn't hugely concerned with Shoulders's separation anxiety. She was more concerned with the fact her eyes seemed to have gone mad.

"Dullard?" she breathed incredulously.

The prince glanced up at her with a half-hearted, breathless flash of a grin. True, he looked in a state—his dark hair was tangled and matted with dried blood and a series of unpleasant-looking scratches had torn down one side of his cheek and his arm. But he looked extremely intact for a man who had purportedly been ripped into tiny chunks in front of a watchful Narrative.

But it was *impossible*, completely impossible, there was no way that he could be...

"Dullard!" she exclaimed again. "How...?" She shook her head. "But you're in shreds, The Narrative said, you..." She blinked hard as her mind reeled against her. "This *can't* be real, it can't..."

"Flirt!" The snap of his voice twanged against her senses, shaking the edges of the insistent certainty of his demise that her mind refused to release. "The Narrative's got into your head! You need to shake it off!" Slender fingers smacked down on her shoulders as his familiar face and the intense gaze of his eyes filled her vision. "It told you I was ripped up and eaten and now you can't disbelieve it. Well, I'm right here, Flirt. The Narrative was *wrong*."

It was like a smack in the face. Flirt forced herself to focus, to stare at him, to clear the invasive fog she hadn't even realised had got into her mind. She took a heavy breath.

"Bloody hell," she breathed. "It *got in*. And I didn't even notice, did I?"

"That's how it works." There was a distracted air to Dullard's manner but something purposeful was gleaming like fire in his eyes.

"It's powered by belief and you believed it, and that belief ingrains itself. I imagine that's why Fodder is a little less than himself as well."

Flirt's eyes darted with concern to her friend. He was still staring in dull silence at the floor.

"What do we do?" she breathed.

But Dullard was shaking his head. "For now, we have to keep him out of The Narrative. Beyond that, I'm sorry but we'll have to worry about him later. My friends can only buy us so much time." His eyes were distant as he gazed into the Narrative-lightened mist behind them. "I've made arrangements so that we can get back on track. But you have to go at once or it will be too late."

Flirt was sure he'd meant to slip the word in quickly, hoped they wouldn't question it; but, urgency or not, she was not about to let this one pass.

"You?" she queried pointedly. "Not us?"

His wince told her that she'd hit the mark. He bit his lip. "I was going..." he started, and the look that flashed for a second across his features was enough to tell Flirt far more than she needed to know. "I hoped...I wanted to try..."

Bloody hell. Now that's *going to complicate things...*

But it didn't change one simple fact.

"She's gone." His bluntness had startled her from her distraction— it was her turn to return the favour. But at the genuine pain that welled behind his eyes, she softened herself to the practical. "She's on horse-back, isn't she?" she added more gently. "Bumpkin'll have her well away by now. You'll never catch up."

He knew what she'd done. But he did not call her on it, merely ducking his head for a moment to gather his composure. "You're right, of course," he replied, his tone steadier but his eyes far away. "I don't know what I was thinking."

"Fascinating as all this is"—abruptly, Shoulders's head was thrust between his hands into their line of sight—"do you think we could discuss it when we aren't *fleeing for our bloody lives?"*

The prince gave a violent start at this wake-up call. "The mist's getting lighter!" he exclaimed with alarm. And it was true: strands of creeping brightness were turning the mundane dullness of the mist into the gloomy grimness of Narrative fogginess in darting tendrils. "It's The Narrative! Run!"

Shoulders didn't need telling twice—pointing his head firmly forwards, he set off at an awkward stumble. Fodder needed rather more prompting—Flirt jammed her hands into his back and gave him a hearty shove that set him rolling hypnotically in the right direction. As Dullard broke into motion at her side, she could see that the fog was thinning, the air developing that vivid tang as a hail of angry shouts rose from behind them in the murk. Hoofbeats sounded on the foggy turf as the ripples sent the ground beneath them shuddering.

Shoulders's head was lifted frantically back over his shoulder. "They're catching up!" he screeched.

And he was right. The greens were greener, the greys were greyer, the air was heavier and bit at the lungs as piece by piece the light of The Narrative pierced their protective veil. Shadows and shouts of fury echoed in their wake, closer, louder, sharper, brighter...

There was nowhere to go, nowhere to hide, and this time they weren't ready; any second, any moment and they would be...

"Get in!" The bellow came from Shoulders. And suddenly, shockingly, his body barrelled sideways into Flirt and Fodder. Flirt gasped and staggered but the effect on Fodder's more inert form was far more dramatic—with a sideways lurch, he tumbled straight into the thick, green pool to their right. Even as Flirt scrambled to a shocked halt, her mouth half-open to berate Shoulders for his clumsiness, the Disposable stumbled away from her, his head clasped almost protectively against his chest beneath crossed arms. His nose wrinkling within the cradle of his own arms, he braced his body and hurled himself in after his friend with a mighty splash.

"He's right! In!" Dullard's hand clamped against Flirt's arm—before she even had time to protest, she was off her feet and falling and suddenly once more she was plunged into the viscous murk of the swamp. The vile taste of what could only vaguely be called water filled her mouth and her nose, her eyes blinking against the dizzy haze of green that filled them as she struggled in the thick ooze that clung to her skin and dragged at her clothing. Dullard's hand vanished from her arm at the impact of the gunk, and she was left struggling alone in greenish concealment, unsure even which way was up or down. It was horrible, it was bitter, it was claustrophobic and unpleasantly sticky— but, most important of all, it was only just in time.

Vivid light skimmed across what Flirt, disorientated from her fall, had not even realised was the surface. Her gasp gave her another clogging mouthful, but she could do nothing about it except silently gag and struggle to stay under as the hooves over mossy ground sent ripples through their liquid hiding place. Shadows scudded across them as unseen figures passed in an unseemly rush, churning their very world for an unsteady moment before first they and then the light faded out of view once more.

Surface, surface, surface...

She clawed at the swamp as it clung to her body tenaciously, fighting her way desperately towards where the light had gleamed moments before, her hand breaking into glorious air as she groped blindly for something solid to hold on to. A mossy hummock caught against her fingers and she clamped upon it, nearly dragging it down with her as her face broke free of the murk at long, long last. She took several precious, gasping breaths before trying to wipe her gunked-up eyes with her fingers—unfortunately, since her hands were as filthy as the rest of her, it made very little difference. Determinedly, she yanked a handful of scrubby grass out of her anchor point and used that to clear her eyes instead.

To her left, Fodder was sitting, dripping, on the mossy turf, a gasping Dullard treading water below him, having apparently just finished shoving him out. To her right, Shoulders's head rose from the quagmire like an apparition, gasping and spluttering on the end of one hand as he slapped it safely down on solid ground. It rolled for a moment before coming to rest beside her.

She glared at his mucky face. "Nice plan," she hissed.

He glared back, the expression strange on his horizontal face. "Saved us, didn't it?" he retorted with a gurgle.

"Indeed it did. Well done." Dullard was the first to clamber back out of the murk—turning quickly, he caught Flirt's hand and hauled her after him. A moment later, both of them manhandled the chain-mailed Shoulders onto dry land as well. As Flirt lifted the Disposable's head, he stuck his tongue out at her. She stared at him darkly. "Do you want this back?" she said deliberately. "Because I could always..."

"Don't bicker. Not now." There was an unfamiliar edge to Dullard's tone, less puppy and more bite as in one swift motion, he lifted the head from her hands and passed it matter-of-factly back to the body it belonged to. A moment later, he had the blank-faced Fodder on his feet as well. "We have to go." His eyes scanned the mist in a hurried circle. To Flirt's relief, there was no hint of glow, but the prince seemed less happy about it. "Did anyone see which way The Narrative went?"

Shoulders gave him an incredulous look. "Yeah, that's right, I stuck my head up to see after going to all that trouble to hide us. Of course not!"

A look of sincere irritation flashed unexpectedly across Dullard's features as he pressed an anxious hand to his mucky forehead. "If The Narrative's around, they won't come," he said absently, almost to himself. "They can't risk being seen but without them we'll never be able to get enough of a head start..."

Shoulders and Flirt exchanged a bewildered look.

"What the bloody hell are you talking about?" Shoulders asked.

Dullard glanced up. "Our lift," he said as though this fact should be self-evident. "I told you I'd made arrangements. Well, sort of, anyway."

"Lift!" Shoulders declared, raising his head between his hands as his eyebrows arched incredulously. "We're in the middle of the Stinking Marsh! What bloody lift?"

And Shoulders was gone.

It was as quick as that. One moment the dripping Disposable had been waving his angry head and the next, a grey streak descended out of the concealing fog like a thunderclap and there was nothing but a pair of feet vanishing upwards and the echo of a keening screech. Even as Flirt gasped, Fodder too was gone, hauled into the fog, and she caught only a brief glimpse of Dullard's relieved face before clawed feet clamped down on her shoulders and yanked.

The entire world turned into a rush of up. Her stomach dropped a mile—it took everything she had to swallow down a wen...*W-wordish* screech as fog battered past her in a dizzying rush, shooting downwards as she hurtled up with a sickening velocity. Suddenly there was light, not the vivid brightness of The Narrative but simple, normal light as the enshrouding fog turned into a pillow of shifting cloud that sank away beneath her dangling feet. The world spread out beneath her: the bubble of cloud shrouding the Stinking Marsh, the green expanse of the Grasslands and the scrubbier Battle Ground beside it, the towering Savage Mountains in one direction and their Least Savage cousins in the other and the lifeless emptiness of the Barren Wastelands beyond the Treacherous Gorge, the Brooding Volcano spitting out a fog of ash that turned the shadowy shape of the Dark Citadel into a menacing silhouette.

Bloody hell. This was a bit high…

And then a scaly, bat-eared head thrust upside down into her field of vision, an inverted toothy smile upon its lips.

"Strange things I'm finding on the wind today. Old Frenzy had better put them somewhere safe, I reckon."

There were leathery wings flapping around her, the shapes of four AFCs flying in lazy circles over the epic view. She saw Shoulders dangling from one set of feet as he clasped his head desperately against himself, his eyes wild; Fodder hanging limp and motionless beneath another; and Dullard holding on gently to the scaly ankles of a third as he stared around at the cluster of his friends with a thoughtful expression.

"So," the prince said deliberately, his breath snatched a bit by the insistent breeze caused by the altitude. "You've captured my friends and me. Oh dear me. And what with my having barely escaped your clutches only yesterday."

"I know." The scaly figure grasping at his shoulders nodded sagely. "Strangest thing it was too. Your uncle Primp and some of the others, you see, they seem to have got it into their heads that we *ate* you."

Dullard shook his head solemnly, barely concealing his smile. "Now, Fang. I wonder where they got a strange idea like that from?"

"No idea," said apparently Fang with apparent confusion. "'Cos after we mauled you a bit and pushed you into the river, they came running up and asked us where you were. And what I said, you see, what I said was, well, *he's all gone*. And Gibber burped."

"It was a good burp too," Fodder's carrier, presumably Gibber, intervened. "Real belter."

"It was," Frenzy agreed from above Flirt's head. "It had resonance and everything."

"And the next thing you know, poor old Primp's scraping up the blood from when The Narrative had us scratching you and he's got us promising to collect our dung and keep it together just in case they'll let him take it to a pixie." Fang nodded, his expression genuinely sorrowful for a moment, and Dullard also looked distinctly remorseful at the news of his uncle's unnecessary distress. "Poor chap. We thought about telling him but, well, we felt he had enough on his plate running off to marshal Slurp. He's no easy job at the best of times."

"So we thought, why don't we help?" Shoulders's carrier stepped in. "Now they didn't need us for a bit, we thought—why don't we go find Prince Dullard ourselves?"

"So, like Chomp said, we did," Fang continued. "We saw you getting hauled out of the river by those Servant types and we saw you rushing off after The Narrative, so we thought, well, we'd better keep a discreet and careful eye on *that*."

"I had no idea you were there," Dullard offered, his expression pure innocence. "I saw neither hide nor hair of you watching me from the branches of that dead tree, or from under that leafless bush or even from behind that goat. You had me completely fooled."

"We were like the wind," said presumably Gibber sagely. "Invisible. Trailing you like phantoms out of the wotsit."

"It was astounding," Dullard agreed. "I really had no idea when I loudly discussed with my friends what we were planning to do and how useful it would be to have a lift out at the end of it that you were sitting so close by, listening to every word. I thought that strange voice on the wind that told me you wouldn't come near us if The Narrative was still involved was merely my feverish imagination."

"These things happen," Chomp offered. "Can't explain 'em."

"But the question is," said Fang solemnly, "what are we going to do with you now, hmm?"

"It's a puzzler." Flirt's stomach gave an unpleasant lurch as Frenzy banked, rubbing his chin, the fan of his wings ruffling her mucky hair. "'Cos you see, lads, I thought we was told we had to hand 'em straight to Strut."

"I don't see Strut anywhere," presumably Gibber exclaimed. "Do you see Strut?" Four sets of beady eyes raked the dome of cloud below, four sets of intensely powerful ears, Flirt noted with amusement, conveniently rolled up.

"Can't *see* him at all," Fang agreed. "Could be anywhere. So what do we do?"

"If I could make a suggestion?" Dullard's diffident tone intervened. "Well, we know the ultimate destination of the Merry Band is the Dark Citadel and Strut will be with them. If you could take us there and leave us on the highest tower before flying off, at whatever pace you feel is appropriate, to tell Strut what you've done, well, I'm sure no one would feel you have in any way done anything but exactly what would be expected."

There was a thoughtful pause. And slowly, one bat-eared head after another began to nod.

"Nice idea."

"Yep. Exactly what they'd want."

"Dark Citadel it is then. Off we go!"

What the...? But she was given no time to even ask what the prince was playing at. Flirt's breath was snatched away and her stomach plunged again, but this time she was at least braced and ready as their four lifts swung them round in the breezy air towards the might of the Brooding Volcano and the stone monstrosity it shadowed. The Dark Citadel loomed out of the rocky, grey, barren ground in front of them, rising from the earth atop a jagged-walled pinnacle of harsh grey rock. The solid blocks of its vast walls seemed to rise from the very stone to curve into pointed arches and twisted spires, spiky towers and rugged battlements merged together in one great amorphous whole that reached upwards like skeletal clutching fingers to scrape at the ash-choked sky. Gargoyles and grotesques leered from every edifice, faces screaming in agony, animals bent in pain, beasts that savaged and creatures that soared coating the walls as though seeking to burst free from them and subdue the world with an army of rock-hide warriors. And there was one tower that rose above the others, shrouded in ashy cloud as it scraped against the heavens, a harsh red light glimmering in the highest window that looked for all the world like a burning eye hunting its prey.

All in all, if one was looking to find a home for a being more monster than man, consumed by magic, whose only aim was the utter destruction of everything that was good in the world, it was a hard place to top. A giant arrow and the words *Here Be Evil* might as well have been carved into the walls.

"Good, isn't it?" Flirt started violently as Dullard's windswept head appeared abruptly beside her, Fang banking considerably closer to Frenzy to aid the prince's sudden need for conversation. His voice was raised over the rush of air. "They can take bits out or add them in depending on the kind of Dark Lord they've mustered. Horribly bad taste of course, but that is rather the point!"

"Charming!" Flirt agreed, her voice straining against the wind as her moist curls battered at her cheeks and tangled wildly amongst themselves across her face. "That's why you're dragging us there, is it? For the architecture?"

Dullard's expression dropped slightly. "No, I have a plan," he said, suddenly oddly subdued. "I'll explain once we've landed, so everyone can hear. So far I've only told Ple…"

His voice trailed away into the sky. His expression wavered painfully for a moment—he swallowed down a deep breath before forcing himself to continue. "I only told Pleasance and the Servants who helped us to take the Imposing Castle. We persuaded them of the merits of helping us, you see, and they've been magnificent, the way they stood up to the Royals and Nobles and held off the Merry Band so we could escape…"

His voice tailed off once more at the sight of Flirt's face. "What happened?" she asked softly over the thud of wing-beats.

But he shook his head. "Not now… I *can't*… It was my fault, I knew she was struggling, I shouldn't have left her alone with them…" He looked away, his pained face vanishing briefly beneath a sweep of dark hair before emerging into the cathartic cold of the air. "And she fought to stay herself until the very last…" He closed his eyes for an instant, teeth digging painfully into his bottom lip, before shaking his head once more. "Not now," he repeated softly. "Please not now. I need to concentrate."

But Flirt had spotted something else, something that Dullard, despite his intelligence, had lost beneath his emotions. "Pleasance knows, does she?"

Dullard nodded wearily. "Yes, she was there when I suggested it."

"So now the Merry Band know too?"

He looked up sharply. "She would never…" he started, almost instinctively, but his head dropped with aching resignation. "She wouldn't," he said softly, close to too softly for Flirt to hear. "But would Islaine?"

The sudden flash of light behind gave them their answer.

Vivid light, Narrative light, arced up into the sky like a beacon. It was restricted in its scope by the narrow confines of the Treacherous Gorge that wound through the barrier of mountains they had just flown over, the only gateway to the Barren Wastelands and the Dark Citadel for those not wearing wings. The Merry Band were heading for their Final Confrontation in the dark hall of their nemesis.

And by the book, the book Flirt had read and squirreled away, now damply she assumed, with Shoulders, they were too early. Why else would they blow this final moment without even an epic battle fought unless they knew for sure where their enemy was headed?

Dullard met her eyes. He didn't say a word. He didn't have to.

"Can't see nothing," Fang's voice echoed over the leathery beat of wings, his eyes fixed firmly on the ashy horizon ahead. "But I got this feeling that we might need to go like the clappers."

Air rushed faster, battering Flirt's skin as they raced away from the shaft of clear, bright light behind them and into the gloomy clouds of darkness.

* * *

Well. This was fun.

Another gust of violent, chilly wind slapped against Shoulders as he fumbled with his head. Leaning with his back against the wooden door that provided the only survivable entrance or exit to this, the open roof of the tallest tower of the Dark Citadel, he struggled, mostly unsuccessfully, to try and reattach his beleaguered head to his shoulders. But the straps holding the helmet to his neck had suffered vast amounts of wear in the last few days and were hanging in green-tinged threads that refused to secure themselves with any consistency. Never had the phrase *end of his tether* been so literal.

Of all the stupid, boneheaded... What had possessed that idiot Dullard to have the AFCs dump them up here? He could have suggested taking them anywhere; somewhere warm, stable, on the bloody *ground*, it wasn't as though there wasn't plenty of choice! But no, Mr Resident Genius had a plan, a plan he had yet to reveal to anyone except, apparently, the *enemy*, and that plan involved having the AFCs deposit them here, on this windy pillar of grotesque architecture, and fly away before anyone bothered to check if the only door out of there was *locked*.

Which it was. Of course.

And as had been long established, none of them knew how to pick locks.

When this was over and if he was alive and solid enough to do so, Shoulders vowed he would track down some of the professional Thieves from the Magnificent City and take a course in lock-picking. After this mess, he wasn't taking any more chances.

Not to mention they were being speedily hunted down. The Narrative light could be seen approaching rapidly in a glowing shaft of brightness that leaked upwards from the crooked scar that was the narrow Treacherous Gorge. If they carried on at the rate they were going, it would be a couple of hours at most before they were storming the giant gates below.

And then there was Fodder.

If Shoulders was entirely honest, he'd been trying not to think about his friend. Or what little seemed to be left of him.

He swivelled his head in his hands to glance over to where Fodder, still glassy-eyed and blank-faced, was propped unceremoniously against a looming gargoyle, the red glow from the window beneath them washing his face in scarlet. Nearby, Flirt, dressed in her green-stained Barmaid's outfit, was glaring at his unresponsive form fiercely.

"Fodder!" she screeched, her hands suddenly clamped on his shoulders as she shook his lolling head ferociously back and forth.

"Fodder of Humble Village, if you don't knock this bollocks off and answer me, I swear I'll..."

"I'm really not sure that's going to help." Dullard's intervention sounded uncharacteristically weary.

Fists clenched, eyes blazing, Flirt wheeled instantly on him instead. "Well, what do you suggest? He's just leaning there, isn't he? You're supposed to be the genius; why don't you stop fannying about and work out what the bloody hell is wrong? Then we can fix him and get on with this, can't we?"

Dullard frowned. Cross as Shoulders was with the prince for getting them into this mess, he couldn't help but notice how *tired* the man looked. He sighed.

"Partly, I think he's in shock," he said quietly. "I would imagine being defeated and eaten—especially after achieving some previous measure of success at wielding limitless power—must be a jolt."

"A jolt?" Flirt's face darkened further. "This is what a jolt looks like, is it? Well, I'd hate to see a ruddy lurch!"

Dullard ignored this interlude, to Shoulders's surprise. "But it has to be more than that. Mere shock alone wouldn't do this."

Flirt's dark expression slipped away, replaced by a sudden edge of fear. "Earlier, at the swamp, when I was...confused. You were hinting, weren't you? That you thought...you thought Fodder might be planted too?"

Planted? Shoulders felt his stomach give an uncomfortable lurch. Fodder? Planted? Oh bloody hell, if The Narrative got him, there really was no hope for the rest of them...

And if he was, his friend was...

"Can't we do this later?" The words snapped out of his head, chasing the end of the thought away like a rabid dog. "Let's batter this door down, find somewhere to hide from the Merry Band, and sort him out after! We're too bloody exposed up here!"

Flirt wheeled on him this time. "We're a thousand feet up, Shoulders! Do you want to take a guess how many stairs are between us and the ground? Now, how about you imagine guiding our comatose friend manually foot by foot down each and every one of them..."

"All right! All right!" Shoulders snapped back. A weird clunk and squeal caught his ear for a second, but he had no time to seek out the source as he stepped away from the door slightly, clutching his head as securely as he could as the wind gusted fiercely once more. "Then we wake him up! How? Throw a bucket of water over him? Oh wait, we can't get one because we're *locked up here!"*

"Please can we focus?" There was an element of strain to Dullard's tone. "I need to think; we have to work out what's going on inside his head. He must have been in The Narrative too long. He must have given it something to use. We have to find a way to reach him so we can work out what it was and get him free of it." He glanced over to where the shaft of Narrative light was creeping ever closer. "Quickly."

Shoulders sighed as he stared at his blank-faced friend. Gods, this was... It couldn't just be being eaten that had caused this—as a man who'd been eaten himself, Shoulders was very much aware that, while it was not a joyful or fulfilling experience, it hadn't turned him into a witless zombie either. And Fodder hadn't even been digested. He was all there, body intact, so why would his head have wandered off to la-la land without him when...

Wait.

A thought, chilling and alarming in one, darted into Shoulders's head. He stared at Fodder, stared at the empty eyes and shivered as his mind drifted back to his various encounters with The Narrative as every step became a leaden challenge, every word a fight. And he remembered as his head had parted from his body, that familiar urge, that soundless voice that whispered into his bones...

You're dead now. Lie down. Collapse. Do not move. You're dead. So why would you want to?

He knew it so well. But it wasn't until the last, insane few weeks, when, for the very first time, he had tried and mostly failed to fight off the siren call of that smooth, insidious command, that he had realised how pressing that urge to obey could be. And if Fodder was mixed up with some planted thoughts...

He glanced at Flirt and Dullard and knew at once they wouldn't get it. Flirt had never been killed, he knew that for sure—about Dullard he was less certain, but he was willing to bet the prince hadn't died more than once or twice at the most, if that. But he was a Disposable, death's best friend, killed off once or even twice a day for most of his adult life. He knew how it felt. He knew its power.

And it was Narrative power. And like with those bonkers Gods or even back at Camp with the lads, that stuff was potent when it got in your head. You couldn't slap at it and hope for the best. You had to work around it. You had to play the delusion...

And Fodder thinks he's dead...

Okay. Great.

Gripping his head in his hands, Shoulders hurried forward, shouldering his way past the surprised-looking Flirt and Dullard as he stood in front of Fodder.

"Got an idea," he said swiftly, cutting over the questions that hung from their parted lips. "Just run with this, okay?"

Holding his head up in his cupped palms, Shoulders rolled his eyes and began muttering some random mumbo jumbo. "Oooohhhh! Hear me, restless spirit! I am the headless zombie sorcerer of...Bloodicoldtowerinaria...and I command you to speak!" Out of the corner of his rolling eyes, he saw Flirt staring at him like he'd drop-kicked a chicken, but there was a spark in Dullard's eyes that suggested the prince at least had cottoned on to what he was doing. "Come forth from the nether-realm, spirit! Come forth in the name of...stuff...and mysterious things! Come forth and...ummm..."

"Speak your name," Dullard hissed in his ear.

"Speak your name!" Shoulders repeated more dramatically. "Speak your name to us, spirit! Return to a semblance of life and speak!"

Fodder's cheek twitched a bit. The fingers of one hand clenched and unclenched reflexively.

Flirt's expression of scepticism melted suddenly. Dullard had already started making rhythmic drumming sounds on the walls with the flats of his hands as he nodded his encouragement.

"We summon the..." Waving his head and rolling his eyes was severely limiting Shoulders's ability to improvise. "The...ummm... *help!*"

"Dark Gods!" Flirt stepped in at his whispered plea, wiggling her fingers back and forth in the air. "We summon the Dark Gods of death to bring forth this spirit with the drumming of his lost heartbeat!"

"Yes, we do! We very much do!" Shoulders quickly snatched back his mantle as leading necromancer. "We call you forth! We call you forth right now!"

And Fodder blinked. Something resembling awareness slipped back into his features as his eyes fixed, somewhat sceptically, on the severed head gibbering in front of him.

"What are you doing?" he muttered irritably.

Yes, yes, yes! "I'm summoning you forth?"

He blinked again. "Why are you doing that?"

Shoulders was on the verge of abandoning the weird charade but Dullard caught his eye, still determinedly drumming on the wall, and shook his head. Apparently he thought it too early to break character. *Name*, he mouthed.

"Who have we summoned forth?" Shoulders was starting to feel dizzy from waving his head about, but he kept it up. "Speak!"

"Everyone knows who I am," his friend said suddenly, and even apparent death did not mute the un-Fodder-like disdain, a wave of cocky assurance rippling out against the cold wind. "Why do you need to ask my name? You should know it."

"Make him say the name," Dullard hissed at Shoulders again.

"Oooh! I...want you to tell me anyway!" Shoulders wiggled his fingers against his chin, trying to be mysterious and occult but suspecting he looked like a twonk. "I command you, spirit!"

Fodder rolled his eyes, sticking his chin into the air. "If I must. I was Fodhelion, the all-powerful man of Sleiss!"

"Oh...*bugger.*" Flirt's quiet, despairing exclamation neatly encapsulated Shoulders's feelings on the matter. He struggled to keep his face appropriately contorted as fear for his friend, the man who used to be his friend, surged through his veins. The drumming stopped abruptly.

"I agree on that," Dullard muttered in response. "There's no question about the planting now."

But paying them no attention, Fodder—or *Fodhelion* rather; what fool had come up with that stupid name?—was apparently not done with his monologuing. "I was the evil threat arisen from nowhere, a humble man with a secret past of blood and fate, who fought against the forces of good for mysterious reasons of my own!" His tone was swelling, his voice developing a timbre that was completely not his own. "I made inexplicable, mad pronouncements and threatened an unseen, unknown foe with my amazing stolen powers! I was out to destroy all that was good in the world and it cost me my life! I was all-powerful and almighty, the greatest threat ever to brave the wrath of goodness, and I intended to displace, to destroy that unknown foe to be master of *all the world* and shape it to my will!" His words were accelerating now as he strode forwards. Arms outstretched, he placed himself dramatically in front of the doorway, framing himself with the gargoyles that peered down from around its spire as his friends backed away from him in alarm. "I would have been the greatest, the most magnificent, revered and feared, the highest, the bringer of my justice, the writer of my laws! I would have *ruled you all!*"

The words echoed from the towers and spires below them, dancing through the air as though to taunt the three slack-jawed, shocked faces that were staring at him.

"Double bugger," Flirt whispered fervently.

"But clever," Dullard whispered back. *"Very* clever. With due respect to the Taskmaster, that's very well played."

"Respect?" The vehement hiss that slipped from Fodder's lips caught them a little off guard. "For the Taskmaster? Respect? Never."

The wild look in his eyes was so utterly unfamiliar that Shoulders had to fight to remember whom he was looking at. The thudding of his heart sounded like footsteps on stone.

"You know me!" The sudden recognition was a touch alarming. "You're my allies, my friends! Is that why you've helped me rise from the grave? So my maniacal plans can be restarted? Because they must!" His eyes were gleaming with furious passion. "The Taskmaster deserves no respect! That manipulator, that monster, that thing that makes us dance like puppets in a sick game—this has to stop! We must rip the grasp that fiend has on our world asunder, we must remake it as it should be, as I see it should be! We will burn this world with our righteousness and make it over new, with no place for any Taskmaster who wants to dole out instructions to precious favourites, to send strutting idiots in stupid shoes to tell us what to do, to ignore those with talent in favour of those who happened to be born looking right! Down with the Taskmaster! Death to the Taskmaster! I will find where that coward is hiding, and payment will be swift for the wrongs we've suffered!"

The shiver that ran through Shoulders's body had nothing to do with the cold wind. He stared in desperation as the raving nutter who had once been his closest friend railed against the world. Angry words of injustice were one thing, spoken often by Fodder since that fateful night in the Bandit Pass that felt like forever ago. But this wasn't Fodder. It was his voice and his face, but the compassion behind his words was gone, the yearning for justice and fairness—and without those, the ideas that had driven them into this mess were nothing more than the ravings of a madman.

Fodder was planted as *himself.* His ideals, his beliefs, and to an extent, his character. But the Taskmaster had only kept the villainous bits of him that were needed for the plot. The good bits, the bits that made him Fodder and not a maniacal nut job, were gone.

And probably so was Fodder. Unless they could rein him in and drag him back.

Dullard was right. It was very clever. But also bloody evil.

Flirt had apparently missed it. "Fodder, please," she cut in, her face reflecting the desperation that Shoulders felt, but still not seeming to see she wasn't talking to their friend anymore. "You need to calm down and try and focus, don't you? This isn't you..."

Fodder's wild laugh filled the air. "Isn't it? It feels like me to me!"

Clunk.

It was a small noise. A nothing noise. But it was more than enough to catch Shoulders's ear over the horrified roaring in his mind at his friend's maddened ranting.

It was a key. Turning in the door. Behind Fodder.

Shoulders opened his mouth as the door rattled slightly. "Ummm..."

"I am *Fodhelion!*" Fodder's bellow crushed his diffident opening. "I am *almighty!* I am going to crush the Taskmaster and I will rule this world! You hear me? *I will rule this world!*"

SMACK.

With a painful shriek of rusted hinges, the door slammed open. Solid wood smashed into the side of Fodder's head, glazing his eyes as he smacked into the floor, out cold.

Dullard, Flirt, and Shoulders froze in place, eyes wide, terrified as the open door exposed a huge black shape looming in the shadows, filling the doorway, an enormous jagged sword grasped in a meaty hand. A giant head, dwarfed beneath the epic massiveness of a black, pitted helmet, cocked as it regarded them with slow, thoughtful care.

And one hand whipped up and pushed the terrifying visor open. A face, craggy, dark, and sunken, was etched in shadows in its depths. And then, it happened.

A broad, beaming smile broke out over the looming face like sunbeams at midnight. The cracked lips parted cheerfully.

"All right there!" the figure proclaimed, his voice a homely, friendly bellow. "How are you folks doing? And for the sake of asking, you know, what are you doing up my tower?"

* * *

Soon.

Oh soon, so soon at last, the horror would be over.

One way or another.

Erik would be a liar of the highest order to claim he did not feel the sting of fear deep within his breast as they careened down the narrow, twisted gorge that led to the terrible blasted home of the greatest evil ever to have walked their world. Knowing that his power might be all that stood between the Six Kingdoms and the rise of Craxis once again was the most horrific of prospects. But what else could they do? They were the last beacon of hope for peace, the last chance to avoid a terrible future, and he could only steel his courage and his fortitude and ride.

For he had Islaine.

Oh Islaine. His poor, brave flower. It was her bravery that had given them this lead, her revelation of foul Tretaptus's boasting that he and the man of Sleiss would ally with the abomination that was Craxis to further their foul ambitions that had placed them on this fearful path, and she seemed to carry the weight of that knowledge like a stone around her beautiful neck. Could it truly be that she felt the power of their love as he did, that her guilt at leading him and his companions to danger could already be so strong? But she had done it, for it needed to be done; and now they rode, to death and the end of all things, or the light of a beautiful future. There was no way for this moment to say which.

He glanced down at her, cradled still within his arms, her slender hands wrapped around his body as her eyes, haunted by the ordeal of her long kidnap, stared into the distance in lost loneliness. But at the sense of his gaze, she turned and met his eyes and her face contorted out of pain into a stunning smile that filled his darkened world with blazing light.

His Islaine. For all his fears, for all the horrors that lay before them, her strength would carry him onwards. He could do anything with her at his side.

* * *

Dead. Floating. Dead.

He was dead again. This was becoming a habit.

But what he couldn't figure out was why the figures hovering around his imaginary body had chosen to tie his incorporeal corpse to a chair. On the whole, given his return to the cool embrace of death after his brief and fiery reincarnation, it felt unnecessary. He was dead. It wasn't like he was going anywhere.

"Fodder?" Again that name, nagging at him, a prickly itch that poked him like a frantic bird from within the deep recesses of his mind. That name, it meant something, something that used to be important before the mission, before the cause, before the fun of watching the heroic fools squirm, before he was dead and floating and everything was done with...

"It's no good, is it? He can't hear me." The hands remained but the face was turned away, the familiar face, the face that was right with the clothes that were wrong. "He's gone back to being *dead* again."

"Should we try another mystical ceremony?" Another voice, again familiar, but should it be, why should it?

"After what happened earlier, I'm not sure that would be the wisest idea." Another voice and this one, oh this one, it was all, all wrong and shouldn't be and the sense of that burned against his mind as the prickly itch ignited into a shallow rip of flame. "It would appear that particular ploy will only summon his character. We want to find the real Fodder underneath." The voice sighed. "I think he can hear us. I'm just not sure he wants to. Try again. Make him think of who he is."

"Fodder!" This time a shake that scrambled the body he knew wasn't really there. "Come on, you stupid bugger! Stop messing around, will you? Honestly, if I had a horse trough here, I'd dump you in it, wouldn't I, like I did when we were Urchins! Remember? Fodder!"

Horse trough. Yes, he'd been a boy and she'd been a girl and he'd pulled her plaits and laughed and run away and she'd caught him in three strides and tipped him into the water like a rag doll and stood there glaring down with hands on barely formed hips and told him sternly if he ever did anything that stupid again, in he'd go, wouldn't he, again and again until he saw sense.

Except...

Was that real? It had been so dull, so grey, it felt a thousand miles away, like a memory that belonged to someone else...

Flames sparked in his head. He winced.

"It was cold. And there was a frog."

He'd spoken. Had he spoken? No, he couldn't speak, he was dead and floating, no, he couldn't have spoken unless summoned to do so but it sounded like his voice and her eyes *(Flirt)*, her eyes *(Flirt's eyes)* widened as though he did.

"I remember the frog." Not her voice but another, a head, a severed head was talking to him but that really wasn't right and he really must be dead for that to be the case. "You remember, Flirt saw me laughing at what you did and tipped me in right after you? That frog sat on my head and croaked at me."

"You haven't got a head." Words again, were they his, could they be his, could it be that he was dead and floating and could speak? "It's been cut off."

The expression on the head's face darkened noticeably. "Really?"

it drawled mordantly. "You don't say! Well, I'd *never* have noticed if you hadn't bloody well pointed it—"

"Shoulders." It was the wrong voice and it sounded wrong, firm and abrupt. "Not now, please."

"And you're all wrong!" His mind was simmering on a low heat but he ignored the burn growing beneath his brain as his dead lips felt compelled to protest at this injustice. Shaking off the hands from his dead shoulders, he attempted to jab a dead and floating finger at the lanky, battered figure who was staring at him with an air of concern. Unfortunately, the unnecessary restraints got in the way. "You and him—all wrong! He's dead, he's got no head! And you! You, *Tretaptus!*" The name erupted much to the protest of his flaming itch, which said this wrong was wrong but the wrong was right, he knew it, even if it was wrong, it was right! "I'm dead! I'm dead and eaten and floating and I've got the good grace to stay that way! But you and him, walking around and talking and saying things when he's got no head and you've been eaten, it's all wrong! All wrong, all wrong, *all wrong!*"

Pain.

It exploded across his face like a fist in the chin, which, in fairness, was exactly what had caused it. Even as his head ricocheted back with an unexpectedly substantial smack against the chair, his own hands still clenched into mad claws being jolted by the impact, he saw her *(Flirt!)* standing over him, wringing her right hand painfully, her face a furious mix of pain and anger. The lanky prince *(Dullard. Dullard!)* was leaning over her shoulder, his eyes concerned.

"You know, that would hurt less if you braced your thumb against—"

"Yes, thank you!" The snapped retort put fervent pay to the rest of the prince's sentence. "I wasn't exactly thinking about technique, was I? I just wanted him to shut up." She shook her head, her eyes despairing. "I can't *believe* he called you *Tretaptus.*"

His head was reeling. There was pain. How could there be pain if he was dead? And that burning at the back of his mind, throwing names at him like daggers, was screaming at him to get a grip. He knew these people. So why didn't he know them?

The prince *(Dullard! Come on, think it, will you?)* winced. "I know. Pleasance did the same. The planting has deep roots."

"What do we do about it?" The head *(Shoulders! It's Shoulders! How long have you known the miserable sod?)* spoke with unexpected softness, his face pale and his eyes worried. "I want my mate the bloody nutter back, not some bloody nutter my mate used to be."

"He's in there." As he struggled to focus, dazed and dizzy with a throbbing chin, he saw the prince staring down at him with disconcerting thoughtfulness. "Once Pleasance had gone, she went completely." For an instant, his eyes were a world of strange pain, hurriedly pushed away. "But Fodder isn't the same. Earlier, he said *the Taskmaster*. That's not a phrase any Narrative construct or character would ever use, would ever be allowed to even *think*. I think…" He tapped his chin thoughtfully for a moment. "I think what Fodder wants and what the Taskmaster tried to make him have got mixed up. And I suspect I know how…"

Slowly, the prince *(You're not going to think it, are you? Oh, for goodness' sake…)* dropped to a crouch at his side, as he tried to focus his bleary, dizzy eyes on the unusual contours of his face. "Fodhelion," he said softly. "Interesting name. Where did that come from?"

"I said it." Honest words. He had, hadn't he? He'd said it. "It was a joke."

Joke. Joke? His name was a joke. And yes, it had been a joke, the fire in his mind was blazing now, it *had* been a joke, a silly aside, a mockery of the daft explanations they'd used and made to cover up the chaos he was causing and he'd used it again for his puppet spirit to poke a little more fun at them all…

When had it stopped being fun? When had it stopped being a joke and become his name?

"You said it?" The prince's face was intense now. "In The Narrative?"

"On the cliff." Dizzy, he was so dizzy and his face was screaming and he really didn't feel like he was floating anymore. And his mouth was answering without him, hot words, unprompted, from the fiery recesses of his brain. "I was making fun of them. I said I was Avikhelion's illegitimate heir by a maidservant."

The prince closed his eyes, his mouth pursed with apparent pain.

"And there we have it," he muttered almost to himself. His eyes opened once more and they were strangely steely. "Fodder," he said firmly, and this time that nothing of a name sent a violent jolt of fire down the length of his spine. "You've been *planted*. And I'm sorry, but you rather brought it on yourself." He shook his head wearily. "You named yourself," he said quietly. "You gave yourself a character and a purpose that The Narrative could use, that the other characters could believe in. It had struggled to pin you down, your motive and who you were, and that gave you freedom. But you shouldn't have played its game by weaving yourself into its Quest-lore. Even said in jest, that would be deadly."

Through the daze, the fire was burning brightly now, the flames licking at the madness, at the maelstrom, and dispersing it to ashes.

"Planted?" he gasped hoarsely. "Planted…"

"It seems to have been done very cleverly." Dullard's voice was soft but his eyes were sympathetic. "You probably didn't even notice." A flicker of a smile touched his lips. "I had a chance to look at Quibble's book a while back and I saw some of the things you've been up to. And I'm in no doubt they came from you. But I suspect that every time you went into The Narrative, it caught you a bit more, building your confidence to dangerous levels with each victory, boosting your ego, putting a swagger in your step and mockery into your voice. It still fought you, but it didn't let those victories go unpunished. It let you pump yourself up with self-belief, gave you enough rope to let you hang yourself. By the end, I can imagine you really did believe that you could and should rule the world. Just as a *villain* should."

Villain? Villain. No, but he wasn't, he wasn't a villain, he was trying to save people, he was trying to help…

"I'm not a villain," he gasped.

Dullard smiled sadly. "You are to the Merry Band. You were their nemesis, indestructible and untouchable, and you knew that, didn't you?"

So confident, so assured it would always work; whatever the plan, he had their measure, whatever he did he would emerge unscathed, there was no reason to fear The Narrative, to take care in its honey warmth, because he knew, he just knew, it would always, always,

always go his way...

Until there was no magic. Until jaws and floating and dead.

How could that have happened? How, how, how was he supposed to cope with that?

"I don't know how they beat me." The words sounded pathetic to the fire that had erupted across the entire of his mind. "I should have won. I *always* win. How could I be killed?"

"I imagine that was a shock to an ego as pumped as yours was." Dullard nodded carefully. "Enough of a shock for you to lose grip on yourself for a moment. Enough of a shock, perhaps, to let The Narrative's version of your character take you over completely. As it did at the top of the tower, and again, here and now. But you can come back. You simply have to want to."

It had seemed so easy, too easy, and yes, a small itch at the back of his head had whispered it had been too good to be true, but Swipe had fallen over and Bob had gone so beautifully and they'd floundered in that river, utterly fooled, and the cross-eyed look on Erik...on *Bumpkin's* face when he'd considered his bladder for the first time in far too long...

He'd gone so far. He'd got so carried away in the fun of it all.

And when it had finished...

The shock, the pain as the jaws began to close and that final moment in the light, he'd felt the syrup of The Narrative flow into his heart and tell him who he was and how he was so very, very dead.

Dead. Fodhelion's thought.

Floating. That had been his.

It had got so mixed up. All alone, with no one to notice, to prod him, to toss him in a horse trough and to point out how stupid he'd become, he'd flown on fake confidence straight into the brick wall marked Swamp Monster. How the hell was he supposed to find the parts that belonged to himself in this mess?

"I don't know who I am." He'd spoken. Had he spoken? Had he said that? "I don't know what I want."

Hands caught his shoulders, easing him out of the chair and the ropes and back against a bench leaning by a wall he hadn't even seen. He hadn't noticed that Dullard had even risen and stepped back until he saw Flirt's hands, yes, *Flirt* and *Dullard,* he'd *thought* Dullard, been *thinking* Dullard and there was *Shoulders* too, yes, his friends, *yes,* Flirt's hands against his arms. A moment later, she slid down beside him to his right, her head lolling on one side as she looked at him crookedly.

"You're Fodder, aren't you?" she said.

The flames lapped at the name. "Am I?"

"Course you bloody are." With a grunt and a mutter, Shoulders dropped down awkwardly onto the bench to his left, his head clutched carefully in his hands as he lifted it to face height. "You're a Disposable from Humble Village who drinks at the Archetypal Inn. You're always the first to ask if we're all right and the last to stop looking for someone's missing kidney. You drink too little and you think too much. You're the bloody nutter who dragged me into this mess entirely against my will by buggering off with someone else's princess. And above all, you're my mate." A smile touched the severed head. "Now stick your bloody hands out before I change my mind."

"What?" The question came easily and so did the hands, an act of instinct. And then from the cradle of his own palms, Shoulders's head was staring up at him.

"You've had me with my head in my hands enough times lately," he said wryly. "About time I put my head in yours. Because—and I almost can't believe this myself, but I've done this so it must be bloody true—I trust you. I trust you not to turn on a mate and chuck my head out of a window. Even when you've dragged me to hell and back. Even when you've been planted. Even when you're being bloody stupid. Because you're Fodder and I've known you all my life. And Fodder wouldn't do that."

He stared at the face of his oldest friend nestled in his grasp, trusting his head to his hands. In a final blaze of cleansing glory, the fire in his mind died.

"I dunno," he said quietly. "There were a few moments back in the Wild Forest when I'd have happily chucked your head out of a window and been done with it. You were bloody annoying, you know."

* * *

Bolstered by Islaine's silent love, Erik glanced up from his tumultuous ride to catch the eye of each of his companions in turn. First he found Zahora, bold and forthright, tensed over her saddle, locks of her dark hair peeking out from beneath her helmet and whipping in the wind of their wild ride. Her smile was tight and hard, the smile of a warrior braced for battle. She would be fearsome when they faced the foes upon whom they closed.

* * *

There was a long moment of pause.

"Oh *nice!*" Shoulders's face crinkled irritably as Flirt burst into a peal of sudden laughter. "I make a grand gesture of trust and friendship and what do I get? Abuse!"

Fodder couldn't help but grin. "You did sort of ask for it, mate." Carefully, he lifted the head and handed it back to Shoulders's groping fingers. "But it was a good gesture. And it helped."

"I should bloody well think so." Shoulders gave a huff.

Dullard, who had apparently backed off to give the older friends a chance to work their magic, dropped to a sit on the abandoned chair, his eyes intent. "How are you feeling now?" he asked carefully.

"Better. Clearer." It was true. Faced with bald facts, his gifts from The Narrative had not found any safe place to hide from the fire of himself. He checked his finger and found with a mixture of disconcertion and relief that the Ring of Anthiphion was still there. "I think I know what was me and what was it now anyway." He sighed, fighting the pounding in his temples that was his legacy from the mental warfare. "I'm so sorry, I…"

"Oh, shut up." Flirt's interruption was affectionate, her prod to his arm slightly less so. "Don't beat yourself up. We've all been there, haven't we? Even Dullard's had his moments with The Narrative."

"Not as many as the rest of us," Shoulders muttered darkly, giving the prince an irritable look.

Dullard's eyebrows rose as his face flooded with genuine surprise. "Well, of course not," he said with a mild shrug.

There was no mistaking Shoulders's dark look now. "What's that supposed to mean, you smug git? If you're saying you're better than us Ordinary plebs…"

"No, certainly not!" Dullard's hands flew up in a placatory manner. "It's just, well, The Narrative will never hook into me as easily as all of you because…well, I don't want anything from it."

Fodder blinked. He wasn't the only one.

Dullard sighed at their blank looks. "You started this because you felt overlooked, correct?" At their nods, he continued. "And you felt overlooked because of your sparse Narrative time. You wanted The Narrative, to be a part of The Narrative, a bigger part because to you, that was what was important, that was what would get you recognised for the talents you have. That was how people would recognise you were worth something more; and for her airs, Pleasance was exactly the same. But me…" He shrugged again, loosely. "The Narrative doesn't really matter to me. I'm much happier out of it because it can't really give me what I want. If anything, being chosen as a Principal rather gets in the way of my hobbies." He smiled gently. "There's nothing in my head for it to hold on to. You can't be tempted by what you don't want, you know."

Fodder stared at him, the man they'd met what felt like forever ago, happy in his world of books and rock samples, who'd bundled his way into their chaotic adventure because he wanted to learn how the world worked. Oh yes, he'd protested at the way his peers had treated him, but not once, not ever, had he bemoaned his lack of Narrative time.

Whereas they…

"Hang on, though." Shoulders lifted his head carefully. "I don't give a toss about being some Hero in shiny armour. All I want is not to get my bloody head cut off. So why the hell does it always pick on me?"

Dullard looked at him thoughtfully. "Because you believe it's picking on you," he said simply. "You expect it to win. You expect the worst to happen and so you can't fight it when it does. You know yourself and you've decided you can't fight it, even though you really can, of course, if you want to. You only need to realise that."

Shoulders opened his mouth. Then he closed it again. His eyes narrowed.

"Bollocks," he said finally, although his voice lacked conviction.

Dullard gave a shrug. "If you say so. It's only my theory, so I could be completely wrong, but I came with you to work this through and that's what I think to be the case. The rest is up to you really. It's about what you *believe.*"

* * *

Next Erik's gaze found Svenheid, strong and powerful, the last of three noble barbarian brothers left standing; and perhaps that loss did play upon him now, for his eyes seemed distant and haunted as he spurred his horse on their helter-skelter ride, his thoughts far away or far ahead, it was hard to really tell. He did not even catch Erik's look, preoccupied as he was, but Erik was sure his mighty strength would rend their enemies apart when the moment came to act. He would find his true self once more in what lay before them.

* * *

"I know what I believe." His brain was still a mush of aches and dizziness, his thoughts working to unravel, but as he struggled to put his brain back in order, one thing was blazing loud and clear in Fodder's mind. "Sod being a villain. And you know what? Sod being a bloody Hero too." He shook his head slowly, his eyes drifting to Flirt, his mind fixed upon a long-ago conversation in a noisy pub over beer and stew. "I wanted some respect when this started and I thought respect came from being the Hero on the shiny horse, the Narrative star, a character. But I don't care if I spend ten seconds in The Narrative, ten minutes, ten hours, ten Quests from beginning to end as long as I'm *myself* at the end of it. If the price of being a Hero is to be something I'm not, they can bloody well keep it."

Flirt's nod was fervent. "Agreed."

Dullard's eyes were sad. "Agreed."

Shoulders's face was thoughtful. "Yeah. Agreed."

Firming his chin, Fodder hauled himself tenderly but determinedly to his feet. "So we all agree. This has to stop."

They rose too, Shoulders juggling with his head as he struggled to lever himself upwards, Dullard unfolding his lanky limbs warily, Flirt rising swiftly with alarm on her face. She was the first to speak.

"What do you mean?" she said carefully.

Fodder frowned. "I mean *this.*" He tapped his own temple pointedly. "Planting! All this getting into our heads and working us like puppets! Making us be who we aren't! A bit of guidance is one thing, but putting an entire other person in your head without even asking? Leaving it there to mess you up? No." He shook his head stubbornly. "I'm not going to let this happen anymore. And maybe I was mental when I said it, but if that means we have to go right the way up, that we have to take down the Taskmaster..."

"No."

The violent strength of Flirt's exclamation was enough to kill his sentence stone dead. As he stared at her in shock, he saw the sudden determination in her eyes, her fist clenched and her jaw locked as she stared right back with a gaze that could pierce a soul.

"What?" he managed.

Flirt shook her head, slowly, strongly. "We can't do that, can we?"

His brain scrambled to catch up with his senses. He'd expected that Shoulders would swear and call him a nutter, that Dullard might offer up a hesitant argument as to why it might not be wise, but Flirt...Flirt was supposed to be with him. Flirt had been with him from the start, the one who'd got it, the one who'd *understood.* She'd been the first one to say it that night back in the pub, the first one to wonder...

Why do we have to obey the Taskmaster at all?

"But you said it." The words were nearly accidental. "Why obey the Taskmaster, Flirt, you were the first to..."

"And now I've changed my mind, haven't I?"

* * *

Sir Roderick, noble and steadfast, was a harder man to read for his face was shrouded by his metal visor but his stance was so magnificent, the set of his shoulders so strong, the gait of his horse so powerful that Erik did not need the further reassurance of meeting his eyes. Sir Roderick was a hero in the truest sense, a knight who embodied all that was good about their world. He would not fade or falter in the face of the confrontation to come—he would stand firm, their rock, against that which would assail them.

* * *

Flirt twisted her lips but her eyes did not waver. "I agree with you, don't I, that something's got to change. But you've been faffing about in The Narrative, haven't you? You haven't seen what it's been like behind the scenes." She shook her head again. "I saw what happens when the instructions get taken away and, Fodder, it isn't pretty. *We* may be ready but the rest of the world isn't. Everyone's too much in their place, aren't they? The Gods, the Disposables, their habits, the way they think, it's too ingrained." She sighed deeply. "It'd be chaos, wouldn't it? Somebody would have to be in charge, and I'm telling you, I'm not going to be the one to rise from humble beginnings to rule the world. It'd be a bloody great pain in the arse." She smiled gently. "The Taskmaster's been doing the job for a long time and I think we still need those instructions. We just need the instructions to be fairer."

"But without the Taskmaster whispering in their ears, once they were given a chance—"

"They'd fall back into the same old comfy ways, because they don't know what else to do." Flirt cut him off sharply. "I've seen it, Fodder, I've watched it happen. I tried to start a revolution with the Disposables and it turned out all they wanted was a piss-up. I tried to rally an army to a cause and they wouldn't follow until I said the instructions were okay with it. I tried to lead a death-or-glory charge and they ran away because they thought they couldn't win if we outnumbered the enemy!"

Fodder blinked. "You tried to turn them against the First—"

"One more word about those bloody rules of yours and I'll punch you in the gob again, won't I?"

"Understood." Fodder knew when was the time to shut up on a matter and he took it. "But I used to think like that and…"

"No, you didn't." Shoulders's interjection was so uncharacter-istically soft that Fodder almost missed it. "You've never thought like that, Fodder. You're one of the lads and you always will be. But the rest of us—we settled for our lives. You never did."

Fodder hesitated, drinking in Shoulders's words. He thought back over his life, to the questions he'd asked of his father even as an Urchin, to the nagging sense that had dogged him all of his life that things weren't quite right. It was a fair point.

"You changed your mind," he pointed out to his fellow Disposable.

A pair of headless shoulders shrugged. "You didn't leave me much bloody choice. You want to behead the entire Disposable army and drag them to hell and back to convince them, though, do carry on. It'll be funny."

"I believe people can be made to see." Dullard stepped delicately into the debate. "After all, Pleasance and I managed to persuade the Servants of the Imposing Castle to defy their masters."

Fodder grinned triumphantly. "There! You see…"

"However, I do wonder if the task would have been possible if the words had not been coming from their established social superiors," Dullard continued carefully. "And those content with their lot, such as the Disposables or the Nobles, or those unable to see beyond it, like the Gods, would have no incentive to be persuaded." He sighed. "I do not believe it's a task that can be taken on by only four people. Flirt is correct. We need someone they are used to listening to."

Fodder's grin collapsed. "But we also need someone worth listen-ing to and that isn't the Taskmaster! The Taskmaster is cruel, plays with our minds and our lives, forces us into roles against our will! The Taskmaster is willing to let us be burned to nothing and left that way! Is that the person you want running our world?"

Flirt cocked an eyebrow. "Actually, Squick doesn't reckon the Taskmaster knows anything about that. He thinks it was Strut and Poniard, doesn't he? The Taskmaster wasn't consulted."

Fodder snorted. "You really believe that?"

"I do." Dullard's statement was soft, but the steel behind it quiet-ened Fodder's attempt to scoff instantly. "In fact, I believe there is a great deal about our world that the Taskmaster is not entirely aware of."

Fodder and Flirt exchanged a sudden look of bewildered solidarity. Shoulders proved the verbal equivalent. "What's *that* supposed to mean?"

Dullard pinched his lips together. "It's not easy to explain. I had a chance to take a look at Quibble's book a short while ago and...oh dear." He pulled a face. "If only I still had it, it would be so much easier simply to show you..."

"Here you go." It had to be said Dullard's face was a picture. He blinked hard as he stared down at the originally brown and now rather sticky green book that Shoulders had rooted out of his pouch and held out under his nose. Its pages curled uninvitingly.

"You have a book?" In spite of the state of it, the prince politely snatched it out of Shoulders's offered hand.

"Preen's, isn't it?" Flirt was grinning again. "We nicked it off him. Twice."

Dullard's eyes were glued to the pages as fervently as the gunge. "It may not be the same as Quibble's, of course," he muttered to himself. "But I need an example... Aha!" He held out the book's slimy pages as Flirt and Fodder gathered round, Shoulders lifting his head to get a better view. "Good, it's the same. This is what I noticed earlier."

Fodder glanced down at the smudged writing, running his eyes over the familiar text. He frowned.

```
Okay, right...the man of Sleiss has escaped again,
the hall is on fire and there's a stampede...why a...? Oh
never mind, let's just get this back on track. They'll
need to chase him because they still need that bloody
Ring and they need him to help find the princess, even
though he probably doesn't know where she is because she
was dragged off by Tretaptus and could be any-bloody-
where by now and maybe they should be looking for her
because they can't go to the noble's castle and start
the battle until she's...
     God, why is this happening to me? It's like bloody
Quickening all over...
     Come on. CONCENTRATE. Sort this mess out.
```

Fodder was so used to the instructions. Familiar, dry words that dictated his fate, emotionless, structured, controlled. But this?

"Maybe I'm wrong." Dullard spoke softly. "Maybe I'm misreading it. But when I look at this, I see a person who is struggling to understand what is happening. A person who doesn't understand our world and how it works. I know the words of the Taskmaster come down to us through the Golden Tome at the Sanctum, but no one speaks to the Taskmaster or vice versa, not in person. What if all we are to the Taskmaster is words in return?" He took a deep breath. "I'm not sure the Taskmaster understands that we're *alive*."

* * *

Erik's searching eyes found Slynder next, the cunning and quick-witted thief riding behind him, and the little man was quick to flash him a smile. Perhaps the cleverest of them but for Elder, Slynder would not let them down—he would read the truth in the situation they were riding so frantically into, he would see the possibilities and he would find the right way to go. How could he not?

* * *

Fodder blinked. The words rang against his ears, setting off bells in his brain that tolled with loud abandon. He'd spent all this time thinking of the Taskmaster as some malevolent entity, peering down at them, laughing, moving them around like pawns on a chess board, sacrifices to the Narrative cause. But if Dullard's ponderings were true—and Fodder had to admit that they generally turned out to be—the Taskmaster he'd been so determined to tear down might be just as confused by this as he was. What if the Taskmaster really was like the Gods as he'd once speculated, but more so, so lost in some distant place that the truths of life itself became unclear? What if the Taskmaster had no more idea of what was going on than they did?

No personal vendetta. No vindictive attempt to squash them. Only a bewildered person struggling to set their story straight without a clue that they were playing with the lives of living beings.

Was that possible?

"If that's true…" Flirt was the first to venture into the echoing silence that had followed Dullard's pronouncement. "That'd mean the Taskmaster might understand, doesn't it? If planting isn't on purpose, if we could make ourselves heard, make the Taskmaster understand what The Narrative does to us, how unfair it is…"

Unfair.

Because that had been it, hadn't it, his vague intention back at the beginning before he even really knew what he was getting himself into. Get attention. Make people listen. Make the world a fairer place. As the fight had turned nasty, it had become more sinister somehow, more of a struggle for mental independence, but could that original thought, of being heard, of getting people—one person—to listen, really be enough to change the mind of the Taskmaster?

"Even if that's right," he said sceptically, "you really think the Taskmaster will listen to us? Power goes to the head even if the person doesn't know they have it. What if by waking up the Taskmaster, we create even more of a monster?"

"I think the Taskmaster is scared of us. I'd be scared of us, wouldn't I?" Fodder grinned at Flirt's statement. "We've shown what a mess we can make, haven't we? I reckon if we offered a truce and a bit of reason…"

"I think it may be more than that." Dullard stepped forward suddenly. "The basic fact is much more straightforward. We need to get the Taskmaster's undivided attention. Simply put, first and foremost, the Taskmaster needs to know we're *here.*" He smiled gently. "We can worry about persuasion when we've made contact. But for now, perhaps we'd best get the lay of the land."

Grasping the slimy book firmly, he leafed hurriedly towards the back and his eyebrows rose. "Oh dear," he murmured. "I think the Merry Band might be getting a touch close to us now. The AFCs have just been rallied to offer fierce resistance at the Citadel gates."

It was at that moment that a severe attack of missing the bloody obvious struck Fodder straight across the chops. Lost in sorting out his head and nailing back down what he needed to do, he hadn't really paid more than token attention to what was actually going on around him. But hang on…

"Wait a minute," he said abruptly. "Where the hell are we?"

* * *

And of course, finally, Erik sought out his mentor, Elder, the magnificent master of sorcery himself, ancient and profound and indefatigable. The old man's face was a wash of stubborn determination, his beard flying in the wind as he gripped his reins in a vice-like hold. The bastion against evil for generations, finally approaching the end of his long, hard mission—no force of heaven or earth would cause him to fail in that purpose now. Craxis and the man of Sleiss might hold a surfeit of evil to be unleashed, but how could any evil stand against the shining light of so much good?

Some way ahead, the narrow, treacherous gorge was converging upon towering pillars, the final obstacle in their heroic surge. Bracing his nerves with courage, Erik took a firmer grip on lovely Islaine, grasped his reins, and whipped his loyal steed to travel faster.

By tonight, it would be over and done.

Forever.

* * *

Two pairs of eyes darted in his direction. Dullard did not tear himself away from the book, but it was he who took a moment to reply.

"We're in the basement of one of the towers of the Dark Citadel," he said, his tone so matter-of-fact that one might have thought that being at the root of all Narrative evil was something that happened to him every day.

"Okay." Next, an important question. "Why?"

"No idea." Flirt shrugged.

"*His* idea." Shoulders jerked an accusing thumb in the oblivious Dullard's direction. "Some great plan, he said—genius, fix everything, he reckons."

Dullard's eyes flicked up. "I did say I'm sorry for keeping you in the dark, but I will explain as soon as we are all..."

Fodder decided to head off the latest round of sniping versus apology before it hit its stride. "Okay," he repeated. "So we're in a tower of the Dark Citadel because Dullard has a plan. And from what you said, the Merry Band are on their way to get us and closing fast?"

"So it says here," Dullard admitted. "Though it would appear that they are cobbling together a delaying scene because..."

"Just let me see."

Dullard nodded. "As you wish." He handed Fodder the book, and he scanned the instructions written below carefully. A heroic ride to death or glory was indeed mere minutes away, albeit with a skirmish planned to slow them down.

"Right." Fodder nodded, still clutching the book. "All clear. So, one more thing..." He gave a slightly manic smile. "If we have a mystery plan that is yet to be executed and we are being rapidly closed down by the Merry Band before we have done so, why the bloody hell have we been sitting in a tower *having a chat?*"

There was a long pause. It stank of guilt.

There was nothing else for Fodder to say but... "What?"

"Well, we had to stop and sort you out because your head was buggered up, wasn't it?" Flirt pointed out bluntly. "And...Hauteur is here."

"Hauteur!" Fodder's eyes widened. "As in, Officious Courtier for the Dark Ones, Hauteur?"

"The very same," Dullard confirmed. "But luckily he doesn't know we're here."

Fodder shook his head. "Not to turn into Flirt, but we can take one Courtier out without breaking a sweat. Why are we hiding instead of grabbing him and tying him up?"

Dullard gave an awkward shrug. "Our host asked us not to. He's not sure if he wants any trouble."

Thrusting the book unceremoniously into his belt for safe-keeping, Fodder mustered the best impatient glare that he could. "Our host?"

Flirt nodded. "He caught us up the tower while he was checking his glowing eye was switched on. He's been very kind and he hasn't turned us in yet, but we don't want to push our luck, do we? Not when Dullard's been hinting we're going to need him onside."

"Plus he's got a bloody huge sword," Shoulders added fervently.

Fodder gritted his teeth at this lack of getting to the point. "Need who?"

Dullard's smile was annoyingly friendly. "Why, Doom the Dark Lord, of course. Who were you expecting?"

* * *

It was as though he was staring into the very maw of death.

The gateway loomed ahead of them, sealing the exit to the gorge like snapped teeth, twisted stone that lurched out of the rock face as though dragged, screaming in pain into the dim and rancid light. Shapes seemed to claw out of the rocky curve: faces, semi-formed, grotesque and contorted; claw-like hands and inhuman bodies, gazing, half in shadow, down at the heavy iron gates that barred their path with grim fortitude. Beyond them, visible above the looming visage of the gateway, a massive up-thrust of dark stone walls lurked in the twisting mess of clouds.

With a shiver, Islaine pressed her delicate form more closely against Erik's chest.

"What a vile place this is!" she whispered fervently. "I wish you had not brought me here!"

Erik's heart reflected that sentiment. This was no place for his beautiful flower to come and risk her life. But it was too late to go back, and he knew that his whole soul would be devoted to her protection. No horror would claim her again.

Zahora was staring at this barricade to their progress with angry eyes. "Now what do we do?"

"Knock and ask nicely?" Slynder drawled with a sardonic smirk.

Zahora gave him a violent glare but Sir Roderick ignored their banter. "I am certain between Svenheid and myself, we can scale this beast and lift the barrier from the other side. What say you, noble barbarian?"

"Huh?" Svenheid glanced up from his persistent reverie, his bearded face distant. "Sorry, what?"

Sir Roderick huffed with impatience. "We stand at the gates of hell and you do not even do the courtesy of listening?"

"It is of no matter." Elder's wise eyes raked across the pitted, scarred wall of metal as he intervened to halt the squabble. "This gate is enchanted. You would be dead before you climbed six feet. No, this is my task. I must untangle the enchantments." He sighed deeply. "But be aware that once I begin, there must be no interruptions. If I cannot complete this task cleanly, it will not be completed at all."

"We understand, noble Eldrigon," Sir Roderick proclaimed. "We will keep away any intrusions."

Elder nodded. "Be sure that you do. For doubtless, there will be many as soon as Craxis feels me begin."

And then a gentle, golden glow began to rise from Elder's skin as his eyes fixed upon the gates with cold intensity. The iron gates began to glow too but with a sickly red flicker that resembled old blood.

And the sky filled with screams.

Even as Erik started, clutching the shivering Islaine tighter as he groped for his sword, he heard Slynder swear loudly, saw Sir Roderick loose his mighty sword, saw Zahora swing her bow to hand and Svenheid scramble for his axe. The too-familiar flap of leathery wings slashed the air as dark shapes plunged out of the misty cloud above, their mouths agape with vicious teeth, their clawed fingers outstretched, and their eyes wild and without reason.

"Protect Eldrigon!" Roderick roared as the knight swung his horse to the glowing sorcerer's side. "We must keep them away from him!"

With Islaine clutched to his breast, Erik focused on the sword within his hand, calling on the now-familiar tug of energy as he aimed the blade at the first swooping creature with grim intensity. Calling on his magic, he thrust white lightning along the length of the blade.

It struck the beast full on. For a second, Erik saw the surprise in its cruel eyes before it ignited into flames and exploded into ashes.

Above, a creature was clawing at its chest as, one after another, three of Zahora's arrows thudded into its leathery body. Another screeched as Slynder's dagger plunged into its eye socket. Another already lay squawking and bleeding where Roderick's blade had pierced it near through while Svenheid swung his axe around his head with a bellowing war cry as he drove the assailants back. But above their heads the sky was thickening with dark shapes, with cold eyes and sharp claws. They were very much outnumbered.

Casting a glance at Elder's glowing, concentrating form, Erik took aim once more. They had to hold them off long enough for Elder to get them inside...

* * *

"You folks can come in if you want to!" The booming baritone voice echoed into the tower room from down the corridor, catching the end of Dullard's sentence and punctuating it neatly. "Hauteur's gone!"

Fodder glanced at the prince, suddenly painfully aware that their choices and timeframe were limited. "Doom? You know him pretty well, right?"

Dullard nodded enthusiastically. "Oh yes, I was his prisoner for most of a Quest. He was kind enough to let me join in with his latest amateur dramatic project, which I must say was the most wonderful—"

Fodder cut swiftly through the rambling to the chase. "Can we trust him?"

Dullard caught himself mid-deviation and settled instead for nodding. "I would say so, yes. I'm certainly sure he won't turn us in."

"You sure?" The nagging image of Poniard's twisted face shouldered into Fodder's mind. "After all, he's been planted as a huge number of raging psychopaths over the Quests, and that didn't do Poniard any favours."

The prince shook his head at once. "You've nothing to worry about there. Unlike Poniard, Doom's Narrative persona is so far removed from his character as to be laughable. Since he's almost never seen except as a heavily armoured monstrosity striding briefly through Final Battles and crushing hapless foes, the fact that he's a big, friendly softy behind it doesn't really seem to matter to his job description. All that matters to The Narrative is that he's mastered the art of archaic proclamation, he can swing a sword in wild fury whilst wearing vast armour, and does a masterly sibilant hiss and deep boom of rage. And his dramatic deaths are unparalleled. No one can collapse into a heap of ash quite like he can." He shrugged slightly, either missing or ignoring Fodder's get-to-the-point glare. "And his Narrative time being so slight and his characters so undefined, he's never really been affected by it. Most of his time he spends here, rearing prize-winning bunnies, organising the Barren Wastelands Amateur Dramatic Society, and managing the AFC Melee team; I understand they are unbeaten in six tournaments, which is a very impressive streak. Not to mention he was telling us earlier as we were bringing you down in his pulley lift that he's recently taken up handicrafts..."

Shoulders snorted. "He sounds like you."

Dullard pursed his lips. "Well, we've always got along well," he conceded. "I think it comes from being far more involved in our non-Narrative interests than our characters, I suppose."

"But that might be a problem, mightn't it?" Flirt pointed out. "Slippery bastard as he was, Cringe was adamant he wouldn't be interested in helping us. Said he was perfectly content with life the way it was."

The prince's strained expression told Fodder that this was a fair assessment. "I'm sure we can work around that," he said without much conviction.

"Are you folks coming? I could use a hand down here!" The deep boom echoed through the stone corridors once more, a voice that had sent whole armies—armies that had included Fodder himself—running for cover alongside countless terrified Heroes and Heroines, but it was filled with such jolly friendliness as to be deeply disconcerting. No rumbling, harsh-edged, world-destroying baritone should ever sound so chirpy.

"Come on," Flirt said, shoring up her shoulders, her green-stained blouse hanging limply over them. "Let's get on with this."

Shoulders took one last, wistful look at his ruined helmet contrivance and then, head grasped in his hands, fell in beside her. "Whatever *this* is," he added, swivelling his eyes towards Dullard as they moved out of the tower room, "you still haven't explained."

The Rejected Suitor nodded. "I can explain it to you at the same time as Doom. There's no point in repeating myself."

They headed down the dark, gothic-arched corridor, Fodder hurrying his friends along in an effort to inject a little urgency to what was, after all, verging on a life-threatening situation. They passed through a gargoyle-lined doorway that opened out into what could only be described as the seat of all evil. The hall was vast, towering to physically impossible heights, the columns, ceiling beams, and walls carved and painted with the familiar grotesque images of torture, maiming, blood-letting, and freakish creature-dom that were so standard to places of darkness. An enormous dais erupted at the head of the hall, and sprouting from it was a massive throne carved of shining jet, black as a starless night and twisted as though deformed, truly designed for the resting of the buttocks of purest villainy.

And indeed it probably would have been a terrifying and imposing sight had it not been for the multi-coloured macramé throw that had been draped over the throne's twisted form. Two bright cushions, also with rainbow macramé covers knotted in the shape of smiling bunnies, nestled in the seat next to an enormous, engraved black helmet with a visor shaped like a snarling dragon. A very ordinary-looking wooden table was resting alongside the throne, scattered with a cork board, pins, and a variety of colourful cords alongside a gigantic, jagged-edged black sword leaning against one leg. Pots of paint and brushes were propped up beside them, and behind the throne, apparently in the process of being packed away, was a series of canvas backdrops: a half-painted fairy castle, a cut-out tree with a prop pair of fairy wings hanging from one branch, and what looked like the beginnings of a meadow scene stretched out on wooden poles to dry.

And stacked below the dais's front edge, in a series of spacious hutches and wooden runs, were a quite extraordinary variety of bunnies.

There were big bunnies. There were small bunnies. There were white bunnies and black bunnies, speckled bunnies and patched, with floppy ears and adorable twitchy noses. And kneeling amongst them, looking more like he ought to be biting their heads off than affectionately stroking their fuzzy ears, was a toweringly out-sized figure in black-lacquered armour.

The Dark Lord, the terror and scourge of so very many stories, was, with tender care, lifting the bunnies one by one from the runs and securing them with palpable reluctance in the hutches. His craggy, hard-lined, deathly-white face was filled with softness and his dark hair, worn bald in a patch at the back from Quests of heavy helmet use, was cheerfully wild, his beard trimmed not into an elegant goatee as might be expected, but left as a rambling hedge. As he captured his latest victim, a black-patched white bunny with a broad collar that said "Percy", the dinky blighter wriggled free of his light grasp and hopped away back into the run with cheery insolence. As he sighed with resignation at this small failure to obey, Doom glanced up and caught sight of the new arrivals. A broad, beaming smile broke out across his face and he beckoned them enthusiastically over.

"Be good folks and give me a hand, will you?" he boomed cheerfully, his voice a good number of decibels louder than the average human being's. It wasn't so much that he was shouting as that he simply operated at a greater natural volume than the rest of them. "I've got to get my darlings under lock and key or they might escape into Narrative like last time! Strut wasn't impressed..." He pulled a comically contrite face. "It was quite funny, though! The look on old Magus's face, bless him! Middle of a dramatic confrontation and a bunny on his foot! The Narrative wrote it off as a magical hallucination, though, no harm done. But I'm under strict orders to keep them out of the way from now on."

For a brief, tantalising instant, Fodder allowed the vision of a swarm of bunnies overwhelming the Merry Band to dance in front of his mind's eye. But a look at the tender expression on Doom's face and the likelihood of a vast, squishing Clank- or Thud-powered foot descending on an innocent fuzzy head told him this was not a plan to which Doom was likely to be persuaded. Reluctantly, he let the happy scene go.

Dullard headed forward at once, catching hold of the escaping Percy and passing him gently to his master. With a quizzical glance at Fodder and a slight shrug, Flirt followed suit. Shoulders, on the other hand, had no other hand but the ones he was using to hold up his own head and hung more reluctantly back. Fodder debated frustratedly with himself for a moment—helping to prepare for a tidy, orderly Narrative scene wasn't really top of his agenda at the moment—but in spite of his anxiety to get on with things, in the end he too moved forwards to scoop up rogue bunnies as best he could. After all, proximity and helpfulness were a good precursor to asking for help, and they really hadn't much time...

* * *

"Ha!"

With a violent flash of light, the gates blocking their path exploded in a maelstrom of fire and ashes, collapsing in a sighing, glowing heap before them, blocking the path to horses but passable for a man. Startled by this sudden wave of magic, the freakish creatures that assailed them at once lost their nerve—shrieking and clawing at the sky, the surviving monstrosities turned and fled into the cloudy air. Erik, panting hard, his sword still drawn in one hand and Islaine clasped in the other, exchanged breathless looks with his companions-in-arms before turning his gaze slowly to what lay before them.

And there it was. The same monstrous citadel that had filled his dreams for as long as he could remember, dark and shadowed, carved with twisted shapes as the gates were, shrouded in cloud, the light from the highest tower a vicious red that seemed to rake across his soul like a piercing eye. A vast gateway sliced into its lower regions where it rose from the ashy, lifeless ground.

Teeth gritted, Elder clung to his saddle for a moment before pulling himself to the ground and straightening into his usual noble stance. Staff gripped in one hand, he gestured forwards.

"We shall leave the horses here," he said, his voice soft but echoing profoundly. "But the way is clear. It is time to put an end to this."

And then, united as one in their great cause, Erik and his companions dismounted, armed themselves, and charged through the gateway...

* * *

Doom spotted Fodder as he moved in to assist. "Back to yourself, now, are you?" he asked chummily. "That planting—it can be a nasty old business."

Fodder knew an opening when he heard one. "Actually..."

"Never had much trouble with it myself, mind." Fodder wasn't sure if his voice was pitched too quiet to register on Doom's wavelength or if the Dark Lord was deliberately veering off the debate. "My characters never have much character to worry about. Threaten, smash, kill, die—that's about all there is to it, you see! I've not had any trouble separating what's me from what's mindless, psychotic evil."

"About that, I..."

"I mean, you don't get many evil Dark Lords who can do macramé, do you?" Yet again, Fodder's words failed to register as bunnies were handed over and secured. "Do you like my cushion covers? I only finished them yesterday!"

"They're lovely but..."

"And I've been working for weeks on the props for our latest production—see them, up there? We haven't had a chance to rehearse for a while, though; the poor old AFCs have been out on duty pretty much constantly lately, what with you folks kicking off trouble and all. Such a shame—I think this play's one of my better works and I'd like to show it off to folks. I do love a good piece of theatre!"

"And that's nice but..." It was impossible to interrupt that voice. The rolling, high-decibel rumble flattened the attempts of any lesser voice to make itself heard. Frustration seeped into every pore of Fodder's body as yet again his words were dashed away.

"But now I've got to pack everything away! Just when I was nearly done and thought I had weeks yet! And I've had almost no notice of The Narrative bundling over, no time to clear up—Hauteur had to scribble in his book and run off to arrange a delaying scene, to give me time to pack my bunnies away so Magus don't get his foot hallucinated on again! Strut's not impressed at the holdup, he told me. But it's not my fault they gave me less than two hours to get sorted!" With a creak of armour, the vast form of Doom hauled himself to his feet, his final bunny contained at last. "And I've had to tell them I'll never get my scenery moved before they arrive. Hauteur's accepted I'll have to lower the backdrop and keep them Merry Band folks away from the dais. Come on, you can give me a hand! Dullard, you remember how it works, right?"

"Absolutely." Dullard moved swiftly into the gap in the conversation that Fodder had singularly failed to find. "Shall I take this side?"

"That'd be grand." The Dark Lord strode off towards the far side of the hall as Dullard made a beeline for a long rope dangling down the near wall.

"You might want to stand back," he called to his friends in passing. "The backdrop comes down with quite a clatter!"

Flirt glanced up as Shoulders tilted his head. Fodder, following the line of the rope upwards, found a distant, gothic beam high above their heads, rigged with what looked like a giant roll of canvas. It was directly over their heads.

Flirt and Shoulders backed off hurriedly as the canvas shifted, but Fodder was more determined to get to the point. He moved quickly to where Dullard was shifting a gargoyle aside to reveal a rope pulley system.

"What the hell?" he hissed. "We need to talk to him if we can get a word in, The Narrative is right outside waiting to come and crush us, and we're helping him *tidy up?*"

Dullard gritted his teeth as he nodded across the room to Doom and began to wind the pulley. A slither and rustle of canvas descended from above.

"Bear with him," he said, the strain on his face sneaking into his voice. "He isn't going to talk to us until he's comfortable, and he won't be comfortable until this is done. Please try to be patient."

"Patient? The Narrative is right outside!"

"Trust me, I know!" The sudden, uncharacteristic snap caught Fodder off guard. "Do you think I don't know they are here? That they came because Pleasance...because Islaine told them my plan and brought them?"

Fodder was speechless for a moment at the flash of pain on the prince's face. It had nothing to do with the pulley. "Dullard, I..."

With an echoing smack, an enormous, heavy curtain of canvas slammed into the floor a yard to his left. Fodder jumped violently as Dullard, his mouth a grim line, tied off the pulley, pushed the gargoyle back into place, and secured the bottom of the canvas wall against one of the vast columns. Backing up, Fodder stared at the curtain that had completely blocked off the high end of the hall and blinked.

It was a painting. A perfect, beautifully rendered painting of the dais in its full evil glory, a macramé-free twisted throne surrounded by shadowy carved columns and horrific imagery in perfect proportion to what lay behind.

"Good, isn't it?" Doom strode back over cheerfully, helmet in hand, though without his sword. "I made it a couple of Quests back when I had the *Maid of Mercy* kit arranged on the dais and didn't want to move it. The AFCs, bless their hearts, they helped me with it and Dullard here was a godsend for rigging it up. The Narrative laps it right up as long as no one actually tries to go up there. It never knows it's looking at a picture." He shook his head. "That Narrative, it's like a piece of theatre. Happy to see what it wants to see to make the illusion complete. As long as the show goes on."

"Speaking of which…" Dullard had hurried back over, looking more determined. "I did say we needed to talk to you."

Thank you, at last! Fodder restrained himself from punching the air. At last, the point! The Narrative couldn't be far now…

Doom's craggy face took on a notable reluctance. "Dullard, I know what you folks have been up to. Fang dropped by earlier and filled me in and so did Hauteur. Though he was a little ruder about it…" He sighed. "Thing is, you see, I like things the way they are. I like it here, I like my job well enough. I don't know if I want to stir things up for you. I know it's selfish but I'm happy."

"We're not." Dullard echoed his sigh. "We don't mean any harm, Doom, and we shan't disrupt your life. You can stay here and carry on as you have if we get our way. The thing is we need to get the Task-master's attention, to get in touch somehow and make it understood that things need to be different. We don't want to tear things apart, we just want to be listened to, and the only way we can think of to do that is to stop the Quest in its tracks. We've been trying and trying but The Narrative keeps finding a way to work around us. So perhaps we can't do it. But maybe you can."

Doom's vast brow furrowed. "How do you propose I do that?"

Dullard firmed his chin. "Sue for peace. When The Narrative arrives, tell them you give up. You've sent your armies home, you're sick of fighting after so many centuries, and you don't want the Ring anymore. Tell them you can't be bothered and you want to settle down.

Don't get into the fight to the death with Bumpkin. Surrender and ask for a truce."

"That's *it?*" Shoulders's tone was cynical. "That's the master plan? Peace talks?"

But Fodder could see the merits. "That's not a bad idea. They've been building up to this epic confrontation. Where could they go if it didn't happen?"

Shoulders pulled a face as he lifted his head. "Won't they set Bumpkin on him anyway?"

It was Flirt who shook her head. "They can't, can they? How would it make the noble and perfect Merry Band look if they barrelled in and brutally murdered a peace-wanting enemy who's surrendered and doesn't fight back?"

"It would lead to stalemate." Dullard rounded it up neatly. "They can't attack, they daren't agree, and they can't just leave. Where would The Narrative be able to go?" He turned to Doom with a hopeful smile. "Are you willing to give it a try?"

But the look on Doom's face was neither the enthusiasm Fodder craved nor the reluctance he feared. Instead it was one of intense thoughtfulness.

"If you folks will forgive me," he said gently, "I think you've gone into this wrongheaded."

Shoulders frowned at him. "If you don't want to help, say so. There's no need to be insulting..."

"No, no, no!" Doom waved a dismissive hand. "I'm not insulting you, not at all. I can see why you're doing what you're doing—if I was in your boat rather than in mine, I'd probably be doing it too. But the thing is, you see, like I said before, The Narrative is like the theatre and I know the theatre. And what's the first rule of theatre? The show must go on."

Fodder stepped forward, eager to urge out the point before time got away from them. "What are you getting at?"

Doom sighed again. "In a show, if your wig falls off, you go on. If the scenery falls down, you go on. If you fluff your lines, you make up new ones and go on. Because as long as you do, the audience can suspend their disbelief and play along, you see. The show only stops when they can't."

"We've been trying to..."

"But you haven't, though, not really." Doom's interruption was oddly sympathetic. "Because, you see, the thing is..."

A shaft of vivid light burst down the corridor at the far end of the hall, piercing through the cracks in the giant iron-bound doors as something heavy slammed against it. Time was up.

There was nowhere to run. The other door was too far, and short of hacking through the wall of canvas behind them, there was nowhere to conceal themselves. Even as Shoulders frantically struggled to position his head in some kind of convincing proximity to his neck, as Dullard and Flirt drew their swords, one face saddened, one determined, Fodder gritted his teeth, wrapping himself up inside as best he could to keep Fodhelion at bay. Doom, his sentence stolen by circumstance, did nothing but quietly and resignedly pull on his helmet.

With a final slam, the locks shook apart. With a crack, the doors burst open in a hail of iron splinters and the hall was filled with...

Light...

The room exposed by Elder's dramatic unlocking of the citadel doors seemed more to Erik like a cavern than a hall, a vast chamber of dark stone carved with horrors from every age that...

"Erik!" Elder's voice cut into his astonished musings forcefully. "We don't have time to daydream about the scenery!"

"Goodness me. They're learning."

Still wrapping his love protectively in the cradle of his arm, Erik felt Islaine stiffen like a corpse, her gasp of indrawn breath a thing of purest shock as she raised her head from its resting place against his chest to turn and slowly face the room before them. He saw her eyes widen and her cheeks blanch as her body began to tremble.

"It can't be..." she whispered desperately.

And following her gaze, Erik felt his own blood turn to ice. For how could such an assemblage be before them? How could that man be standing there and daring to breathe when he had himself witnessed his grisly demise? True, his face and clothes were scratched and battered, his whole body smeared with some kind of strange green slime, but his very intactness was a vile affront to Erik's senses.

"Tretaptus!" he gasped, for the mad prince of Mond it was! "You live! And..."

For his company was no less extraordinary. A bizarre figure, a soldier of Sleiss, capered to the mad prince's right, his hands clasped desperately around his own throat as though to strangle himself alive. Beside him, the woman who had challenged Zahora, once in chain mail but now more modestly dressed in her peasant skirt and blouse from the swamp, was watching her contorted companion with one nervous eye as the other fixed upon Erik and his companions, her beautifully wrought sword extended warily before her. And to the prince's left, conscious and apparently lucid, the mad man of Sleiss, the Ring of Anthiphion glistening on his finger and a tatty book jammed in his belt, was watching them with resolve writ large across his face. All bore the same odd greenish stains as their prince.

And standing behind them was a vast, armoured figure who made Erik's very soul feel hollow and whose mere presence turned his blood to lead.

He stared at the towering form wrapped in armour of the blackest night, his helmet wrought in the image of that same dreadful dragon that had assailed them in the mountains and...

With a casual flick of a surprisingly ungauntletted white hand, the monstrosity raised its visor to reveal a craggy face, eyes deep sunk within...

"Hello!" The interruption boomed and echoed across the vast hall, but oddly, in spite of the deep, guttural nature of the tone, the intonation of the words did not contain the violent threat that Erik felt they ought to. Indeed, the giant man's own companions were staring at him with pleasant surprise. "Sorry to interrupt, but you see, that description? It's pretty and all, but it's time-wasting. Under the circumstances, getting to the point might be an idea..."

"Oh, now he thinks that..." Erik heard the man of Sleiss mutter under his breath. Foul Tretaptus, who had until that moment been staring intently at the pale, drawn face of Princess Islaine as though searching for some secret there, glanced up distractedly and politely but firmly elbowed him in the arm.

"Oooh...bollocks!" The rude cry came from the man who was grasping his own throat. Erik's eyes narrowed—there was something very odd about his neck... "I...I can't... They've seen..."

"Fight it!" his female companion encouraged. "Believe in yourself, shoulders, you can do it!"

"Nooo! No, I..." Erik felt his eyes widen in horrific shock as he finally caught a proper glimpse of the man's neck, or at least the severed gap where head and neck should have met. But how, how could he be standing, speaking when his head was not attached to his body?

"Oh...arse..." With that final, inexplicable exclamation, the headless man's eyes rolled, his body crumpled, and both halves of him slumped to the ground and lay still.

"Oh dear." Mad Tretaptus gave a gentle sigh as he stepped forward and nudged the arm of the corpse with his foot. "Shoulders, it doesn't have to be this way. Fodder defied death and so can you. Just concentrate and believe. You can do this. Come on now, get yourself up..."

But Erik could only stare at this insane scene and he was not alone. Svenheid, his axe clasped in his hands, was glaring at the corpse with wild eyes, Slynder beside him with his features twisted in disgust. Zahora looked appalled, Sir Roderick astonished, Islaine sickened, and as for Elder...

Elder's blazing eyes were fixed firmly upon the monster in armour.

"Craxis!" he hissed. "For all your strange games on this day, here are your true colours for us to see! Dare I even try to probe the perverted recesses of your mind to understand why you would use your foul magic to sever this man's head here before us? What was it? A warning to us? A punishment for him? Or another of your games, a murder for your own sick amusement with no point but the suffering of others? Well, it matters not! You will not trick us with your fake smiles, foul fiend!"

The mad prince, the man of Sleiss, and the woman exchanged a long, weary glance at Elder's words. Then as one, they rolled their eyes.

"I told you." The psychotic Lord Craxis gave a sigh. "It sees what it wants to see, the narrative does. Reality doesn't come into it."

The woman shook her head. "Even though he's clearly the same bloke clank beheaded back by the river? And the same bloke who was with us in the village and who fought the dragon and who fell from the cliff with me and who lost his head again helping pull me out of the swamp monster? This is what, his fourth narrative death now—fifth if you count the rambling woods—and it's clearly always him, isn't it? All it has to do is look and see!"

"He's a disposable." There was a cold edge to the man of Sleiss's voice. "They don't look at us that closely. If they did, we'd be out of a job."

"Enough of this nonsense!" Elder's voice cut viciously through their ramblings. "I don't know why you persist in speaking in such riddles, but you, you who would call yourself Fodhelion, you have no..."

"I bloody wouldn't." The vehemence of this exclamation halted Elder's building declaration in its tracks. "Fodhelion is not my name, you got that? It was a joke, a facetious little game, but I know what you did with it and I'm not playing anymore. I know exactly who I am. I'm a disposable from humble village and there's not a drop of royal blood in me. And my name is Fodder."

"And I'm Flirt," the woman added. "Not much of a name and not really me, but it's better than *woman*, isn't it?"

The man of Sleiss—apparently called Fodder—grinned slightly. "I don't know about it not being you. You spend enough time flirting with danger."

"And let's put an end to this Tretaptus nonsense, yes?" chimed in the mad prince, ignoring as the woman fixed her other companion with a faux-steely glare. "Everyone here knows I'm really called Dullard."

Erik heard Islaine give a squeak of shock and tightened his grasp around her reassuringly. To his surprise, she tensed violently, glancing at him with a vague hint of disconcertion before casting her searching gaze back to the lanky form of her former kidnapper.

"You going to get up and introduce yourself, mate?" The woman— Flirt, as she would have herself called—addressed this bizarre remark to the headless corpse slumped at her feet. Unsurprisingly, there was no answer.

Flirt sighed. "That's Shoulders," she said with a jerk of her thumb to her dead companion. "Hopefully he'll get himself together enough to introduce himself soon."

"Introduce himself?" Sir Roderick's voice had an unnatural shrillness to it. "He is dead!"

Flirt shrugged, a grin teasing the edges of her mouth. "Yeah, for now. But he tends to get over it."

"But... Get over it?" The infuriated roar was Svenheid's. "Death is not something that can just be gotten over! Ask my two poor slaughtered brothers!"

The wo...Flirt's grin spread. "I would, if they weren't both you. Honestly, thud, you didn't even bother to change your costume."

"How dare..." Svenheid turned purple, a violent contrast to his red beard. His hands tightened around his battle axe. "Enough of this!" he screeched, an odd sound in his rumbling voice. "I'm tired of you people messing with my head! I don't feel like what's right is right anymore, and enough is enough! Time to die!"

"Truer words were never spoken!" Sir Roderick's vast broadsword swung in a threatening circle. "Let's put an end to this!"

"Or will you flee once more like cowards with your craven magic?" Zahora hissed, her twin swords whistling from their sheaths. "As you ever do!"

But the man of...Fodder was shaking his head. "We're not running away, not this time," he said firmly, with a nod to his companions. "This has to end and the dark citadel's as good a place as any for a grand finale, don't you think?"

Prince Tretaptus, he who had called himself Dullard of all things, gripped his sword more tightly but leaned his head closer to his companions. "Fodder, I don't think a sword fight is going to help matters. We need to be stopping this finale, not driving it on."

"Hear the fear in his voice!" No one could smirk like Slynder could. "They dare not fight us!"

Erik's companions were advancing now, even Elder with his staff aglow, and only the sudden, vice-like grip of Islaine against his arm kept Erik from summoning the full power he could muster and following.

"Oh, don't!" she gasped breathily. "Don't leave me! This place, these people...I feel weak and strange! There are voices in my head that whisper at my very soul! I have naught but you to cling to! Stay! Stay and protect me!"

Erik felt the strain of twin tugs at his heart, his love and loyalty for his noble companions against his adoration for his Islaine. But her beautiful eyes consumed his resistance and though he remained braced to help, he stayed where he was.

And his noble friends advanced upon the odd quartet and the corpse at their feet with inexorable tread, their eyes intent, their weapons braced, and who could stand against such bravery and...

"Drop your weapons." Stepping from the silence in which he had watched recent events, the towering figure of Lord Craxis moved suddenly forwards, easing his way between Flirt and Dullard with surprising gentleness. His voice was firm.

Sir Roderick's retort was a scoff. "You think we will simply obey you and back away? You know nothing of our..."

"I wasn't talking to you folks." Craxis's retort was vaguely amused. "Fodder, Dullard. Flirt. You need to drop your weapons. Quick as you like."

This statement surprised his lackeys as much as his enemies. Flirt in particular gave him a most deathly stare.

"You what?" she retorted.

The prince of whatever name's eyes, however, had widened in realisation. He smiled. "Oh, of course!" he exclaimed. "What was I thinking?"

And then, he tossed his sword to the floor with a gentle clang.

Flirt gasped. "Dullard!"

Craxis was watching her kindly. "Peace talks, remember?" he said easily. "You wanted a stalemate. They can hardly slaughter you in an epic fight to the death if you're not even armed. That's butchering the defenceless. It's just not done."

Fodder glanced at him at once. "He has a point," he conceded.

Flirt almost growled. "We won't have a point if we throw our weapons down!"

But she had apparently been outvoted. Fodder followed his prince's lead and dropped his weapon too. Flirt, after a breathy sigh and a glare at Craxis—who, despite his vast armour, did not seem to be wearing the gigantic jagged sword one might expect—followed suit.

But although Erik's warrior companions did hesitate in their advance at this abandonment of physical weapons, Elder, his great magical mentor, did not, his staff still aglow as he continued his stride forwards.

"Fodder, drop the Ring too!" The prince's voice sounded slightly anxious. "Quickly!"

The man of Sleiss, as was, cast an oddly forlorn glance at his greatest weapon. "But..."

"Greatest weapon!" the prince emphasised. "Drop it!"

"Oh, bloody hell!" With a huff, Fodder reluctantly pulled the Ring, that most precious and dangerous of objects, from his finger and with a distinct lack of respect, allowed it to tumble with a surprisingly straightforward tinkle to the stone slabs below. It glittered innocently.

Elder froze in his tracks. "What trickery is this?"

"No trickery," Craxis said gently. "We don't want to fight you—we want to discuss making peace. No more wars, no more fighting. We want to be friends and here's our good faith to prove it." He smiled, the expression perverse on his grim features. "So here's a little moral dilemma for you. Can you kill four peaceful and completely unarmed people in cold blood?"

"I can!"

The fervent screech was Svenheid's. Erik gasped as he stared at his noble companion, for there was some wildness in his eyes that defied reason; a desperation at all costs to rid himself of the horror before him. His eyes bloodshot, his hair tangled, and his face frenzied, he hefted his giant battle axe and with a roar, he charged.

"Svenheid!" Roderick's cry at this flagrant breach of the rules of good conduct went unheeded as the shrieking barbarian hurtled forwards with the force of a hurricane. The prince and Fodder exchanged an anxious look before they both, as one, darted to the side, away from Svenheid's path of rage with Craxis hard on their heels. But Flirt was more resilient—with a fiery look in her eyes, she lunged towards her fallen sword.

"No, you bloody don't!" she hissed.

"Naaaah!" It was too late for Flirt to grab her sword—her grasp for it missed, but though she was unable to parry the vast overhand blow that Svenheid launched, with an agile twist she did manage to dodge out of the path of the swing. Insanely, Erik heard the powerful blade slice through the air, a tearing sound almost like ripping canvas as the very hall itself seemed to shiver and ripple under the power of his blow.

"Oi!" Craxis sounded distinctly peeved. "Careful! You've ripped it now!"

But in his rage, Svenheid was beyond such scolding. Yanking his axe free of the ripped air, he wheeled angrily on the unarmed Flirt.

"You did this!" he cried frantically. "When I was Halheid, I was fine! Even Torsheid was fine!" Erik had no time to absorb this bizarre statement as Svenheid ploughed on. "But you killed them! You killed one and he killed the other and now I'm stuck like this! You did this to me, you stupid wench!"

Silence, deathly and terrible, flooded the hall like an avalanche. Why this word should have brought such horrendous, doom-laden quiet Erik could not be sure, but he heard the shocked draw of Fodder's breath, saw the prince's wince, and felt the icy cold that enveloped Flirt. In Erik's heightened state, he even imagined for a moment that he saw the headless corpse give an alarmed twitch.

Even Svenheid paused in his raging, for the look on Flirt's face would have frozen even the fiercest monster in his tracks. But then, something in her eyes bubbled up past the fire—she straightened herself, her face melting from angry to strangely resolute as she relaxed her jaw.

Slowly, somewhat wryly, she smiled.

"You know what?" she said softly. "That word really used to bother me. You know why? Because it stood for you."

Svenheid flinched at the tone behind that last word, his anger draining away to disconcertion at the sight of her expression. "Me? What did I do?"

Flirt's smile did not waver, although a hint of hardness tightened its edges. "Same as everyone else who came in the archetypal inn looking for some narrative fun, didn't you? You treated me like a thing." One eyebrow arched pointedly. "And that word was how you did it, didn't you? That word, there to grind me down into what everyone wanted me to be, dismissing me as a person and making me an object, a plaything, a bit of entertainment, good for nothing but giggling and getting brainlessly groped. Well, you know what?" She laughed softly, seemingly to herself. "You can call me *wench* if you want, try and dismiss me with it, can't you? But it doesn't matter. I know who I am and I don't care what people call me. I'm me, I'll always be me, and I know I'm nobody's wench. That name isn't me. It's just a bloody word."

Silence echoed once more in the wake of this astonishing speech. Erik saw Islaine's gaze was fixed upon Flirt with a sudden intensity, as though trying to drink in the confidence that was radiating from her and take it for her own. Zahora too was staring at this woman she had loathed with new eyes. Slynder looked vaguely uncomfortable, Sir Roderick affronted, Elder distinctly frustrated. And Svenheid...

Was staring at Flirt with round, shocked eyes, his expression, half-hidden beneath his beard, an odd conglomeration of horror and dawning realisation.

"You mean it wasn't fun?" he hoarsely whispered. "When we flirted, you didn't enjoy it? Even when I was Halheid?"

"Are you trying to have me on?" Flirt's eyes widened incredulously. "No, of course I bloody didn't enjoy it! You were rude, you were rough, and you smelled! You bruised my thighs when you slapped them! And your beard bloody reeks, doesn't it?"

Svenheid stared at her blankly for a moment. Slowly, strangely gracefully, his tree-trunk-like legs crumpled beneath him and he slumped to a sit on the floor.

"Ummm..." Flirt stared down at him in confusion, leading the gazes of the rest of the room. "No offence, but I never got the feeling you were looking for some spiritual connection, were you? What's the problem if I didn't enjoy it? Offended your masculinity, have I?"

Svenheid's eyes whipped up towards her in horror. "My...masculinity?" he breathed anxiously. "I..." He swallowed hard, closing his eyes for a moment as he apparently struggled to gather his thoughts. "It isn't only now," he whispered, half to himself. "It was Halheid too. And the others. I thought it was some strange enchantment cast by the man of Sleiss but it's not. It's always been there."

"What has?" Zahora's voice cut into the strange scene and the sound of her voice triggered some odd spark of realisation in Svenheid's eyes. "What is this madness?"

Svenheid shook himself, struggling to articulate the source of his distress. "I just...the thing is..." He paused again, chewing his lip, almost seeming to try and bite back what he was saying. But it failed and the words escaped.

"I didn't enjoy it either. In fact...I hated it."

The latest bout of silence was so desperately profound that it rang against Erik's ears like a peal of bells. He stared in virulent shock at the form of his barbarian companion, he whose masculine bravado with women had encapsulated his personality. Zahora, for whom Erik had some time ago suspected that Svenheid had harboured feelings, looked no less taken aback. But oddly, shocked as she seemed, she did not look surprised.

"But that's what a barbarian does!" The exclamation that burst from Svenheid's lips shattered the silence into pieces and spoke aloud the thoughts of those around him. "Barbarians flirt with women! They slap them on the thigh and kiss them and drag them off for some fun! That's the barbarian way! So why can't I enjoy it? I was doing all the right things!" There was an anxious note to his breathing now. "I did everything I could to be a proper barbarian. I made sure I always stared at their breasts, trying to muster up...something! I slapped and snogged and groped like I should! And I thought...I thought as long as the women enjoyed it, that was good! I was doing it right and I didn't need to worry that I...that I..." He dragged in a desperate gulp of air.

"That I wasn't feeling a thing."

"Svenheid, stop!" Elder's commanding voice thrust itself into the moment. "Enough of this nonsense! Take up your axe and rejoin your companions and ponder no more on these strange—"

"Oi, shut up!" Fodder's somewhat less grandiose injection nonetheless halted Elder's speech. "Let him speak! Let him get this off his chest and stop trying to drag him back into character! He needs this!" He turned to Svenheid, with an odd sympathy for this enemy written on his face. "Go on, thud," he said more gently. "We're listening. Find what's yourself and tell us. Believe it."

"It's all about the beard, you see." There was a distant quality to Svenheid's voice now. "When you're a barbarian, the beard represents everything we stand for, masculinity, rough and tumble, violence in war and fervour in lust." He sighed once more. "Maybe I've been hiding behind my beard for too long. And, lately...well, not only lately, but I've not let myself see it until now. Those feelings I should be having for women..." His eyes drifted up, his head twisted as his gaze raked slowly from Erik, to Sir Roderick, to Slynder, noticeably skipping Zahora altogether. "I've found I feel them...elsewhere..."

Erik felt a tingle of sudden discomfort as he recalled the number of times in the last few days when Svenheid's eyes had lingered on him or Slynder or Roderick for a few moments longer than had felt appropriate for chummy companionship. The long, disconcerted look exchanged by Slynder and Sir Roderick suggested he wasn't the only one having these recollections.

Svenheid must have seen their expressions as he pulled himself to his feet, abandoning his axe as his gaze swept his male companions apologetically. "And I'm sorry to you all, but I had to know if I was right and the only way was..."

"So this is why you reject me?" Zahora's harsh words cut away his apology. "This is why you have pushed me aside and slighted and ignored me in spite of our chosen destiny?"

Svenheid shuffled his feet like a scolded child. "I tried not to. But I don't know, the last few days it didn't feel...right anymore."

Zahora's expression defied description. "So I am pushed aside for...them?" She gestured disdainfully at Slynder, Roderick, and Erik.

"Not them specifically." Svenheid kept shuffling. "Just, you know...men."

"Men?" There was a shrill, tremulous note to Zahora's voice now. "But we are destined! It is meant to be, it has long been meant to be, and now you tell me...men?" She almost howled. "It is not to be borne! Am I to be so humiliated, so abandoned, so rejected, so..."

"Hang on, though." Flirt's voice intruded upon Zahora's frustrated lament. "Did you really, you know, want him?"

Zahora's eyelid twitched. "That is beside the point!"

Flirt's returning look was cynical. "Is it, though?"

"We were destined!" Zahora screeched.

"And you're off the hook," Flirt retorted easily. "I'd be celebrating, myself." She sighed. "The thing is, I've always thought that if I had my narrative choice, I'd love a job like yours. But the only drawback is they never let the warrior woman just be a warrior woman without hooking her up to some hairy brute like him. I'd take the escape you've been handed and run with it, wouldn't I?"

"Escape? When I am rejected so humiliatingly before my romance has even begun..."

Flirt's expression hardened. "You haven't had to get up close and personal with him yet," she said, somewhat coldly. "I have. You've got a way out, which is more than I ever got. Be grateful."

Zahora met her longtime battle rival's stare for perhaps the first time and Erik could see the dawning realisation on her face of what the life of this counterpart of hers had been. Her eyes widened slightly. "Oh," she said quietly.

In his arms, Erik could feel Islaine's tension straining against his body. As she watched the two women, she glanced at him, something strange within her gaze.

It was then that Erik noticed Sir Roderick, who was shaking his head slowly in disbelief at this strange turn of events. His expression was strained.

"This is not how it should be," he was muttering to himself. "This is not how it should be..."

Svenheid was looking nervously at his companions. "I'm sorry I've upset everyone," he said quietly. "But I've been carrying this for so long and I..."

"Enough!" Elder's violent roar shattered Svenheid's quiet statement; with a ruthless slash of his staff, he thwacked the apologetic barbarian roughly over the head and sent him tumbling to the floor, knocked cold.

"Elder!" Slynder's cry reflected the shock of all concerned. "What are you doing?"

"We will have no more of this!" There was a wildness to the sorcerer's gaze now, a frantic desperation, as there had been on Svenheid's face before his confession had brought him peace. "This is a trick! A distraction from our mission! Our enemies try to deceive us!" He cast a deathly glare at Craxis and his lackeys, lurking together by the strangely ripped air. "They may have parted themselves of earthly arms, but the strange, invisible arts of Craxis are here at hand, meddling in the mind of our noble Svenheid, trying to dissuade us from our necessary task!" He gritted his teeth, bearded chin hardening. "They have invaded his thoughts—what choice did I have but to fell him before he turned on us? And I know it is distasteful to us when they have thrown their weapons down, but they will pick them up again without question if we leave them the means to do so! For what need have they of physical arms when they can contort our minds? I'm so sorry to ask this of you, my fine companions. But armed or not, we must advance! The unnatural fiends must die!"

Craxis gave a sigh. "Now, here we are," he said with resignation. "I can see the peace thing was a good idea, but like I said, the show must go on. I really think the best thing would be to..."

"Pick up our weapons?" Flirt interrupted pointedly. "Before they slaughter us?"

For Sir Roderick, at least, had felt the fire of Elder's call, stepping forward with his broadsword raised. Erik too could not resist it, the necessity of the destruction of these weird tricksters pressing upon him as he eased his way out of the startled Islaine's embrace and reached for his short sword. But Svenheid's motionless bulk held the attention of

Zahora and Slynder as the pair exchanged a wary, uncomfortable glance.

"Elder, I don't know that we should..." Slynder started tentatively, but the sorcerer's glare dried up his words.

"Attack!" Elder screeched. "Now!"

Slynder sighed as he reluctantly grasped his knives. Zahora reached unhappily for her swords beside him. Erik, his own weapon raised, began to reach within himself, summoning his powers to enhance the blade as he...

"So you would slaughter the defenceless then? Is that what you have become? You who claim to be worthy of my love?"

The voice cut to the very depths of Erik's soul like a knife. Agonised, he turned to find his beloved Islaine striding to catch up with him, her eyes fierce but her voice alight with disbelief, sorrow, disappointment, even disdain, throbbing into the air as though to crush his soul to powder. With a swish of her purple skirts, she swept in front of him and his companions, hands resting on her hips as she faced them resolutely.

"I will not permit this!" she declared, her expression rich with dismay at their lack of chivalry, and her anguish did indeed halt their unworthy advance in its tracks. Both Slynder and Zahora, looking almost relieved at this moral excuse not to continue, sheathed their weapons and stepped back towards Svenheid's unconscious form as Elder and Roderick reluctantly and frustratedly ceased also. "For your own sakes, how can you even consider such butchery in cold blood? Are the finest heroes of these lands come to this?" Her eyes shifted to Erik, although, strangely, she seemed unwilling to meet his eyes and fill his world with her beauty. "My truest love would not behave like this."

"You urged us to attack them at the swamp!" Erik exclaimed, trying to conceal his confusion and despair.

"I was not in my right mind! One who shared my soul would understand that!" Her breath hitched painfully. "You disappoint me."

It was as though she had plunged a dagger into the depths of his heart. His Islaine, disappointed in him? She, who was his universe, whose love made him whole and pure, had found him wanting? How could this be? How could he live with himself if this were so?

He had to make things right. He could not bear it if he did not.

"My Islaine!" He stepped forward, his voice passionate as he rested his hands against her delicate shoulders. To his dismay, she still did not meet his eyes and stiffened at his touch. "I would not wish to disappoint you, not for all the world! You who are the radiance that lights my life!"

"You would stain that radiance with blood!" Islaine was shaking now, seeming to fight with herself to keep her chin down, her eyes lowered from his pleading face.

"Never!" Gently, Erik reached out, cupping her porcelain chin with his fingers and tenderly lifting her face towards his. "But sometimes in the name of a greater good, small evils must be done! You are my conscience, Islaine, my guiding light; but for the sake of our kingdoms, this has to end. You must see that."

Still, she would not meet his gaze, her eyes fixed downwards. "I...understand this has to end."

"Please look at me." Erik threw his heart and soul into those four words and, to his joy, she could not resist so much love—her eyes lifted and met his, her lips curled into a reluctant smile. Erik could feel her soul melding once more into his and, unable to help himself, he leaned forwards and with warm passion pressed his lips to hers.

For a moment, she tensed in shock at this touch, but then he felt himself melt against her, losing himself in the glory, sharing all that he was with her in this most precious of instants. He felt her hands grasp his arms, felt her lean closer, pull him nearer, felt the rustle of her skirts against his hose and...

The pain was so vivid and so sudden that Erik barely managed to register it before he felt himself crumple, staggering back from Islaine, his hands clutching his suddenly agonised groin as he slumped to the floor with a whimper that longed to be a scream. Even as he writhed on the floor, hands clasped protectively over his wounded manhood, he saw Islaine, his Islaine, lower the sharply risen knee that had driven him downwards as she gagged and spluttered, wiping her fingers across her chin, her features twisted in disgust.

"Slobber!" she hissed in revulsion. "I hate slobber! Dear lord, it's like kissing the family dog!"

Bewildered, shocked, and in some considerable pain, Erik stared up at his beloved, as did the rest of the room, managing to outstretch one plaintive hand as he yearned to understand.

"Islaine!" he gasped. "My love! I..."

Islaine's gaze snapped down to face him, her eyes burning with some strange conflict, seeming torn between reaching back to him and kicking him in the gentleman's region for a second time.

"Oh, do shut up!" she retorted with uncharacteristic ferocity. "Both of you!"

Erik blinked. Both? But no other had spoken! What could she mean by...

"Now listen to me, you planted harpy!" Islaine's eyes, no longer on him, were instead burrowing with a violent intensity into the floor. She stood alone, her fists clenched against her sides, her shoulders trembling with tension and her face strained.

"I am not his love! I will never be his love! I don't even like him! That's all you and you're not me!" Her eyes wheeled back towards Erik. "You hear me? I don't love you, bumpkin! Before this, you didn't even really like me! So this isn't going to happen!" Her gaze fixed upon his yearning hand. "And stop waving that thing at me! I just saw where it's been!"

Erik could only stare in confusion as the love of his life changed before his eyes, ranting at him and dismissing their indisputable feelings in a mad tirade.

"But...why?" he managed to rasp out. "Our love is eternal! Why do you say such things? Why say you do not love me?"

Islaine stared at him with distaste. "Why would I love you? You're a self-important, self-deluded, brainless little boy! Your breath smells like clank's armpits and your armpits smell worse than your breath! I would sooner marry a dead hedgehog than spend the rest of my life with you! Oh, you think you're something special with that planted heroism and since urk's ramped up your maturity, with that floppy blond hair and those pert features and those grafted-on muscles you kept squeezing me with; don't think I didn't notice you took every chance for a grope when we were on horseback together! Regal, my pert royal behind! Underneath all the physical improvements, bumpkin you are and bumpkin you will always be. Handsome comes and goes but it's nothing next to being kind."

Recovering slowly from his shock and his injury, Erik managed to stagger to his feet, reaching for his troubled beloved desperately.

"You are confused again," he breathed. "My love, they have interfered with your mind! Dearest Islaine, you know not what you say..."

But Islaine slapped his words away with ruthless fervour. "I know exactly what I damned well say! And you know what else? Stop calling me by that name! I am not bloody Islaine!" She turned her furious gaze towards the heavens, but her eyes were screwed tight shut. "I'm not you, you imaginary bitch! I'll never be Islaine again! I'm myself, do you hear me? And my name is PLEASANCE!!!"

Pleasance, pleasance, pleasance, pleasance...

The word echoed around the vast hall, dancing from wall to wall as though to mock Erik's stunned heartbreak. He could feel everything he cared for crumbling, feel his world break into dust, and he desperately rallied his vast love as he reached once more for his poor, confused Islaine, frantic to make this one last chance count, to make her realise that she was being duped, that they were meant to be together; and as he watched her, eyes open now as she lowered her head, he could feel her fighting to turn to him, to abandon her maddened rantings and return to his arms where she belonged and yes, her head began to turn to him, her eyes rising to meet...

"That's it! Enough is enough!" Tearing her gaze away from Erik, Islaine turned sharply on her heel...

"It's Pleasance! Get it right!"

...and, insisting on being called by her own odd new name, she marched over to where her former captors were huddled, watching her with wide but happy eyes. In particular, the prince, Dullard as he now called himself, was staring upon the woman he had tried to force to love him with distinct joy, his face awash with relief, with nervous hope and satisfaction and with a strange tenderness that seemed out of place on the features of such a madman. And indeed, this expression did not waver, switching only slightly to confusion in the final strides as the princess marched right up to him, grasped the front of his doublet in one delicate hand, yanked him close, and kissed him.

Even acknowledging his own horrified disgust at this sight, Erik had to admit that, initially, the kiss did not seem to be going that successfully. Dullard had clearly been caught by surprise by this affectionate assault and, given the vast impediments of his nose and chin, it took several moments of clumsy manoeuvring for both parties to get comfortable and into the swing of things. But they persisted anyway and after a few more harmonious-looking moments, they gently parted.

Pleasance stared up at Dullard. Dullard stared down at Pleasance. Both blinked.

A look of nervous apology crept across the prince's features. "That wasn't very good, was it?" he offered awkwardly.

Pleasance smiled at him fondly, wrinkling her nose as she shook her head. "Not really, no."

Dullard sighed. "I'm terribly sorry I made such a mess of it, but as I'm sure you must realise, I've never really had much of a chance to practice." He bit his lip in mild embarrassment. "Or...any, really."

But Pleasance was still smiling at him, warmth radiating from her features in a way that had never happened for Erik. She snuggled against his side and patted him affectionately on his chest. "Oh, don't worry. You weren't hopeless; we can work on it." Her smile turned a touch cheeky. "I know how good you are at picking up new skills."

The prince's face ignited with a fervent blush. "I... Goodness..." He swallowed hard. "But I mean...Pleasance, are you sure about this? About...us? I mean, I'd like...of course I'd very much like...but I don't want you to do anything you might regret and..."

Pleasance actually laughed. "Oh, stop worrying and relax, will you? Didn't you realise that insulting someone repeatedly and biting their nose is a sign of affection?" Dullard smiled at that and to Erik's amazement, he could see the depths of the prince's feelings reflected in that smile. "If you're really sure..."

"Completely." Pleasance rested her head on his shoulder with a satisfied grin. "You're kind, you're clever, and you care. You keep me myself and loving you for that is the one thing I'm certain makes me different from Islaine. And most important of all…"

And then suddenly her gaze turned to Erik, meeting his eyes with a vivid confidence. Within her suddenly hard and pointed stare, he found no trace of his beloved Islaine whatsoever.

"You don't slobber," she said firmly. "That kind of thing matters to a girl."

Erik felt his world tumble away. He staggered backwards in desperate shock at the sight of his glorious beloved locked in the arms of that foul, terrible, ugly fiend. Sir Roderick too was staring at his noble mistress in appalled shock, the facial twitch Erik had earlier noticed growing ever more pronounced.

"What is this…insanity?" he breathed desperately.

Elder's face was one of pure, indignant rage as he caught Erik by the arm, all that kept him from falling in shock. But they could only watch, bound by dreadful morals not to attack the unarmed as the awful pantomime unfolded. Flirt was patting Pleasance almost proudly on the shoulder.

"Welcome back," she said wryly. "Never thought I'd be glad to see you, but here we are, aren't we?"

Pleasance cocked an eyebrow at her. "I could say the same about you. I might even concede to being glad to see Shoulders, especially since he's definitely at his best silent." In the depths of Erik's bewildered grief, he yet again let himself believe for a moment that the headless corpse slumped on the ground had twitched.

Fodder was also beaming at the princess. "And that was beautifully done," he added, gesturing to Erik's limp, grief-stricken state. "The stuff that dreams are made of!" He turned his face towards the cavernous roof of the vast hall. "What are you going to do now, then, hmm?" he shouted inexplicably towards the ceiling. "No more kingdom-inheriting love interest for bumpkin! Where does that leave your happily ever after?" He grinned cheekily. "Want to call it quits now? That way we can have a little chat."

Although the words tumbled into his brain, Erik found he was only half-registering them and could certainly not grasp whom Fodder thought that he was talking to. He could feel himself freefalling in a spiral of despair for Islaine, oh Islaine, she was gone and this strange Pleasance had stolen her form and taken her love to that monster Tretaptus or Dullard or whatever. What strange arts had he used to warp her mind, to believe herself another person...

"Erik!" As it ever was, it was the powerful, immutable, unswayable voice of Elder that cut through his musings and roused him, shaking him roughly by the shoulder he grasped. "Do not slump there in defeat like a coward! You are the heir to the greatest powers of the universe! Can you not see what this is? Your Islaine has not forsaken you..."

"I assure you, she has." Pleasance's cool intrusion did not stem Elder's latest attempt to try and drive them into action.

"It is Craxis, don't you see?" the sorcerer ploughed on fervently. "He has used his mind-bending powers to try and dissuade us from our task, first by...confusing Svenheid and now by warping the mind of your love into a sick infatuation for his lackey! He fills us with doubt and confusion—for have you ever seen noble Slynder and proud Zahora retreat from a fight before?"

He glared viciously at the pair in question, still lurking by Svenheid's unconscious form, Slynder carefully leaning down to check the state of the large welt growing on his barbarian companion's temple. Zahora, however, returned his glare.

"I have never seen you strike one of your own!" she retorted harshly. "What does he do to your brain, old man, to make you act so abominably?"

"You've turned on one of us." Erik had never seen Slynder look so serious before. "You've broken the cardinal rule of companionship. How can we be sure you will not turn on the rest of us?"

Elder swore appallingly, a sound Erik had never before heard from his noble lips. "See how he erodes their minds with distrust!" he screeched. "Do you not see as I do that this has been his plan all along? These lackeys of his have played his game, provided extensions to his powers as they have used their strangenesses and mind games to confuse us and drive us from our destined path! We must fight against this madness, we must rise up and defeat..."

"Now I do hate to say *I told you so*..." His huge hands extended apologetically before him, Lord Craxis turned to face his servants with a wry shake of the head. "But here we are again. I appreciate what you're doing and I can see your logic, but carrying on like this? It isn't going to work."

Ignoring Elder, who was spluttering furiously at this further interruption, Craxis turned to Fodder, who was staring at him with a mixture of confusion and curiosity.

"But it is working!" the man of Sleiss protested. "Look at them, they're in disarray! The narrative's losing control of them, it's..."

"Irrelevant." The word dropped with the force of a falling star. "Because Elder's explained it away. It's me and my mysterious powers. Whatever happens now, whatever you or they do, it can be explained as my evil enchantments messing with their heads. Heck, we'll probably turn out to be hallucinations, eh? Just like that bunny of mine."

Fodder's expression tightened. "But if we keep trying, keep pushing them..."

"I did try to tell you this earlier, but now do you see?" The lord of all evil continued as though he hadn't spoken. "It doesn't matter what you change and how you twist the story. The narrative will always find a way to justify it and carry on in the end." He shook his head slowly. "I'm sorry, Fodder. But I don't think what you want can be done."

There was a long silence. Even Elder's exhortations to attack seemed to have been stilled by the strange power of Craxis's inexplicable statement; and with Zahora and Slynder reluctant, Svenheid unconscious, Roderick in a tangle of bewilderment, and Erik himself only able to blankly listen over the numbness of his broken heart, no one made any move to attack as Fodder, Flirt, Dullard, and the enchanted Pleasance stared at their master with expressions of dawning comprehension on their faces.

"You know, squick said something similar to that," Fodder stated slowly. "He said we could change the details but the narrative would always adapt."

Craxis nodded. "He's a canny little beggar, is squick. Been around the block more times than anyone. He's always worth listening to."

Erik saw an oddly disconcerted expression flit across Flirt's face at this statement. She frowned thoughtfully.

But Fodder's gaze was even more distant, lost in faraway thoughts. "Wait a minute..." he muttered almost to himself. "I always reckoned we'd have to break the quest to stop the narrative. But what if...what if we haven't broken the quest because the quest is too much in our heads? Whatever I've tried, I stayed a part of the story—I even let them make me their villain for a while! I thought I was thinking outside the quest but I wasn't outside it at all." He turned suddenly to his companions. "We've been going about this all the wrong way."

Pleasance gave an incredulous snort. "Now you decide this? After all you've put me through?"

Flirt was staring at him. "But we have to break the quest to stop the narrative. It's the only way to..."

"Breaking the rules within a quest won't break the quest itself!" Fodder was highly animated now. "It's only going to change its direction. I mean, look at how we've done this—we've played this exactly as we would if it was a narrative plot. We've formed ourselves a merry band." Fodder swept his hands along the line of his friends, dipping to even include the slumped corpse. They exchanged oddly uncomfortable glances at this strange description of their company. "It's a bloody unconventional one, but that's what we are. I never meant to, but I've cast myself as the oppressed rebel taking on a mighty, all-powerful, and unseen foe that cannot possibly seem to be defeated. I've acquired powerful, unexpected magic in the form of a quest object..." He gestured to the Ring, glittering next to the heap of discarded weapons. "And you a fancy sword..." His finger flicked towards Flirt's impossibly beautiful stolen blade. "And we've won battles against impossible odds, fought off the unseen foe's henchmen, had narrow escapes and wild adventures. Doesn't that sound familiar?" He switched his gaze to where Dullard and Pleasance were still pressed closely side by side. "You two have even accidentally given us the traditional antagonistic relationship!"

"Ummm…" With tentative diffidence, Dullard raised his hand. "I would like to point out that I was never antagonistic."

"I was," Pleasance chimed in fervently.

"Do you see what I'm saying?" There was an odd plea to Fodder's voice now. "Peace talks, changes of heart and character, even death—it can be written around. We've been playing to the Taskmaster's rules and our Taskmaster's been doing this a lot longer than we have. Playing along with the story, however much we twist it, is never going to work. There's only one thing that will."

Dullard was watching the man of Sleiss shrewdly, eyes narrowed in thought. "Are you saying what I think you're saying?" he said carefully.

Fodder exchanged a long look with the prince, a look of shared comprehension, before turning to Craxis, whose smile was oddly gentle on his heavy-browed face.

"You think you've found a way?" the dark master of evil said with a nod.

Fodder nodded. "I do. I think we should stop playing along. Completely."

Pleasance was staring at both prince and man of Sleiss with crinkled brow. "Stop playing?" she repeated. "What on earth does that mean?"

"He means go on strike, doesn't he?" There was an expression of grave apprehension on Flirt's face. "Stop talking, stop interacting with the narrative or anyone in it. Sit down and ignore it all."

Craxis nodded. "The show can't go on if the actors won't act."

"Sit there? That's your plan?" Pleasance's voice rose an incredulous octave. "Sit there while my erstwhile companions slaughter us in cold blood? Because, in case you hadn't noticed, magus seems to have left Elder's conscience about cold-blooded murder at the gates! Even if we stop, what about the merry band?"

But Erik could see a light in Fodder's eyes that hadn't been there before. "No, I think this could be it. The only way!"

"Fodder, I don't know about this, do I?" Flirt's intervention was nervous. "I spoke to squick earlier and he said we had to keep things going or it'd end up like quickening again. What if this is what he meant?"

"But that's good! Quickening is what they're afraid of!"

"Yeah, but personally? I'd prefer not to invoke some mysterious disaster unless I know what it is! Plus, squick was very clear that being in narrative when it happened was a bad idea."

"But if we just—"

"Oh, for the love of all that's holy!" Sir Roderick's angry bellow cut away the strange conversation. "Elder, for pity's sake! Why are we standing here as if useless cowards letting them jabber like old women about nonsense? Why can't we butcher them?"

Lovesick and bewildered as he was, Erik had been depending on Elder's grasp on his shoulder, and when it was yanked away abruptly so that the sorcerer could wheel on their knight companion, he found himself staggering. As he turned towards his erstwhile support, he saw that the greatest sorcerer of their age was shaking with frustrated rage.

"You think I haven't been trying?" he screeched, his voice sounding oddly normal with the sudden loss of its usual booming intonation. "I've been driving and driving to get on with this and every bloody time something gets in the way! We're the merry band, we're the root of all that's good, we're supposed to feel sad and regretful even when killing murderous psychopaths! Do you know how hard it is to work past that?" He drew a furious breath. "And of course, it would be about all that's left of this stupid narrative—I can hardly feel a damned thing to guide me anymore, I don't even know if we're supposed to attack or not, I don't know what I'm doing! But still I've been trying my heart out and what do I get? Our barbarian decides he fancies men! Our thief and our warrior woman decide to wuss out of the rumble!" Zahora's angry gasp and Slynder's huff of resentment were ignored. "And now our hero gets rejected by our princess deciding she'd rather love the freak who hit his face on every branch when he fell out of the ugly tree!"

"Hey!" Pleasance's indignant screech, unusually, was lost to Elder's rage.

"So, what's your bright idea, hmm?" He hurled the words at Roderick. "What do you suggest we do, O brains of the outfit? What's your master plan?"

With his teeth gritted furiously, Roderick wrapped his hands frantically around his broadsword. "We charge them and kill them!"

"Yeah, that worked so well for Svenheid." Slynder's drawl cut coolly across the argument. "Break it to me gently, Roderick—is it me or Erik you've been yearning to cuddle up to?"

In the fervour of the argument, a true argument between companions that Erik never thought would be possible, the air around them started to feel strange, harder, colder, as though the very atmosphere was fleeing in horror at this breakdown of companionly fortitude. He tried to shake the odd feeling off but it tickled at his skin, almost seeming to tighten against him.

"You impudent wretch!" Roderick was seething. "I should carve your bones like a butchered hog if we had not so long ridden together!"

Zahora scoffed. "Oh, do try. You never did practice enough. Without guidance, you'd probably trip over your own spurs!"

"Stop sniping at each other!" There was a desperate edge to Elder's voice. "This does no bloody good!"

"And what will?" Slynder snapped back. "What the hell are we supposed to do when the narrative gives us nothing?"

"We do what we started this to do!" Worked up into a blazing rage, Sir Roderick swung his gaze and his blade to the watching and distinctly amused-looking cluster of their enemies, although their expressions did waver at the twisted look upon his face. "We kill the threat!"

He wheeled like a metal tiger towards the slightly alarmed-looking enemy, although there was a sudden, oddly thoughtful look on Fodder's face. "This is their fault, all of it! They've spoiled everything! They have tortured us, tormented us, ruined our noble ride with their foul vendetta!" He began to advance now, teeth clenched, eyes virtually whirling in their sockets as his knuckles, grasped to his sword hilt, turned white. Erik saw Flirt's hand twitch towards her sword.

"No!" Craxis hissed. "If you touch the weapons, you'll be playing along!"

"So, what do you suggest? Stand here and get repeatedly

murdered? Get chopped into bits so they can throw our remains in the fire?" Flirt hissed right back. "He's not looking much burdened by morals right now, is he?"

"No, he's losing it!" Fodder joined in the hissing. "And if the whole band lose it, maybe, just maybe..."

"The world will tremble when it learns their fate!" Sir Roderick ignored their words, too intent upon his tirade. "I shall chop them into fragments and feed their innards to my dog! I shall hand what pieces are left of them to strut to face the fire that will cleanse the world of their villainy forever! They shall rue the day they victimised us in our innocent desire to obey, that they so unfairly persecuted..."

"You what?"

It had seemed to Erik that this situation had little scope to get much stranger. As it turned out, he was wrong.

For from its position on the ground, the decapitated head of the corpse earlier addressed as Shoulders was glaring at Sir Roderick with the fiercest, most indignant fury that Erik had ever beheld.

And then, even as he stared at this bizarre sight in shock, one arm of the slumped body rose slowly, tremulously, as though fighting some desperate urge to lie still in death, before slapping its hand down upon the ground with resolute fervour. The second arm followed, smoother than the first as the corpse's elbows bent and pushed the torso slowly up to sitting. Legs twitched, curled, and braced the booted feet attached against the ground, the corpse bending sideways to slap one hand forward and push its bottom up into the air. With an awkward stagger, it stumbled to its feet, reaching down to scoop up the fallen head, before wheeling on the furious-but-now-also-perplexed form of Sir Roderick.

"You metal git," the head snapped. "You arrogant, head-chopping, self-obsessed bastard! Us persecute you? You don't know a damn ruddy thing about persecution! You know what persecution is? Let me tell you what it is!" With a furious grimace, the corpse thrust its own decapitated head into the air. "This, this is persecution! Every time, every single bloody, messy, stupid time I have fought you for the last six quests, you have chopped my head off!"

Erik, along with Elder and the rest of their company, was staring at the animated corpse with blank, resigned shock. The corpse's own companions, however, seemed delighted with his sudden rise. Indeed, Fodder, observing their shock as well as his companion's apparent resurrection, looked distinctly satisfied.

But Sir Roderick, at whom the dead man's ire was aimed, was watching the bizarre spectacle with growing indignation.

"What are you doing?" he screeched. "You are a headless corpse! You shouldn't be standing up!"

The corpse smirked at him grimly. "You're absolutely right, bloody shouldn't, should I? Everything this light's got left is telling me to lie down and shut up. But you know what?" He snarled the words. "I am sick of being overlooked and ignored and pushed around and killed! You hear me?" As several of his companions had before, he appeared to address his remarks to the very sky. "And if you think I can stay silent and dead and ignore it while you, you who have made my every narrative experience a misery for quests now, moan on about being sodding persecuted, you can bloody think again!"

Sir Roderick was staring at him incredulously. "I was doing my job, you stupid peasant!" he retorted fervently. "You were there for me to kill; that was the point!"

"But you didn't have to go for the head, did you?" was the sharp response. "You didn't chop anyone else's head off every single time, did you? No, you always, always, always went for mine because you knew I didn't like it! That's a ruddy vendetta, that is! It was deliberate, try and deny it!"

"Why should I deny it?" Sir Roderick drew himself up furiously. "You insulted me to my face! You called me a pillock!"

The head snorted. "You are a bloody pillock!"

"I am no such thing!" Roderick screamed. "I am a principal! I am the knight of this realm! I am the highest of the high, the noblest of them all! And to be insulted by the likes of you, common disposable gutter scum!" He gave a near-hysterical peal of laughter. "Why should I not seek retribution? It gave me great satisfaction...nay, great amusement to see your foul-featured head fly from your grotty body every time my sword crossed your path. You who speak to me thus when you are nothing, a commoner who should know his place, why should it not be so? I have the right to do so if I choose!"

The headless corpse stared at him, his face filled with indignation at this rather unworthy speech. And, with a twitch against his fingers, his jaw hardened.

"Flirt?" he called out grimly.

"Yeah, Shoulders?" The woman was at his side instantly. Erik noticed that in spite of Craxis's earlier insistence, she had picked up her sword.

"Swap you." With a tight grin, Flirt accepted custody of the head, holding it carefully up to allow a clear, sweeping vision of the room. In return, her beautiful sword was passed into the corpse's hands.

"One has armed himself!" There was a shrill, desperate note to Elder's voice. "Now at last is the time to strike! We must..."

"He's already dead, Elder." Slynder's tone was a weary drawl of submission. "What do you want us to do, kill him a bit more?"

But Sir Roderick was apparently past such considerations. At the sight of a sword in the corpse's hand, he lost his last hint of reason and, dragging his giant broadsword through the chilly, hardened air, he swung angrily, irrationally at the risen corpse before him. But the motion lacked his usual, natural fluid skill and the corpse was ready, blocking the blow easily and pushing it aside as his head grinned wildly.

"So, you think it's funny, do you?" With a straightforward, proficient swing, the corpse wielded his own sword around and delivered a vast, over-neck blow that Roderick barely staggered to stop. "Chopping someone's head off for your own sick amusement?" The next sweep slashed at his knees, clanging off his armoured protection. "Tormenting them day after day, week after week simply because you can?" Roderick stumbled as the flurry of blows bounced off his raised sword, off his armour, finally catching the side of his head and knocking his vast helmet awkwardly askew. "Just because you think you're better than me?"

With a harsh slam, Roderick's sword tumbled from his grasp as the head gave a bark of laughter, its eyes suddenly intent.

"Well, you know what, clank? Laugh this off!"

The blade swung. There was no avoiding its destination.

Sir Roderick's eyes widened in horror as he realised what was coming, but it was already too late. The blade sliced cleanly into his neck and sent his head flying neatly across the chamber.

Sir Roderick's body hesitated a moment in its upright state, before apparently deciding that it at least was going to do death-by-beheading properly. It crumpled to the floor with a vast clattering of armour and was still.

There was a shocked pause. And then...

"Oh YES!!!!!!!" With a violent scream of triumph, the headless corpse known as Shoulders dropped to his knees, tossing his borrowed and bloody sword to one side as he leaned back and shook his fists to the sky in glory. His head's expression was equally exultant, almost holy in its reverence at this apparent dream fulfilled. "Oh yes, oh yes, I did it! I finally bloody did it! Did you see his face, his smug face when I swung my sword? Did you see the way his head flew off? It was beautiful!" His features slipped towards beatific. "I've never been so happy..."

Erik was stunned. Stupefied, he stared blankly, disbelievingly at the remains of the greatest knight of the six kingdoms, of the noblest soul to walk the world, now slumped in two pieces and apparently unable to gather himself to rise as his enemy had. The odd feel to the air only grew, reflecting the horror of what had befallen another of their band. And Erik was not alone in his horrified astonishment, for Elder's mouth was agape with shock, Zahora's expression oddly irritated, and Slynder's one of weary resignation.

"Oh, bloody hell," he muttered.

Craxis, strangely, was equally stoic. However, Shoulders the corpse's companions were rather more effusive.

"About bloody time!" Flirt exclaimed as she helped him to his feet, handing him back custody of his own head. "The walking dead! Talk about the ultimate narrative defiance!"

"I'm proud of you, mate!" Fodder slapped the corpse on the back cheerily. He grinned. "That might be exactly what we needed!"

"You see, I told you!" Prince Dullard exclaimed happily. "You needed to believe you could do it!"

"It took you long enough," was Pleasance's less-than-generous addition. "But nevertheless..." Her lips quirked slightly. "I'm glad you've finally pulled yourself together. Perhaps you'll finally stop moaning about it!"

"I doubt it." Fodder chuckled. "The world hasn't ended yet."

Elder's breath was shrill as his beard vibrated beneath his trembling chin. "They...they have killed noble Roderick! A corpse, raised by foul enchantment, has slain him! We must...avenge him... We..."

"Oh, sod this." With a sigh, Slynder dropped to a sit beside unconscious Svenheid, shaking his head tiredly, as he curled his arms around his drawn-up legs. "I give up. I can't be arsed with this farce anymore."

"Nor can I." Carelessly tossing her precious blades to the ground, Zahora dropped down beside him. "There's no point in killing them if they don't stay dead! There's no point to any of this!"

"But...but..." Elder grasped Erik's arm roughly. "But we must! We must fight, the point is to fight, we..."

And it was then, into the icy, sparkling air that caressed at Erik's very skin, that the man of Sleiss turned and faced the two remaining upright members of Erik's noble company with eyes that burned like beacons.

"Really?" he said softly. "Really, you're going to keep this up? Because you must see it now, right? We're not playing along anymore and as Shoulders has shown, even killing us in cold blood won't keep us down." He shook his head gently. "We might as well sit on our arses and twiddle our thumbs, because this quest? It's over. There's nowhere left to go."

The air seemed to shudder at this awful realisation as noble company of heroes and foul band of villains alike stood opposite each other without anywhere to go or anything else to say or do. Even as Fodder slowly turned, wandering back to where his friends were gathered by the strange, ripped air, Erik found himself fighting a sick, lost kind of feeling in his stomach. He felt adrift, lost, unable to focus, unable to find where he should be and what he should do. The air closed in around him,

God, it did...

making his limbs heavy and his head pound and

Something wasn't right now, Fodder could feel it, the air felt suddenly *tight*, like a straightjacket, closing around his limbs, restricting him, and now he was *thinking*, thinking properly in spite of the

the light, the light

and it was dimming, The Narrative was *dimming* and it

seemed to flicker and

"Fodder! Fodder, what the hell is happening?"

there was nothing

Shoulders's yell was strangled, oddly muffled, and he could see Doom looking bewildered, could see a look of sudden, horrified comprehension on Dullard's face as he clutched the suddenly shrieking Pleasance closer against him and Flirt

else left

was watching him, her eyes were filled with horror and with realisation as her earlier warning about Squick's words darted into his head and suddenly she was lurching towards him through the calcifying syrup of the Narrative light, her hands outstretched and her features desperate

to do

as her hands slammed into his body, shoving him backwards through the solidifying air, tumbling with agonising slowness as he saw her face, almost frozen in a rictus of horror, her mouth forming a single gasped word.

but

"Out!"

stop.

"Oof!"

With a painful smack, Fodder felt himself slam into the stone floor of the chamber, as Flirt's shove propelled him through the rip in the canvas backdrop that Thud's axe had accidentally cleaved earlier. For a moment he could only lie, writhing and gasping, the sudden constriction that had engulfed him past but close enough in memory for the discomfort to linger. For several moments, it was all he could do to catch his breath after the thick, cold air that had choked his windpipe; but after a few moments of coughing, he found his voice and his old, Disposable instincts kicked in.

"Everyone else all right?" he managed.

There was no answer. But for the scratching of bunnies near his head, silence and stillness echoed like thunder around him.

Slowly, warily, Fodder pushed himself onto his elbows. "Flirt?" he called out cautiously. "Shoulders?"

There was still no response, not even a gasp or a moan. Cold fear began to clutch glacial fingers around his chest with the same force as the strange air from which he had been so unceremoniously hurled.

"Dullard? Pleasance?" But there came no deferent assertion, no shriek of indignation. There was nothing at all.

Slowly, painfully, and using a convenient bunny hutch for support, Fodder dragged his bruised and aching body to its feet. Blinking his strangely sore eyes, he shifted his gaze to the narrow rip in the canvas wall just beside him. The dazzling light of Narrative he vaguely expected to find creeping through the gap was gone, a strange, dimmed flicker like a dying candle in its place, glittering slightly with an icy, disconcerting sparkle that made his blood run cold. There was something familiar about the way that light danced.

But that didn't matter now. All that mattered was why his friends wouldn't answer.

Carefully, fearfully, he reached for the tear in the canvas and parted the wall.

He couldn't help but jump in shock, his eyes not fully registering the truth of what he was seeing for a second. The pair of hands thrust into his face made him startle but after a moment, it dawned that the hands were not moving, frozen in outstretched mid-thrust, glittering, and beyond them...

Fodder stared as his mouth dropped open, the true horror of what he was seeing trickling like poison into his consciousness.

"No..." he heard himself whisper.

Directly before him was Flirt. Her posture was exactly as it had been mere moments before when she had barrelled into him and hurled him backwards, arms outstretched before her, body poised in a desperate lunge, her green-stained skirt rippled, her dark curly hair flying behind her, her eyes wide. Her mouth was fixed in the last tsk of the letter T, her face wild with alarm and determination as one.

Doom, armoured and huge, was a bewildered statue to her left. Beyond him, Dullard's arms were wrapped around Pleasance, his cheek flattening her hair as she burrowed against his shoulder, her mouth locked open in a silent shriek. Shoulders was crouched beside them, his head juggled between his hands, his expression one of confused, indignant terror. And across the room, both parts of Clank and also Thud remained unconscious, motionless lumps, with Swipe beside the Barbarian, his arms curled around his legs as he stared up at the ceiling in utter confusion. Harridan was half on her feet, one sword instinctively grasped too late. Magus and Bumpkin, frozen in the act of grabbing each other's arms, reflected her horror in their expressions.

And flowing motionlessly across every inch of their bodies, moulding them into the floor like some vast, bizarre ice sculpture, was glittering, solid crystal.

And he knew. He knew right then and there exactly what had happened and he felt the pit of his stomach drop away into a yawning chasm that clawed to drag his struggling heart down too. In his mind's eye, he saw the hacked-up crystal that had coated the floor of the village hut; the glimmery, hypnotic, disturbing flower and the piece of meat; Gods, it had been crystal, crystal right down to its core...

Squick had tried to warn them. His words to Flirt, to all of them... He'd *known*...

Why hadn't he just *told* them? Why hadn't he just *said?* Fodder knew if he had only known that this was Quickening, this was the consequence of a broken Narrative, a story run out of steam, he would never in a million Quests have mindlessly pressed on...

His friends...

Guilt and horror clawed at him like an AFC on the attack, threatening to pull him down. He'd killed the Merry Band. Really, truly killed them when they'd been doing nothing but pressing on with the only way to live they knew.

And Doom too, Doom who'd wanted nothing more than to pet his bunnies and put on a show. He'd killed Doom.

And his friends...

He'd killed his friends.

Flirt and Shoulders, his friends as long as he'd known what friendship was, who'd stuck by him through thick and thin and reminded him who he was when even he had struggled to recall. Dullard and Pleasance, bright and kindly meeting fiery and vulnerable, burning bright with newfound love and a whole new world to discover together.

But this couldn't be happening. It couldn't. This wasn't the way that it was supposed to be.

What had he done? What had he *done?*

Stepping as carefully as he could onto the ice-like, slippery surface, his eyes raked over Flirt's frozen face, searching desperately for something, for anything, some spark of life, some hope.

"I'm so sorry," he breathed, the words barely shuddering past his lips. "I didn't listen. You were right and I didn't listen. Oh Gods, Flirt, I'm so..."

And then he saw it.

It was so brief, so slight, so minute, that for an instant he thought he'd imagined it. But, even as he stared intently, he saw again that briefest of motions, that tiny hint of movement.

Her eyes had moved. Slowly, awkwardly, and with great effort, but they had rolled from staring blindly straight ahead to look directly at him. She'd moved. She'd *moved.*

She was *alive!*

"Flirt?" Frantically, he grabbed both of her outstretched hands as he leaned around them into her face. "Flirt, can you hear me?"

The expression on her face didn't, couldn't change, but the eyes shifted again, slowly, painfully, but distinctly towards his new location. Whether she could actually hear him or was only responding to the sight of him, Fodder had no way to know, but she was responding and, in that instant, that was all that mattered.

"Wait here," he exclaimed, realising an instant later what a stupid thing this was to say and that she'd have clocked him for it if she could. "I'll be right back."

The crystal was worse than ice, flowing in smooth curls that offered absolutely no purchase, but after two tumbles onto his arse, he found a kind of stumbling skate that allowed him to make his way. First he checked Doom and Shoulders's juggled head. Pleasance's eyes were unfortunately screwed shut but Dullard's were open, as were those of the conscious members of the Merry Band. And in each case, it was there: brief, difficult, but distinct movement of the eyes.

Relieved euphoria bubbled into his chest as he skated to a halt in the centre of the crystal's spread. True, they were still encased in this odd substance, but the previous victims had clearly been chipped out and removed so there had to be time. Maybe if he could find a way to...

"You."

Never in his life had Fodder heard one word expelled with such utter venom. Struggling to hold his balance, he managed to turn.

Framed in the massive doorway, the stick-thin shape of Strut the Officious Courtier was staring at him with thick, unbridled hatred. His slender body was shaking like a twig caught in a hurricane.

"I hope you're proud of yourself," he hissed viciously. "You...*murderer.*"

Fodder opened his mouth to protest, but before he could speak, another voice interrupted.

"Sir?" Fodder recognised the voice of Pious the Priest as it echoed from the corridor at the foot of the shadowy steps descending behind Strut, moving closer up the hidden stairs as he did. "Sir, what's going on? Do you need—?"

"Stay there!" Strut's voice slashed out like a whiplash. "Come no further, you or any of you! Stay where you are!"

There was a pause. "But, sir..." Pious's voice replied cautiously. "I—"

"Didn't you hear me?" Strut interrupted harshly. "I want this area sealed off. No one is to come into this room! Except..." There was a brief pause. "Find Squick. I believe he is repairing AFCs down at the Gates of Wrath. Bring him and allow him in. After that, no one, not even a glance, on pain of burning! Do you understand me?"

There was a nervous silence. When Pious's voice came, it was full of bewildered fear. "Yes, sir. I understand. I'll fetch the pixie."

Carefully, deliberately, Strut turned his back on Fodder, striding to the nearest of the flung-wide iron-bound doors and grasping its enormous bulk as his weedy, whip-thin frame struggled with its weight. But after a moment, the hidden counterweight system that allowed them to be hurled open by a manfully striding Hero swung into action and first one door and then the other creaked closed. They thudded together with an ominous crunch.

Fodder made his cautious way to the edge of the crystal expanse as Strut worked. He had a feeling he'd need solid ground underfoot for this.

And Strut wheeled. His eyes were as icy as the crystal.

"Do you see now what you've done?" The fury in the Courtier's voice was only barely suppressed. "I tried! I tried everything I knew to stop you, to prevent this abomination from happening again but..."

"You threatened us, tried to lock us away, and set loose a nutter Assassin who tried to kill us!" Fodder retorted sharply. "Didn't it occur to you to just *tell* us this was what happened during *The Chalice of Quickening*?"

Strut looked distinctly taken aback. "You've heard of..." He shook himself. "It is of no matter! And when was it the place of common scum like you to know of such things?"

"So what? Another coverup?" Fodder gestured to the hurriedly closed door and the presumably confused souls behind it. "Another big secret? You think you can put everything nice and neat back in its box and pack it away? You're going to build another village, is that it?" He shook his head. "You can't hide this. You tried hard enough to hide Quickening and we found the edges of it. Too much has happened this time. People will *notice*."

"They will notice you!" Strut's anger was losing its restraint. "You, as you burn in the pyre for your heinous crimes, for the murders you have committed! No one will care about the means when they know you are to blame!"

Fodder snorted. "You want to set me on fire and you're calling me a murderer? They aren't even—"

"It is the will of the Taskmaster!" Strut's screech interrupted

Fodder's revelation. "The Taskmaster commands all who defy the instructions will perish by fire! The Taskmaster's will is—"

"Bollocks."

The crude intrusion brought Strut's rant crashing back to earth. His eyes blazed. "How dare..." he started.

"Oh, shut up." Fodder had had quite enough of yelling politely. While this idiot yammered on making excuses for himself, his friends were trapped. "You know what? I'm not holding any of this against the Taskmaster, not anymore. Because I know, that burning business? It's all Poniard. And that means the order to have us brutally murdered came from *you*."

The vague alarm in Strut's eyes was quite satisfying. *"Given* by me on behalf of the—"

"Oh, give it up!" Fodder cut into his words once more. "The Taskmaster doesn't know a damned thing about it and we both know it." He caught the Taskmaster's taskmaster's gaze and held it with steel. "You're trying to cover your own behind in case *you* end up the murderer. Aren't you, Strut?"

Strut drew himself up but Fodder could tell he was faltering. "You dare to presume to know the words of the Taskmaster? You who deny..."

Fodder didn't say another word. He didn't have to. He simply pulled Preen's battered, green-stained book out of his belt and held it up.

Strut blanched. Fodder didn't see fit to mention to him that he'd really no idea if it mentioned burning or not. In the short time he'd had it, he'd barely had time to glance at it. But he knew Dullard had and Fodder was pretty damned sure the prince wouldn't have come to the conclusions he had if there was talk of burning them to death inside these pages.

Strut's face shifted, telling Fodder at once that fresh bluster was on its way. "Do you believe that idiot Preen was privy to everything?"

Fodder gave a grim smile as another piece of their world came sharply into focus. It was as though the glittering light of the crystal had scoured his mind and got down to the core of everything. "No, but I reckon I've got your hierarchy figured out. This is all you get, isn't it?

These words, telling you what people should be doing, getting vaguer and vaguer as we messed it up. There're no real names and real locations, nothing specific to our little behind-the-scenes world because I'm not even sure our beloved Taskmaster knows any of that *exists*." He shook his head. "All of the rest of it—who goes where and when, all rules and regulations set in place for this or that position—that's you lot, isn't it? It comes from the Courtiers. The instructions guide your actions for The Narrative, but the restrictions, the class system, the personal stuff? It's all *you*. And all you have to do is say it's in the instructions and everyone believes you." He laughed, a strange, soft, weary, angry sound. "So, what the *bloody hell* gives you that *right*?"

There was an echoing silence. The crystal glittered in the limited light.

Strut had gone deathly pale, his angry bravado withered by the exposure of Quests' worth of organised deception. "You can't prove anything," he said shakily.

Fodder wafted his commandeered book casually. "Think you'll find I can."

Strut swallowed hard. "I could destroy that. You too. I'd only need to call for help."

Fodder simply smiled. "Try," he said.

Strut stared at him, a strange kind of defeat glimmering in his eyes and slumped in the set of his shoulders. "What do you want?" he said softly.

Fodder gritted his teeth. "Right now? All I want is my friends back."

A strange sadness settled over Strut's face, startlingly out of character. "That's impossible."

Fodder felt his chest constrict. "I don't believe you."

But Strut was still shaking his head. "It doesn't matter if you believe me or not. The facts are indisputable. They're dead. There's nothing anyone here can do."

"But..."

"Laddie, I'm sorry, sorrier than you can know. But he be right."

The interruption, sorrowful, haunted, and so familiar, snapped Fodder's head around. Squick the Duty Pixie hovered just inside the smaller door from which they had earlier emerged, watching him with weary misery as his eyes swept the room. How long he'd been listening for, Fodder didn't know.

"I should never have let yon lad and lass out." The pixie was shaking his head sadly as he stared from Flirt's frozen figure to that of Shoulders. "I should have left them in that damnable stockade. Mayhap they'd have been safe there after all. But that bastard Poniard was coming back for them and..." He gave a gusty sigh as his eyes drifted up to meet Fodder's. "I was trying to keep them alive, lad. All of you, always trying to keep you alive, from burning one way and this the other." He closed his eyes. "I failed you all."

Fodder blinked at the guilty-sounding pixie's despair. He had to realise there was hope, he had to see. "But, Squick..." he started, yearning to hear a different truth from a voice he actually trusted. "Their eyes..."

"Are moving, aye." The pixie swooped over to where the Disposable and the Courtier were stood, his face set with sorrow. "That be how it started before, up in yonder mountains. We had hope then too." He sighed deeply before wheeling in mid-air to face Strut. "I'm going to tell the lad," he told him resolutely. "But I'm bound by yon oath I made, sworn on their poor crystal bodies, and there be magic in an oath like that, leastways for a being like me. Old Edict, he ain't around no more to free me of it, but you've his blood in you, laddie, and you can do it for him." He smiled slightly. "If you're quite done being stupid."

Strut tightened his jaw but, to Fodder's surprise, didn't argue. "Fine, I free you."

Squick nodded in brief gratitude, turning back to Fodder, who suddenly understood why the pixie, desperate as he had seemed to warn them at times, had been so cagey.

"The Chalice of Quickening," Squick said softly. "It was a long time ago. One of yon early Quests, one of the first really." He smiled wearily. "We were still finding our feet in those days, still learning yon ropes. So, what happened—it came as a Godsawful shock." He shook his head. "Old Edict, he was the Courtier in charge back then, he spotted right from the start that something was different about this Quest. The instructions were vaguer and the ending—well, to tell the

truth, there weren't much of one at all, some random guff about a standard confrontation. Somehow, it felt like yon Taskmaster's heart weren't really in it."

He sighed deeply. "What happened, laddie, it weren't like it was with you and yorn. There was no great rebellion, no deliberate faff to stop the Quest. Yon Narrative got weaker and weaker, the actions on yon Merry Band less pronounced, more repetitive—they were running out of things to do. And, up on yon cliff one day, it just petered out. The Narrative, it flickered, it dimmed, and it *died*. And there they were, left behind, frozen in the moment it ended, the whole Merry Band. Encased in crystal."

"It just stopped?" Fodder stared at the pixie incredulously. "Why?"

Squick shook his head. "Never really knew, did we? We think the Taskmaster ran out of plot. And like I said before: for a while, we had hope. The Quest's Tome was in place in yon Outer Sanctum, down at the City Temple. We thought The Narrative would come back, mayhap revive them, and it would go on. And we could tell the Merry Band were alive at first—their eyes were moving and they were aware of us. At first, we thought they could be saved."

Fodder did not like the words *at first*. They were settling unpleasantly in his chest. "Then what?"

"Then nowt." Squick closed his eyes in brief pain. "Yon Narrative never came back. And every day, their eyes got stiller and stiller. We tried to chip them out, but the crystal was like diamond—it chipped our tools rather than t'other way around. Higgle, he built the pass and the village to hide the truth of what we were doing, in the hope it could be fixed and no one would need know. But we couldn't free them. The crystal wouldn't break." He drew a ragged breath. "Not until it were too late."

"Too late how?" Fodder was struggling to hold down the horrible panic rising once more within him. "How was it too late?"

"The Tome fell." Squick swallowed hard. "The Golden Tome should never leave its pedestal until yon Quest be done. But a few weeks after yon incident, *The Chalice of Quickening* Tome fell to yon floor unfinished and a new Tome, a new Quest, appeared in its place. That was the day the Taskmaster abandoned *The Chalice of Quick-*

ening and moved on. And those that were frozen got left behind. The crystal, it finally broke that day. But them that was trapped inside had turned crystal through and through, and there was nowt that any folk could do to help them." He drew a shuddering breath. "Even me. Poor souls."

"Word couldn't get out." It was Strut who took up the story with surprising softness. "That's always been made clear to every new generation of Courtiers. That was why their...bodies were extracted and taken to the Sanctum in secret for safekeeping. Edict knew it must be hidden—that was why he had the oath sworn upon all that remained of that poor band by those who knew the truth and concealed their disappearance with a story of isolation and intense comradeship. If people found out that this was possible—that for no reason and with no warning at all, The Narrative might *kill* them..." He shook his head. "Who would ever dare to enter it again?"

But Fodder was only half-listening. He was fighting to control the urge to shake, to scream, to be sick, to do something that could some-how relieve the cold, sickening horror that threatened to drag him down and consume him forever. They couldn't be dead, their eyes were moving, they were *alive*, there had to be some way...

But Strut and Squick knew more of this than he did. And they both seemed so sure that no one here could...

Nothing anyone here could do. Strut's words. Nothing anyone *here*...

Wheeling sharply, Fodder caught Strut's arm, ignoring the indig-nant look on the Courtier's face at his daring to take such a liberty. "You said anyone *here*. Nothing anyone *here* can do. Well, what about someone who's somewhere *else?* What about the Taskmaster?" His eyes darted to Squick. "You said it too, you were waiting for The Narrative to come back, you thought that would fix them! Would it fix them if the Taskmaster brought The Narrative back?"

Squick shook his head. "The Taskmaster *didn't*, laddie. It was a hope. I dinna know."

Strut too looked deeply sceptical. "The Taskmaster offered no help before," he injected, with a hint of his familiar disdain. "They were abandoned and the Quests moved on. Why would this time be any different?"

But Fodder was not to be dissuaded, the hope running rampant once more inside his mind, all that was keeping the swamp of horror at bay. He needed that hope. "But you both said yourself this time was different—last time, the Taskmaster just ran out of steam. But this time it was *me*—I broke it. The Taskmaster wanted to continue, but I made it impossible." He swallowed down a deep, guilty breath. But he hadn't known, if he'd have known... "If I could persuade the Taskmaster to try again..."

It was then he realised he still held Preen's book in one hand. Abandoning his grip on Strut, he shifted the rag Flirt had used to keep the book from locking again and leafed rapidly through the sticky contents, past pages and pages of ever more confused and bewildered instructions. But how did it end, he needed the end...

And there it was, the Merry Band told to storm the citadel and start a fight, things that they had failed to do, things that had not happened, breaking up into confused sentences about suddenly gay Barbarians and *what the hell* and question marks and such bewilderment until...

Oh, bloody hell. This is PANTS.

The instructions stopped at this strange sentence. Only a few rogue words, almost like afterthoughts, were scribbled beneath it...

Need to GET A GRIP on characters.
Where is this even going anymore?
Is it even worth salvaging?
What's wrong with me?
Oh, sod this.

Fodder felt his blood run cold. If the Taskmaster decided there was nothing worth salvaging, if these characters were abandoned in the name of moving on...

The real people behind them would die too.

And the Taskmaster didn't even know that.

Fodder felt an urgent desperation flood his veins. If the Taskmaster gave up on them, ignorant to the damage done, if the Tome fell and the world moved on...

Keeping the rag in place, he shut the book and tucked it back into his belt as determination flooded through him. It was what he'd always wanted really, what he knew he needed, but a part of him had wondered if it would ever be possible; and even so, he never imagined it would happen under circumstances like these. He'd never imagined that lives, genuine, to-be-extinguished-forever lives belonging to people he loved, would depend upon what he said, upon his need to have this conversation. In one way, his whole life had been leading to this, certainly the recent times, and he'd always assumed somehow that he'd have time to think, to prepare and brace himself for it. But there was no thinking and there was no time. It had to happen and it had to happen *now*.

And only one man could help him do that.

With burning eyes, he turned on Strut. "I need to talk to the Taskmaster. Now."

Strut stared at him as though he'd grown an extra head. "I beg your pardon?"

"You heard me." Fodder was in no mood for Strut's incredulity. "I need to talk to the Taskmaster, myself, directly, and you are going to take me to wherever it is I can. Now."

Strut gave a disdainful snort. "You dare to presume that..."

Fodder had had enough. Without even hesitating, he thrust out one hand, grasping the front of the Courtier's tunic and dragging his lanky frame down so as to be nose-to-nose.

"Laddie!" Squick's alarmed exclamation was ignored.

"Now you listen to me." Fodder didn't shout or bellow or scream in his face. His voice was calm and cool and so steely that it could have beheaded armies in one swipe. "Either you do exactly what I asked or I am going to march out that door and show every Servant you've ever cuffed, every Disposable you've ever disdained, every Ordinary face you've dismissed that there's not one word in the precious instructions to say that they should sit back and take that from you and yours. And then I'll find every Principal, every Interchangeable, every Narrative regular and let them know that any time it fancies, The Narrative could freeze them into crystal and steal their lives just because, beyond their control, the Taskmaster runs out of ideas." He cocked an eyebrow pointedly. "How smoothly do you think your next Quest will go after that?"

The blood drained from Strut's face like a ruptured dam. "You wouldn't dare."

Fodder pulled him closer, squashing their noses together in a weird amalgamation. "Bloody try me."

Strut was shaking. "But...it isn't even possible! No one *speaks* to the Taskmaster! Not even *me!*" He took a gasping breath. "It comes through the Golden Tome! That's all we ever get, I swear! Simply words on a page, with no way to write back! I've never spoken to the Taskmaster, no one has! I wouldn't even know how!"

And damn it, Fodder believed him. This was not an admission, he was sure, that proud, controlling Strut would have made if it were not true. But if this was the case, if there really was no way...

A walk along a riverbank in the half-lit darkness of the Magnificent City. Dullard, a newly made ally, telling him of his visit as a boy to the Sanctum of the Courtiers, the Outer Sanctum of the Golden Tome and the secretive Inner Sanctum, where only Strut and a chosen few had ever been.

"What about the Inner Sanctum?" He loosened his grip slightly on the shaking Courtier, but did not release him. "The big secret back room that only you and a few others have ever been allowed inside? What's in there?"

Strut, given some latitude to move, immediately shook his head. "I can't, it's forbidden, I—"

Fodder grimaced and tightened his grip on the man's doublet once more. *"What's in there?"* he cut him off sharply.

Strut gave a rage-riddled, fearful gasp. *"The Narrative* is!"

Fodder blinked. Of all the answers, he had not expected that one. "What?" he exclaimed. "But The Narrative's *outside*, it follows us around, it—"

"Not the light!" Strut huffed impatiently. "For the love of all that's holy, will you let me go? It's hard enough trying to explain without you shaking me around!"

Grudgingly, Fodder released his grip on Strut's doublet. The Courtier staggered a moment and shifted his weight, drawing himself up as he smoothed his much-abused silks back into some kind of order.

Fodder wasn't in the mood for prissiness. "Stop faffing and talk."

Strut shot him a venomous look but obeyed. "When you are in The Narrative, there are the *words*," he began grudgingly. "You don't see or hear them, but they are there and you *feel* them, you *know* them..."

"I know what being In Narrative's like," Fodder interrupted. "I know about the words. What does that have to do with...?"

But Strut was shaking his head. "But didn't you ever wonder what those words *were?* Or where they *came* from?"

"I..." Fodder's sentence dried up. Quite honestly, he never had given much thought to the flow of words that meandered through his head as The Narrative washed over him. That was just *The Narrative*.

Strut pressed on without bothering to wait for his question to be answered. "What happens in the Inner Sanctum while The Narrative is flowing, I do not know and cannot tell you, for no one has ever been able to pass into it at such a time. But when a Narrative is done and the Quest is over, the barrier drops away and one of us few who are permitted enters the chamber. Inside there is a closed book. And in that book are the words of The Narrative's Quest, every one, exactly as we who took part in that Quest have known them, written down and finished with. I put the book away and I leave. A new Quest begins and the barrier returns and the cycle begins anew. A new book will be wait-ing the next time a Quest is done—sometimes more than one if a Quest runs particularly long—never positioned or placed by us, simply *there*. And that is all I or anyone knows of the Inner Sanctum."

Fodder stared at the Courtier for a moment. "But who puts it there? How do the words get on the pages?"

The look on Strut's face was the most sincere Fodder had ever seen. "I don't know. We see the writing of the Golden Tome appear. But we know nothing of this."

Fodder's mind was racing. A link directly to The Narrative, to the Taskmaster's very instrument; surely that had to be the place, there had to be a way from there.

His jaw hardened. "Take me to the Inner Sanctum."

Strut rolled his eyes. "You do not listen. I told you, we cannot enter while a Quest is in progress..."

"Does this look *in progress* to you, laddie?" Squick's voice cut in before Fodder had the chance. "Let him do it. It can't hurt to try."

Strut's face contorted violently as a number of emotions did war across his face. "How can I leave this mess?" he exclaimed, gesturing with a certain lack of respect to the crystal shapes frozen around them. "Go yourself if you must, why should I..."

"I'll watch the lads and lasses." Squick once more cut in, much to Fodder's gratitude. It was good to have his support openly at last. "This be more important. Get to yon Sanctum before yon Tome falls, lad, or it's for nowt." His expression was haunted. "I canna lose any folk like this again."

"And you know bloody well I won't get in the Sanctum without you," Fodder added, addressing the reluctant Courtier firmly. "You're coming with me. And don't try anything or you know what I'll do."

"And if you silence the lad, I'll do the telling for him," Squick added with unexpected fervour. "Not again, Strut. Not again."

"We'll have to get there." Strut looked desperately uncomfortable. "It's a long ride, even with fast horses and the terrain..."

"We aren't riding." Grasping the Courtier by the arm, Fodder gave Squick a grateful nod. He paused a moment longer, his eyes sweeping the room and lingering on the trapped forms of his friends as he tried to ignore the tight fear that gripped his heart.

"I'm coming back," he called out, his words echoing around the crystal and the vastness of the hall. He had no idea if they could even hear him, but if there was any hope they could... "I'm going to save you."

And then, still dragging Strut by the arm, he hauled the Courtier to the small doorway through which they had entered the hall.

It didn't take long to find a staircase—the Dark Citadel was pretty much made of towers—and soon they emerged onto a rooftop, the wind whipping around them as the permanent cloud cover overhead continued its frenzied whirl. Praying that someone was in hearing range, Fodder ignored Strut's confused protestations and grasped the battlement, leaning out as he bellowed at the top of his voice.

"Fang!" he roared. "Gibber! Anyone! Please, I need your help! My friends are dying! Really, truly dying! Forever! Please!"

For a horrible moment, he wondered if they had been hurt too badly at the battle of the Gates of Wrath, that they couldn't hear him, that they couldn't come. But against the raging sky, he saw one black dot circling and then another and another and suddenly two shapes were plummeting from the sky as talons stretched, grasping the battlements, and AFC wings batted at the air as they settled on their perch. Two pairs of beady eyes fixed on Strut nervously.

"Hope you know what you're doing, mate." Fodder was sure it was Fang who spoke, his wings twitching as he eyed Strut's suspicious, fruitless-hunt-understanding expression with distinct discomfort. "If you hadn't said *forever...*"

"It's okay." One glare from Fodder was enough to loosen Strut's expression and ensure nothing would be held against his AFC friends. "And thank you."

"What do you need?" probably Gibber chimed in. "A lift?"

"Yes. Both of us. To the Sanctum behind the Temple in Magnificent City. As fast as you can."

Strut gaped at him. "You want to travel with *them?* You cannot be serious."

Fang and Gibber exchanged a bewildered look. Both shrugged. "You got it," said Fang easily. "Hang on to your backsides."

Clawed feet clamped down on his shoulders. And with Strut's horrified shriek ringing in his ears, Fodder felt himself yanked up and into the sky.

Finally, he was moving. He could only pray that he still had time.

On returning, Erik finds Islaine is now Queen of
Nyolesse and, since genealogy, the prophecy, and his
unique ability to use the Ring have proved that his
ancestor was Avikhelion, making him the rightful
king of the Six Kingdoms, he is crowned High King of
all the lands. Myhessia, freed from her duty,
marries Sir Roderick; and Halheid, who turned the
tide of battle with his brave charge, marries
Zahora. Astonishingly, at Erik's coronation,
Eldrigon's ghost appears and blesses him with a long
and glorious reign. Erik and Islaine's first son is
named Eldrigort in honour of those who gave their
lives.

Darkness had fallen by the time Fang and Gibber stooped over the glittering ball of torchlight that was the Magnificent City and deposited
the resolute Fodder and the mildly hysterical Strut on the steps of the
City Temple. Newly lit braziers circled the outer colonnade of snowy
marble, the Temple itself glimmering like a jewel on its island where
the rivers of the Realm met. The light glinted off the fast-moving
waters in a spinning dance that redoubled its brightness.

It would have been a stunningly beautiful image if Fodder had
been in the slightest mood for sightseeing. As it was, he simply nodded
his thanks to Fang and Gibber, hauled Strut away from the statue
plinth he was pressing his face into for a quiet spell of hyperventi-
lation, and strode up the marble steps and past the row of towering
columns into the arched entrance.

He knew they were getting looks. Ordinary folk used the Temple,
not as a place of worship, since the Gods were a pack of deluded luna-
tics living on a mountaintop on the other side of the Realm, but as a
place for a quiet sit and a bit of peace. Occasionally they helped out by
tidying up the benches and prayer cushions, freshening the flowers,
polishing the gilt gold decoration, and touching up the frescos in the
hope that the Priests who lived there would remember these small
kindnesses when the time came to hand out a couple of lines or a
Narrative moment.

Fodder couldn't help but smile wryly to himself. He'd gotten used to having too lofty a perspective, sending the blame too high. Perhaps if he'd thought back to his Ordinary roots, he would have seen where the prosaic truth about their culture truly lay much sooner. The Ordinary folk had always known, in their own way, where the power behind the Taskmaster really started.

The eyes were intensifying as he strode down the aisle. It was only to be expected given he was hauling the gasping and alarmed-looking form of the most powerful man in the Realm along by his arm. One or two faces even flickered to Fodder with a hint of recognition, although given the all-purpose nature of his face, he suspected they were noting the well-worn chain mail and applying common sense to his being the Disposable causing trouble rather than having any specific knowledge of his features. One Priest, his expression concerned, started towards them nervously, but Strut by this point had recovered sufficient wits to wave him away with a measure of his standard contempt.

"Let go of me, will you?" the Taskmaster's taskmaster hissed in his ear. "I'm hardly going to do anything at this juncture and you'll spark a panic if word of you dragging me into the Temple starts to spread."

"Well, we can't have a panic, can we?" Fodder tried and failed to suppress the urge for sarcasm. "I know how much you Courtiers hate those."

But his arm was starting to hurt from reaching up to grasp the taller man anyway, and Strut was right—what could he do? If he tried anything, Squick would take care of the panic-making for him, and the pixie's word carried more weight than his own in such things. Fodder couldn't risk starting trouble that would delay or prevent him from helping his friends. He let go.

Strut, caught by surprise at this sudden freedom, stumbled briefly, but it took only seconds for his dignified instincts to kick back in. Straightening his silk doublet, he flowed into his usual long, sharp strides, which took him past Fodder in moments, his superior gaze flashing back over his shoulder.

"Come," he commanded in his best clipped tone. "The Sanctum is this way."

As Fodder followed, he felt the strange, silent sigh of relief that rippled through the Temple as what they had grown up to believe was the proper order of things was restored. Much as he loathed to admit it, Flirt was right. These weren't people who were ready for a sudden and dramatic cultural revolution started by a Disposable. The change would have to be gradual and Taskmaster-led.

Strut strode rapidly to the golden, jewel-strewn altar, hurrying up the steps. Fodder followed as he rounded the altar and brushed aside the rich scarlet hangings draped behind it to reveal a small, prosaic-looking wooden door behind them. With a touch of his fingers, the lock clicked, and with a tinkle of bells and a golden glow just like those of the Courtiers' books when fresh instructions beckoned, the door swung open.

Fodder bit his lip. The Outer Sanctum. Home to all that had ever pushed him down.

He followed Strut inside, down a short grey stone corridor which opened out into a much larger, oval chamber, brightly lit and full of bustling people in priestly robes or Courtier silks, talking in anxious huddles as they waved pieces of paper or non-tinkling books around. Though this was no match for the pomp and ceremony of the Temple, the involvement of Courtiers in its creation had insured a certain grandeur had crept in—the floor was paved in marble slabs and the ceiling, with its vast golden chandeliers, was clad in glittering quartz that reflected the candlelight and cast it sparkling back like daylight. Marble staircases rose in four carefully equidistant locations to a balcony that ran the circuit of the room, golden railings gleaming in the chandelier light. And the walls of the balcony were lined with book-shelves, Courtiers' instruction books, presumably now defunct, nestled in their grasp, the remnants of the Quests that had gone before. Below these balconies, on ground floor level, a series of alcoves plunged beneath, mostly occupied by intent-looking Scholars and Scribes, working at paper-strewn desks. But there were also doors in some of the spaces, one beneath each staircase, not to mention the door through which Fodder had himself stepped. And there was one more mystery entrance too, a simple burgundy curtain in the alcove directly opposite the archway where he stood.

And there, in the very centre of the room, was a reading pedestal.

It was raised on a marble plinth, carved into an oval of three steps.

The pedestal itself was glittering gold, as Fodder had come to expect, and resting on it...

He felt a tension he had not even noticed unknot just a little. A vast book was resting, fully open, against the pedestal's surface. The Golden Tome had not fallen yet.

He still had time. His friends still had time.

The gold-and-marble room glittered at his nerves mockingly. He thought about the muddy hovels in which he had grown up and felt a sudden wave of resentment.

"Don't think much of yourselves, do you?" he remarked caustically. "Such a humble abode for the simple mouthpieces of the Taskmaster..."

Strut shot him an angry look and parted his lips to retort, but at that moment, a Priest in white vestments glanced up and spotted the sudden arrival of his boss.

"Sir!" he exclaimed with the mixture of alarm and relief typical of someone who has spotted an authority figure mid-crisis—it was good to know he didn't have to fix it by himself but bad that he would have to explain it. Nonetheless, the Priest took the plunge and abandoned his companions to hurry over. "Sir, the Golden Tome! The instructions have stopped, sir, everything has frozen and..."

His eyes found Fodder. Both his words and his advance dried up instantly.

To give him credit, Strut didn't miss a beat. "Everybody out!" he exclaimed, his steely voice echoing the length of the chamber. "Into the private chambers, everybody, at once. Do not emerge until I say so." His eyes flicked to the Priest. "Devout, check the Library of the Golden Tomes is clear and follow them." The startled Priest nodded, bit back the questions Fodder could see hovering on his lips, and darted to the doorway beneath the staircase to their right. Fodder caught a glimpse of shelves of large golden books like the one at the room's centre before the man darted out again and vanished after his bewildered cluster of hurrying companions through the right-hand doorway on the oval chamber's far side.

"There should be no one in my office—if there is, they will be sorry," Strut muttered to himself as he glanced at the near door to their left. "The same goes for the Chamber of Quickening. I want no witnesses to this."

"The Chamber of Quickening?" Fodder caught on to the name at once as he followed Strut out on the marble floor towards the pedestal. "You have a chamber for it? Why?"

Strut's expression wavered. "That's where we keep them," he said with unexpected softness. "The last companions to suffer this travesty, along with their unfinished instructions, are stored in that room." He gestured to the far left door. "We show them to our new initiate Priests and Courtiers to express the importance of what we do."

Fodder fought back a shiver as he stared at the simple door. Would that be the fate of his friends and the Merry Band if he couldn't save them? Would they spend the rest of eternity as crystal statues, shown off as a salutary lesson to newcomers to this arrogant chamber of deceit?

No. No, he wasn't going to let that happen.

Strut was mounting the steps to the pedestal. Fodder rushed after him, bounding to his side in a sudden rush of impatience.

"Where's the Inner Sanctum?" he demanded. "Because unless it's pretty bloody tiny, I doubt it's up here."

"A moment's patience, if you would." Strut was staring at the tailed-off instructions, written exactly as Fodder had seen in his book. For all Strut's bluster about Preen's book not being complete, it seemed the instructions had been going out unedited and verbatim to the Courtiers for some time now.

But Fodder had had enough. Time was ticking by—who knew how soon the Taskmaster would give up completely and let this tome fall from its pedestal? "You know what I bet?" he said abruptly. "I bet it's behind the mystery curtain. Let's find out, shall we?"

"No!"

But Fodder ignored the Courtier's cry of alarm, the grab his skinny fingers made for the Disposable's arm. Leaping down from the pedestal, Fodder rushed across the marble floor. He heard a shriek and a thud—Strut's curly slippers had apparently betrayed him on the slick surface—and he pressed home his advantage, hurtling to where the unremarkable-looking curtain hung. If this had been The Narrative, perhaps it would have rippled mysteriously via an invisible wind or whispered to him in an unheard voice. But this wasn't The Narrative and the curtain offered no mysterious powers of resistance as Fodder pulled it aside, shoved open the door behind it—which gave with a sour screech like broken bells—and plunged into the dark opening beyond.

"Wait! Hold, you fool!"

Fodder didn't wait. But he did feel the sudden surge of warmth around his body, slowing his advance as a tingling sensation and liquid-like ripple washed across his skin. Strut's voice, calling warnings, turned distorted and distant in his ears. Fodder stumbled forwards and then suddenly he was free again, the strange feeling abruptly gone. He gasped for a moment, bending over to catch his breath, feeling half-drowned in honey, half-scoured with grit. Shaking himself, he turned.

Strut's astonished face stared at him from beyond distorted air. A pale shimmer, rippling in downward waves, washed the Courtier's skin in a tincture of gold and refracted his image and the room beyond into strange, twisting shapes. It was like staring at the world through a slow-moving, gold-washed waterfall.

"How did you do that?" Strut's voice was muffled and far away, but Fodder could hear his amazement. "The last person who touched that barrier was unconscious for a fortnight. You shouldn't even have been able to open the door without my help. It's keyed only to three people."

Barrier... So this *was* the Inner Sanctum. And he'd apparently just defied some mysterious force to get inside. Fodder wasn't entirely sure if that was a good thing, but at the moment he wasn't going to argue the toss.

"No idea," was his frank response. "But I did it. It's probably lost its kick with The Narrative breaking down. Are you coming?"

Strut shook his head violently. "I can't risk being made unconscious now. Too much needs to be watched."

"I'm fine," Fodder pointed out. "Come on, don't be a wuss."

Strut raised a distorted eyebrow. "I am a...*wuss*, as you call it, because you are a freak. I have seen too many unnatural things occur of late to assume that I will pass through as easily as you did.

Besides..." His muffled voice took on a sardonic edge. "Given your heroic tendencies, I suspect you would prefer to make this journey *alone*."

Sarcasm aside, Fodder had to admit Strut had a point. Not about any heroic solo venturing-forth into the mysterious unknown, but about wanting to speak to the Taskmaster without the Courtier muddying the waters.

"Suit yourself," he simply said, turning his back on the Courtier. Ahead, a narrow, shadowy corridor of plain grey stone stretched away. A little way along, a simple arched doorway held a plain wooden door. A light, a vivid, over-bright, familiar light was glowing gently around its edges.

Fodder took a shuddering breath. *The Narrative*. That was Narrative light, still here, not faded, not frozen into crystal. And if there was still light, there was still hope.

He walked forward, approaching the door with caution, given what he had since learned about the barrier he'd so easily swum through. He wasn't surprised, though, when the door opened easily at a gentle touch. Cautiously, he pushed it wide and stared.

It was not a large room, simply a round chamber lined with book-shelves, like a less-pretentious version of the oval chamber outside. Books lined perhaps a third of the shelves but they were the strangest-looking books Fodder had ever seen, flimsy things with no visible binding or leather cover, wrapped instead in thick, shiny, colourful jackets of paper. And on each spine were the names of Quests, shorter Quests holding one book alone but longer Quests stretching through three, four, or five different volumes. The newer, shinier ones were Quests that Fodder remembered taking part in, the older names of legend or even names unknown.

But the books were not what held Fodder's interest. That honour fell to the pedestal.

It was a simple thing compared to the one outside, a small stone plinth in the chamber's centre that came to waist height, mounted with a wooden reading stand. On the left-hand side of the stand, one book like those on the shelf was already closed, the title "The Ring of Anthiphion, Part One" blazed across its garish cover. Squinting at it,

Fodder could see a stylised painting of Magus and Bumpkin as their Narrative selves gazing back at him with heroic fierceness. To the right, a second book, which lacked the paper cover of its companion, lay open.

And the light...

The Narrative light enclosed the pedestal, reading stand, and two books whole, a vivid, column-like shaft that plunged down from a strange, glittering, chimney-like hole in the ceiling. It gleamed at him.

Fodder stared for a moment. He wasn't an idiot—it was obvious what he had to do, where he needed to be to do this. But to have this conversation in Narrative light wasn't something he'd anticipated. Would he be able to think clearly in there or would the conversation be a fight? Would he have his mind changed without realising it?

He could only hope not. Newfound belief in a benevolent Taskmaster was the only thing he had to cling to. It was all his friends had left. Whatever happened, he had to go ahead and do it.

Closing his eyes and drawing a deep breath, Fodder stepped into the light.

And it was different. Instantly, he could feel it, the lack of that feeling of being manipulated, the honey-like embrace not all-encompassing but a gentle stroke against his skin, no words tumbling unseen and unheard through his brain. He could still think straight. It was The Narrative light but not The Narrative *content.*

He opened his eyes. Light surrounded his body. The open book was right in front of him.

Now what?

Did he speak and wait for a response like a penitent appealing to a God? Was he supposed to genuflect and whisper a prayer or something? That didn't sit too well after what he'd been through. But what else was he supposed to do? How could he make contact when...

Movement caught his eyes. It was the slightest thing, a whisper, a hint of motion, grey like smoke and just as illusive. He looked down, really looked at the pages of the book, and there was The Narrative as the Taskmaster had been forced to leave it, frozen as his friends were frozen in those terrible, faltering last moments:

The air seemed to shudder at this awful realisation

```
as noble company of heroes and foul band of villains
alike stood opposite each other without anywhere to go
or anything else to say or do. Even as Fodder slowly
turned, wandering back to where his friends were gath-
ered by the strange, ripped air, Erik found himself
fighting a sick, lost kind of feeling in his stomach. He
felt adrift, lost, unable to focus, unable to find where
he should be and what he should do. The air closed in
around him, making his limbs heavy and his head pound
and the light, the light seemed to flicker and there was
nothing else left to do but
```

Stop.

But there was more. There and then gone, for merely a second, a string of words, pale and grey and spectral, zipped across the blank page below that final, terrible word, passing too fast to even read, tumbling in all directions like wild and scattered thoughts, unable to fix themselves in place. Another followed, then another, darting like frightened birds briefly stripped of cover, and hard as Fodder tried to read them, they were too quick, too faint for him to see.

He felt his breath catch in his throat. Was this the Taskmaster trying to continue the story? Or was it the final death throes where words would no longer stick and the Quest would be abandoned?

He had to know what they said. But how? How could he...?

Why did he do it? Even Fodder himself didn't really know. But as the next string of ghostly letters spun across the page, he darted out one hand and pressed his fingers to the page.

```
maybe it's a sign, maybe I need to get away from
this? I need a holiday maybe? Or a sport. I'll take
up a sport. I used to like sport, before chocolate
got in the way
```

With a gasp of shock, Fodder yanked his fingers back and the...voice? If it was a voice...cut off instantly. For a moment, he could only stare at the page, breathing hard as he reassembled his shattered thoughts.

It had been... It was like The Narrative. Words, unseen and unheard, streaming through his head unbidden, but like with this new kind of light, there was no guidance, no aim to control. And unlike the strong, decisive words of his Narrative experience, this voice was fractured, rambling almost, sounding confused, uncertain…

`Lost.`

Was that the Taskmaster?

And if he could hear the Taskmaster…could the Taskmaster hear *him?*

Carefully, hesitantly, Fodder reached out once more, fingertips to paper…

`can't be a good thing when even your own characters won't listen to you! I need to get out and about, take a break from writing. I need a break, this story hasn't been relaxing at all, it's been so hard! Even the damned Chalice of Quickening didn't give me grief like this! If I hadn't promised myself never to give up on another book, I would have dumped this mess by now. Maybe if I take a break, I can think of a way, I can decide what to do next. I can decide if I should press on with this or just bail and have done with it`

He knew he had to say something. The Taskmaster was wavering, on the verge of giving up on this Quest, and if it was abandoned, what would become of his friends?

He had to speak, he had to try it, to see if this odd communication worked two ways. But what did one say to the lost and rambling voice of the all-powerful guider of their Realm? He considered some bold statement or a demand, some forceful cry against abandoning them, but that felt cold in the face of that sort-of voice ringing in his head. His pride refused to consider any kind of plea or supplication and to be honest, given what he could hear, it hardly seemed appropriate either. Really, when it came down to it, there really was only one thing he could say.

"Hello?" he called. "Hello, can you hear me?"

And there was a pause. Just for an instant, the rambling sort-of voice hesitated.

`What the…? No, God, don't start that. We do not listen to the random voices in our head.`

Fodder felt his breath catch. The Taskmaster… The Taskmaster had *heard* him!

"Hello!" he called out again. "Hello, listen to me! I need you to hear me! I need to talk to you!"

And now I'm hearing things. Wonderful. So much for having a break, maybe I need to see a doctor. Or a psychiatrist. Perhaps this is a symptom of some kind of illness. Maybe I'm having a breakdown...

"You're not ill!" Privately, Fodder didn't know if that was true, but he couldn't allow the Taskmaster to dismiss him as a symptom. One thing was becoming very clear, though—as ever, Dullard had been right on the money. If the Taskmaster was dismissing him as an illness, it didn't seem likely that the ins and outs of their Realm were familiar ground. "It's me, Fodder! From the Quest you were guiding? I need to talk to you! It's important!"

There was a long, long silence. It echoed in Fodder's head as profoundly as the sort-of voice had. And then...

Fodder?

"Yes!" The word couldn't have exploded from Fodder's lips faster. "Yes, that's right!"

From my story?

There was a part of Fodder, he had to admit, that could completely understand the reluctant astonishment of that tone. That part of himself shared it. For all his talk and his will and his determination, a corner of him had never truly believed a conversation with the actual Taskmaster could possibly come to pass. The feeling was apparently mutual.

"Fodder from your story," he repeated firmly. "Sort of sometimes Fodhelion or the Man of Sleiss, but they weren't me. Fodder's me. I'm Fodder."

And you are...talking to me?

"I will if you'll let me. I kind of need your help."

Another echoing silence lingered in Fodder's brain. This one was starting to become uncomfortable.

"Hello?" he called out a little more tentatively. "Are you still there?"

Oh God, it's happened. I've cracked. I've officially cracked.

This was not going as well as Fodder had hoped. "You haven't, honestly, I just need to..."

My brain is broken. It's ruined. Is this how this

stuff starts? Is that why this story turned into such a mess, because I'm losing my mind?

"No, that was me!" Fodder stepped in quickly to try and head off any further steps in that direction. "I…"

But the Taskmaster was apparently not listening. The character who got written in my story out of nowhere, ran rampant with it, and killed it dead is now apparently talking to me. I think I need to go lie down.

It reminded Fodder of trying to talk to Grim or Doom—his words didn't seem to be hitting the Taskmaster's wavelength. And the thought of where Doom was now, where his friends were, struck him with renewed force and hardened his resolve.

"My friends are *dying!*" The words burst from his lips with sudden fervour. *"Please*, can you listen to me?"

Again came one of those strange, profound silences that seemed to still the very world. The Taskmaster's sort-of voice, when it came once more, had lost its edge of hysteria, although incredulity remained rich within it.

What did you say?

"My friends are dying," Fodder repeated himself once more, willing himself to keep cool, keep calm, not to spook the Taskmaster having made this connection. "When The Narrative stopped with them inside, it trapped them inside this crystal stuff, like happened with *The Chalice of Quickening* back in the day. The Merry Band are stuck in there too…"

The merry who?

"And last time this happened, the people inside died when the Golden Tome fell…"

Golden tome?

"I need to save them—it's my fault, I'm the one who started trying to disrupt the Quest, but I've been told that no one down here is capable of getting them out. But you're *not* down here and since you're the Taskmaster…"

I'm the what now?

"I thought…maybe you could…" Fodder felt his words trail away at the bewilderment in that tone. "You have no idea what I'm talking about, do you?"

Not really, no. Sorry.

Fodder felt a pool of desperation swelling in his chest—how was he supposed to have this conversation with no points of reference in common? Although he'd accepted the idea of the Taskmaster's possible ignorance, it hadn't really occurred to him how difficult it would make things to explain his issues about the world to someone without the slightest clue how his world worked in the first place. "You don't know *anything* about the Realm? About The Narrative or those of us living down here to work with it?"

Wait a minute. You're talking like...like you have some kind of world in there.

Fodder didn't really know what to say to that. He settled for simply saying, "We *do.*"

A world...other than what I write.

Writing—the words of The Narrative flowing through his brain, the words on the page in front of him, written by an unseen hand. The Taskmaster thought that The Narrative was all there *was.*

"What you write—we call it The Narrative." Fodder struggled to pull his brain into gear, trying to explain life to someone who'd never seen it. He also forced himself to hold back on his complaints arising from it for the time being. "It passes through the landscape and we make sure the right people are in the right places at the right times for what it wants. For what it says in the instructions. Instructions we've always been told came from you." He drew a breath. "You know —*local guards try to apprehend the heroes but are tossed aside*—that sort of stuff."

My plans. The Taskmaster's sort-of voice contained a sudden, glorious hint of comprehension. That sounds like how I write my plans. I always make plans, really detailed ones. That's what failing to finish The Chalice of Quickening taught me. I never start a story these days without knowing exactly where it's going. I never stray from the plan. Even if...

The pause echoed briefly, then suddenly turned sour.

No. No...a world? You can't possibly expect me to believe there's a whole world inside a world inside... Oh God, listen to me! I'm doubting the veracity of the voice inside my head.

He was losing the Taskmaster again. Fodder leapt in. "Why don't you let me tell you about it?" he exclaimed desperately. "If you let me explain..."

There was a hollow, distant sense of laughter, not joyful but strangely weary. Tell me about it? The character speaking inside my head would like to tell me how his world works. Okay, knock yourself out. This ought to be good.

So Fodder told. He explained about The Narrative, about the all-purpose landscapes and the pixies that kept people and places in keeping with the Taskmaster's needs, the social structure of their world, instructions led and distributed by Courtiers, the breeding of different families, the limitations that entailed, and the culture that grew out of different roles. He expressed his views quite fervently on the character-contorting nature of planting. And finally, a bit guiltily, he explained his own actions and how he had done everything in his power to disrupt the Quest in order to get himself a fair hearing and an equal chance, including the fate that had befallen his friends because of it.

"That was why I started it all, you see," he rounded up, rather hoarsely. He had no idea how long he'd been speaking but his dry throat implied it had been some time. "I felt overlooked, like no one—especially not you—considered me to be worth anything because I was a Disposable. That would be my life forever and it didn't seem like enough somehow. At first I thought I wanted a shot at glory myself, but I'm not so sure about that anymore. I want to be listened to and allowed to be myself. I want a fair chance to be heard." He smiled wryly. "I had no idea that all the time I was clamouring to get your attention, you didn't know I wasn't just a *character*."

Well. The Taskmaster sounded shell-shocked. That was more than I expected. I didn't know things in there were so organised.

"And *alive*." Fodder felt that needed to be drummed home—there remained a deeply sceptical feeling to the voice he could feel. "Very alive."

Alive. There was a strange edge to the unheard voice. A whole alive world hanging around on the edges of my imagination. And what, I didn't even notice?

"I don't think you were supposed to notice," Fodder pointed out. "We kind of assumed that you knew."

And you've been leaping around in there and messing with my plot?

Fodder gave a guilty shrug, albeit without the slightest clue if the Taskmaster could see it. "It seemed the only way to get your attention at the time."

Oh, you got it, all right. What almost felt like another laugh echoed silently in the ether. I thought I'd gone completely round the twist. I couldn't even keep my own story straight. The silent words turned wryly resigned. If I ever tell anybody about this conversation, they'll lock me up as a nutcase, you know.

Fodder gave the practical answer. "I wouldn't tell them then."

I think you can rely on that. The Taskmaster went quiet for a moment. I'm really not quite sure if I believe any of this.

Fodder fought down the urge to bang his head against the pedestal. "I'm getting that impression."

I still think I might be having a breakdown. I probably shouldn't even be talking to you.

"I'd prefer that you did."

Hmmm. There was a slightly disconcerting edge to the Taskmaster's murmur. But, suppose I run with going crazy for a moment... Why have you been so desperate to talk to me? I mean, you said your friends were dying, but judging by your monologue earlier, you've been after a chat since well before that.

"I have." Fodder took a deep breath. "Because like I said before, I don't think our world is very fair. The way things are...it's not *right*. Everyone deserves an equal chance and right now, most of us don't have one. Only you can give us that."

There was a soundless sigh. Okay. I just...I can see that unfairness thing, I guess. But, look, I don't know what you expect me to do about it. I don't even understand how you can exist, let alone how I can make a difference.

Fodder blinked. "You're the *Taskmaster*," he replied stubbornly.

In the nicest possible way, that doesn't help. That
name doesn't mean anything to me.

Fodder sighed wearily. "Well, it means a heck of a lot to *us.*" He
struggled for a moment, trying to articulate his point while barely
knowing what his point was. "The thing is, you are *everything* down
here. Your instructions guide how we live our lives. The way you create
your characters has shaped our culture. And any changes in it, they'll
have to come from you."

You can't work it out for yourselves?

Fodder allowed himself a quiet, tired laugh. "Oh trust me, I tried.
The people down here aren't ready to think outside of the instructions.
Perverse as it sounds, my friend Flirt was right when she said people
will only think for themselves if *you* tell them to."

You're right. That does sound perverse.

Fodder smiled dryly. "Welcome to my world. Or *your* world." He
gave another wry laugh. "We've lived our lives by the instructions for
too long, with set patterns of behaviour—we're too used to it to live any
other way. You must know the drill—guards are easily overcome,
mysterious powers right any plot-related wrongs, princesses are
always beautiful, heroes always rise from humble origins to discover
their true birth and save the world. The barbarians flirt with the
barmaids, wily thieves hide a heart of gold, the henchman always
sneaks and smirks, the dwarves live underground and the elves live up
the trees. Servants don't matter and the ordinary folks are just ordinary. And it always ends the same—everyone knows that the smaller
force in battle will always thrash the larger and the Dark Lord will
always be obliterated. To you, that's story. To us, it's nature. It's *life.*"

This time the pause resounded like the space between peals of a
bell. The Taskmaster's silence lasted so long that Fodder almost
wondered if the much-touted breakdown had occurred. When at last
the non-voice returned to his head, there was a strange, thoughtful
quality to it.

You're right. I hadn't realised...but you're right.
God, I really do repeat myself, don't I?

"You do a bit." Fodder put it as politely as he dared, not wishing to
alienate the Taskmaster at the cusp of this potential breakthrough.
"Well, a lot, to be honest. And we based our culture on those repeti-

tions. We evolved into what we expected you to need and the Courtiers arranged the rest. And now we're stuck with it."

Maybe I have become too rigid in my thinking. I've been wheeling out stock characters, stock ideas, only changing the names and the landscape. I've become so predictable... Fodder could have sworn he felt an invisible shake of the head. Bloody Quickening, that's what started it. I ran out of steam, out of plot, out of interest, right in the middle of the damn story. So since then, I make a plan and I stick to the plan, no deviating off or writing myself into corners like I did when I started out. And if the characters seem a bit forced sometimes, if they don't evolve, that was the price to pay to know where I was going, you know? For making sure I finished it.

"Maybe you need to try something different," Fodder offered gently. "New characters and new ideas, more flexible plans that can evolve with your character. Maybe that would help you *and* us."

Bloody hell. My breakdown is giving me writing advice. Good writing advice.

Fodder wasn't sure whether to take that as a compliment. "I'm just trying to help."

That's what the voices say right before the body count racks up. But still...maybe I do need to start making my plans more flexible, letting the story flow instead of trying to force it. I mean, *The Ring of Anthiphion* was chaotic and nuts and frustrating to write but it was strangely fun sometimes. I kind of liked not being quite sure where I was going, having to think and follow rather than pushing when it didn't feel quite natural.

"Then why don't you let *us* guide you?" Fodder was starting to get an inkling on the edges of his consciousness as to how the forces that had driven his world had, albeit accidentally, come to work. "Let us make your characters—if nothing else, my friends and I have proved it's possible to do that. Because if you were forcing the characters like you say—maybe that's how planting happened. Maybe if you stop pushing the characters and let them lead you, the planting will stop too."

But how am I supposed to do that? I don't know any

of you down there and I need some kind of plan to start with, even if it's subject to change. I can't leap in blind. That's how Quickening never got finished. I started before I knew where I was going.

Fodder pondered for a moment. "Well, hold auditions," he suggested suddenly. "Any or all of us Realm folk come in here, introduce ourselves, and share any ideas we have for what we could be. We get a fair chance and you see what resources you've got. You can pick whichever of us you like the idea of for your characters and let those characters guide the story. You give us a back story to learn and we run with it. There're plenty of us down here to try out, so you won't be short of material. That way you get new characters and no one gets planted with personalities that aren't theirs. It'll be nice and natural and flowing along. All we ask is that you always finish whatever you start. Fair enough?"

I suppose so. As much as letting the voices in my head audition to be my characters is a worrying development. And I guess I can manage bringing anything I start to a conclusion. It might be a crappy conclusion if the story doesn't go well, mind.

"Makes no odds to us," Fodder replied honestly. "As long as we don't end up trapped, you can finish how you like. Speaking of which..." He took a deep breath. "What about my friends?"

This time the hesitation was deeply disconcerting. We're back to where we started with that. I'm sorry, but I don't know what I can do about it.

"I thought...if you restarted The Narrative, resumed the story..."

And go where? *The Ring of Anthiphion* is dead in the water. I don't know where else to go with it or what to do with those characters. That's why they're frozen, I guess. I can't continue so I don't need them anymore.

Fodder could feel his heart drumming with terrified anxiety in his chest—was a statement like that enough to have made the Golden Tome fall? The book he was touching was open, so surely that meant they were okay, didn't it?

"Can't you find a way?" He hated to beg or plead, especially with an entity that didn't seem entirely convinced he was real, but these were his friends. "Find another use for them, in a new story maybe?"

A new story? It was the strangest sensation that Fodder had ever felt, as though invisible eyes were raking him over with thoughtful deliberateness. You know, what you've been saying, about repeating myself, being too rigid, needing to let the characters lead...I think I knew it. I think there was a part of me that...I wonder...

Again Fodder felt the unseen eyes bore into him. He felt without seeing a slow, wry smile spread through the light.

Fodder. There was something very contemplative in the Task-master's non-voice. For all that you might be a figment of my warped imagination, you seem to be a figment that's had a bit of an adventure. Why don't you tell me exactly what you and your friends have been doing behind the scenes?

Fodder hesitated. "Now? We still need to find a way to get the others out."

Trust me. The tone of the Taskmaster was irresistible. Tell me your story, Fodder. I think it will solve both our problems...

* * *

It was like reliving a nightmare. In his mind's eye, Squick could always see them, that long-ago Merry Band of *The Chalice of Quickening*, sallying forth with less and less direction, less and less drive until that terrible day when the light had faded and they'd been frozen forever.

And here they were again.

And this was worse somehow. He didn't really get to know the Merry Bands so well; after all, they rarely needed a patch-up except in the case of dramatic demise. And while he felt for Bumpkin, Magus, Thud, and the others, he wasn't close to them. Doom was a once-a-Quest acquaintance, usually reassembled from ashy remnants, which didn't make for great conversation, and even Prince Dullard and Princess Pleasance, although they were Fodder's friends, weren't really well known to Squick, professionally or personally. But Flirt always had time for a chat and a catch-up when he was doing a butchery patch-up in Humble Village, and Shoulders...there was a regular customer! Hell's teeth, he'd probably spent more of his life re-attaching that lad's head than he had on patching up any other Disposable, and despite his moaning, he liked the laddie. Squick had risked the wrath of Strut to make sure the Disposable and the Barmaid hadn't gone to Poniard's vindictive pyre by letting them out of that stockade. And to see him now, like this, trapped in the crystal prison that had haunted Squick's nightmares for Quests now...

They didn't deserve it. None of them did. If Squick was honest, it was a fate he would not even have wished on Poniard, who up until recently he would probably have classed as his only real dislike. Luckily, the nasty laddie's run-in with the flaming oil had apparently doused his fervour for murderous, pain-causing death—once Squick had reluctantly patched him up, his enthusiasm for fire, for pain, and indeed for death had definitely waned. It seemed he was much less inclined to give it out now he'd taken it.

So, most likely even Poniard would not deliberately have caused this now: a long, trapped, suffocating, helpless death. Slowly, as he had done in the hours since Strut and Fodder's departure, he flitted from face to face, checking that their eyes continued moving, stating words of reassurance he had no way of knowing were either audible or true. He moved from Swipe to Harridan, Thud to the detached head of Clank, Magus to Bumpkin and the bound-together forms of Dullard and Pleasance, Shoulders in his awkward crouch, Doom's towering figure, and finally to Flirt, still frozen in her last-ditch push. He landed gently on her outstretched arms and watched as her eyes shifted awkwardly towards him.

"Hang in there, lassie," he whispered gently. "Hang on in. One way or the other, it'll be over soon."

Was it possible Fodder could do this, could talk to the Taskmaster, could fix what Squick, the Realm's healer, had failed to fix before? He could only hope, he could only pray, he could only...

Light surged through the room, sudden, sharp, and unexpected. Squick launched into shocked flight, his heart pounding as the hall blazed—The Narrative, was it, could it be The Narrative? But the light did not consume the room in vivid fervour—instead it plunged, carving like lightning streaks through the crystal, cracking it open with a burst of gold. And then with a final spark, the crystal covering shattered.

Squick flinched back, raising his arms to cover his face as pieces of crystal rained through the air. He blinked as the tinkling noise of their fallen remnants faded, and looked. And stared.

And whooped.

"Oh yes! Alive, they're *alive!*" he shrieked at the top of his voice, his words echoing throughout the chamber. "You did it, laddie, *you did it!*"

For there was Swipe clambering awkwardly to his stiff feet as he offered a hand to Harridan. Thud sat sharply upright, sending a cascade of broken crystal from his vast form. Clank's armoured body was already scrambling on its hands and knees towards the resting place of his head as Magus and Bumpkin clung, shivering, to one another. Doom was brushing pieces of crystal wreckage from the crevices of his armour as he smiled with relief. Prince Dullard was staring down at a handful of crystal, his eyes alight with curiosity right up until the moment when Princess Pleasance grabbed hold of him, pulled him down to her lips, and turned his mind to other things. Flirt lowered her arms slowly, breathing deeply as she gazed around the room and stretched her stiffened limbs. And Shoulders...

There was an awkward clattering of crystal fragments as Shoulders's body, head clasped in his hands, made his way hurriedly over to where Squick was hovering. He beamed up at the pixie hopefully.

"Given your declarations of support," the Disposable began breathlessly, confirming to Squick at once that the prisoners had indeed been able to hear what had earlier taken place, "I don't suppose you could see your way to..."

He hefted his head with an ingratiating grin.

Squick couldn't help but chuckle. And after all the lad had been through, the world owed him this one.

"Aye, I could," he replied, rummaging in his pouch for a needle and thread. "Come on, laddie. Let's get you back in one piece."

Shoulders's answering smile could have outshone The Narrative.

And they lived happily ever after....

Of the things that Fodder would remember from that strangest of days, the one that would always stand out with the strongest fervour was the moment he first saw his friends were safe.

His conference with the Taskmaster had been lengthy and involved and, if he was honest, what the Taskmaster had suggested had taken the Disposable somewhat aback. It had been his turn for incredulity but the guider of the Quests had been utterly insistent that this would be the best way forwards for all of them. So Fodder had done as he'd been asked, explained as best he could, but it was quickly clear there were questions he couldn't answer, gaps he couldn't fill. They needed his friends.

Were they still crystal, were they still trapped? Fodder hadn't known. In the desperate hope that the Taskmaster's need might have freed them, he'd excused himself for a few moments and hurried back to the Outer Sanctum, where an impatient Strut had battered him with demands for answers. Fodder had ignored him and instead issued one simple statement. The Taskmaster wanted to see his friends. If it was possible, get them.

Strut had stared at him like he'd grown an extra head. He'd opened his mouth and half-started the much-expected protests, about their condition, about having no way of knowing he spoke for the Taskmaster, about...

With an echoing crash, the vast Golden Tome of *The Ring of Anthiphion* on the pedestal behind them had slammed shut. It rocked, teetered, and fell to the ground with a smack.

Fodder's heart had plunged. The Tome had fallen. Oh Gods, the Tome had fallen...

Then had come the tinkling of bells. The flicker of golden light. The rustle.

But no new book shimmered into life on the stand's top. Instead, with a tiny pop, a single sheet of paper drifted down onto the pedestal and came to a gentle rest.

With a single glare at Fodder, a glare that seemed to encapsulate a whole universe of distrust, discomfort, and resentment, Strut wheeled away and strode over the marble floor to the pedestal, snatching the piece of paper from its resting place. He read it. He froze. He turned white. His fingers began to shake.

And with a strangled gasp, he hurled it down, turned on his heel, and actually ran towards the door through which he'd dismissed his fellows earlier. In a shuddering voice, he called for Devout and told him he needed to find the AFCs. He had an urgent job for them...

As the Taskmaster's taskmaster wrangled, Fodder had slipped forwards and snatched the piece of paper from the marble floor where it had drifted to a halt. It was almost blank, but for four words, written in the familiar script of the instructions.

`Get Fodder's friends. Now.`

Fodder couldn't help but grin. So the Taskmaster was starting to believe in them after all. Poor Strut—he'd waited so long to speak to his mysterious boss and this was what he'd got.

But there had been more to do and more to say. Satisfied that Strut would do as he'd been told, Fodder had ducked back through the shimmering curtain and resumed his talks.

When he re-emerged, his friends were there.

The relief was indescribable. There they were, a bit battered and flattened at the edges but unharmed, their eyes raking, as his had, across the opulence of the chamber. It was so odd to see Dullard and Pleasance holding hands and odder still was Shoulders's beatific smile as he ran his fingers across his newly reconnected neck with a look of near bliss. Beside him, Flirt saw him and caught his eye, her face filled with a whole world of *I told you so, didn't I's?* and Fodder had to admit that she'd earned them. She'd been right on so many things in the end, staying down to earth while he'd got carried away. He owed her. He owed them all.

He didn't consider himself a particularly demonstrative kind of man. But he just couldn't help himself. Breaking into a sudden run, he crossed the floor in moments and grabbed them all into a shocked, lopsided group hug.

As an experience, it could have gone more smoothly, Fodder was honest enough to admit. The look on Pleasance's face suggested she was participating only under sufferance, and he definitely caught the incredulous look that flashed between Dullard and Flirt, but surprisingly, Shoulders, beaming with contentment, was the most enthusiastic. His return to a single whole had definitely bolstered his mood.

After some awkward disentangling, Fodder took another moment to rake their faces.

"Are you okay?" he asked in concern. "The crystal…"

"Was damned claustrophobic, but it didn't hurt us." Flirt raised her hands reassuringly to ward off his worries. "It was bloody frustrating, though, wasn't it? I hated not being able to move or help when you took on Strut."

Well, that answered the question as to whether those in the crystal had been able to see or hear what had gone on. "So you knew what was happening then? You were aware?"

"Yep." Shoulders was wearing his vague smile as he caressed his own neck with embarrassing lovingness. "It wasn't nice, mate."

"It was vile," Pleasance sniffed with a shudder. "I had my eyes closed so I couldn't even see what had happened. And what that horrible crystal has done to my *hair*…"

"Actually," Dullard offered mildly, "while the situation was concerning, I did find the whole experience to be somewhat fascinating…"

He trailed off at the three incredulous glares he received from his fellow ex-statues. Fodder smiled quietly to himself. Ah, Dullard, always in his own little world.

"But nobody's hurt?" he asked, unable to keep the anxiety from his voice as he recalled not everyone who had fallen victim was in front of him. "You or Doom and the Merry Band?"

"A bit stiff and sore," Flirt stated as the others nodded their agreement. "But otherwise unharmed."

"They're fine, laddie." Preoccupied with his friends, Fodder hadn't noticed Squick was hovering behind them, wearing a broad, beaming smile that wiped away Quests' worth of helpless pain. "Doom and the Merry Band too. I fixed up yon Thud and Clank once they got free." Shoulders's face lost a touch of its blithe joy at the memory of Clank's restoration—Fodder suspected his friend had wanted to leave the Knight that way a bit longer in an act of natural justice. Ignoring the

Disposable's huff, Squick continued. "They be tucked up warm and cosy at the Dark Citadel with Pious keeping an eye out. They be shaken up and a bit bewildered. But they be *alive*."

Flirt placed her hands on her hips. "So," she said firmly. "With all that out of the way, are you going to tell us what the hell is going on?"

That was fair enough. So Fodder did.

His invitation—or rather the Taskmaster's—surprised them. Dullard, it had to be said, quickly allowed his academic curiosity to swamp his wariness, but Pleasance, Flirt, and Shoulders looked decidedly unsure when he outlined the agreement he and the Taskmaster had reached and why their input was so necessary. But his assurances that their participation was vital poked Pleasance's vanity and Shoulders's pride, and even Flirt's practicality drew her to the benefits. And so they followed his lead through the shimmering golden curtain and into the Inner Sanctum.

The meeting within had gone well. The meeting without went less so.

Having seen what the Taskmaster had achieved with the piece of paper, Fodder was quick to request a contingency plan to insure what had been discussed was believed. The Taskmaster agreed to try but since the piece of paper had been half an accident as it turned out, generated by the frustration of waiting, there could be no promises. And the notes made from the discussions that would form the basis of the new Golden Tome would take a bit longer to clean up. For a while at least, they were on their own.

And Strut was not a happy bunny. For so long, he had been the leader of the pack, the commanding force, the issuer of instructions, and he'd had a great deal of leeway about how he chose to carry them out. But the big boss had just stepped in and taken a look over the books. As they emerged once more from the Inner Sanctum, Fodder could see in Strut's face that he was feeling sidelined. And he could see even more clearly that he didn't like it.

Fodder tried to explain. Strut didn't care to listen.

"You expect me to believe this nonsense?" he outright hissed. "Opening the Sanctum? A break with the traditional family roles—roles, I should stress, that go back to the dawn of the Quests themselves? *Auditions?"* He spat the word like it had bitten his tongue. "I respect that you have freed those imprisoned from the crystal and I am grateful." He didn't sound especially grateful, but Fodder opted not to comment. "But for the rest?" He peered down at him as though he was a specimen trapped in a jar. "We have Quests' worth of tradition..."

"Tradition your family made up," Flirt pointed out acidly. After all, she'd heard every word spoken at the Dark Citadel. So, it occurred to Fodder at that moment, had Doom and the Merry Band. "And then you inflicted it on the rest of us, didn't you?"

Strut ignored her, keeping his eyes fixed on Fodder. "Nonetheless, tradition. And against it we pit your word. The word of a troublemaker, a rebel and a nobody. Who do you think people will listen to?"

"I think they'll listen to the Taskmaster," Dullard injected mildly. "As they always have."

Strut snorted. "And everyone knows I speak for the Taskmaster. Not you."

On the edge of his vision, Fodder became aware that the door through which the Priests and Scholars had retreated was still open, and he could see a cluster of them in the shadows, witnessing proceedings with a mixture of anger, confusion, and curiosity. Devout was at the front, watching the head of his family through narrowed eyes. Next to him, having accompanied his AFCs back to the Sanctum, was Dullard's uncle Primp.

Pleasance fixed Strut with her best look of disdain at this arrogant statement. "I think you'll find the Taskmaster can do the speaking, actually. And we'll all see what's said when the new Tome appears."

"And I'll be speaking too, laddie." Squick's voice was steely. "I said I would and I ain't gone changing me mind. I be with them."

Strut gave the pixie a fearsome glare. "You would help them destroy everything this world stands for? Being blackmailed into helping to free those trapped is one thing. I never agreed to this."

Shoulders grinned at him. "I'm pretty sure blackmail means you don't have to agree at all. You do it or we tell the world you're a manipulative shit and you've been lying to everyone. Simple."

Strut opened his mouth to respond to this offensive statement when the tinkle of bells and the glow of light over the pedestal cut him off. A glow of gold, but oddly streaked with silver, arched across the pedestal. There were two thumps.

Two new Tomes, one gold and one silver, sat side by side on the suddenly expanded pedestal.

Strut stared at this unique double-header for several seconds. Carefully, he started forwards. His eyes raked over the title of the silver book and he gave a notable start. They switched to the title on the gold book.

The palpitations that followed were strangely entertaining under the circumstances.

At their boss's distress, the watching Courtiers and Priests finally stepped in. As Strut was helped back to his office for a fortifying draft of wine, Devout and Primp moved forward instead and reverently opened the new books of instructions.

Fodder had to admit he was greatly relieved at the Silver Tome's appearance. Despite his conversations with the Taskmaster, the tone of scepticism at their existence had never quite been shaken off. And he was gladder still that a number of independent witnesses—Primp and Devout and several other Priests lurking in the door and, best of all, Squick—had seen it appear. The last thing he needed was for anyone to doubt what it said was truly from the Taskmaster.

"It's as you've said," Devout admitted after leafing through the Silver Tome from cover to cover. "It contains a new way of life. The Taskmaster does not wish us to be restricted by our birth, in The Narrative or outside of it. Once this new Quest is done, we are to arrange audiences in the Inner Sanctum for whoever wishes to offer a suggestion. The Taskmaster will audition any Principals personally and they can come from any family—we can decide amongst ourselves for the rest as long as we do not trap any person regularly in a role they do not want. The Sanctum is to be an open book so everyone can see who the instructions are coming from. And no one is expected to live their Narrative life when The Narrative has gone. Nothing must restrict the imagination." The Priest took a heavy breath. "This isn't going to be easy. Strut is correct. We're working against Quests' worth of tradition—our very way of life. And for our next Quest..." He nodded to the title embossed on the huge Golden Tome that Primp had just closed, somewhat shakily, beside him. "That's really going to be a challenge. Certain people..." He shook his head. "They won't like it. In certain roles, we may even have to recast."

"But you'll do it?" Fodder was painfully aware that this was the big test. If the Courtiers and Priests, the glue that held a Quest together, refused to participate... For the first time in a long time, he found himself willing someone not to disobey the instructions.

Devout smiled at him. "Of course we will. These are the instructions. It's what we do."

And thus began the oddest few weeks in the history of the Realm.

* * *

"You still wish me to be in charge?"

Strut, it was safe to say, had emerged from his small apoplexy well-fortified and ready for a confrontation regarding his position. He'd been most surprised to find there wasn't going to be one.

Fodder shrugged, glancing at Squick, who was hovering at his shoulder as a precaution. "We want you to stay on as supervisor, yeah. Trust me, Strut—there is no force in this Realm that would make me or my friends want your ruddy awful, thankless job. I've said from the start we don't want to run this world, we just want it fairer. As long as you stick to the new instructions, we won't get in your way."

Strut looked both bewildered and mollified at the unexpected prospect of remaining nominally in charge. After all, when it came to the crunch, he was a man designed by nature to carry out instructions, even if he didn't like them. But there was a hint, a gleam in his eye...

"Don't think we aren't taking precautions, though," Fodder added, too pleasantly. He gestured to where Dullard—who, rather to Pleasance's annoyance, had temporarily abandoned her to return to his first love affair with academia—had settled down with the Silver Tome and started to scribe his own copy of its contents in one of his many notebooks. "I know that a Tome can't be moved, harmed, damaged, or destroyed," he said, watching Strut's eyes very carefully as they narrowed. "But we know the word spread from it can be selectively edited. So we'll be taking our own copy—just in case."

"As you wish." Strut's expression was one of deathly control, concealing, Fodder suspected, a certain disappointment, and Squick's steely look suggested he'd seen it too. It was time to deliver the final blow.

"And the original will be available for anyone who wants to view it, once we open the Sanctum doors to the public."

It took a moment for this to dawn on Strut. When it did, Fodder wondered for a moment if further palpitations were on the cards.

"What?" he hissed.

A loud tearing noise echoed through the Outer Sanctum from the direction of the Temple. There was a loud whump and the sound of dragging material. A moment later, Flirt and Shoulders appeared, hauling the rich scarlet hangings that had concealed the Sanctum door behind them.

"All done!" Shoulders exclaimed cheerfully. "The door's out in the open, everyone in the Temple can see it now. Did you want us to wedge it open yet? There's a good crowd gathering out there that'd love a poke around in here."

Strut went white, so white in fact that Fodder wasn't sure there was a drop of blood left in his face. *"What* are you *doing?"* he gasped.

Fodder dropped the faux friendliness. "Making a point. Just because you're the best person for the job doesn't mean we simply forget everything that you and your family have done in the past. The curtain has come down, the door will soon be opened—no more secret chamber, no more lies. Do that and we'll be fine and dandy. Start hiding things and dictating people's personal lives again and there will be consequences."

Fodder didn't consider himself a hugely threatening man. He hadn't been sure, even now, how seriously Strut would take him. That was why he'd brought backup.

"Laddie." Never had so congenial an address sounded so dark. Squick's voice barely rose above a whisper. It didn't need to. "I've known you from a babe in arms. And I know from that look on your face, you ain't planning on taking this lying down. But if you stray one inch from what that book says, I ain't keeping my mouth shut for you anymore. Everyone will know what you did when yon Quests were in your care—how you dominated their world and their lives and tried to murder innocent souls in the nastiest of ways. And mayhap you may recall, I ain't the only one who heard what was said in yon Dark Citadel and neither are the lad here and his friends. Doom and yon Merry Band heard every word as well." He smiled with crooked glee. "Yon laddie Thud, he weren't so happy to learn he'd hidden his true self all his life to fit in with what some Courtier thought was right for him. He asked me to say he'd strongly like to have a word."

Fodder hadn't thought it was possible for Strut to go any paler. He was wrong.

"So if you be thinking you can still get things back to the way they were before," Squick rounded up, his voice threateningly soft, "remember that. And remember too that whatever yon nutter bastard Poniard thought, there's no getting rid of *me*. I'll be here and I'll be watching. Forever."

The Officious Courtier hadn't moved throughout Squick's piece of Strut-traumatising theatre, his back ramrod straight, his face frozen. Slowly, carefully, he breathed out.

"Very well." When Strut spoke at length, his voice was slightly weaker but contained the familiar edge of terse steel. "Then I suppose I'd better get started. But you can't open the doors. Not yet." When Fodder moved to protest, the Courtier cut him off. "I said *yet*. But this is a major change and there is a great deal that needs to be done. New instructions mean that word needs to be spread, the right people informed of work that needs to be done, and we can't do that with a rabble underfoot. We need to issue notices, tell the people who need to know…"

"Which would be *everyone*," Fodder interjected pointedly. He had known all along they'd have to let the Courtiers and Priests do the initial groundwork. Their word was trusted—if they said this was what was to be, it would be believed in a way Fodder knew from bitter experience he wouldn't be. But he wasn't going to let their boss slip anything past him.

"True," Strut drawled, his voice brittle. "But there is an order to it. We will get our Scribes and Scholars to draft leaflets explaining what has happened and announcing the nature of the new Quest and what will follow it…"

"Dullard can help write those," Fodder pointedly insisted.

Strut sighed. "As you wish, I suppose I can trust his judgement." Fodder noted the slight but let it pass—after all, Dullard was the best man for such a job. He wasn't bothered by Strut's disdain as long as the task got done. What mattered was that once the leaflets went out, everyone would know soon. Unlike their illiterate Narrative counterparts, if there was one thing everyone in an instruction-driven Realm could do, it was read.

"So when does the door open?" Fodder said instead. Beside him, buzzing from side to side with agitation, Squick pointedly folded his arms. "Let's pick a day and publicise an invitation to the Outer Sanctum in the leaflets so we know where we stand."

"I need to meet with the Courtiers first," Strut retorted stiffly. "They are the instruments by which these arrangements are made. Once they are here and the leaflets are made…"

"How long, laddie?" Squick cut in coolly.

The Courtier frowned grimly. "To summon them and draft enough copies of the leaflets—three days perhaps?"

Fodder nodded. "Three days it is."

Strut returned his nod. "I will issue a Courtier summons. In the meantime, perhaps you and your companions would care to return home. I'm sure you will find this most tedious…"

Fodder had been expecting that one. For all the idea of what he was about to say worried him—it would be too easy to get isolated from those he needed to reach if no one chose to step through the opened door—he knew it was the wisest course. "Actually, you might need to find us five bunks somewhere—my friends and I are going to stay here and keep an eye on things," he said, secretly rather enjoying the slight crease in the corners of Strut's eyes that implied he'd ruined the last shred of his day. "Just in case."

* * *

"Wait. They've *lost* him?"

Dimly, somewhere behind him, Fodder could hear the sound of Shoulders collapsing into gales of laughter. Biting his lip, he fought to keep a straight face himself at this bizarre piece of news.

He wasn't the only one. Fodder couldn't help but note that the lips of Reverence the Priest were also twitching at the corners as he continued the explanation that the Disposable had curiously requested when he'd heard Strut's curt statement that Preen's absence from the imminent Courtier gathering would have to be temporarily excused.

"I'm afraid so." The Priest didn't sound desperately distraught. "Thrash and Donk assure me they are searching as hard as they feel able to. All they know is that he was tied up and stowed away somewhere in the Final Battle Camp when they marched off to your assistance in the marshes. The trouble is no one can remember exactly where it was he was put." He couldn't quite restrain his strange sense of cheer. "But not to worry, they are certain he'll turn up. Eventually."

* * *

It was fair to say in hindsight that Strut's Courtier gathering could have gone better.

The incident was over. The screams and rage-riddled shrieks of Quibble, Officious Courtier to the Royal and Noble families, had faded as Primp and some of the sturdier Priests dragged him away down a distant corridor for either fortification or sedation. As the horrified hush across the Courtiers, Priests, and Scholars who remained turned into a sudden wave of shocked chatter, Fodder, Flirt, Shoulders, and Pleasance drew together.

"Well, I always knew he idolised us Nobles," Pleasance remarked, brushing her hands down the front of her creased dress as she stared in the direction of the retreating echoes of Quibble's paddy and reached down to replace the shoe she had just clocked her former Courtier over the head with. "But that was ridiculous."

"All that over his precious posh set not getting special treatment anymore?" Shoulders shook his head as he examined the fingernail scratches up his wrist. "Blimey, what a nutter."

"I guess he feels since they've been effectively demoted, he's demoted too," Fodder remarked, rubbing the slowly blossoming bruise on his temple. "But still..."

Shoulders snorted. "I don't know about demoted. *Demented* would be closer."

"Is Dullard okay?" Flirt asked, stretching her arms out to restore circulation after the incredible physical efforts she, Fodder, and Shoulders had had to make to haul the enraged, slavering Courtier away from the glittering object of his hatred. "That loon went for him like an animal when he tried to help us pull him off."

"Well, between us, Dullard and I did knock him unconscious and lock him in an oven quite recently," Pleasance admitted. "We may not be his favourite people. But I hit him with my shoe before he got close enough to do Dullard any harm."

At that moment, the prince himself bounded over, his hair dishevelled but his expression relieved, as though a mad-eyed Courtier hadn't moments before launched at him in a wild frenzy of rage.

"No harm done!" he exclaimed, apparently overlooking Shoulders's scratches, Flirt's stiff arms, and Fodder's growing bruise. "I knew there couldn't be, of course, but I thought I'd better make sure."

"Seriously?" Shoulders blinked incredulously. "After that lunatic went ripping into that book like a rabid dog, he didn't even damage it?"

"The Silver Tome is quite as indestructible as its counterpart, it seems," Dullard confirmed. "Which is fortunate under the circumstances." He smiled. "Squick's gone to find something to calm Quibble down, but once he's back, he said he's happy to heal any damage we sustained. It'll soon be like it never happened."

But it wasn't the physical damage that worried Fodder. It was lucky, really, that Quibble had taken the worst of his anger out on the one thing he couldn't actually hurt—the Silver Tome itself, containing the words he found so hateful. But to Fodder the incident had illustrated vividly what they were facing.

Fodder was no fool. He knew that the deal he had reached with the Taskmaster for a fairer world would not please a lot of people—principally those the old world had benefitted most, as Quibble had so violently demonstrated. He knew any change would have to be gradual and careful and most likely would take more than his lifetime to implement. But he'd made a start. He'd made a difference. His Quest wasn't over. It was about to begin.

And tomorrow, the leaflets would go out and the Sanctum door would open. And then they would really see.

* * *

"Thought I'd take a look, really." Fodder watched as Cringe's curious eyes swept the lavishly decorated walls of the Outer Sanctum. "When I heard about the new open-door policy around here and all—well, I thought it might be a lark to come and poke around."

The professional Henchman couldn't quite disguise his nervous edge, which Fodder sort of understood, given the events at the Grim Fortress—but he wasn't a man to hold a grudge and whatever side Cringe had been on in the end, he seemed genuinely pleased by this turn of events. The former Disposable smiled reassuringly at his first— well, vaguely—ally.

"You're not the only one," he replied frankly. Indeed, any worries that people might be too afraid or too angry to come and Fodder and his friends might be isolated based at the Outer Sanctum had quickly been assuaged. For whether out of average nosiness or true curiosity, soon lots of new faces were slipping through the opened door from the Temple and poking around, much to Strut's visible, if restrained, horror. Many an informative chat had been had about the content of the leaflets and the Silver Tome—indeed, even now, Fodder could see Flirt and Shoulders bidding farewell to Doom as he headed back to his Citadel and his bunnies, happy to keep the life he had in spite of the help he had given them to change theirs.

Cringe gave a quiet chuckle. "Yeah, nosiness—it's a powerful draw," he admitted dryly. "Though, it's not just that, I don't think. People are interested in what you're doing too." He frowned slightly. "In fact...I don't know how you'll feel about hearing this but...based on something I saw, you may have a convert in Grim."

* * *

Grim the Dark General stared for a long time into the full-length mirror, running his eyes over his heavy dark brows, his thick black hair, and his angular features with a thoughtful frown. Slowly, one hand reached out towards the chair beside him, grasping the thick forest-green cloak and drawing it slowly up and up and up until it hung upon his shoulders with a rebellious flourish. The hand reached out again, this time finding a pointed green hat topped with a slanted single feather that he placed with almost reverent care upon his head.

And he smiled.

* * *

After a brief chat, Fodder let Cringe wander off to indulge his curiosity, genuinely pleased by what he had heard. Although Grim had betrayed them, it was good to know even he was thinking outside of the villainy box after all. Nearby, Dullard and Pleasance chatted enthusiastically with Fang and Gibber from the AFCs. Judging by the amount of gesticulating going on, something they were saying had definitely caught the prince's interest. Moving across the chamber, he headed to join them. He knew from his earlier conversations with them that, like Doom, the AFCs had no desire to change their way of life—their careful aid had been motivated solely by a desire to help their friends. And help they had—Fodder had not even been able to begin to express his gratitude for all they'd done. They'd negated his attempt at thanks with a dismissive flap of a clawed hand apiece and insisted he could show how grateful he was if he must by attending their next amateur dramatic performance. He'd laughingly agreed.

And as he approached, he realised that the aforesaid performance was apparently the subject that had so caught Dullard's attention.

"...not only inviting me to perform! We wouldn't have to spend time apart if you joined the production too!" Dullard was bristling with big-eyed enthusiasm as he beamed in Pleasance's direction. The princess, by contrast, looked a mixture of bewildered, alarmed, and, oddly, secretly pleased by whatever was afoot. "Once the new Quest is over, wouldn't it be wonderful to have a proper joint project like this we could work on together? And I know with your acting talents, you would be magnificent in the performance! Gibber, Fang, don't you agree?"

"Yep." Probably Gibber added his gruff, to-the-point assent.

"It'd be fun," likely Fang agreed more verbosely. "It'd be nice to have an actual maiden in our show for once instead of Mania in a dodgy wig."

"Well..." Pleasance preened subtly. Fodder got the feeling she was protesting rather too much in the name of a little compliment fishing. "I suppose that's very true. But still...I'm really not sure I'd be *right* for the role."

Fodder couldn't help joining in, and the slight smile on Dullard's face as he did so told him the prince wasn't fooled by the princess's protests either.

"Go on, Pleasance," he said cheerfully. "Why not? After all, you were raised to play the female lead."

The broad smile on Pleasance's face told him he'd just sold it perfectly.

* * *

"So to my knowledge, those are our only refusals from the general cast." Reverence the Priest rolled up his scroll with a hitherto uncharacteristic flourish. Aware that the Priest was unused to having any Narrative time that did not involve walking in a line, swinging incense and chanting, Fodder suspected he was practising being slightly more noticeable.

Flirt shrugged. "Well, Quibble's no great surprise," she stated frankly. "And no great loss either, is he? We can ask around for someone to cover that, hold an audition or something. And if a few minor Nobles want to kick up hissy fits, that's their problem. Their like are ten a penny—this Quest won't miss them." Her face flickered, an odd expression that combined dislike with concern. "But Poniard..."

Shoulders gave an incredulous snort. "Are you going to miss him?"

"Gods, no." Flirt gave a shudder, the memory of her conflicts with him apparently fresh in her mind. "But he's a bit crucial and he's got a pretty unique skill set, hasn't he? How can he be replaced?"

It was a good question. Fodder couldn't pretend not to be relieved that the professional Assassin and psychopath who'd made a damned good attempt at destroying them forever in the most painful way imaginable was not in the mood to play anymore after his full-body roasting, but Flirt had a good point. No one else had his skills.

"What about some of the Grim Garrison lads?" Shoulders chipped in suddenly. "They've got the look and can do the slavering-psycho bit without a problem. I know Thrash is spoken for but Gurgle's pretty handy with the small weapons. He does that whole picking-his-teeth-with-the-blade bit when he's being snuck up on, to make himself look hard."

Fodder blinked. "Didn't he cut his own nose off once?"

"Swipe made him jump."

"It still doesn't fill me with confidence."

Flirt was gazing thoughtfully at the glittering wall. "What about one of the AFCs?"

Shoulders gave her an incredulous look. "Flirt, they aren't human. And though Poniard is a slavering nutter, he's definitely that much."

"Yeah, but they fit the bill," the former Barmaid pointed out. "They've got the skills and the role isn't far off what they do anyway. There's just more talking." She grinned broadly. "Hey, we know they can act, don't we?"

Shoulders was still shaking his head, but Reverence didn't look as though he thought her suggestion was so absurd.

"It could be done," he offered thoughtfully. "Urk has adapted them to near-human looks before now."

Fodder nodded. "It's definitely worth considering. We'll gather up the candidates, see who wants it and who does best. Isn't that what this is all about?"

An exchange of wry smiles occurred. But Flirt suddenly frowned and turned to Reverence.

"You said the general cast, didn't you?" she said. "Does that mean there've been refusals from the Merry Band?"

Reverence's pasty brow creased. "To be honest, I'm not sure. I've been compiling the list but Strut insisted on handling those negotiations in person—he thought they might be tricky. He hasn't told me the outcomes yet. I think Pious has been helping him—I could see if he knows how things stand?"

"If you could, that'd be great." At Fodder's smile, Reverence turned and hurried off. Flirt gave a little snort and shook her head.

"You know, even though we said we didn't want to be in charge, it feels a lot like we're running the show, doesn't it?" she remarked dryly.

It was a thought that had crossed Fodder's mind too and he spoke the words aloud that he had already used within to assuage his personal concerns. "It's only temporary, until things settle down. Besides, when it comes to this Quest, we're the ones best suited. We know the plot." He sighed as he glanced after Reverence once more. "I only hope the Merry Band are willing to run with it. We know from experience it's not their idea of a damned good time." He glanced at his friends. "So the question is, who is likely to refuse?"

"Well," said Flirt, "I'd say the ones who've swallowed their pride and been down here are more likely to say yes, aren't they? So between us, who've we seen?"

* * *

"Would that be acceptable to you?"

Flirt blinked. She had long ago gotten over her Heroine worship of Harridan the Warrior Woman. However, there remained a small part of her brain doing happy cartwheels at this turn of events—they were not cartwheels of admiration but of vindication. At last.

She restrained her satisfied smile as best she could, though she suspected it was escaping at the edges. "Sounds good to me, doesn't it? I'd be happy to train with you once the new Quest is done."

Harridan's smile was hesitant, pleased in the context of her new circumstances but tainted by a struggle to move past the feelings of the old. "That's good. If these events have proved anything, it is that you are a most worthy opponent. And besides…" Her smile flickered. "After my recent…rejection, I am quite content to avoid the company of big, sweaty menfolk for the time being. It is a strange sensation to mourn the loss of a love I did not even want."

Flirt felt a glimmer of sympathy. "Those feelings—they weren't your own, were they? They were Zahora's. They'll pass."

Harridan's smile turned brittle. "I am aware of that. But if you are able to inform me where Zahora stops and I begin, I would be most grateful."

* * *

"His name's Swash." Fodder could honestly say he had never in his life seen Thud the Barbarian look so happy. Beneath his now neatly trimmed beard, he was positively beaming as he stared unashamedly across the room to where the handsome, moustachioed Buccaneer who had entered the room on his arm was gazing at the glimmering ceiling of the Outer Sanctum with unabashed curiosity. "I've never met anyone like him. He told me he's always had those same feelings as me but being a Buccaneer depended so much on sweeping beautiful women onto the decks of ships and the like, he didn't dare say a word until now." He sighed wistfully. "Isn't he magnificent?"

That was not a subject on which Fodder felt qualified to comment—with a glance at Shoulders, who was stood beside him, he moved things along. "What are your plans?" he asked instead. "For after the Quest, I mean."

"We're going to find a nice place in the City." Thud smiled. "Actually, Swash's cousin Bard has a few ideas. Apparently, he and Preen are looking at doing the same—Preen's not so keen on living with the Courtiers anymore. Strut's *very* unhappy with him since he found out some of the things he'd said."

"Really?" Shoulders's voice was laden with revelatory irony. "Well, isn't *that* interesting?"

* * *

"Apology accepted." Fodder was surprised at how magnanimously Swipe was prepared to take Flirt's halting, distinctly reluctant expression of contrition over the thigh-stabbing incident in the Ruined City. She hadn't been keen to make one, but in the name of smooth waters and, if he was honest, minor revenge for her getting herself into that situation when he'd definitely told her not to, Fodder had insisted. The Thief in general seemed somewhat quieter and more restrained than his formerly cheeky and self-satisfied personality.

"And for that matter, if we're doing apologies..." he said suddenly, looking at Fodder with a distinctly uncharacteristic awkwardness. "I'm sorry about the whole nearly-let-them-burn-you thing, yeah? I hadn't really realised what it might mean and how serious it was. I've never had to die before and I didn't really understand until..." He pursed his lips, his eyes oddly haunted. "Let's say that being trapped in a thick block of crystal unable to move or speak and never knowing if you'll escape is one hell of a reality check."

* * *

"So Swipe, Thud, and Harridan should be in." Shoulders's grin faded. "Mind you, that's just three. Doesn't make a Merry Band, does it?"

Flirt sighed. "So no one's seen Magus, Gruffly, Bumpkin, or Clank?"

An exchange of shaken heads produced a definite no. "That's not good, is it?"

Shoulders shrugged. "After how they behaved, would you expect them to show up? Magus ended up a raving nutter intent on slaughter, Gruffly tried to turn us in, Bumpkin got it in his right royal jewels from Pleasance, and Clank..." He gave a beatific smile, presumably letting his happy vision of Clank's head flying across the room flit over his mind's eye. "They're probably too embarrassed to show their faces. It doesn't mean they'll refuse the Quest. They're too bloody vain to."

A hustle of gentle footsteps heralded the return of Reverence to halt the debate. His instant smile put pay to Fodder's concerns in an instant.

"Pious says they've all agreed so far but Gruffly," he told them cheerfully, scribbling on his scroll as he talked, adding the names to his confirmed cast. "Some not as happily as others—Clank, in particular, was reluctant but Strut won him round in the end by playing the duty card. He couldn't ignore that." He shrugged. "As Pious said, in the end, they are the Merry Band—they would never turn down Narrative time, it's who they are. Where would they be without it?"

Shoulders grinned. "Told you so."

Fodder smiled but his heart wasn't entirely in it. Happy as he was to have the Merry Band on board, the sentiment behind it indicated that their little cultural revolution still had a fair way to go. And hadn't Reverence said...

"What about Gruffly?" he pressed. "He's refused?"

Reverence's smile wavered. "He's not refused as far as I know. We simply don't know where he is. He and his wife packed up and left the tunnels a few days ago. No one seems to know where he's gone."

Fodder, Flirt, and Shoulders exchanged a series of looks. It was

Fodder who spoke up.

"Actually," he said, "we may be able to help you with that."

* * *

"I won't have to go back into the tunnels?"

On the windswept plateau above the Place of the Quickening, Primp the Officious Courtier responsible for the Minions of Darkness and Mystical Beings clutched at his feathered hat to prevent its theft by the wind and smiled down at Gruffly, official Dwarf of the Merry Band. The dwarf's bearded expression was a mixture of belligerence and fear, his fists clenched stubbornly and his eyes filled with apprehension.

Primp moved quickly to reassure him. "Only as required as part of the plot, which shouldn't be a great deal. And once the Quest is over, you and your wife will be left alone here. You have my word on it."

Gruffly was shaking his head. "I'm not going back to those tunnels to live. Never, you hear me? It was bad enough before, but now the missuses have come up from the Deep Mines, it's so...crowded."

Primp had to admit he had a point—the bustle of the tunnels had greatly increased since the female half of the dwarf population had taken the opportunity to move a step closer to the surface. It had also resulted in a number of more carefully shaven beards, a great deal less conspicuous consumption of mead, and a great deal more covert trips to the Mystical Forest caves for interspecies card games and a round of Cackle's good stuff.

"It's not to live," Primp repeated. "Only a brief visit for plot purposes and never again if you don't want to, I promise."

Gruffly regarded him cautiously, but was unable to hide the flicker of hope in his eyes. "All right," he said warily. "I'll do it. Brief, yeah?"

Primp nodded. "Just a couple of scenes."

"Okay." The dwarf turned abruptly and started to stride away. "Come get me when it's time. And then, I'm done. Solitude and open sky is all I want."

With a nod and wrestling to retain his hat, the Officious Courtier let him return to his much-valued solitude and open sky and turned back towards the tunnels.

* * *

Primp had to admit he understood Gruffly's feelings as he made his way back towards the Magnificent City to pass the news, foolishly choosing to do so via the dwarfish tunnel system. After a few hours' ride in a rickety cart, he too was feeling distinctly claustrophobic and on reaching the access for the Mystical Forest, queasily requested a halt.

He couldn't help but smile as he stepped out into the beautiful, enchanting surrounds that had until very recently contained the treetop residences of the elves. The high rope walkways and soaring branch residences were still there, ready for any future elf-based stories, but even as he approached, he saw the last of the elves scrambling awkwardly down the tree trunks with bundles of their things as they moved en masse to the secluded, ground-level dell on the forest's edge where Windblossom and Moonbright had already secured the services of Lathe the Artisan and his friends to build them a series of nice, sturdy, and very much single-storey houses. Several of the elves had collapsed, sobbing, at his feet when he'd broken the news to them that their longed-for move to the forest floor was finally allowed.

But as he took a few moments to breathe in the clean air, Primp spied a lone figure moving off in a different direction to his fellows. Curiosity overtook him.

"Leafstar?" he called out. "Aren't you going with the others?"

The handsome elf, his arms full of rather battered and green-stained clothing, jumped and gave a gentle blush.

"Actually," he said shyly, "I've had an invitation to live somewhere else. Cackle and I..." His blush deepened. "Well..."

Primp, a man of the world, did not need a picture painted and was very much aware from his nephew that love took all sorts. He smiled. "I see. She's a lucky woman."

The elf looked genuinely taken aback, his eyes filled with a sudden affection that was almost embarrassing to witness. "Oh no. *I'm* the lucky one."

And smiling blithely, the elf regathered his clothing and scurried away into the trees.

* * *

"What do you mean, there's nothing you can do?"

Pleasance knew that voice in an instant. How could she not? She had grown up listening to every weight and measure of it, every melodramatic roll, every indignant shriek, every shrill reprimand, and every honeyed word. It was more familiar to her than her own.

Oh lord. It seemed her sewing lesson was over.

Beside her, Menial raised an eyebrow as she wordlessly lifted away the slightly crooked shift they'd been working on. It was both disconcerting and pleasing that her expression no longer contained the shiver of fear it would have once shown at that familiar tone, though from what Pleasance had gathered of events at the Palace, the days when the Royals and Nobles had been deferred to and shrunk from were well and truly over. With a grateful nod to her former Maid, they both rose.

"We demand action! This is intolerable!"

Nearby, Dullard, who had been talking to Scrape about a prospective audition piece, let out a weary sigh as he recognised the lower, more strident voice of the first's companion. With a pat to Scrape's shoulder, they both moved over to join his princess and Menial.

"Well, we knew this day would come," Pleasance declared wearily. "Did either of you know they were coming today?"

Both Menial and Scrape shook their heads. "Those two don't tend to mingle much, Pleasance," Menial pointed out. "Along with Vanity, they're pretty much the worst, Pleasance."

The princess sighed, taking a moment to drink a quart of reassurance from Dullard's face. "Of course they are. Come on then. Let's get this nonsense over with."

A strange scene was unfolding beside the central pedestal. Strut, his expression steely and immovable, stood on the lowest step staring down at the two scruffy and hysterical figures yelling their grievances into his face, waving their hands at him, stamping their feet, and generally making idiots of themselves. And the first was Pleasance's bitchy, treacherous sister, Sweetness. Her hair was down and wild—after all, without her Maid, she had no knowledge of how to fasten it—her dress looking in dire need of a clean, her face smudged clumsily with rouge and smeared with badly applied lipstick. Beside her, her husband, Count Bold, looked little better, his beard untrimmed over his purple, angry face, his doublet fastened crookedly, his hose hanging loosely, and his boots scuffed. His eyes, still somewhat unfocused after his undignified fall, were rolling.

"How can you stand there and tolerate us being degraded in such a manner?" Sweetness was in full, furious Heroine mode, her fingers making sweeping gestures, her eyes shining with the rage of ages. It would have been more effective if she hadn't looked like she'd fallen through a few dozen hedges backwards. "With even Quibble now denied us, they have full rein of our Palace and they disdain our commands as though we are nothing! Do you have any idea how those foul dogs we once deigned to honour as our loyal Servants are treating us?"

She couldn't help it. A broad grin spread across Pleasance's face, mirrored by Dullard, Menial, and Scrape. For they knew very well indeed and as far as Pleasance was concerned, it couldn't happen to a nicer group of obnoxious relatives.

* * *

"Will you stop laughing at me?"

From the work table where she had been gently instructing Lord Dauntless on the best way to knead dough, Jolly the Plump Cook glanced up to find her husband, Sour the Thin Cook, curled in a heap in the corner, laughing so violently that Jolly feared he was going to take Quests off his life. The subject of his amusement—battered, dishevelled, and pasted in flour and what looked very much like pieces of eggshell—was none other than the great and renowned double Heroine Princess Vanity. Unfortunately for all concerned, Vanity's recent flattening had done nothing to improve her temperament, and it was only her husband, Valiant's, refusal to ever enter the kitchens again after what had become known as the *spatula incident* and her own imminent starvation that had led her to enter what she had referred to as *this despicable place* in the first place. Her demands for service had been ignored but her insults had not.

"You told me to do that!" Vanity's voice was spiralling ever more towards the melodramatic as she picked eggshell distastefully out of her hair. The consummate professional was losing her cool. "You said it was a *helpful hint!*"

Sour's laughter redoubled as Jolly bit her lip and noticed to her amusement that Lord Dauntless was doing the same. Once he had been reassembled after his long and messy fall, Dauntless was one of the few Royals and Nobles who had become wise to the new balance of power, realising that practical skill was more valued than prestige and courtesy more effective than authority. He had also caught the measure of what were becoming known amongst the Servants as *helpful hints* and their correlation with a Servant being insulted and threatened and the insulter suffering a domestic calamity. As the insults calmed, so the help became more helpful. Some of the Royals and Nobles had learned the new way of things and were willing to work with it. Others, however...

Vanity's chest inflated. Clearly she was working herself up to some full Heroine projection. "How dare you trick me in this manner?" she declared regally. "Your fat wench offers no such falsehoods in assisting Dauntless!"

Jolly had been called worse but she silently noted to offer Vanity a helpful hint as soon as she was able. "Aye, but Lord Dauntless has been nowt but polite and courteous," she pointed out reasonably instead. "He listens to what we have to say and ain't afraid of learning to look after himself."

Lord Dauntless cocked a somewhat reproachful eyebrow at his niece as he worked his hands through the dough just as instructed. Jolly suspected he'd make a decent baker. "Not to mention I didn't call the person helping me a filthy, traitorous gutter maggot who deserves to be whipped and fed to the mongrels because they wouldn't make supper for me," he added sternly. "Strangely enough, Vanity, that doesn't endear you to people."

Vanity turned a fascinating shade of purple. "Uncle! You..." Jolly jumped violently as the respected and noble princess released a shrill, enraged shriek towards the ceiling. "Wretches!"

And then, with her best dignified sweep, Vanity started to stride from the room. It would probably have worked better if she hadn't tripped over the slop bucket and shoulder-barged Bow the Serving Man as he met her in the doorway, but you couldn't have everything.

Rubbing his shoulder, Bow stepped into the kitchen. "Cooking lessons are going well, I gather?"

Sour collapsed into another burst of laughter. Jolly simply smiled. "Well, Dauntless here is well on the way to a fine loaf of bread. Duchess Vanity, though—she may be going hungry for a while. How are things above stairs?"

Bow gave a slight grin. "It's not going too badly. Lady Gracious has actually started listening and asking nicely, so I showed her how to clean her clothes and helped her fill her washtub. Baron Stalwart, however, has not, so I gave him some helpful hints about lighting his chandelier." Bow's grin turned wide. "After he was so kind as to call me a foul, treacherous cur and threaten to thrash me yesterday, it was the least I could do."

From a distant corridor, the inevitable came, a tremendous crash and a drawn-out screech as Bow's helpful hints and the disrespect that spawned them reaped what they had sown.

* * *

Dullard had to admit that watching two princesses go to war was a fairly remarkable sight.

When Pleasance had announced she'd wanted to indulge in a *quick scream* at her sister, Dullard had tentatively suggested it might not help matters. But oddly enough, not only Pleasance but Sweetness seemed to be enjoying herself as the Outer Sanctum echoed with shrill insults and infuriated exclamations as the sisters let rip with their respective grievances. Dullard knew his princess was very keen to prove herself no longer one of the spoiled elite—indeed, her sewing lessons with Menial and the cooking lessons she'd requested from Dullard himself were part of an unashamedly smug and fervent effort on her part to show her domestically challenged relatives up. In this particular bout of one-upmanship, nothing was beneath her.

And the rift was going public. Very much so.

"You dragged me into The Narrative against my will, you hag-faced bitch! I almost lost myself!"

"It was for your own good! You were delusional! And now look what you've done! You *stole* our Servants! I can't dress, I can't eat, I can't even *bathe! Look* at the *state* of me!"

"I can see the state of you! I can also *smell* it!"

"How dare you insult me when this is all your fault?"

"How is it *my* fault that you are utterly incapable of doing anything for yourself? Did it not cross your tiny mind that if you stopped bitching about your situation and asked the Servants nicely to help you, you might be able to fix this?"

"Did it not cross your mind that if the natural order was restored, I wouldn't *have* to?"

"There was nothing natural about *your* orders!"

"Well, what about your precious new Quest? Do you expect us to appear in it in this disgraceful manner? Bold and I are of a mind to join Lord Stance and his companions in their boycott of this self-aggrandising nonsense!"

"Oh, please, do carry on! We'd be delighted! In fact, I'm sure some of the female Servants would be thrilled to audition for your role—some of them do excellent impressions of you and they'd *love* to wear your dresses..."

Sweetness gave a horrified, hiccupping shriek and grabbed her husband's arm. "You *wouldn't!*"

Pleasance's smile was predatory. "Try me."

Sweetness drew herself up in an attempt, Dullard supposed, to gather her scattered dignity. It wasn't as impressive a sight as it used to be.

Pleasance smiled at her sweetly. "So we'll be seeing you and Bold at the plot run-through next week?"

Sweetness and Bold exchanged a long, shaky look. Although they were proud, stuck-up, and arrogant, Dullard also knew that at their core lay the hungry souls of a pair of fervent glory hunters.

Carefully, deliberately, Sweetness raised her chin to gaze down her nose at her shorter sister. "We'll be there," she brusquely said.

Count Bold glanced up and caught sight of Dullard, standing with the grinning Scrape and Menial behind Pleasance. His eyeball twitched.

Dullard made sure to give him his friendliest smile in return. "Bold, as we discussed at the Castle, if you'd like me to show you how to hold your stance better..."

The twitching in Bold's eye redoubled. His jaw hardened like a rock.

Grasping each other's arms as though they were pulling themselves free of a raging ocean, Count Bold and Countess Sweetness turned and swept from the room with a great deal less oomph than they'd entered it.

* * *

"Really?"

Fodder wasn't sure why he was surprised, but of all ways of life, the Barbarian one had felt the most ingrained. Flirt's expression was particularly smug.

"Oh, Braid and I had a very long chat, didn't we?" she said cheerfully. "And once I convinced her that wandering eyes and a slap on the arse was best met with a slap in the face, the amount of bosom staring has reduced dramatically. It may take a while to sink in, though. Barbarians aren't the brightest, are they?"

"They aren't bred to be," Dullard pointed out, somewhat sadly. "And a generation of training is hard to breed out. Hopefully with many of the mothers converted, the next generation can work on it. I suspect this one will be more inclined to stay with what they know."

"You know, it may not need to wait that long," Fodder chipped in. "I have seen a couple of Barbarians in textiles rather than animal skins recently. One had even shaved off his beard."

"Blimey, that's a step." Flirt's eyes widened. "Oh and I meant to say, didn't I? Did you hear about Froth?"

* * *

Cleave the Woodsman folded his arms, eyeing up the burly figure ranged before him in a huge woollen tunic, chin shiny and freshly shaved. "You were an Interchangeable, right? With proper Narrative time? So how come you want to chuck that in to become a wood-cutter?"

Froth the ex-Berserker smiled beatifically. "I needed a change," he stated wistfully. "The idea of the woods and the peace and quiet, no one yelling at you to fill your beard with spittle and head-butt AFCs, just a simple chop, chop, chop... It's *bliss*." He sighed. "I need a less *pressurised* career."

* * *

"It's not only him, you know," Flirt remarked as Fodder's smile broadened at the news of Froth's career change. "I've been hearing loads of stories. Plenty of folks out there want to audition for a part or try a whole new profession. It's great what some people have been up to…"

* * *

Reel the Seadog stared down at the strange apparition in rusty chain mail balancing on his gangplank, beaming at him with crooked teeth as he cradled his helmet in his hands. "So yer from the Watch, lad," he said slowly. "And yer want to be…a Buccaneer?"

The pale little Watchman nodded. "Yep. Love the sea, always have. And if there's any swinging from long ropes with cutlasses gripped in my teeth to sweep beautiful maidens off the deck, I'm up for that too."

Reel's huge, knotty eyebrows ground together for a moment. "Well, we tend to work up to that kinda thing, lad." But nonetheless he held out one salty, callused hand. "So we'd best get started."

* * *

The Desert Nomad lowered his hood and smiled at his friend. "You're moving to the Magnificent City?"

The Exotic Islander nodded with determination. "I've had it with being ignored. No more being stuck on the sidelines—I'm getting my face up front and centre. I'm going to show them who I am and what I can do." He cocked a smile at the Desert Nomad. "Want to come?"

* * *

"I'll try *anything.*" The Buccaneer's exclamation was fervent as he stared around the assembled group of Artisans. "Smithing, carpentry, anything. As long as it's off the water. *Very, very* off the water."

* * *

The hard-faced Grim Garrison soldier beamed as he stared at the enormous silk-and-feather concoction that held pride of place in the window of the milliner's shop. It truly was an *epic* hat.

"So, my pretty," he breathed. "Now you're *mine.*"

* * *

"I don't think they'll even let us in, Giggle."

Giggle the—until that morning—Tavern Wench stared up at the Royal Palace with fervent eyes for a moment before switching her gaze to her nervous friend. "The Servants will, Coquette, I bet you. They'll think it's brilliant." Her voice hardened. "And why shouldn't we? They said anyone can be anything, right? So why shouldn't we try out to be princesses?"

* * *

The Tavern Keeper stared at the stately Priestess who was eyeing his smoky bar with a strangely liberated gleam in her eye. "Well, if you really want to work here," he said cautiously. "It happens I am a couple of Wenches down."

* * *

Pluck the Squire folded his arms. "I mean it."

Sir Fealty stared at his former adherent and general dogsbody with horrified eyes. "But who'll help me into my armour?" he declared in horror. "Who'll clean my sword and curry my horse?"

Pluck shrugged. "Reckon you'll have to do it yourself. But it won't change a thing. Sir Gallant's already agreed to train me. I'm going to be a *Knight.*" He gave a half-smile. "So it looks like you'll have to manage without me."

* * *

"I'm just so tired of staring into mirrors and wafting around in the background." The minor Noblewoman carefully took her seat amongst the circle of smiling Seamstresses, picking up a needle. "You have no idea how much I've longed to do something useful."

* * *

Lathe the Artisan clapped his hands together. "The elves want some simple houses built out by the Mystical Forest," he said cheerfully. "So, as my new apprentices, are you up for the challenge?"

The burly farm lad from Fertile Fields gave a happy nod. The chop-weary woodcutter shrugged. The female Barbarian was already eyeing the tools with a gleeful gaze.

"Well," Lathe declared. "Let's get started."

* * *

It was no use. Pleasance had to smile.

"And he's enjoying it?" she enquired, peering out through the doorway of the Outer Sanctum into the impressive edifice of the Temple itself to watch her former Palace-mate work.

Reverence the Priest smiled. "He thinks it's wonderful. Have you ever seen someone smile so much? And you have to admit, he has an eye for it. We definitely want to keep him on."

That much was true. Pleasance's smile widened at the beautifully arranged floral displays now decorating the Temple, each one carefully and precisely created by the blissfully beaming ex-Sir Venture.

* * *

"That kind of change isn't for everyone, of course," Dullard remarked rather sagely on hearing of the various changes of direction. "An awful lot of the Ordinary Folk in particular I've spoken to are quite happy and contented with the lives they have."

Fodder nodded. "I respect that. Change isn't for everyone, and we're all muddling through this. We need to be sure everyone knows the choice is there."

* * *

"I'm sorry. We tried, we really did. We spent hours trying to explain it all to them. But they refused to believe they weren't divine. They didn't *want* to."

Devout the Priest looked genuinely sorrowful. Fodder gave him a wan smile. "It's not your fault. You gave it a good try."

"We did." Devout sighed. "It doesn't make me feel any better about it. It's such a long time since anyone from the Sanctum has even thought to go up there. They weren't asked for in the Quests so we left them alone. We hadn't realised what a *state* they'd gotten themselves into."

Fodder could see the guilt in the man's eyes and he knew the feeling well. The Gods had been nagging on his conscience for a while. With their participation in the Quest requested, and fearing the sight of him and his friends wouldn't help after their unceremonious flight, he'd asked Devout and several companions if they'd travel to their mountain and gently try to bring them into the new reality. But hearing it from the Priests was apparently no different than hearing it from any other mortal. The Gods refused to believe they weren't Gods.

He wasn't sure, even now, if anything could be done for them. The Taskmaster had agreed to halt the forcing of character that had led to planting, but for those already planted, there was no easy solution, no clean fix or conjuring trick. They would keep trying, but faced with a Taskmaster whose belief in their existence was still undetermined and whose power was not entirely conscious, there was no magic wand that could be waved to repair the damage. There was only time and hope.

"Did you tell them about the Quest?" Fodder asked as he glanced at Dullard, who was stood beside him. The prince's eyes were thoughtful and distant.

Devout nodded. "Oh yes, what they understood of it. They were *very* keen for their precious light. Much as it pains me to admit it, though, you may have to speak to the Taskmaster about a slightly heavier hand with them. I doubt they have the ability to run with The Narrative themselves."

Fodder groaned. A return to the old brain-crushing way was exactly what they *didn't* need. "That's not going to help."

"Actually, it might." Dullard's pensive interjection caught Fodder by surprise. At his shocked look, he cocked a thoughtful eyebrow. "Well, think about it, Fodder. They always believe their glorious light. And think what the light will give them this time. It'll be showing them the *truth.*"

Fodder caught his meaning and felt a tiny, flickering spark of hope. It would be painful, to be sure, and they'd have to make certain someone was there to help them through it afterwards, but...

"Maybe..." he muttered.

"Maybe," Dullard agreed. "Just...*maybe*, they'll see."

* * *

"You buggered off." Flirt's glare was steely as she raked it around the sheepish-looking gathering of men around the table in the dark and smoky tavern.

"It was a tactical retreat!" Clunny insisted for about the fifth time, although Fodder noticed he had resisted looking up from his tankard from pretty much the moment they'd walked in. Fodder wasn't quite sure what was on his mind.

"Yeah!" Dunny backed him up. "And you won, didn't you? The First Rule worked! So what are you complaining about?"

Flirt gave a long-suffering sigh. "Nothing, boys. Never mind."

Fodder couldn't help but smile. The pub might have been different—they had decamped to the closest one the Magnificent City had to offer—but the feel, the friendly camaraderie, that never changed. It had been strange to see his old band of mates arrive at the Outer Sanctum along with Thrash of the Grim Garrison, staring at the fancy décor and the glimmering architecture as they handed back the battered and whimpering form of Preen to be led away by kindly relatives as Bard fluttered around him in concern. The lads hadn't said where they'd found the Officious Courtier in the end but Fodder suspected it might have been a hidey-hole of Preen's own making, given the noticeable twitch he developed at the sight of Strut's glare. Word of his diatribe at the Final Battle Camp had clearly gotten back to his cousin.

It had been oddly relaxing to see his friends again. Only Midlin was absent, which was no great loss to Fodder anyway—he had apparently been recruited to help spread the word of the new instructions by one of the Priests, and Tumble reported he'd never seen him so happy. And since it seemed only right, Fodder, Shoulders, and Flirt had taken their old mates out of the Temple and headed to the nearest pub for a chat.

"So what do you lads reckon then?" Fodder said. He was surprised at how nervous he was to pose the question. "Do you think you'll want to audition or try a new career?"

A flurry of looks, containing a mixture of expressions, was exchanged. It was Thump who first spoke up. "I think we're all right, mate, to be honest," he said with a shrug as he hefted his pint. Tumble, Dunny, and Donk were nodding with him. "We kind of like what we do—we're out in the fresh air, having fun with our mates—it's wholesome, you know?"

"I know what you mean." Shoulders's admission was a surprise. "But, lads, what about the mud, the beheadings, entrails up trees?"

"Don't really mind that," Tumble said easily. "As long as we get a bit more respect from now on."

"And no more ruddy Preen!" Dunny added with fervour. "I was against giving him back but Donk insisted."

Flirt snorted. "After that fiasco at the Camp? After this Quest is done, Preen'll be lucky if Strut ever lets him loose in any official capacity again, won't he?"

"I feel a bit sorry for him," Donk admitted, to general astonishment. "Maybe this new Quest will help him. Maybe it'll let him see where he's gone wrong."

Shoulders pulled a face. "Big maybe."

The door to the tavern creaked appropriately as the bulky form of Thrash of the Grim Garrison appeared in the door. "Heard you were here," he said with a grin as he sauntered over and dropped into the empty chair next to Clunny. "And I just wanted to say…I'm in. I want to try out."

Fodder gave a broad smile. "Thrash, that's great. I wish you all the best."

Thrash chuckled. "I wish me all the best too. I fancy showing up that little turd of a Minstrel. And it could be fun."

"Actually." Fodder couldn't help but notice that Clunny was looking everywhere but in his direction, words creeping painfully over the
threshold of his lips. "I think...I might...try out too? You know, once
this next Quest is done?"

Fodder smiled deeply. He remembered Clunny's fervent criticism
back when this had begun, his insistence that Fodder couldn't change
the world; and now, here he was, wanting to be part of the new adventure. It was the best of outcomes.

He glanced around. Though it wasn't the Archetypal Inn, it was
close enough to some of its guises and it felt right, sitting with his old
mates, as he had at the start, somehow unable to shake the feeling that
with Clunny's words, the world had come full circle.

"You go for it, mate," he said with feeling. "You give it everything."

* * *

So that was how it was. Part of the Realm happy to change and take the
new opportunities, part with no choice but to change due to the choices of those who'd once served them, and part content to live the life
they already had. But everyone knew it could be different if they wanted. And that was important.

And then, as the strange new shape of the world began to form,
something familiar rose to settle it back down again. It was time for the
next Quest to begin.

* * *

It felt strange to be back at the Palace.

True, it was not precisely the Palace he had left, filled as it was
with his highly disgruntled distant relatives and a pack of cheerful and
amused Servants, but as work had begun to tidy up and prepare for the
new Quest, things had slipped back a tad into an older pattern. Dullard
had even spotted several of the Royals and Nobles trying to resume
giving their Servants orders and being met by a number of upraised
fingers. It was crude, but it got the message across. There was no going
back.

In other quarters, given the piteous state of some of the Nobility and the need to get them into at least a reasonable state before the Quest began, a few Servants had, mildly, relented. Jolly the Plump Cook had started giving cooking lessons to those willing or desperate enough to learn without sneering at her. Menial had set to work teaching some of the less bitchy ladies how to mend their own clothes and fix their own hair. Bow and Scrape were leading tidying parties amongst those Nobles who were willing to pull their weight and keep their Palace residence in a liveable condition. Compromises were being reached, alliances were being forged and new boundaries marked out. The Nobles and the Servants were, grudgingly, starting to work as a team.

It had been a relief, to be honest. Dullard had been worried that the antipathy between the two groups might affect the preparation and progress of the new Quest. But for all that went on behind the scenes, when it came to The Narrative, the Nobles and the Servants were professionals. It would be as it should be.

And it had also meant that, for the first time in what felt like forever, he'd had a chance to sit down and think.

His room hadn't changed a jot. It had been an odd feeling, returning to his chambers, the place where his part in this adventure had begun, sinking into the chair at his desk and seeing his papers and rock samples exactly as he'd left them, the gap in his sword rack where Flirt's sword had rested, and that bizarre, freakishly ruffed Tretaptus outfit hanging in his garderobe. The moment when he'd found Fodder's head poking out of his toilet felt like a lifetime ago. He supposed that in a way, it was.

So much had happened. So much had changed. And here he was, right back at the beginning and ready to start over again.

Gently, he picked up the long-ago-dropped sapphire necklace he'd retrieved from the floor shortly before and smiled.

Except this time, he wouldn't be starting alone.

There was a knock at the door. Dullard smiled.

"Come in, Pleasance."

It still filled him with a bewildered kind of joy to feel the rush of warmth that surged through him as his princess appeared, stepping briskly inside and pushing the door shut behind her as she started towards him. For a moment he half-expected her to leap into his lap as she had taken to doing of late, an act that had filled him with a mixture of pleasure, amused embarrassment, and occasionally, if the leap was badly timed, pain. But instead, slightly to his surprise, she hesitated, coming to a halt a few yards from his chair with her hands resting rather charmingly upon her hips and her face distinctly quizzical.

"I was aware you were clever," she said with a smile. "But I hadn't realised you were omniscient. However did you know it was me?"

Dullard beamed fondly. "You knock like a princess. It's very firm, authoritative, quite unlike the more tentative way the Servants knock when they call. And it's simple deduction from there—if it's a Royal or Noble knocking, given most other persons of Noble blood in this building aren't desperately keen to visit me..."

"It had to be me. Good grief." Pleasance folded her arms and arched an eyebrow at him, her lips tugging at the corners. "Master sword-smith and swordsman, geologist, chef, gardener, actor, academic, and now capable of assessing former social status via a door knock?" She shook her head. "What have I gotten myself into loving you?"

Her tone was playful but he knew her so well now, too well, every motion and mood, and he saw it at once, the flicker behind her eyes, the vignette of emotion that didn't quite match her outward façade. It passed so quickly he couldn't quite pin it down but the context in which it had appeared quelled the warmth in his bones in a rush.

No. Surely not.

But yet...it would make sense.

"How were your chambers?" he asked instead, as lightly as he could. A part of his mind was yelling at him not to change the subject, to go back to that flicker, to trace it, to follow it to its source. But another part was yelling with equal fervour to hold his tongue.

If it's true...you know what it means. You've been waiting for this from the first moment she kissed you. Do you really want to hear it?

"Just as I left them, but for a bit of dust. I tidied it up." There was sweet, undeniable pride in her tone at this simple achievement. She'd taken such joy in learning to look after herself, more than he'd expected, and it'd been so lovely to watch her blossom through her newfound skills. "Self-sufficiency is turning out to be rather fun. It's nice to be in control of things around me for once. At least there's no more waiting for someone to answer your bell."

"It has its benefits." Dullard kept his tone mild but his brain was whirring.

If she's regretting her choice, I won't hold her back, it wouldn't be fair, but...Gods, it'll be difficult. Has everything between us been down to the adrenaline and intensity of our adventure? Has her love for me faded along with it? Perhaps she wants to wait until after the new Quest to break it to me so as not to make things awkward.

"All right, what is it?" Dullard jumped as Pleasance's terse tone cut through his silent maelstrom of anxiety. Her eyes were boring into him like spear-points.

"What do you mean?" The prince was quite proud of how calmly he got the words out.

There was that eyebrow again. It was distractingly appealing on her lovely face. "You." The single word was clipped and determined. "You aren't the only one in here who can read faces, you know. You're wound up tighter than a bowstring and trying to pretend you're fine. And you're going to tell me why."

"Really, I..."

"Are you going to do this?" Her pointed expression wasn't helping his composure, made even worse by the hint of concern hidden behind it. "After all the times you've badgered me about not hiding my true feelings?"

"I..." No, she was absolutely right. He was being a hypocrite and he'd upset her in the process. Dullard had to admit the fact he found her to-the-point approach to confronting him charming was a mark of how besotted he was and it would make this harder. But it was only fair.

"It's just..." He took a deep breath as he tried to steel himself internally for what was to come. "I wasn't sure if *you* were all right. You looked a little...*odd* when you made that joke about what you'd gotten yourself into and..." Her eyes were hurting him—that mixture of confusion, annoyance, and barely contained worry—and he ploughed quickly on. "I...wondered if perhaps you'd started to...change your mind?"

Her nose furrowed as she stared at him quizzically. "Changed my mind about what?"

Dullard swallowed hard as he braced himself for the inevitable. "Us?"

There was a vast silence. Pleasance stared at Dullard. Dullard stared at Pleasance.

And slowly, fiercely, like a hangman drawing a noose, Pleasance expelled a single, ferocious word.

"What?"

Oh dear. He was in trouble.

As it turned out, being in trouble wasn't vastly objectionable. For a mere moment later, Pleasance plunged forwards into his lap, grabbed his face, and kissed him.

For all that they'd had very scant time to be alone in the last couple of weeks, they'd managed to find their moments to practice their previously unsuccessful kissing technique. As a result, it really didn't take more than an instant for Dullard's newfound instincts to kick in and his brain to switch off. The world and his worries faded gloriously into the distance.

When he finally resurfaced, he became slowly but painfully aware of how much Pleasance's knees were digging into his thighs, and the grimace on her face as she pulled back told him that she was feeling the discomfort too. Grabbing the high wooden arms of the narrow chair, she eased herself stiffly back onto the floor.

"This chair has to go," she told him firmly.

Dullard blinked, still fuzzy after their moment of passion. "Pardon?"

"The chair." Pleasance stretched herself out in an extremely distracting manner. "It's abominably uncomfortable for two. The only reason I didn't pounce on you when I first came in was because I was convinced we'd both do ourselves a mischief if I did. And I was absolutely right. And since we're going to be doing this on a regular basis, you need a new chair."

"I... All right." Dullard's brain was struggling to catch up with events. If this was a case of actions speaking louder than words, he'd been blasted at high decibels. "I'll speak to Lathe. I'm sure he and his new apprentices will be happy to make us something roomier."

"It'll need cushioned arms."

"I'm sure he can manage that."

"And something to soften the head."

"Easily done, I'm sure. I'd be happy to try and design it myself, if you'd like."

"Are we really going to keep talking about the chair?"

"Only if you want to."

Silence fell once more. Dullard watched Pleasance stare down at him, her eyes filled suddenly with a world of swirling emotion.

"You think too much, you know," she told him, her voice suddenly soft. "You notice I'm distracted and immediately assume I've stopped loving you? Why?"

Dullard felt a wash of shame rush over him at her obvious distress. "I suppose because I've never been entirely sure why you loved me in the first place. And...well...we've never really talked about it. We kissed and we were frozen in crystal and then everything's been so frantic, we've hardly spoken properly." A thought occurred to him. "Do you know, other than our moments here and there, this is the first time we've really been alone together since our kiss at the Dark Citadel?"

Pleasance's playful smile flooded him with relief. "It had crossed my mind. But honestly, Dullard, why do you always need to *talk* about everything? Love isn't something to analyse or study. It's something to *feel.* Believe me, I know."

And there it was again; that same flicker behind her eyes that had started his mind racing. He opened his mouth, intent on tracing it properly this time, but Pleasance got in first.

"Do you love me?"

He smiled sincerely. "Very, very much."

She returned his smile gently. "I love you too. You always say you have faith in me, so have faith in that. Please don't ever doubt me."

And there it was again, stronger than ever, rippling through the pleading vulnerability of her final words. He met her eyes, rising from his chair and placing his hands carefully on her shoulders.

"What is it?" he asked softly. "What's wrong?"

Pleasance didn't answer for a moment. Instead she reached up, lifting his hands from her shoulders and holding them for a moment in her delicate grasp. Gently but firmly, she began to lead him towards the bed.

His flicker of panic at this potentially vast development must have shown on his face because she chuckled slightly.

"Don't look so worried," she said with a hint of a smile. "It's the only place in here where we can both sit comfortably. Only one chair?" She shook her head. "You aren't used to having visitors, are you?"

"Not unless they crawl up through my toilet," Dullard answered with wry honesty.

"Or they arrive intending to make you grovel and you kidnap them." Pleasance grinned at him ruefully as they sat side by side on the bedspread. "What a pair we make."

"And we are a pair. I promise." Dullard sighed. "I'm sorry I doubted you. I was being foolish." He smiled at her tenderly. "Will you tell me what's wrong?"

It was Pleasance's turn to sigh as she stared down at their still-joined hands. "I don't know. I suppose I'm being a hypocrite too, in a way, when I think about it. But I can't stop worrying." Her eyes rose to meet his once more. "It's the new Quest. I'm just scared of being in The Narrative again, of going right back to how things were, to how I was..." She bit her lip. "Oh, Dullard, what if I forget how I feel? What if Islaine comes back?"

Despite his earlier uncertainties, on this matter and now in her feelings too, Dullard was confident. The no-longer-Rejected Suitor reached forward and pressed his lips to hers for a moment. "Islaine is *gone*. There's only you."

Pleasance smiled at him wanly. "I know but..."

He squeezed her hands tenderly. "Pleasance, you wanted me to have faith in you and I do. You defeated her at the Dark Citadel and you will always defeat her again in the unlikely event the need arises." He frowned as a question, mixed with an idea, flashed across his mind. "I have to admit, I've actually been meaning to ask. How did you defeat Islaine?" He smiled at her. "After all, it should have been impossible."

Pleasance shook her head, her eyes oddly haunted. "I'm not really sure. I know I was lost at first. Even in those brief moments when I wasn't in The Narrative, I was in shock. I thought you were *dead.* I couldn't surface." Feeling the shudder that passed through her, Dullard abandoned her hands and gently drew her into an embrace. He felt her fingers press gratefully into his back as she laid her head against his shoulder, her voice unusually quiet.

"All I knew was there was no more me. There was only...*her.*"

There was silence for a moment as they simply held each other. But Pleasance took another deep breath, raised her head an iota, and continued.

"But...I don't know, it was like the little part of me that had survived began to wake up. I could see and feel how wrong it felt." She smiled wryly. "I became my own inner Islaine—I *was* the nagging voice at the back of my own head. And do you know how it started?" She gave a dry laugh. "It was Bumpkin. All those lovey-dovey moments we had to share, all that gazing and adoration blown up out of absolutely nowhere. I'd always been told by my family that Narrative love was like nothing I'd ever felt, and they were right about that." She met his eyes suddenly, her smile dazzling him. "Because I knew what real love felt like by then. And I knew what I was feeling for Bumpkin wasn't real. Because it wasn't a patch on what I felt for *you.*"

Dullard knew he was an amateur at being in love. But even he was aware that this was definitely the right time for another kiss.

When he returned to his senses a while later, Pleasance had rested her head against his shoulder once more and was snuggling against his neck with a slight frown creasing her delicate features.

"Your shoulders really are dreadfully bony, you know," she remarked. "I may have to fatten you up when this new Quest is over."

Though it was said in partial jest, Dullard was glad Pleasance was looking towards the future. "You'll be fine, you know," he told her simply. "You know how you kept yourself free before, so you can always do it again. And if the Taskmaster does as we agreed, it won't be an issue. You won't be planted again; you'll be acting. And I'll always be there if you need me."

Pleasance stared up at him. "I know you will." All at once, a hint of cheekiness slipped across her features. "You know, given loving you helps me to feel myself, the best way to ward off Islaine might be to do lots and lots of kissing." Her expression turned to faux innocence. "After all, we agreed we needed plenty more practice." The innocence vanished from her face in a rush that made Dullard's insides turn somersaults. "So, if you can spare some time for...rehearsal?"

* * *

So this was the Royal Palace. Although Fodder had never really seen much of it outside of its plumbing, the grandeur of it couldn't help but nag at a distant, instinctive corner of his brain and whisper that any second, some appalled soul was going to scurry over, rake their eyes over his and Shoulders's scruffy chain mail and Flirt's cleaned-up Barmaid attire, and unceremoniously toss them out on their arses. It seemed even he had a way to go with adapting to the new order.

They hadn't been tossed out, though. Dullard's friend, the ex-footman Bow, had met them at the gates when they pulled up in Pleasance's overwrought and fully repaired monstrosity of a carriage and cheerfully led them inside—in Quibble's necessary absence, he had apparently taken over as unofficial organiser of the Palace preparation and, to Fodder's untrained eye, appeared to be doing an excellent job of it. Seeing Lord Dauntless cheerfully polishing a suit of armour and Queen Eminence reluctantly, if determinedly, rearranging the hanging tapestries with Scrape was a bit surreal, but it was good to know that everyone was getting used to things.

He got a few dirty looks, of course. But he was getting used to that too.

He was glad to have a guide—the Palace, with its ever-changing architecture, was a bit of a labyrinth. But after innumerable sets of stairs and corridors, Bow finally led them over to a particular door and gestured to it with a smile.

"That's Dullard's room," he told them. "But mind, I'd have a quick listen before knocking. Menial said she saw Pleasance head in there earlier, and no one's seen her since." He waggled his eyebrows cheekily. "They may need a few minutes..."

Shoulders's face contorted disconcertingly—apparently he had been too slow to halt an attack of mental imagery. Fodder could see his point—he had nothing against the prince and princess's relationship, far from it, but they were his *friends*. He really didn't need a picture painted.

Flirt, however, spied their faces and rolled her eyes. She smiled to Bow as he grinned wickedly and headed away before turning towards the door and raising her hand and knocking. Fodder heard a surprised squeak from inside, some rustling, and a clatter of footsteps before Pleasance's surprisingly tidily coiffured head appeared around the door.

"Oh, it's you." Fodder would have been deeply touched by her enthusiasm if there had been the slightest hint of it. She gave a resigned sigh. "Is it that time already?"

How the world turns, Fodder thought to himself. Just a few weeks ago, the woman staring at him from Dullard's doorway would have battled her way through the unholy hordes of hell for a starring role in The Narrative. And now here they were to pick her up and escort her to the starting point of her big moment and she was regarding them not with raptures of joy but as a downright inconvenience to her love life.

"It's that late? I hadn't realised." Dullard ducked into view over Pleasance's shoulder—in contrast to her tidy poise, Fodder couldn't help but notice he looked a little flustered. "Ummm...sorry, we..."

"We were practising for later." Pleasance didn't miss a beat. "But I suppose it'll have to wait now."

Fodder noted wryly that the princess hadn't specified exactly *what* they'd been practising, and Dullard's blush was worrying. He decided to hurry things along.

"We collected your carriage from the Artisans' sheds," he said with determined matter-of-factness. "It's as good as new and waiting outside. Do you mind if we catch a lift with you?"

"I suppose I can put up with that." The flicker of a smile on Pleasance's face denied her resigned tone. "And that being the case..." The princess laid a gentle hand on Dullard's arm. "Could you give us a moment?"

Shoulders happily obliged, retreating to the stairwell hurriedly with Flirt and Fodder a few steps behind. Fodder kept his face discreetly turned for the most part, although when he did happen to glance, he saw that Pleasance had wrapped her arms around Dullard's neck, her face resting against his shoulder with his hands upon her hips. It was oddly sweet.

A few words drifted over too. Fodder definitely heard Pleasance mention Islaine with unmistakable concern, heard Dullard using his most reassuring tone. He heard inaudible sentences, rich in gentle tenderness, from both sides. He heard kissing noises and retreated a step further around the corner with Flirt and Shoulders to give the prince and princess more privacy.

Finally Dullard's voice called out and summoned them back. Pleasance was standing in the corridor, giving a damned good show of being composed, though her expression contained a hint of wistful sadness and a tiny smidgen of worry. Dullard looked somewhat downcast as well, in spite of the fact he was smiling.

"Well then," he said with a slight shrug as he offered Fodder his hand. "I suppose this is goodbye—until The Narrative comes, at least."

Fodder took the hand and shook it, staring back with a smile at the definitely no-longer-Rejected Suitor who had stared at him so quizzically and accepted him so readily the day he'd happened to climb up out of his toilet. Who'd have thought on that day when he'd accidentally met that strange buffoon of a prince with his rock collection and his academic enthusiasm that they would come to this?

Shoulders was next to shake hands. "I guess you're not such a prat after all," he conceded with a smirk to the prince. "I got my head back eventually, so I can forgive you now."

"Indeed." Dullard took the mock insult gracefully. "It's a very kind concession for you to make."

He turned to Flirt. "Now, you know what I'm going to have to ask…"

Flirt's pained face suggested that she did. "I really have to?"

Dullard grimaced. "You do. I'm sorry. But it needs to be here. I promise I'll take exquisite care of it until it's time for you to get it back. I'll polish it up like new and get the blade properly sharpened."

With a grudging noise of defeat, Flirt reluctantly reached down and unstrapped her beautiful, Dullard-forged sword from her belt.

With even more potent reluctance, she held it out to the prince.

"You'll look after it, won't you?" she said plaintively.

"I most certainly shall." Dullard smiled at her sympathetically. "It'll be back in your hands soon enough, better than new. You have my word."

"You know..." Flirt looked suddenly thoughtful. "I'm not sure I ever thanked you properly for giving that sword to me, did I? So just in case—thanks, Dullard. That sword means the world to me, and you went ahead and gave it to me when you barely knew me. It helped me to stand up for myself. I really appreciate it."

Dullard merely beamed in reply as he placed the sword carefully back inside his rooms and emerged to shake Flirt's hand as well.

"Well, I'll see you all soon in a manner of speaking," he said warmly. "Not quite properly for a while, of course—or perhaps so, it's so hard to say quite how this is going to work. I have to admit, though, finding out is going to be *fascinating.*"

Fodder couldn't help but laugh. "I had a feeling you might think that," he said. "Whichever way it turns out, we'll definitely see you on the flip side for your academic opinion."

"Of that you can be sure." Dullard held out his hand one final time, but this time, it was Pleasance's delicate fingers that he took hold of.

"Honestly, it'll be fine," he told her gently. *"We'll* be fine. And there'll be plenty more time for..." He cleared his throat, looking slightly awkward. "Our *practice* when this is done."

Pleasance firmed her chin. "Not so much, given as soon as this Quest is over, we'll be getting married," she told him matter-of-factly. "You said find something to hold on to, and I'd say our impending nuptials should do it. You've a few days off before we reach here—try and arrange something, will you?"

Dullard looked surprised but a definite hint of joy flickered behind his expression too. "I'm not sure how your family will feel about that," he replied cautiously. "Several of them do rather hate me."

Pleasance shrugged. "Stuff them."

"That'll be fine." Dullard nodded happily. "I will see what I can do."

He kissed and gently let go of Pleasance's hand. Smiling at him one last time, she turned and swept abruptly up the corridor.

"Come along!" Her voice drifted back from the head of the stair-well. "The carriage is waiting!"

Dullard gave his friends one last smile. "She's a little nervous. Keep an eye on her for me?"

Fodder smiled back. "We'll do our best. See you soon, mate."

"You too." As Shoulders and Flirt also headed for the stairs, Dull-ard started back into his rooms, glancing around wryly before nodding at Fodder, who had half-turned to go. "Here we are, heading back to where we started. Who would have thought?" The prince shook his head with a rueful grin. "I suppose that means I'd better get back to sorting out my rock collection. You never did get to see it."

Fodder laughed. "Maybe next time, huh?"

Dullard laughed in reply. "Not many people are interested in seeing it, you know. I may hold you to that."

As the prince disappeared back into his rooms, Fodder, still chuckling, headed down the stairs, leaving the first of his own personal Merry Band behind.

Pleasance was oddly quiet as their carriage rumbled out of the Magnificent City towards the old gallows junction. At the stone bridge where the roads to Humble Village, the Battle Ground, and the Bandit Pass parted ways, Fodder couldn't help but remember how he himself had parted ways with this carriage last time he'd ridden it by hurling himself into a river and being knocked unconscious by Shoulders's plunging arse.

He'd been so fresh, so naïve, so utterly clueless. Defiance had been so shiny and new. And now…

The carriage rattled to a halt at the crossroads. It was time for another parting of the ways.

With a glance at the subdued Pleasance, Fodder pushed open the wooden door and jumped out, Flirt and Shoulders on his heels. He nodded his thanks to the coachman, who was checking the sharpness of the spear that would soon once more need to be plunged into his chest to pin him to the carriage, before turning back to the wan princess.

"It *will* be fine, you know," he told her through the open door, aware his wasn't the voice she wanted to hear say so but hoping to help all the same. "Honest, it will." He gave a rueful grin. "I never thought I'd hear myself say this, but I'm sure we can trust the Taskmaster. It'll be done how we've asked."

Pleasance's head jerked up at his words. For a moment, she flashed a tiny smile at his attempt to reassure her before her poise kicked back in.

"I know you're probably right," she said with a careful nod, but there was a sudden mischief behind her eyes. "But I think it was foolish not to have asked for a gag for Shoulders. The pain we could have saved ourselves…"

"Oi!" Shoulders's retort was instant but Pleasance's sudden grin deflected any further retort.

"Oh, don't moan," she told him with cheery dismissal. "You enjoy my insults, you know you do. You'd miss them if they were gone. What would you have left to feel indignant about?"

"He'd find something, wouldn't he?" Flirt inserted dryly.

"Oh, that's nice!" Shoulders crossed his arms as he glanced from one woman to the other, though Fodder did notice he didn't look particularly put out. "The more things change the more they stay the ruddy same. What is this, *Pick on Shoulders Day?*"

Pleasance smiled sweetly. "I wasn't aware we needed a special occasion."

Flirt snorted at that and Fodder had to struggle not to join her. Instead, he felt obliged to step in.

"Okay, peace," he said with faux firmness. "It's a whole new world, remember. Why don't you two take this chance to part as friends?"

Pleasance's sniffed "Hardly!" battled with Shoulders's "Not bloody likely!" and came out even.

Fodder shook his head. "Fine, I'll settle for a truce. Agreed?"

There was a distinct lack of response from either party, although Fodder could see they were both trying not to smile. Deciding he'd probably best not press any more to deprive them both of what was clearly a slightly weird mutual pleasure in their lives, he gave up.

"Well, then I guess this is it," he said instead, reaching out to push the carriage door shut. Pleasance peered out of the open window instead. "Time to part company, for now at least."

The princess frowned suddenly. "Before I go, I'd like to put in one request," she declared, her eyes flitting from Fodder to Flirt and most pointedly to Shoulders. "Be a bit more gentle with me, will you? I didn't particularly enjoy being tossed around like a trussed-up sack of potatoes and have no desire to repeat the experience. So, if you wouldn't mind...I'd appreciate you taking a great deal more care with me this time."

Fodder smiled at her—that was fair enough, to be honest. After all, it wasn't like he loathed her anymore. "I'll take it easy."

Pleasance raised a pointed eyebrow, her lips twisted wryly. "I wasn't just talking to you, Fodder."

Flirt grinned too. "All right, I'll see what I can do, won't I?"

Pleasance nodded graciously. "Thank you. I know we didn't always see eye to eye, but it would be much appreciated."

The Barmaid nodded in reply. Pleasance's gaze shifted.

There was an expectant silence, not filled by Shoulders's agreement. The pointed eyebrow sharpened dramatically but the Disposable, apparently up and ready for round two of their little spat, was unmoved.

"What?" Shoulders shrugged at Pleasance's fierce glare and Fodder and Flirt's pointed looks. "We can't be too airy-fairy, can we? We have to make it look good! I'll see what I can do but..."

"*Shoulders*," Flirt admonished.

But it was Pleasance who stepped in first. "Do you know, I think you are *absolutely* right," she exclaimed with a sudden worrying fervour. "We *do* have to make this look good and I would *hate* to be responsible for any lack of realism creeping in. So!" She beamed at the open-mouthed Shoulders regally but there was a cheeky, not-so-regal curl at the corner of her lips. "Instead of toning down my screaming, as I was planning, so as not to rupture your eardrums and make your ears bleed when you carry me, I think I'll have to *see what I can do...*" She straightened herself royally, squaring her shoulders and tossing her hair with an elegant sweep. "Flirt, Fodder, I will see you shortly. Shoulders, I suggest you wash your ears out. If for nothing else, your *hygiene* still needs work. Drive on!"

With a clap of her hands, the coach driver whipped his reins. Fodder caught one last glimpse of Pleasance's broadly grinning face before the carriage trundled away and carried her back up the Bandit Pass.

Shoulders was staring after the carriage with a look of great offence. Fodder fought not to smile.

"She was joking about the screaming," he said, clapping his Disposable friend on the shoulder. "And about the…hygiene."

Shoulders pulled a grouchy face. "She bloody *wasn't.*"

Flirt was also struggling not to laugh. "He might have a point, mightn't he?"

Fodder shook his head. "Flirt, don't encourage him. Shoulders, you're a terrible cynic."

Shoulders huffed loudly. "Oi, I resent that!" He straightened his shoulders pointedly but, like with Pleasance's, Fodder could see a hint of cheek beneath his smile. "I happen to be a bloody good cynic, thank you!"

And with an insincere humph, he turned and started down the track towards Humble Village. With a mutual headshake, Flirt and Fodder set off side by side behind him.

As they walked down the very familiar trail towards their home, Fodder glanced at Flirt beside him, her curly dark hair bobbing, her Barmaid's outfit, for all it was so well known, seeming wrong for her when put against the memory of her stint as a chain-mail-clad warrioress. The seed of a thought—a thought which, if he was entirely honest, had crossed his mind long before his fireside question had turned into out-and-out rebellion—flickered once more into his mind. He'd never said anything—never been sure he would ever say anything, quite frankly, but perhaps in the context of what was happening, now might be the time. He'd need to move quickly if it was to have the effect he was hoping for, but surely she wouldn't object to that. After all, it would round things off very nicely.

"Flirt?"

The Barmaid glanced at him with a smile. "Yeah?"

"I was just thinking…"

"Don't strain yourself, will you?"

Fodder gave her a long look. She smirked.

"Sorry, it's instinct, isn't it?" she said easily. "I've spent so long with Shoulders, the sarcasm comes naturally."

Fodder shook his head. "Could you try and restrain yourself for a few minutes? I wanted to ask you something."

"That sounds serious, doesn't it?" Flirt raised an eyebrow at him humorously. "Not about to propose, are you?"

Uh-oh.

Perhaps he could have covered it, deflected her and changed the subject; but he hesitated, paused that moment too long. Flirt came to an abrupt halt on the road, hands on her hips as she stared at him, open-mouthed. Her second eyebrow shot up to join the first as her eyes widened for a brief instant before narrowing with worrying intensity.

"You're *not serious*," she drawled incredulously.

It was hardly the ringing endorsement that their close friendship might have led Fodder to expect. The Disposable floundered awkwardly as he thrashed in unfamiliar waters.

"What's so wrong with that idea?" he retorted with embarrassed indignity. "We've always got along so well and…"

"And you think it'll make a nice, neat happy ending for the Quest, don't you?" Flirt's penetrating glare quickly told him he wasn't fooling anyone. "I know you, don't I, Fodder? If this was about you, you'd have waited until this business was done with. But doing it now, right before we start over? You're hoping it might get *included*, aren't you?"

"Well, don't you think it'd be nice?" Fodder could feel himself blushing but there was nothing he could do to stop it. "It's not like I hadn't thought about maybe you and me even before this started and…"

Flirt's expression killed his sentence stone-cold dead. "If…and it's a *big* if, isn't it?" she said, her eyes boring through him with a long, hard look. "*If* anything like that is ever going to happen between us, it'll happen in its own bloody time and not because you feel the urge to contrive a happy ending. Leave the romantic subplot to Dullard and Pleasance—I think they've got it covered, haven't they? I'm not saying never, am I?" she qualified on seeing the sheepish look on his face. "But I am saying *not now*. Okay?"

Fodder decided to gracefully take the offered out. "Okay. Sorry about that."

"We'll talk about it again after the Quest, won't we?" Flirt turned, straightening her apron, and started back down the road. Fodder fell in beside her once more. "And any decisions either way can be made later."

"Sounds good." Fodder carefully swallowed the flicker of disappointment playing through him. The fact the flicker was there implied it was going to be a conversation worth having. The fact it was only a flicker suggested that she was right about this not being the right time to have it.

But whatever happened, she was still his friend and a bloody good one. There was something else that needed saying.

"Thanks," he said suddenly.

Flirt glanced at him quizzically. "For what? Turning you down?"

Fodder smiled. "Kind of. For keeping me in line. For speaking common sense when I needed to hear it. For keeping my feet on the ground when my head was off in the clouds. I'd probably be stuck thinking I was an arch-villain and trying to destroy the Taskmaster if it wasn't for you."

Flirt gave a shrug, but the teasing smile on her lips suggested she was pleased. "Well, that's what I'm here for, isn't it?" She grinned suddenly, gesturing up the road to where Shoulders was strolling ahead of them. "You boys—you lose your heads too much!"

Perhaps sensing the gesture or catching the mention of heads, the now-distant figure of Shoulders paused, turned, and stared back at them with arms crossed.

"Oi!" he called back. "What are you two dawdling about for? It's nearly time!"

"They can't start without us, can they?" Flirt hollered in reply, but nonetheless she and Fodder quickened their pace until they had reached where Shoulders was impatiently waiting. Ahead, the trees parted to reveal the first of the oh-so-familiar cottages of Humble Village ahead of them.

It was strange. He'd been gone for so long, been to so many places, seen and done so much. Yet one glimpse of Humble Village and it felt like he'd never been away. The crooked thatch, the lumpy daub walls, the small, scrubby green with the Archetypal Inn, uncharacteristically in the same location and form that he had last seen it in, parked on its far side. Bessie and Daisy, the village cows, were chewing grass contentedly in their pen. Stout the Innkeeper was rolling barrels into his yard as his son Lank swept the veranda. Fodder could even see the roof of his own cottage a little way further on. He wondered what kind of state it would be in after all this time and the likely attention of Thud's minions during that initial night of searching. There would be no time for a while to go and check.

As they reached the village green, a few faces glanced in their direction. To Fodder's quiet disappointment, several of the people he'd known since childhood scurried away without meeting his eye, although both Stout and Lank smiled in their direction and old Crook the Shepherd gave them a cheery wave. Of course, it could never be the same here as it used to be and he could hardly expect it to be such. He'd torn everyone else's comfy universe to shreds—it wouldn't really be on to come back and find his own home nostalgically untouched and welcoming. The world had to be fair.

There was no sign of his fellow Disposables. Fodder could only assume they were already in place, which meant he and Shoulders probably needed to get a move on as well. Although Flirt had joked they couldn't start without them, he had no wish to be an arrogant diva and stroll in late just because he could.

"Well, this is it, isn't it?" Flirt glanced over to her inn across the green before turning back to her two old friends with a smile. "Time to part company, lads." Her smile turned slightly wicked. "It's a whole couple of hours before you'll see me again, isn't it? Think you can cope without messing things up?"

"Almost certainly not." Ignoring her half-offered hand, Fodder moved relentlessly in for a hug. He was pleased to find that in spite of their recent conversation, it wasn't awkward either. "You'll probably have to pick up the pieces again like usual."

"I know. It'll be awful, won't it?" With a final pat on his shoulder, Flirt pulled free. "See you shortly, Fodder. And as for you…"

She turned to Shoulders, who Fodder noted was looking at her with a rather pained expression. She sighed. "All right, Shoulders, what's the face?"

Shoulders echoed her sigh. "I'm probably going to regret this," he said wearily. "But it's going to be ruddy ages before we get to talk again properly so..." He took a deep, reluctant breath. "I wanted to say...*thanks.*" The gratitude passed through his lips with all the grace and willingness of a pulled tooth, but Fodder had the feeling his friend was playing it up, plying his sentence with forced gratitude to hide the depth of the real gratitude underneath. "For all that you scared me and risked my life and my sanity and my head many, *many* times, you helped me out too. And we did all right in the end, you and me. We made a pretty decent team."

The look on Flirt's face told Fodder that she wasn't fooled by the show Shoulders was putting on any more than he was. She smiled at him sincerely. "We did, didn't we?" she said quietly. "And you know what? Thank you too, Shoulders. For all that you moaned like a champion every step of the way, you got us out of more trouble than I would have expected. You did well, didn't you? Even when you didn't believe it yourself."

Shoulders looked oddly touched for a moment, although he hid it very quickly. "Well, I am pretty damned awesome," he said with casual smugness. "I always knew that, really."

Flirt rolled her eyes. "Of course you did."

"Time to go, I guess." Shoulders offered Flirt his hand. "Sort of see you soon."

But Flirt grabbed his hand instead of shaking it. "Oh, come here, you prat," she exclaimed, and dragged him into a hug. It wasn't entirely successful given both parties were still new to the mutual respect, but a few rounds of shoulder-patting did the job and they parted without undue awkwardness.

"Well, then," Flirt said cheerfully, "I'd better go and pull some pints. I know how you lads need your ale after you've been chopped to pieces."

And with a final smile, Flirt turned and strolled off towards the Archetypal Inn and her new start in her old home. Fodder shook his head. It was ridiculous to feel emotional when he knew they'd be back together in a couple of hours. But would it be the same? He had no way right now to know.

But it was time to find out.

"Come on, Shoulders," he said, clapping his arm around his old friend's shoulders and turning away towards the trail into the Rambling Woods. "Let's go do what we do best."

* * *

A piece of paper.

Fodder had been amazed to find that it was actually the same one. He hadn't really thought twice about what had become of it after he'd shoved it in his pouch before that fateful fight in the Rambling Woods—it hadn't even crossed his mind again until Clunny had sauntered over and handed it to him, saying Lank the Innkeeper's Son had found it on the floor of the Archetypal Inn the day after they'd kidnapped Pleasance. He'd forgotten he'd even had it, let alone realised that he'd dropped it. It was more dog-eared than it had been, but the clear print of those long-ago, now-obsolete instructions stared back at him like a blast from the past. This piece of paper, with its insultingly dismissive summation of his world, had planted that first tiny seed.

Local guards attempt to apprehend them but are tossed aside...

And here he was now. Back on the muddy track through the Rambling Woods, waiting for the chance to start over again.

How would he do? The Taskmaster had been very clear about wanting an accurate portrayal, hideous cock-ups and embarrassments and all—this was to be no edited-highlights or new-and-improved version. It was tempting, he had to admit, to put a better spin on this or that, to make himself look a bit less confused and incompetent or naïve, especially in those early days; but in his heart, he knew that he couldn't. He and his friends would be leading the action and they owed the Realm the right to see it done properly. He had an example to set.

The wind rustled gently through the trees of the Rambling Woods like a whisper of the changing times. To his right, Shoulders was carefully fitting a newly crafted half-tankard to his neck. His expression was one of weary resignation.

"I can't believe it's got to come off again so soon!" he exclaimed suddenly, his fingers running around the line of his neck with desperate anxiousness. "I've only just got it back on again! I like being able to swallow and gulp and turn my head…" His voice was almost plaintive. "Can't we skip this bit and start in the pub?"

Fodder fought not to smile. "It isn't forever, mate. You know you'll get your head back in the end."

"Yeah, *in the end*," Shoulders griped, but Fodder could tell it wasn't only his imminent beheading that was bothering his friend. "And the end is bloody ages away! I can't believe I'm going to have to go through this again." He gave a snorty huff. "It was bad enough the *first* time around."

"It won't be so bad, mate, honestly." Fodder plumped for a bit of reassurance. "You know how it ends now, Shoulders; you know that we'll be all right." In the spirit of optimism, he even added, "Maybe this time, you can try and enjoy it?"

One glance from Shoulders was enough to shoot that prospect down in an epic fireball, but it was still there, that deeper worry, that nagging hint behind his eyes. This was more than Shoulders's standard griping, this was something more, and Fodder knew that when Shoulders was truly worried, there was something to worry about.

"Mate, what is it really?" he asked gently. "Come on, let's hear it before it's too late."

"Too late." Shoulders's tone was suddenly, alarmingly serious. "That's it exactly." He turned to look his friend straight in the eyes. "How do we *know*, Fodder? The Narrative is coming and we're about to put ourselves at its mercy. How do we know we aren't going to get planted and altered and dragged right back under?"

Fodder swallowed hard. Aha.

"We're playing *ourselves*, Shoulders. How planted or forced can we be?"

Shoulders raised an incredulous eyebrow. *"You* got planted as a twisted version of yourself, mate, and you didn't even *notice.* And it didn't do you any favours."

Fodder pushed back the alarming, unpleasant memory flood that accompanied that happy little reminder. "Planting and forcing characters is over," he said instead with as much conviction as he could muster. "I'm sure of it. After all, both the Golden Tome and the Silver Tome state that from now on, the characters are the ones guiding the action and The Narrative has to follow where they go…"

Shoulders's tone was mordant. "Haven't you heard? Instructions can be *broken.*"

Fodder sighed. "Mate…"

"And it's not only this Quest," Shoulders cut off Fodder's next bout of comfort ruthlessly, although to his relief, his friend was keeping his tone low and unexpectedly restrained. "What about the next one? What about when we aren't playing ourselves anymore?"

Fodder mustered up as much conviction as he could, trying to fight off the onslaught of his friend's sincere and, frankly, valid concerns. "Everyone is playing a version of themselves this time out," he said firmly. "That means that by the time The Narrative rolls out for any future Quest, they'll be used to being themselves in it and they can act with more confidence. There won't be any need to plant."

Shoulders sighed deeply. "But, mate—what if it happens again anyway? What if the Taskmaster just *can't help it?*"

Fodder stared back into his friend's anxious eyes. It was a good question. If he was honest, it wasn't one he was sure he could answer because the truth was, he *didn't* know if any of his assertions would ring true once the light of The Narrative took them. All he had were the assurances of the Taskmaster, a guide who only vaguely understood their world and had little conscious control over it.

But as he stared into Shoulders's worried face, as he remembered Flirt's warm hug, Pleasance's parting grin, and Dullard's gentle smile, he could see one fact in their uncertain future with absolute clarity.

He grinned at his suddenly incredulous friend. "Then we know what to do," he simply said.

Shoulders blinked at him, and his own smile slipped almost reluctantly over his features. "Suppose we ruddy do and all," he conceded. "Even if doing it is an epic pain in the arse."

And the air began to flicker above them, tiny sparks, those first of Narrative life, arching through the grey skies overhead and washing them with colour. Behind him, Fodder could hear Preen scuttling nervously about mixed with the grunts and clanks of Clunny and Thump,

Tumble and Donk, Midlin and Dunny as his fellow Disposables prepared themselves for their so familiar yet so utterly different fate. Squaring his shoulders, Shoulders gave his friend a final nod and turned to face the road ahead as Fodder braced himself at his side, the piece of paper still clutched between his fingers.

It was time. In those long-ago days when he'd dreamed of being a Narrative Hero, he'd never dreamed he'd be a Hero like *this*. But now that he was here and after all he'd seen and done, he couldn't have wished it any other way.

"Well, lads," he said softly. "Here we go again."

And then there was…

Light…

THE DISPOSABLE

PART ONE
No, hang on, that's already done with.

PART TWO
Nope, that one's over too. Ah, here we are…

PART THREE
A piece of paper.

That's what it was, when all was said and done. A simple, straight-forward piece of paper, the words upon it written in the familiar, authoritative, unnaturally regular lettering that signified instructions from the Taskmaster. It spelled out a sequence of events that had to be ruthlessly prepared for by every living thing in the Realm, and it was to be obeyed without thought and without question. That was merely the way it was, and to disobey would be unthinkable.

Wouldn't it?

Because there were days, sometimes, when he couldn't help but wonder if the world would really come to an end if he just chucked the paper away and went back to bed.

Probably not. After all, he was only a Disposable. Who would notice? Who would care? For if there was one word that could be used to describe Fodder of Humble Village, it was *ordinary…*

The Beginning

293

TRAPPED BY CRIME. FREED BY MAGIC.

When Skate tries to burgle a shut-in's home, she gets caught by the owner—a powerful undead wizard. He makes a deal with her. Now, she'd better find out exactly where her loyalties lie.

Skate the Thief
&
Skate the Seeker
by Jeff Ayers

TRUE LOVE. ANCIENT CURSES.

Theodora is determined to unravel the mysterious Seth Adler's secrets. No matter how many thousands of years old.

Painter of the Dead
by Catherine Butzen

RIDICULOUSLY MAGICAL. MAGICALLY RIDICULOUS.

Crafted as a slave to serve Time, the clockwork man escapes to seek out his imagination, his purpose, and his name.

The Land of the Purple Ring
by Deborah J. Natelson

A TALE OF THE MYTHUSIAN EMPIRE

Endlessly attacked by accursed beings, the kingdom of Ordyuk relies ever more heavily on four siblings. Under such a weight, their only choice is to grow into monsters themselves—

Or to shatter like glass.

Sand to Glass by **Remy Apepp**

AND YOU THOUGHT COLLEGE WAS TOUGH BEFORE

Try getting bitten by a werewolf. And being hunted by madmen. And being stalked by a very suspicious secret organization.

Hunter's Moon by **Sarah M. Awa**

THE CLOCK IS TICKING

Plans seldom survive contact with the enemy, a truth thrown at Mercedes when an ordinary trip turns into a battle for survival.

Bargaining Power by **Deborah J. Natelson**